TO TAPPUAH

ULIMAN
EMPIRE

ANAB

HABUSH

THE DIMAH SEA

P'RI
HADAR

TO BAOBAB

KATLAV

THE
REPUBLIC
OF SALT

Also by Ariel Kaplan

Grendel's Guide to Love and War
We Regret to Inform You
We Are the Perfect Girl

THE MIRROR REALM CYCLE
The Pomegranate Gate

THE REPUBLIC OF SALT

ARIEL KAPLAN

EREWHON

an imprint of Kensington Publishing Corp.
erewhonbooks.com

Content notice: *The Republic of Salt* contains depictions of antisemitism, assault, murder, and torture.

EREWHON BOOKS are published by:

Kensington Publishing Corp.
900 Third Avenue
New York, NY 10022
erewhonbooks.com

All Kensington titles, imprints, and distributed lines are available at special quantity discounts for bulk purchases for sales promotions, premiums, fundraising, educational, or institutional use.

Special book excerpts or customized printings can also be created to fit specific needs. For details, write or phone the office of the Kensington sales manager: Kensington Publishing Corp., 900 Third Avenue, New York, NY 10022, attn: Sales Department; phone 1-800-221-2647.

Erewhon and the Erewhon logo Reg. US Pat. & TM Off.

ISBN 978-1-64566-095-8 (hardcover)

First Erewhon hardcover printing: November 2024

10 9 8 7 6 5 4 3 2 1

Printed in the United States of America

Library of Congress Control Number: 2024932749

Electronic edition: ISBN 978-1-64566-096-5 (ebook)

Excerpts from *Vulture in a Cage: Poems by Solomon ibn Gabirol* (trans. Raymond P. Sheindlin) reprinted by permission from Archipelago Books.

Edited by Sarah T. Guan
Cover art by Micaela Alcaino
Designed & typeset by Rebellion Publishing

For my mother,
Kathy Walden Kaplan

My pain's too much, my wounds are deadly.
My strength is gone, my vigor all depleted.
Nowhere to flee, no refuge for my soul,
no place where I might find some rest.
Three things have come together to consume
the little flesh and tortured spirit left to me:
Great sin, great pain, and loneliness—
could anyone withstand all three?

— Solomon ibn Gabirol
(trans. Raymond P. Scheindlin)

DRAMATIS PERSONAE

FROM THE MORTAL WORLD

TOBA BET PERES: A half-Mazik from Rimon, daughter of Tarses and sister of the Courser. Toba Bet is the buchuk of the original Toba, who was killed by her sister while rescuing Barsilay from La Cacería. Her mother was also part Mazik, descended from Marah Ystehar, a Mazik who was forced to become mortal. Toba's Mazik name is Tsifra N'Dar: literally, the Splendid Bird.

NAFTALY CRESQUES: A young man from Rimon, the latest in a long line of tailors. He has enough Mazik heritage to enter the dream-world and cast illusions; he also has visions which he cannot control and which often leave him ill afterward. For untold generations, his family were the guardians of the book containing the gate of Luz.

ELENA PERES/ELENA BAT BELADEN: The original Toba's grandmother. She speaks several languages and uses her own brand of mortal magic.

ALASAR PERES: Toba's grandfather, who relocated to Petgal after the exile. A former translator for the Emir of Rimon.

PENINA PERES: Toba's mother, who died in childbirth.

THE OLD WOMAN: A former beggar from Rimon. Her real name is unknown. Her stated goal is to protect Naftaly as long as she's able.

DAWID BEN ARON: A half-Mazik from Luz. He and the other mortals in Luz were convinced by Tarses to pull out their gate and hide it in a book, leading to the Fall. Dawid saved himself and the book by escaping on the back of the Ziz.

THE QUEEN OF SEFARAD: The ruler—with her husband—of Sefarad, newly united after the conquest of Rimon. She is known to put a great deal of confidence in her confessor.

FROM THE MAZIK WORLD

ASMEL B'ASMODA (known in the dream-world as Adon Sof'rim, the Lord of Books): An astronomer and minor Rimoni Adon. Formerly Marah's husband. Asmel was forced to become mortal by pulling his magic into a safira.

BARSILAY B'DROER: The heir of Luz. A former member of ha-Moh'to, and at one point a medical student. Has made an effort to develop a reputation as an indolent wastrel. He is also Asmel's nephew and heir, through Asmel's marriage to Marah.

MARAH YSTEHAR: Former envoy to mortal Luz. Asmel's wife, Barsilay's aunt, and Toba's ancestor. She was the founder of ha-Moh'to and the guardian of its killstone. She was forced to pull her magic into a safira after being trapped in the mortal realm by Tarses.

RAFEQ OF KATLAV: An expert on demons and member of ha-Moh'to. He spent the greater part of the current age imprisoned under Mount Sebah. After escaping with Toba's help, he stole Marah's safira and the killstone of ha-Moh'to.

TARSES B'SHEMHAZAI: The Caçador of Rimon and Queen's Consort. A former member of ha-Moh'to and at one time a close confidant of Marah. He is the father of both Toba and the Courser, and is famous for his prescience, though he is only able to see the distant future.

TSIDON B'NOEM: The Lymer of Rimon, one of Tarses's top lieutenants in La Cacería. He had planned to marry Toba in exchange for freeing Barsilay. He bears a particular grudge against both of them. As Lymer, he commands the Hounds and Alaunts; however, since his failure to secure the killstone and marry Toba, he is presumed to be out of favor.

RELAM B'GIDON: The deceased King of Rimon, who died after riding his horse into the sea.

QUEEN ONECA: Relam's cousin, the Queen of Rimon.

THE COURSER/TSIFRA: Tarses's half-Mazik daughter and personal aide-de-camp. Because she has no use-name, she thinks of herself with her true name, Tsifra N'Dar, which she shares with her half-sister, Toba.

THE PEREGRINE: The Caçador's most trusted lieutenant. She commands the Falcons—responsible for work abroad, consisting mainly of espionage and assassinations—and is widely considered the deadliest assassin in Mazikdom. Originally from Baobab.

ATALEF: A demon with Mazik magic created by Rafeq of Katlav, currently enslaved to the Caçador. His mission is to possess the confessor of the Queen of mortal Rimon, but his greatest desire is to be united with the demons still imprisoned under Mount Sebah.

SABA B'MAZLIA: A prominent doctor and teacher at Zayit's university, and a regular attendant at the Colloquium of the Northwest Cities. Efra, the Savia della Mura, is his sister.

EFRA B'VASHTI: The Savia della Mura of Zayit, responsible for the defense of the city. She commands two forces: the First Division, which mans the city's wall, and the Second Division, which defends outside the city's perimeter. Saba is her brother.

THE PRINCE OF ZAYIT: The man elected to serve as Zayit's leader; however, most of the city's power is held by the Council of Ten. The position is not hereditary.

THE COUNCIL OF TEN: The most powerful Maziks in Zayit, who set laws and policy for the city in addition to electing the prince.

OMER OF TE'ENA: Asmel's former mentor at the University of Te'ena and one of the greatest astronomers in history. Since Te'ena was cut off from the rest of Mazikdom in the Fall, no one has been able to reach him, and it is unknown if he is still alive. Before the Fall, he was a member of ha-Moh'to.

RAHEL (known in the dream-world as Adona Maz'rotha): A former colleague of Asmel's at the university in Rimon. After Asmel's imprisonment and the destruction of the university, Rahel relocated to Zayit.

MIR B'COHAIN: A prominent astronomer based in Zayit. Friend of Asmel's, and a regular attendant of the Colloquium of the Northwestern Cities.

YEL: Commander at Zayit's wall, and Efra's most trusted officer.

GEOGRAPHICAL LOCATIONS

IN SEFARAD

RIMON: City-state in southern Sefarad.

MOUNT SEBAH: The highest peak in Rimon, very near the Rimon gate.

BARCINO: Northern port city in Sefarad, on the Dimah Sea.

SAVIRRA: The former residence of the old woman. Home to a massive pogrom some years prior to the events of the story.

MANSANAR: The capital of the newly united Sefarad.

VERCIA: A minor port on Sefarad's eastern coast.

THE GAL'IN: The mountains between Sefarad and the land of the Franks.

OTHER LOCATIONS

PETGAL: Country that shares the peninsula with Sefarad, and destination of many of the Jews who were expelled from Sefarad by the Queen. Elena's husband Alasar is in Petgal, along with her brother.

THE DIMAH SEA (the Sea of Tears): The sea that rose after the Fall of Luz, between Sefarad in the west and P'ri Hadar in the east.

THE ULIMAN EMPIRE: A great multiethnic empire in the east. Its capital is the gate city of Habush.

THE GATE CITIES

LUZ: Legendary lost city, known as the location in which Jacob saw angels climbing a ladder to and from heaven, as well as the mythical source of tekhelet dye. The former seat of the Mazik Empire. Barsilay b'Droer is the heir to the throne.

P'RI HADAR: The great city of the east. Its queen is the oldest living Mazik.

BAOBAB: The most southern gate city, notable—like Tappuah—because of its great distance to the sea. On the mortal side, it is an important trade hub.

KATLAV: On the southeast side of the Dimah Sea, an important center for education.

EREZ: A city to the south of the Dimah Sea. Famous for its natural beauty and for being surrounded on three sides by a steep gorge, making it a natural fortress.

TAMAR: A city to the south of the Dimah Sea. In close proximity to Rimon, however the two cities are separated by the strait, so travel between them is limited in the Mazik world. An important producer of lentils, the Mazik city is suffering from a blight on their crop.

RIMON: The great city of the west. After the Fall of Luz, it suffered a series of bloody coups d'état that led to the rise of King Relam and La Cacería. After the assassination of Relam and his sons, the throne was taken by Queen Oneca, who made Tarses her King Consort.

TE'ENA: Made an island in the Fall. Located roughly midway between Rimon and Zayit. Once home to a university second in importance only to the school in Luz.

ZAYIT: An important port city north of the Dimah Sea. On the mortal side, it is known in particular for its prominence in the salt trade. The Mazik city is likewise famous for its monopoly on salt—which is poisonous to all Maziks—as well for importing luxurious mortal-made goods that Maziks cannot use magic to replicate, such as spices. After the Fall of Luz, Zayit became the wealthiest of all Mazik cities because of its continued trade with mortals, which was discouraged or forbidden elsewhere.

TAPPUAH: The city of the north. Because of its distance from the other gate cities, its Mazik residents are relatively isolated.

ANAB: An important trade city in the Uliman Empire in the mortal world. The Mazik city is ruled by King Yefet, known for being a just king and the most widely respected of all the Mazik monarchs.

HABUSH: The capital of the Uliman Empire in the east. Several hundred years ago, both the mortal and Mazik cities were sacked by the Zayitis.

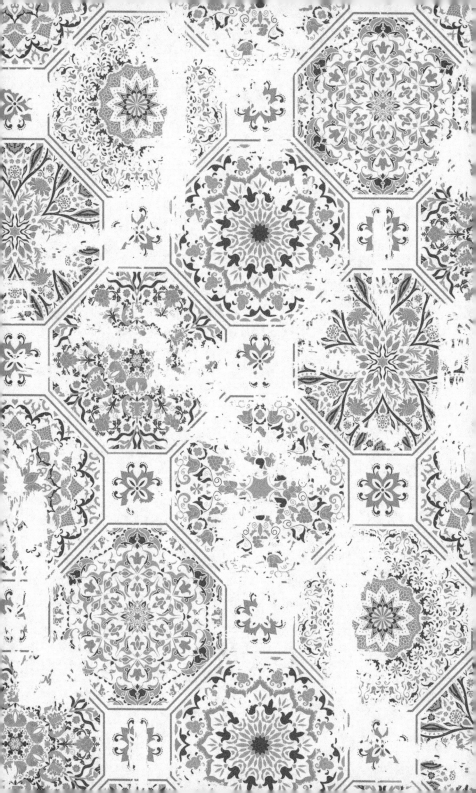

THE
REPUBLIC
OF SALT

ONE

IT WAS THREE nights until the New Year, and in the mountains north of Mazik Rimon, Naftaly Cresques was lying on the ground beside two old women and a Mazik who was mostly dead. The autumn air left the four of them chilled, but not too chilled to sleep, or dream.

Naftaly was there entirely by accident.

He was supposed to be in P'ri Hadar. They were all meant to be in P'ri Hadar, but Asmel, the Lord of Books, had made a mistake. Only days before, he'd been forced to remove his own magic, an act which had left him weakened and with a failing memory. So when he'd opened the gate of Luz, he'd accidentally sent Naftaly and his companions not to the great city of the east, but only a few miles away from his own alcalá in Rimon.

They'd been facing death in the alcalá. Here in the mountains, they were not much safer.

It was worse, even, than that. Naftaly's near-dead Mazik, Barsilay b'Droer, lately Naftaly's beloved and the heir of Luz, had lost an arm and nearly bled to death on the pine-littered ground.

This was why they'd stayed the past few nights in the mountains instead of fleeing north immediately. Elena, the younger of the old women—and, in Naftaly's estimation, the cleverer—had stated rather emphatically that Barsilay, no matter his objections, could not be moved without killing him. They'd managed to gather a little food and enough water to keep them alive. They'd slept, and Naftaly had scouted the area a bit. They'd discussed moving Barsilay farther down the mountain, where there would be easier access to water, but Barsilay had grown feverish. It wasn't until late that night that his fever had broken on its own, and at that point Elena convinced the two men and their elder woman companion to sleep a few hours, to marshal at least a little strength, so that they might discuss moving Barsilay in the morning.

Whether Elena herself slept or not Naftaly was not sure, but as he rested, his dreaming mind found itself called back into the city of Rimon, back to the garden of the King, in the shared dream-world of the Maziks.

Only it was no longer the King's garden, Naftaly recalled, as he opened his eyes to the same courtyard he'd seen the night of the crown prince's oath-getting many weeks before. The King was dead, and his oldest son was also dead, so Naftaly assumed this must be a ceremony for the King's younger son, whose name he had never learned.

Flowers bloomed all around him, strange Mazik flowers that were silver and purple and orange the color of Barsilay's eyes. The dream-world stars whirled overhead, and the white pergola in the courtyard seemed to glow in the pale light. The air smelled, Naftaly thought, faintly of pomegranates.

The place was full of anxious Maziks whispering to one another as they approached the courtyard, and Naftaly found himself very reluctantly carried along with the rest. He wanted badly to escape, but the Maziks were so tightly packed there was no easy way to slip out without causing a spectacle.

He assumed they had all been summoned as he had, and then he realized that Barsilay may have been summoned, too, which would have been disastrous. But before he could go to look for him, all the paths into the courtyard were blocked by blue-clad Mazik guards, who moved at once to trap all the assembled Maziks inside.

From within the main pergola came a woman, very tall and dark-haired, with rubies across her forehead. To her left was a man whose orange eyes marked him as Luzite. A woman dressed in blue came and stood on the dais beside them. She put a hand to her own throat, which seemed to magnify her voice enough to be heard without shouting, though every Mazik assembled fell silent as soon as she appeared.

"The reign of Relam is over," she said. "You will give your oath to his blood and heir, the Queen of Rimon, long may she dream."

A great murmur went up, but the woman, who Naftaly supposed must be some sort of herald, continued. "The oath-getting will not be dreaming. You will all swear your loyalty to our new Queen tomorrow at the royal alcázar. Tomorrow, you shall greet your Queen."

The Queen herself smiled, but only slightly. The man to her left let his eyes scan the crowd, and Naftaly was glad for once to be shorter than the people around him.

Someone near him whispered, "She's to wed the Caçador," and someone else, "They say Relam rode into the sea."

Naftaly's eyes opened, and he was back in the mountains. Barsilay slept at his side; Naftaly thought of waking him, but decided the man was probably too weak to dream, and the immediate danger had passed anyway. Elena, still sitting in the same position she'd been in earlier, said, "You had a bad dream?"

Elena, of course, knew that Naftaly's dreams were as real as most people's waking moments. A bad dream was no passing figment to be forgotten after breakfast.

"Yes," Naftaly said. "I think it was."

IT WAS THREE nights until the New Year, and in the mortal world Toba Bet had been a flock of birds so long she was beginning to forget what it meant to have hands.

She didn't miss them. Wings, she'd concluded, were the better choice. While hands could manipulate, wings provided escape, and escape was not a thing smartly given up.

The horror of her own death was never out of her mind. In the Mazik books Toba Bet had perused in Asmel's library, the question had been posed repeatedly: Was one conscious the moment she entered the void, or did consciousness cease at that precise instant? The scope of the suffering—whether the void of nonexistence was bad enough, or whether it was still worse, and you actually felt yourself inside it, however briefly—was something that had been opined on for as long as Maziks had been writing books, which was long indeed. But the opinions put forth, no matter how well reasoned, were merely philosophical. Or they had been, until Toba had died, and discovered the truth of the matter.

Toba Bet had felt her other self—her original self; some might say her *truer* self—go into the void. The time between her death and the blotting from existence of her mind or spirit or consciousness was little more than an instant. But that instant had existed. Toba Bet had felt it, and she wasn't sure she would ever manage to stop thinking about it, like a whisper in her ear that would not quiet.

"You'd be more helpful as a person," Asmel muttered, which Toba Bet supposed was true. He'd traded his coat and splendid shoes and the ring he wore on his forefinger for simpler clothing and enough money to get them as far north as Barcino. Or it would have, if Asmel had not been too much a Mazik to secure a spot in a cart.

This despite the fact that he had no magic. While his eyes were now a mortal's eyes, he remained too tall, too handsome, and his manner of speech too formal. Everyone seemed to be aware that he was in disguise, though of course none could say how—though everyone seemed to note the combination of his youthful face and silver hair. The effect was enough to make the local farmers and tradesmen and merchants too nervous to allow him to travel with them, and Asmel had been forced to use most of the money they needed for provisions and inns on a sad old horse instead. So Asmel rode and walked alternately to save the horse's strength, and Toba Bet flew, as they put as much distance as possible between themselves and the gate of Rimon before it opened at the next moon.

Asmel had stopped to rest well off the side of the road, because Toba Bet was fairly conspicuous, and made Asmel look even less mortal as she flew around him. "I am growing weary of this," he went on, waving at Toba Bet's many bird-selves. "We're in a bad enough situation without your making it so I can't even talk to you. You know a great deal of what's happened and I am at a complete disadvantage. I don't even know if Barsilay and the elder Toba made it to P'ri Hadar or if things went badly for them." He sat down heavily and pulled his hair back from his face. "And I keep thinking that is why you won't change back, because you don't want me to know the truth."

The truth was more complicated than he'd guessed, and not only because the original Toba had died. Barsilay lived, but he was most certainly not in P'ri Hadar. Instead, he was probably in approximately the same place as Asmel and Toba Bet, only in the Mazik realm, traveling north and trying to get himself away from Rimon. Asmel would blame himself for that, Toba Bet knew. It was a fair disaster that Barsilay was still in grasping distance of the Caçador of Rimon.

They'd also lost the book containing the gate of Luz. Toba's half-sister, the Courser of Rimon, had taken it. Toba's last act, before she'd been killed, was to tear out the last page and send it to Barsilay.

Toba Bet let the part of herself that was airborne bank in a circle around Asmel; others of her were on the ground and in the trees nearby, listening carefully without responding, as she'd been doing for days while she neither ate nor slept, watching over Asmel as he ate salty mortal food and slept on the hard ground.

His eyes had gone far away as he continued his monologue. "I cannot even dream. Do you not have enough pity to tell me if my only kin still lives?"

The bird nearest to him flitted down to land on Asmel's shoulder, and he let out a sigh and turned to meet its eye. "If that's meant to be a comfort, it isn't." He lifted the bird in his palm and held her gently in his lap. "Whatever happened frightened you terribly. I'm sorry I couldn't protect you. I'm sorry I have no magic I can use to protect you now. But please come back to me, and I will do what I can."

Toba Bet felt his warm hand holding her small body. He said, "Shall I make you a trade for your company? I have little left with which to bargain. What would you have of what remains?"

She felt wretched. He was manipulating her, of course, but he had a right to it; no matter how terrified Toba Bet was, she still had more than Asmel. She had her magic, and that meant that while she still had a chance to escape a second trip into the void, Asmel had no other possible destination. And even if he failed to grasp the precise shape of that horror, his imagination could bring him close.

Enough, Toba Bet told herself. She had mourned herself long enough. Toba bat Penina was dead. The person who remained was Toba bat Toba, her own creation, and she would live to protect herself and Asmel for as long as she could, even if what Asmel most needed protecting from was the isolation of his own mind. Gathering herself, she drew in her breath and let her selves come together until she was a woman again, feathers smoothing to a filmy shift—not quite mortal and not quite Mazik, the product of an accidental spell. Asmel's eyes welled and he murmured, "Thank you," and pulled Toba Bet against him. She put her own bare arms around him, trembling in the cold as he pressed his face to her neck, and she stroked his hair and decided that hands had a use after all.

IT WAS THREE nights until the New Year, and three nights since the Courser of Rimon, Tsifra N'Dar, had failed to kill both the heir of Luz and her own sister, when she found herself dreaming of Atalef the Demon.

Tsifra had concluded that her sister had made a buchuk—a twin—and it was one of these versions of Toba Peres that she'd killed. What Tsifra hadn't yet determined was whether she'd killed the original or the buchuk herself. She wondered if it mattered, and had decided to table the question for later pondering; one of them, at least, was still alive and in the mortal realm, and it would be her mission to hunt her down and return her to their father, the Caçador.

If she succeeded, this would be her last act as Courser. The Caçador would replace one sister with another he hoped was cleverer and would better suit his purposes, another half-Mazik who could carry out his will in the mortal world and help him harness the power of the Mirror. Tsifra's entire life had been spent in the pursuit of not being killed by her father or one of his agents, so much so that her awareness of her impending end left her more weary than fearful. Or so she told herself.

Tsifra did not much enjoy Atalef's company while awake, let alone dreaming, and had hoped not to see him again for a very long time after having left him in Mansanar to possess the Queen's confessor. In this dream, he'd taken the shadowy shape of a cat. He paced a circle around her, growing larger until he was the size of a lion made of black shadow.

"Did your master send you?" Tsifra asked, because she could not imagine what Atalef wanted with her.

Atalef said, "No. Our master is content with our work and leaves us alone." Tsifra was glad not to be there to witness the work in question; the real confessor was bad enough even unpossessed. She wondered if anyone at court had noticed the difference.

"Whispering in the Queen's ear?" Tsifra asked. "What does the Caçador want her to do?"

"Nothing, yet," Atalef replied. "Only we aren't whispering now. We are hunting. Hunting birdlings."

"Birdlings," Tsifra repeated, because this was what Atalef called her, too. "What do you mean? Are you not in Mansanar?"

"You know what we mean," Atalef murmured. He had condensed down to the size of a house cat again, and peeked at her through several dozen smoke-colored eyes. "You know precisely what we mean, birdling."

He meant he was hunting her sister, the other Tsifra. The presently considered Tsifra did not know why they shared a name—it was not a typical thing among Maziks—but she suspected that her sister knew. If she found her again, she would have to ask. A problem for another day. To Atalef, she said, "I thought the Caçador was sending me on that mission."

"He changed his mind, decided not to wait," Atalef said. "The Queen can whisper to herself for a bit while we scent the air."

Tsifra did not much like the sound of that, because it meant she was redundant, and being redundant in the service of La Cacería was deadly. It was for this reason she'd killed her sister in the first place—though it turned out she'd only killed half of her. "If you're busy scenting the air, then why are you here with me?" she snapped.

"We wanted to smell you again," Atalef said. "Smell your magic. Birdlings smell different than Maziks."

"Do they?" Tsifra said, and put out her hand, because the quicker he got a whiff, the quicker he would leave; he was bad enough without insisting on calling her "birdling," a moniker she presumed referred to her name, Tsifra N'Dar—the Splendid Bird. She did not like to think that this demon had somehow intuited it. "Well?"

"Hm," he said. "Troublesome, indeed. There is no scent like this in Rimon. Not in the city, not in the mountains."

"Perhaps you're not smelling hard enough."

"No," he said. "She cannot be there."

"She cannot be anywhere else," Tsifra said. "She went through the gate. Fifty Maziks saw her, including the Lymer." The fifty Maziks were all either dead or mad, but the Lymer had been far enough removed not to have suffered from that encounter. "The Lymer said she'd become an entire flock of birds. Can that be why?"

Atalef sat back on his haunches and changed into a shape that was decidedly not a cat. He unfurled his arms and waved his clawed shadow-hands. "It could be. It could be. If she is ten or thirty, then she is too small and too many, like us now."

"Like us? You mean, like a demon?"

"Yes."

Tsifra had never experienced being a flock of birds, and wondered what it might feel like. Did Toba look out of all their eyes at once, or one at a time? She asked, "Her magic is too spread out, you mean?"

"Yes. Just so," Atalef said. "We had not considered that."

"But she can't remain like that for long, can she? Won't she forget how to change back?"

"We don't know," Atalef said, which was probably true. Becoming birds was not a thing that Maziks did, as a rule, making it a clever move indeed. "But if she is with the Lord of Books she will change back soon, I think. She would not want to be his pet."

Tsifra wondered about that. Was Toba not Asmel's pet already? It seemed to her that Asmel must be using Toba the way Tarses was using Tsifra herself, as a tool. What other use did a Mazik have for a half-mortal?

But for all that, he'd given up his own magic before he'd given up Toba to their father.

The Courser did not like plans she could not untangle. It was too much like dealing with a second Tarses.

"But once she changes back, you'll have her."

"Oh, yes," Atalef said. "Very quickly."

And the killstone, she thought, because that was no small part of why Tarses wanted Toba. He believed she possessed the killstone of ha-Moh'to, the stone that contained Tarses's own name, and could be used against him. Atalef would give it to Tarses, because it was what he'd been ordered to do. And for all Atalef made her skin crawl, they were very much the same sort of creature: They were both Tarses's unwilling servants.

Ha-Moh'to, Tsifra had learned through much digging, had been the ancient order sworn to fight the Queen of Luz, their watchword *Monarchy is Abomination*. Their killstone contained the names of every member, and the ability to kill them instantly if only one knew the command-word. Barsilay had given her the command word, under torture. It was only later, when she'd asked the Peregrine about the word he'd said, that she'd learned it had been a mortal word for idiot. Whether he knew the real word or not, she could not say.

"It's a pity," Atalef said, "we don't have the second safira."

Tsifra's mind caught on *we*, as if Atalef considered her an ally. The second safira was the one that belonged to Asmel. "What for? It's a pretty bauble. There's nothing in that one."

"Perhaps. Or perhaps it could be useful, too. The Lord of Books was very wise. Our old master always told us tales of him, before he was put under the mountain. Do you know why our former master was imprisoned?"

"No, I don't."

"He was passing too much time with us. He was doing things with us, to us, for us. So the Maziks came and locked him away, but some of us the Caçador kept for himself." Atalef faded in and out. "He had many ideas about us. What we were, what we could be for. Add a bit of Mazik magic to us and we change. Teach us and we sing, we dance, we learn. The man under the mountain thought, if we can hold a bit of magic, why not more? Why not enough for a whole Mazik?"

This was a lot of information to be freely given; it could not be freely given. She was dangerously close to conspiring with him now, only she did not know how just yet.

She could wake and end this conversation. Nothing he'd told her so far would get her into trouble.

Or she could stay and hear him out, and risk learning things she should not know. She weighed the options in her mind, and decided things could not be much worse for hearing Atalef's suggestion. If either of them managed to catch Toba, she was going to be killed anyway. She said, "How could a demon get a Mazik's full magic?"

Atalef said, "He thought we could be made into receptacles. For safiras."

Tsifra regarded Atalef closely. He was unhappy—even without a face she could tell. "For safiras?"

"Forcing a Mazik to make a safira, it is an old punishment. He forgets himself and goes to the void. The man under the mountain believed there was a way to put the magic into someone, somehow, as long as you were not putting it into a Mazik."

"Why not a Mazik?"

"Too much magic," Atalef said. "It would kill him. But he believed you could put it in a demon. Or a mortal. Or the person it had come out of, if they still lived. And then whatever creature had taken the safira would have all that magic, and all those memories."

"Are you saying," Tsifra said, "that whoever gets Marah's magic put into them will have all her memories? Including the command-word of the killstone?"

"Yes," Atalef said. "We are saying so."

Here, then, was Atalef's plan. And now that she knew, she could either inform Tarses or become Atalef's ally in truth. Tsifra found herself asking, "And did the man under the mountain discover how to put the magic into a demon, or a mortal?"

Atalef said, "If the safira were made into small enough pieces, it could be absorbed, he thought. Only he was never able to test it, because he was put beneath the mountain first."

What Atalef did not know what that she *did* have the second safira. Tarses had thoughtlessly given her the stone containing Asmel's magic for safekeeping, not believing it to be worth enough to guard himself. She whispered, "Does the Caçador know this?"

Atalef hissed back, "He does not."

Tarses only thought to keep the killstone from his enemies. He didn't realize how close he was to being able to use it himself, if he could pass Marah's magic to Atalef. He could kill Barsilay in a moment, and any other enemies who might have put their names into it.

Or Atalef could use it to kill Tarses.

Tsifra considered her next words carefully. "What precisely were you ordered to do?"

"We have three tasks," he said. "Return the other birdling, deliver the killstone, and kill the Lord of Books. And all three are together in one place. Once we find them, there is nothing for us to do but carry out our master's will." Atalef made himself into a facsimile of Tarses's face, which said, "If you are clever, your order will have more empty space."

To trick Tarses into giving her vague orders . . . It was next to impossible. And even if she did somehow manage it, Atalef still didn't know how to absorb the safira. How did you break down an object made of ossified magic?

"The man under the mountain, how did he think a safira could be broken down? Why wasn't he able to try it?"

"What breaks down magic?" Atalef asked. "Surely you must know. Something no Mazik may ever touch. But something that *you* can. Do you know what it is?"

Tsifra startled. Could it be so simple? Atalef laughed, a sound like breaking glass.

"We will keep hunting, little birdling," he said. "And we will see you when we see you, wishing for what you most desire and cannot have."

Freedom, he meant.

"What we both desire," Tsifra said, but Atalef said, "No. We desire something much greater than freedom. Something you cannot understand."

"And what is that?" she asked, as Atalef began to fade.

Atalef whispered, "Unity."

✦ Two ✦

NAFTALY TOLD BARSILAY the details of his dream once he awoke a little later.

"A Queen?" Barsilay asked, a little dazed, still, from his extreme blood loss. "But Relam had three sons, and two of them are still alive, so far as I know."

"Apparently not," Naftaly said, "because there's a Queen now, and all the Maziks have to give her an oath today."

"Today? As in, waking?"

"Yes, that's what they said."

"That's not what I would have expected," Barsilay said, closing his eyes again. "Tell me about the Queen."

"Very tall," Naftaly said. "Dark hair."

"Like this?" Barsilay made a circle in the air with his hand, apparently attempting some illusion that did not manifest. "Never mind," he said. "It can only be Oneca. Dreadful woman. This is worse than I'd feared. At least the younger sons were fools." He sat up on his elbow. "On the other hand, if the oath-getting's being done in person, it might be to our advantage. The Maziks will all be in the city. It will help with our escape."

Elena muttered something in Zayiti, which had been her preferred tongue since she'd suffered a stroke some weeks before. Barsilay said, "Yes, I'm aware—she says we have to do something about my masticated corpse. It isn't a corpse if I'm not dead."

"I did not say corpse," she protested, in La'az Sefardi this time. Turning to the others, she added, "I said body, not corpse."

"You would not have to worry about him mistranslating if you spoke La'az Sefardi in the first place," Naftaly said.

"Zayiti is easier. Not my fault."

"I'm a bit turned around here," Barsilay said. "Is she Zayiti or not?"

"Not," the old woman explained. "She's had a stroke, and it's scrambled her a bit."

"Could you help her?" Naftaly asked Barsilay. "You were studying to be a doctor, you said."

"A *Mazik* doctor. I have no idea what to do for mortal brains. It would probably be easier if you just learned Zayiti."

"This is…" Elena said another word in Zayiti.

"Irrelevant," Barsilay put in. "It is."

"We need to do three things," Elena said, ticking the items off on her fingers. "Clean up blood, get horses, run away."

"Seems clear enough to me," Barsilay said. "You hardly need more words than that. Anything else is superfluous."

Elena scowled. "I miss being su-per-flouts." To Naftaly, she said, "Dig a hole."

NAFTALY DID NOT expect his morning to begin by washing blood from the body of his half-dead Mazik lover while discussing the finer points of horse thievery.

Labeling Barsilay his lover might have been a bit of a stretch. As was the half-dead bit—Barsilay was probably more like three-quarters dead, but it was such a dark thought that Naftaly tamped it down.

The blood bit, that was accurate. It was nothing short of a miracle that Barsilay had bled so much and yet somehow lived, and while most of it had soaked into the ground, enough of it was on Barsilay himself—his skin, his clothes, his fine hair—that they really couldn't do anything else 'til it was addressed.

Elena told Barsilay something in Zayiti, which made him smile faintly, and nod.

"What did she say?" the old woman asked.

"That I'd attract scavengers," he said. "She's probably right."

"There's no saving the clothes," the old woman pointed out.

"We'll have to find replacements," Naftaly agreed. "And quickly, it's cold out here."

Barsilay's shirt had already been cut away, but he objected in the strongest terms to losing his trousers until suitable replacements were located. "Do allow me some dignity," he said. "I don't care how bloody they are."

"Fine," the old woman said. "And where can we get pants in the middle of nowhere?"

Elena made a snide-sounding remark.

"What?" asked Naftaly.

"It's nothing," Barsilay said. To Elena, he said, "You know, I just nearly died, so if you could not make me waste energy translating your asides, I would appreciate it."

Elena glanced over at Naftaly and said, "If he wants *you* to sew him pants, we will be here 'til next spring."

Naftaly thought of mentioning that of course he could sew no pants—he had no fabric, needle, or thread—but decided to let the insult about his tailoring skills pass.

"There will be clothing at the same place as the horses," Barsilay said. "And you'll need replacements, too. You look like a pack of mortals that wandered in through the gate and got lost . . . You know what? Never mind. The clothes are the least of that. You're far too old and your eyes are all wrong, and I don't have enough magic to fix any of that right now."

"So what do we do?" Elena demanded.

Barsilay's head lolled to one side. "I have no idea. Just go steal the damned horses. If we run into anyone between here and Zayit, it won't matter what any of us are wearing or what your eyes look like."

What little luck the universe had granted them was this: They were a scant mile from a ranch near the base of Mount Sebah that was famous for providing the King with horses, which they might be able to use to get out of Rimon before they were all murdered. The owner of the ranch—some minor Mazik lord or other—would not be at home, because he would be swearing fealty to the new Queen. "It won't be well guarded," Barsilay said. "No one would ever steal horses from that ranch; it would be a death sentence. But just to be safe, don't pick the fastest. Pick two they won't be likely to miss right away, that will be harder to identify later."

It seemed to Naftaly that successfully stealing *any* two horses would be an enormous coup, not to mention the clothes and lentils Barsilay had also requested. The wisdom of this entire enterprise seemed especially doubtful as Naftaly crouched with Elena and the old woman behind a thatch of barbed undergrowth looking down at a building of buff stone, surrounded on all sides by a fence of what might have been polished wood or else some Mazik facsimile. Within the fence were dozens of grazing animals. "Those are horses?" Elena asked dubiously.

"Barsilay said so," Naftaly replied.

"Barsilay is nine-tenths dead. He may be confused," the old woman said.

Overlooking the paddock was the largest oak Naftaly had ever seen. On the opposite side of the fence, several shadows were sweeping its acorns into a pile, which had attracted the attention of what must have been Mazik squirrels—red as foxes but otherwise unremarkable. They were taking turns dashing into the growing pile of acorns, each the size of Naftaly's largest toe, whenever the shadows were far enough away not to be a threat with their brooms. Two of the shadows were taking turns working a pair of horses, a bay gelding and a palomino mare, that were both under saddle and being led around in a circle by their bridles.

"I've seen these animals before," Naftaly said, meaning the horses. "When I was nearly captured going through the gate, the Maziks were riding them."

"Could be goats," Elena put forth. "They have horns."

They did indeed … The creatures were at least as much like goats as like horses, but Naftaly thought it hardly mattered as long as you could safely ride one. Apart from the horns and the size of the animals, the thing that gave him the biggest pause was their eyes: square-pupiled like Maziks', but also far too close together. It gave them the air of being too much like a person, or a cat, or even an owl. Horses were not meant to look you in both eyes at the same time. Elena either did not share his discomfort, or else had decided it was too cumbersome to remark upon.

"What difference does it make?" he asked.

"If I am going to sit on an animal," Elena said, "I want to know what it is."

"Well, say it could be either, then. It's a large, tame herbivore that runs fast. The point remains, we have to find some way to steal them without being noticed. Do you have any idea how to do that?"

Elena frowned.

"What?" Naftaly asked.

"Those shadows…"

Naftaly had noticed half a dozen shadows performing various tasks aside from sweeping the acorns. Others were grooming the horses, leading them from one side of the fenced area to the other on long leads, and checking the integrity of the fence. The two that had been leading the saddled horses in circles had paused to help some of the others do something magical to a loose board, leaving the horses to graze. "I have no idea what those are," he admitted. "Magical servants, I expect."

"Barsilay said nothing about those," Elena said. "No idea how well they see or how to get past them." She sat back on her haunches and rubbed at her eyes. "It would be better if the person who knew things was here."

But Barsilay could not have come, because his legs were broken, his arm was severed, and he had lost most of his magic along with the blood that had soaked into Mount Sebah.

"Never mind," Elena said, seeing Naftaly's distress. "Just watch and see. They have not noticed us yet."

"So they may see as well as a person," Naftaly reasoned, "but no better."

"Yes. Good."

"They haven't heard us either," Naftaly added.

"Right," Elena said. "Always claim your assets. The horses are also very big. They'll be fast, if we can get some."

"Won't that make them more dangerous?" Naftaly asked.

"Hardly matters," Elena said. "Even a regular horse can kill you if it decides to kick. It's only a large, tame her-bi-vore, right? It's safe unless you scare it or make it angry."

At that, one of the red squirrels passed a bit too near, and the palomino mare that had been grazing there jerked its head over the fence and snapped the squirrel into its mouth.

Elena and Naftaly met one another's eyes. Behind them, the old woman muttered, "Fuck."

TOBA BET WAS SLUGGISH and weak after her transformation, and she was chilled even in the wool wrap Asmel had traded for the last of his money. She struggled to change lentils into food, and after three tries at making bread gave up and made them into lentil soup, which took less imagination.

"You've overexerted yourself," Asmel said, drinking the soup directly from the wooden cup Toba Bet had made from an acorn, because she was too exhausted to make spoons. "You spent too much time as all those birds. I'm surprised you aren't worse."

But Toba Bet wasn't sure that was the entirety of the problem. "Asmel," she reminded him, "I died."

"No," he said. "You didn't die. Your counterpart died. You are very much alive, and you need to remember it."

"I did die," she insisted. "I felt it, Asmel. I won't believe that's had no effect. Are you so sure that's not why I'm ill now?"

"You're ill because you spent days flapping around. There's a cost to maintaining magic that profound, and worse, you weren't eating or sleeping. Your weakness is accounted for by that alone. Put the rest out of your mind."

"I can't."

"We have limited time," he said. "We are safe now because the Courser is still on the other side of the gate and Tarses has no one else to send after us, but each day we grow closer to the next moon, and we haven't put nearly enough distance between ourselves and Rimon."

He was correct, of course. Toba Bet's ruminations about the void were doing her no good ... She needed to concentrate on not ending up there a second time. But whenever she closed her eyes, she felt herself slipping into it again, the horror of it creeping into her limbs as she went numb from the outside in, until only her mind was left for a split second of terror.

"Come here," he said, and then embraced her—such an uncharacteristic move that it alarmed Toba Bet more than it comforted her. "Dear one, why are we here?"

She pulled back. "What?"

"I don't recall how we left the university. Did something happen?"

Toba Bet blinked at him stupidly. "Asmel," she said, "do you really not remember?"

He cocked his head. "No." He rubbed his thumb over his lip. "What's happened to your eyes?"

"My eyes?"

"They're so dark ..." He looked at her a long time before lowering his arms, saying, "You aren't her."

Marah, of course, would be his dear one. Toba Bet had seen her in Asmel's memories, and she'd had the same golden eyes as Barsilay. Notably, she and Toba—her descendant of more generations than Toba Bet could account for—bore little physical resemblance. That he'd mistaken one for the other was alarming indeed.

"Do you know me now?"

When he gave no response, she said, "Do you remember what happened to Marah?"

He blinked a few times, trying to get his mind to focus. "It's the same thing that's happening to me now. She pulled out her magic and her mind went dark. How long has it been for me?"

"Five days," she said.

"Five…" he said. "Listen to me, whatever happened to Marah was finished before the next moon, else she would have come home. She probably didn't realize her mind would decay so quickly. By the time she was able to return, she'd forgotten how, if not where she came from in the first place. I don't have much time." He pressed the heel of his hand between his eyes. "It's growing more muddled all the time. I can't bear it. What am I? I am no Mazik now."

Disaster on top of disaster. Toba Bet said, "If magic and memory are so linked, would some of my magic slow the decline?"

Asmel let out a shaky breath. "Your magic is different enough that I could not say what it might do."

"Could whatever protects my magic from dying in the mortal world also protect your mind?"

Asmel shook his head. "It's hardly worth a test … You have little enough magic even for yourself right now."

Toba Bet drew a great breath and pressed a bit of magic out from her palm, as she'd seen Asmel do himself long ago. "Just take it." She held out her hand.

He reached for it and let his hand drop. "I can't," he said. "I have no way to hold it as I am now."

"Then I'll give it to you," she said, and pressed the magic into the space over his heart. He jerked a bit as it went in, as if it had hurt him, and after, he put a tentative hand to his chest. "Do you feel it?"

He blinked a few times; his eyes stayed round, but for a moment the pupils shifted, as if they were trying to return to their former shape. "Yes." He glanced up at her. "We're in the mortal world. Barsilay is alive."

"Yes."

"And he's the heir of Luz." Asmel smiled, just barely, as if at some old private joke. "Of all the absurdities. And he's on the way to Zayit?"

"Most likely," she said.

He looked far away again. "I forgot that for a moment." He shook his head. "I forgot a great deal."

"And now?"

"Now I seem to be myself. But this can't be a solution. I won't be drinking your magic like a parasite."

"For now, we have no choice," she said. "We need your mind sharp if we want any hope of getting to Zayit. We'll have to think of another solution after we get there."

Asmel let his hand rest over the spot where Toba Bet's magic had gone in for a minute. "We have to assume my mind may not hold out that long," he said. "I don't know how much time you can safely buy me. Whatever help I can give you, it must be soon."

ALL THAT REMAINED of the squirrel was a tuft of tail, on the ground next to the fence. The palomino mare had gone back to placidly munching the grass, as if nothing of interest had happened at all. An ordinary afternoon for a horse—chew a little grain, get a little exercise, eat a little helpless animal.

"Your Mazik," the old woman said, "has sent us to capture a pair of large *carnivores*."

"It was only a squirrel," Naftaly said, not even convincing himself. "I'm sure it was just an opportunistic meal."

"Right," the old woman said. "You go stand next to one of those beasts for a bit, and we'll see how opportunistic it gets."

"This changes nothing," Elena said. She bobbled her head. "It changes some things. But we still have to *get* them. We can't walk to Zayit. So the question is: How do we get past those shadows, and how do we steal two of those horses?"

"Oh, you're right," the old woman said. "That is so simple. You've convinced me."

"Be helpful or be quiet. Now, the boy is right. It was just a squirrel. The horses are not eating each other; they aren't starving. And we're large. Probably too large to bother with."

"Right," Naftaly said. "And the shadows? How do we avoid them seeing us?"

"Not sure yet," she admitted.

"We could make a distraction," the old woman said. "Set fire to the barn."

"No," Naftaly said. "Barsilay doesn't want the Maziks knowing anyone's been here, and they'd know if someone set a fire. It would have to be something natural."

Elena looked at the scene a while longer. "What are the shadows doing?"

"Tidying," the old woman said. "Either the grounds or the horses."

"Right. Right." She looked back up at Naftaly. "So let's give them something bigger to clean up."

The key to Elena's plan was the great oak near the paddock, which had already dropped about half its load of fruit. The shadows were not wrong to be concerned with tidying the acorns; so many on the ground would wreak havoc on the horses' hooves. Naftaly was surprised the Maziks hadn't simply removed the tree, but it was so old and so beautiful he assumed there might have been a prohibition against harming such a specimen. A human rancher would certainly have cut it down.

The old woman had argued to wait until nightfall, but there was no indication the shadows would stop working overnight, and in the dark they would be impossible to see. So instead Elena crouched in the roots of the oak, while Naftaly and the old woman were at the far end of the paddock in a blind area blocked by the edge of the barn.

Elena was just fixing to use a bit of magic to blow the remaining acorns into the paddock when every shadow within it vanished.

Brooms clattered to the ground, along with the brush one of the shadows had been using to rub down an especially large stallion. From inside the barn, a crash signaled what was likely a bucket or something else metal being dropped.

Naftaly peered out from his hiding place and saw Elena peeking out from behind the oak. He gestured at the paddock and mimed a giant shrug, then pointed to Elena, who shook her head back.

"Are all of them gone?" the old woman asked in his ear.

"I don't see any anywhere," he replied.

"Was it her?"

"Elena? She says not."

"Well, was it you?"

"If I knew how to do such a thing, I'd have done it earlier," he said, standing up. He called to Elena, "Can you see the road from there? Has someone returned?"

Elena said, "Don't think so. All the shadows have gone. Nothing left but horses."

"Lucky for us," said the old woman, getting to her feet with a grunt. "Let's get what we came for before those shadows come back."

BARSILAY HAD MANAGED to sit himself up by the time they returned. He still looked like death, but now it was of a more vertical variety, so Naftaly thought this was probably an improvement. He was massaging one of his calves, which were looking decidedly less crooked. It occurred to Naftaly rather belatedly that Barsilay must have set his broken legs himself after the others left, probably to spare them the sight, and he'd had to do it with one hand.

They'd been more or less gifted the horses by the disappearance of the shadows, but then they'd realized that none of them knew how to saddle a horse, and they would have been afraid to try even if they had. After they'd managed to find lentils and clothes for Barsilay, a lengthy discussion had broken out about which horses to take. There was a pair of smallish gray mares, snoozing in the sun, that looked especially docile but were not saddled. The two that were—the palomino squirrel-eater and the brown stallion that the shadows had been working—were a bad bet indeed. But they'd had to conclude that taking the saddled horses was the only choice, and so they'd very cautiously walked them back up to Barsilay in the hills, since not only did none of them know how to saddle a horse, none of them knew how to ride one.

"Are you less broken?" the old woman asked Barsilay, upon seeing him sitting up. "Will your arm grow back as well?"

"Are you asking if I can regrow limbs like a salamander?" Barsilay asked. He laughed as much as his ill state would allow. "Now wouldn't that be something? No, I'm afraid not. I see you've found us transportation. I'm deeply impressed. If we survive the next several days, I shall reward you handsomely."

The old woman said, "Are you very rich?"

"Not remotely. But you shall have"—here Barsilay was taken by coughing—"my eternal gratitude."

"Will it buy me dinner and a new pair of shoes?" the old woman grumbled.

"Don't mind her," Elena said. "She's only cross because you failed to mention your horses are carn-ivor-ous."

He blinked tiredly. "They're not, they're omnivorous. And of course they are. They're horses, aren't they?"

"Ours eat only grain," Naftaly said gently.

"Do they? No wonder they're so small. But it's no matter. They've been trained not to hunt; just because they can eat meat doesn't mean they do."

The old woman said, "We saw one eat a squirrel."

Barsilay looked slightly nonplussed. "Oh. Really? Well, that is unusual. But I'm sure it was only being opportunistic—"

"Yes!" Naftaly said, pointing.

"And who among us has not opportunistically eaten a squirrel?" Barsilay said.

The old woman looked from Barsilay to Naftaly. "Is he joking? I can't tell."

"Hashem's sake," Barsilay said. "Listen, I told you the horses have been trained not to hunt, and they'd certainly never try to eat a Mazik. You're all lathered up about nothing. Anyway, it's not as if you brought back the squirrel-eater."

The old woman pointed toward the palomino mare. "It was that one."

Barsilay cocked his head to one side. "Ah."

"You just said it was merely opportunistic," Naftaly said.

"It's … Yes, I did say that, in the general sense that it was seizing an opportunity. It's just that, well, to sum up the situation: You saw one of the horses had a taste for fresh meat, and you thought, 'I'll take that one to ride on for the next five hundred miles.'"

"It … was available," Elena said. "We had a hard time. You also failed to mention the shadows."

"The shades? Ah," he said. "I didn't mention those?"

"You did not."

"Well, that's my fault then, but you seem to have found a way to deal with them."

Naftaly put in, "Not really. They just left."

Barsilay sat back hard. "They left? Where the devil did they go?"

"Not left so much as vanished," the old woman said.

At that, Barsilay looked troubled indeed.

"Is that bad?" Naftaly asked.

"It means the Mazik who cast them is probably dead," Barsilay said.

"Is *that* bad?" the old woman asked. "Was he a friend of yours?"

"Oh, no, he was dreadful," Barsilay said. "But a Mazik like that doesn't just die for no reason."

"Especially not on the first day of the reign of a new queen," Naftaly said. "On the day of her oath-getting."

"Right," Barsilay said, then echoed uneasily, "Right…" To Naftaly, he said, "I think we should go. Quickly."

+
+ ++ +
+ · ++ +

THAT NIGHT, TOBA BET dreamt herself into the void.

She had hoped to dream her way to Barsilay or Naftaly, to tell them that she and Asmel lived, that they would find a way to Zayit, the Republic of Salt. Instead, she felt herself trapped, motionless, as the fibers of her mind began to wink out one by one.

Then, a voice: "Why are you torturing yourself this way?"

Toba Bet had no voice with which to answer, but felt herself being yanked back, and suddenly she was a mind and body again, with the complete range of senses. And she was surprised to see that the person who had liberated her from the void was the very person who had condemned her to it in the first place: her sister, the other Tsifra N'Dar, Tarses's younger daughter and the Courser of Rimon.

Tsifra had pulled her into some dream of her own, some deserted walled city that Toba Bet did not know. "I would think one trip to the void would have been enough for you," she said. "I had no idea some version of it even existed here." Toba Bet glared at her own murderer, who went on, "Or maybe it didn't, and you just created it somehow."

They were atop the wall, looking down into the city with no people, and Tsifra picked up a pebble of disintegrating mortar and flicked it into the street below. "For what it's worth, I'm sorry I had to kill you, but if I hadn't I'd be dead and there aren't two of me." She seemed to consider this a moment and then added, "Also, you'd be a monster now."

"I would not."

"Oh, you would. Our father would have your name and he'd have used it to compel you. Probably he would have made you kill the Lord of Books first, and then your Luzite cousin second. Dying a little seems a small price to pay to avoid that."

"Do you want my forgiveness?"

Tsifra thought for a moment, and then said, "No, I wouldn't trust you if you offered it."

"Then why are we here?"

"Would you prefer I put you back where I found you?"

Toba Bet stood, brushing the dream-dust from her skirt, and said, "Never mind. I'm leaving."

"You'll never be free of him while he lives."

Toba Bet paused. "Assuming you mean our father, you're telling me nothing I don't already know. And if you've come to trick me into telling you how to find me, you've hunted me down here for nothing."

"I don't need to trick you," the Courser said. "I'm trying to warn you."

"Then give me some useful information so I can avoid him," Toba Bet said. "Or else leave me alone, unless you intend to cut off my head again, and you're just dragging out the moment."

Tsifra said, "And what will you give me if I offer you useful information?"

Toba Bet spat, "Are you joking? I'll give you nothing!"

Tsifra had risen to walk along the edge of the wall and peered down as if judging the distance. Finally she said, "I'll give you this for free, then: The Queen's confessor is possessed."

Toba Bet tried to make sense of this. She must have meant the mortal Queen—the Mazik Queen would have no confessor. "Possessed by what?"

"By *what* is obvious," Tsifra said. "By *whom* is a more useful piece of information, which I cannot share. But puzzle it out quickly, sister, because I think that you shall meet him soon."

THREE

IN ELENA'S OPINION, their greatest problem—apart from the fact that none of the four was a passable rider—was that three of the four of them looked abundantly mortal and the fourth was wanted by La Cacería, and probably the crown, too. None of them had a face that was safe to be seen by other Maziks, and the only one among them able to generate enough magic to disguise them all was too weak to do it just then. Elena could glamour one or two of them for a handful of minutes and Naftaly could manage a set or two of eyes, but it wouldn't be nearly enough to protect them if they found themselves at the end of a Cacería sword.

Hiding in the mountains until Barsilay's magic returned was an option that had very early been considered and discarded. "The longer we wait, the more Maziks will be hunting me," Barsilay said, and Elena agreed, "If the choice is to run or hide, you must always run. If you hide, you risk being trapped."

They did what they could, which is to say that Naftaly disguised his eyes and the women did their best to shield their faces with hoods made from cloaks liberated from the ranch.

At least Barsilay spoke Zayiti. Elena's La'az Sefardi was passable now, but she hated how clumsy she felt, and in Zayiti, she still sounded like herself. "So tell us," she said, as they made their way north, "now we're underway, why you think the owner of all those fine horses is dead."

Barsilay said, "I don't know. I can think of two possibilities: either he made the wrong person angry, or he was in someone's way. Most likely it's both. Without any source of information, I can't say more. But whenever there's a change in the succession, it's likely to be bloody. It's been that way since the Fall of the Empire."

"The empire to which you are the heir," Elena said.

Barsilay looked quite uncomfortable.

Elena put forth, "Are you unhappy I know this, or with your position?"

"It's only a moot point. I have no intention of resurrecting the throne of Luz, even if I could. Which I can't, since Luz is very much at the bottom of the Dimah Sea." He tsked. "In any case, the Rimoni succession is the issue here, since that city is very much extant. I only wish we knew what was happening."

"And there's no one you can talk to for information?" she asked.

"Oh, loads of people," he answered. "Just none I can trust at the moment, especially if Queen Oneca has it in mind to purge the adonate. Dreadful woman."

"You seem to say that about everyone," the old woman said.

"You do realize when I say 'dreadful' I mean it in the literal sense, as in 'inspiring dread.' I don't mean she's unpleasant company. I mean she'll kill you in the nastiest way possible and won't feel sorry after."

"But surely you know some Maziks who aren't dreadful," Elena said.

Barsilay thought on this. Eventually he said, "Yes, but most of them are dead."

Then there had to be a bit of shuffling, because the horses had gotten too close together and the palomino mare was sniffing at Elena's leg in an alarming way and had to be jerked back just before she snapped her teeth together around Elena's ankle.

"Sorry," Barsilay said. "I'll keep tighter control."

Elena steered her own horse several feet away. "If all the Maziks are as terrible as you say," she said, "I don't understand how there are any left."

"Oh, well, that's easy. There aren't many Maziks, not compared to mortals. Haven't you noticed the miles and miles of empty space we've been traveling through?"

"I supposed you were taking us through a deserted area deliberately."

"There's no need," he said. "There's no one between Rimon and Zayit. It's completely unoccupied except for beasts and the occasional pocket of demons."

She gaped at him. "Empty all the way to Zayit?"

"Indeed," he said. "We are a civilized people, in the sense that we dwell in cities only. We don't require so much arable land as mortals, and we don't need pasturing except for horses. There are no Maziks to be found far from the gates." He paused. "Well, so far as I know, anyway. I suppose there could be some we haven't met. Our travel is a bit circumscribed because of the salt issue, you see. We can't travel by sea, nor can we cross deserts. So what lies on the other side, I couldn't say."

"So there could be ten million Maziks at the other end of the silk road or across the western sea and you would not know?" Elena asked.

"Yes," he said. "That's entirely possible. I suppose if there are, they also believe that we don't exist." He smiled. "What a delightful concept. I shall dwell on it a bit." He gave his full attention back to the road and keeping his mount from eating his companions, and rode the next several miles without saying anything at all.

Elena wondered about all the empty space ahead of them. It seemed impossible that so much of the world here was unoccupied, or that there were so few Maziks. Fewer Maziks ought to have meant they were a more peaceable people: What did they have to fight over, with so much space? And if they could feed themselves like kings for the price of a few lentils, there should also be no hunger and no poverty.

Still, Barsilay had told them the Mazik world was filled with dreadful people—queens who killed their subjects over nothing much, and inquisitions who hunted people down and executed them for even less.

What was the point? she wondered. Suffering, in this world, was an entirely manufactured condition. She wondered if it had always been so, even under Luz. But if Luz had been preferable, wouldn't Barsilay be more eager to resurrect it?

"Barsilay—" she started.

"Not now," he said. "I am choosing not to exist."

TOBA BET AND ASMEL were in nearly the same place in the other world, heading in the same direction.

At that moment, Asmel was riding while Toba Bet walked, because she wanted to conserve Asmel's strength and the horse's legs both. Also, she wasn't used to riding and it hurt her backside rather badly.

"I've been thinking about the Mirror," Toba Bet said. She'd already given Asmel another small burst of magic that morning when he hadn't remembered where they were or where they were going, and she was concerned that the first bit had worn off so quickly, but there seemed to be no point in bringing it up. If there were some other way to treat Asmel's mental decline, they would be using it. Anyway, the parallel between Asmel's loss of magic and Marah's, so many years before, had made her wonder about the Mirror. Asmel could not be a mirror to Marah when so much time had passed between them, but Asmel was a mirror to someone, if she understood the effect correctly. She went on, "If Tarses is trying to manipulate the Mirror, isn't there some way for us to do the same?"

Asmel looked forward to the horizon. "It had occurred to me that there might be some way for us to help Barsilay, but honestly, it's such a nebulous thing I'm not sure what we could do. It's not as if everything here has some analog there, or if it does, it's not obvious what it is. You can see the effect with great figures or events, but among those smaller? I don't know. In any case, if Barsilay lives, his analog here may well be us, in which case the only way to help him is to get to Zayit safely ourselves." He adjusted his weight in the saddle. "I take it that you were unable to dream of Barsilay last night?"

Toba Bet nodded once. She had not been able to decide how to couch her dream of her sister, whose word she certainly could not trust. She supposed she had to tell him, though. "I dreamed of the Courser," she said. "She apologized for killing me."

"Did she? How generous of her. I suppose you forgave her?"

Toba Bet snorted. "She said she had a warning for me."

"That Tarses intends for her to kill me and return you through the gate? We've guessed that already."

"There was more," she said. "She told me the Queen's confessor was possessed."

"Possessed?"

"Mm. And she implied the key detail was not what possessed him but who."

"That makes little sense. Is she implying he's possessed by a Mazik? That's not possible."

"Are you sure?"

"Completely. Demons can possess mortals because they have no body; they simply slip inside. A Mazik is as corporeal as a mortal, or a dog, or a tree."

"Yes, but Rafeq controlled demons, didn't he? Could she have meant something like that?"

"You saw how poorly he controlled them," Asmel said. "And that was after ages of training. I doubt someone else could do better."

"But it is possible? In which case Tarses could have another agent here."

"You're assuming she was telling you the truth. Does it change our course of action, either way?"

Toba Bet hated an unsolved puzzle, and it was worse because it had come from her sister. But Asmel was right, it changed nothing. "I suppose not," she said.

"You're upset," Asmel said.

"Yes, well, dreaming of your own murderer will do that, but there's more. I told you we have the same name."

"You want to know what it means for you, that you share it?"

"Do you know?"

Asmel thought a moment and then said, "On a practical level, it certainly puts you at risk from her and anyone else who knows her name. As to any more esoteric meaning, I could not say. I can tell you this, though: There may be a way out of it for you. There is a tale about the Queen of Luz. One of her adons was tricked out of his name by a scheming lover who wanted to force him into marriage. He agreed to the betrothal and then went to the Queen and begged for help, so she made him a deal: She would grant him a new name, breaking his engagement and the power of his fiancée over him and, in exchange, he was to give the Queen all his lands and serve as the Queen's consort for fifty years."

"Surely he didn't accept that!"

"If he'd refused, he'd have been enslaved to his wife the rest of his days and suffered the wrath of the Queen besides, so he had no choice."

The Queen, Barsilay had told Toba Bet, had been a horror— enough to spawn ha-Moh'to, which sought to mitigate the worst of her rule. Toba Bet asked, "Is it a true story?"

"Marah was the one who recounted it to me, so I assume so," Asmel said. "Barsilay could confirm it."

"He could do more than confirm the story," Toba Bet said. "If that power lies with the crown of Luz, then it's Barsilay's too, or it would be if he were King. You think Barsilay might be able to give me a new name?"

"If he were King," Asmel said.

"Do you think he even means to be?"

"I think if Barsilay had the choice between being King and running to the farthest edge of the earth, we would never see him again. He has entirely the wrong sort of disposition for kingship. And he's far too aware of the sort of things kings are capable of. On the other hand…he may not have the choice to run to the farthest edge of the earth. In which case, at least you'll have a new name."

Toba Bet scoffed. "That would require more things to go right for us than has happened so far."

Asmel said, "Yes, but I know how you enjoy gnawing on a bit of optimism from time to time."

Toba Bet gnawed on it a little while she walked next to the horse. Barsilay, King! But before that could happen, they would have to find the Ziz, repair the firmament, and prevent either herself or Barsilay dying or being enslaved by Tarses. She found she liked the idea of not sharing her name, however, and the more she thought about it, the nicer it sounded—not least because it would mean that her murderous sister would no longer have potential power over her.

They were approaching a crossroads. North would take them to Mansanar, the Queen's capital, and northeast—the direction they were headed—to Barcino and then on to Zayit. The proximity to the crossroads meant there was much more traffic on the road than there had been closer to Rimon, and Toba Bet did not quite know what to do when they passed travelers coming the other way. She'd decided the best course was to keep her gaze focused on the road and appear tired and careworn, which she was. The unfortunate result was that she did not notice the force of men coming from Mansanar until Asmel said, "Toba."

Asmel pulled the horse to a stop and Toba Bet watched as several squads of armed men marched through the crossroads and onward northeast. "They're going to Barcino?" she asked. Admittedly, Toba Bet had been mainly in the Mazik world for months and knew little of what was happening in mortal Sefarad, but so far as she knew, the country was not at war. Then again, the King and Queen had spent the past ten years fighting in Rimon. Now that was taken, they were probably itching to do something else with the soldiers. Bother the Franks by attempting to push the border north, most likely. Regardless, Toba Bet did not think it would be wise to share the road with so many soldiers. Soldiers often got ideas, and if you happened to be around when they did, it did not go well for you.

"What should we do?" she asked. Turning back was no option. "Do you think there are more coming?"

"I think we have to assume there may be," he said. "Perhaps—"

He stopped speaking, because ahead of them a cadre of a dozen mounted men had turned south, toward Rimon. "Do we turn around?" Toba Bet asked.

"That would only draw more attention," he said. "Let's keep going for now." And he nudged the horse and Toba Bet both. "Cover your face."

"Cover yours," she replied. "You're prettier."

Asmel ignored this.

"They're likely on their way to summon troops from the occupation," she said. "They'll pay us no mind." And she believed it, too, until half of the men split off and went to the other side of the road, boxing them in.

Toba Bet glanced at Asmel, who, to his credit, did not look afraid. "Sirs," he said. "I find you are impeding our progress."

It was too cheeky, and Toba Bet would have told him so but the apparent commander of the bunch said, "It does look that way. Where are you going?"

"To Vercia," Toba Bet put in. Not the next town up, but the one beyond, because it seemed less suspicious than two people traveling alone all the way to Barcino. She added, "To see my brother's family."

The commander gave no reply, but stared too intently and for too long into Toba Bet's eyes. He would not be able to see through the glamour that disguised her pupils, but it occurred to Toba Bet that he was checking for them. She saw one of the soldiers creeping closer to Asmel and realized her oversight just as the soldier reached out to uncover Asmel's hair.

She flung out a panicked hand and grasped at Asmel's thigh, throwing out enough magic to darken his hair from silver-white to light brown just as his hood came off. Asmel turned to glare at the man who had uncovered his head.

The commander frowned and said, "My apologies for delaying you." The man returned Asmel's hood, and then they continued south.

When they'd gone on for several minutes, Toba Bet said, "He checked my eyes, did you see?"

"I saw." The glamour on Asmel's hair, which had been cast badly and in a hurry, had already faded out. "I think we had better get off the road now, and I think you should ride for a while."

Ignoring the obvious problem—two people could not cut across open country on a horse for long—there seemed no other option. Someone had sent those soldiers to hunt a woman with unusual eyes and a man with unusual hair on the road south to Rimon. Which meant, most likely, there was another group looking for them on the road north to Barcino.

Toba Bet pulled herself up into the saddle behind Asmel, and he turned away from the road.

"Do you think this is to do with what my sister said, about the Queen's confessor?"

Asmel said, "I think it's likely. Whether Tarses has a demon or not, he clearly has some agent here, and they have sway over soldiers." He glanced back to Toba behind him. "I've been thinking of what avenues of help might be left open to you. You do understand what you must do, once you arrive in Zayit?"

"Find Barsilay," she said.

"Beyond that. You are Marah's heir; you have to do the work she left you. Go into Aravoth, find the Ziz, and replace the gate of Luz in the firmament."

"I'm aware of the task," she said, "only I've no idea how to get into Aravoth."

"I wish I could tell you. The best person to ask would be Omer of Te'ena, but there has been no way to reach him since the Fall. I think our only hope of your obtaining that information now is the dream-world. You must find the Colloquium."

"A dreamed colloquium?"

Asmel said, "Just so. After La Cacería closed the university in Rimon, the remaining scholars began convening a Colloquium in the dream-world. It was the only safe way for them to meet without risking their lives for their work. All those in the cities close enough to dream together meet the night of the new moon."

"Including you?"

"I attended the first Colloquium long enough to realize that the silencing sigils La Cacería had placed on me followed me to the dream-world. After that, I stayed away. I can only hope they continued the meetings. If so, the scholars from Zayit and Anab should be there. There are two colleagues of mine who might help you: Rahel and Mir. I believe both are in Zayit now. They may be able to advise you better than I can. Find them; make yourself known. You cannot rely on me, Toba. You must find someone else."

TARSES MARRIED QUEEN Oneca in the Alcalá of Rimon, in front of the adonate, the Courser, and Tsidon the Lymer.

Oneca looked as she normally did, which is to say like she'd rather have been watching someone die horribly. Tarses, conversely, was exultant. Not that he smiled—he would never, at his own wedding—but his eyes were as bright as they'd been the day he'd learned that his other daughter had wandered through the gate and was now in easy grasping distance.

They were strange, too, Tarses's eyes—subtly dark, so that at first Tsifra thought it was something to do with the light. But when he moved nearer a light-stone she realized they'd been glamoured, the orange dimmed, as if he were trying to make those in attendance forget he was of Luz and not Rimon.

Probably none at the wedding, besides Tsifra herself, knew of the man he'd been there, so long ago—not only an enemy of the monarchy of Luz but of all monarchy, a member of ha-Moh'to. Tsifra wondered what Oneca would think of that, or if it would matter to her at all.

Tsifra wondered what sort of deal Oneca had struck, which had involved murdering her cousin, the late King Relam, and all three of his sons. Oneca got the throne and Tarses got ... what exactly? Free rein for La Cacería, but he'd already had that. He would never be King, not properly; he needed blood to join the succession, or a coup, or a child with Oneca for whom he could serve as regent.

If Oneca were clever, she would never allow herself to become pregnant.

Tsidon the Lymer came to Tsifra after the ceremony, his entire left eye surrounded by a long, winding scar that was likely a punishment for allowing Toba to escape after tricking him with a buchuk and the wrong safira.

"Did Tarses try to take your eye?" Tsifra asked, as if this were normal conversation at a wedding. The Peregrine had warned her once not to ask questions that would lead her into trouble, but the Peregrine was, most unfortunately, not there.

Tsidon pressed his lips together.

"No, of course not," she said. "If he'd tried, he'd have cut it out completely."

"He couldn't afford to lose it," Tsidon said.

"I'm sure he let you think he'd take it."

"Why are you here?" he bit out.

"Guarding Tarses, same as you. Where else should I be?"

Tsidon said, "I'd have thought you'd be holding the demon's leash."

Tsifra schooled her face to blankness. Tsidon smiled, the edges of his new scar puckering around his eye, and he leaned in close. "Everything you're worried I might know, rest assured I have known all along. Who you are." He smoothed a wrinkle from her sleeve. "What you are. What your purpose is."

"At least I have one," she said, not too brightly. "What is yours, with your eyes so easily tricked?"

He laughed dryly. "I have been at Tarses's side since the turning of the age, Courser. Don't worry about my purpose."

"Is that what you told yourself when he ran a blade through your face?"

A heavy hand came down on Tsifra's shoulder, making her jump: Tarses, and she'd failed to hear him coming. "In the time you have been at each other, I could have been killed twice," he said, voice low.

"Not easily," said Tsidon.

"No, not easily," Tarses snapped. On his left forefinger, he wore a ring with a ruby in the shape of a teardrop: a gift from his bride. On his other hand were several other, smaller rings—smaller, but still impressive. Oneca had been generous. "Hold your tongues." To Tsidon, he passed a folded piece of paper marked with the Queen's seal, saying, "I have a wedding gift from Oneca and I need you to take possession."

Tsidon broke the seal and read the paper. "Horses?"

"For your Alaunts."

Tsifra wondered. Alaunts were not mounted fighters; they worked for La Cacería murdering dissidents and heretics. Tsidon said, "I'll manage this straightaway," and he nodded to Tsifra, as if paying her respect, and left.

When he was gone, Tsifra said, "I thought you'd sent him after Barsilay b'Droer."

"Tsidon? Oh, no. No, someone else is cleaning up your mess with Barsilay, don't worry. But I have a gift for you as well." He slipped off one of his smaller rings, a pomegranate ruby that was a mark of the House of Rimon, and slid it onto her forefinger.

"You are no longer just the Courser," Tarses said. "You are the aide-de-camp of the King Consort of Rimon." She looked down at the jewel on her finger. She hated ornaments of any kind, and one on her hand was worse; it was heavy, and would be always in the way. There was no way, however, to refuse it. "You will not see me again before the moon," he said. "I will be gone on a mission of my own."

Tsifra tried to mask her surprise, both that he would leave Rimon so soon after his wedding, and that he would tell her his plans.

"Sir," she said, "I am at your service—"

"Not this time," he said. "I can entrust this particular work only to myself. Your task is to pass through the gate at the next moon."

"Your mission," she said. "I would help—"

"Do not interrupt me again," he warned. "You will bring the surviving buchuk back to Rimon, before—"

"Are you trying to conceive another heir?" she asked, and at that he slapped her, whipping her head sideways and catching her lower lip against his ring. The blow was loud enough that Oneca, still on the other side of the room, stopped speaking to watch them. Tsifra's lip was split clean open.

"Do you understand what you are to do?" he said quietly, and Tsifra could hardly believe her luck. Her only orders were to pass through the gate and bring Toba to Rimon.

"I will do as you have said," Tsifra answered, and turned her bleeding face away, and smiled.

THE SUN WAS setting on the dawning of the new year, and Barsilay was so fragile Naftaly was afraid that if he looked away the other man might die.

He'd never seen Barsilay healthy in the flesh, but the man before him bore little resemblance to the person he'd been in the dream-world. His face was nothing but ash-colored skin stretched too tightly over the bones beneath. If not for his eyes, Naftaly wasn't sure he'd have recognized him at all.

They'd stopped at sunset, and Naftaly had done his best at praying, with no minyan and no shofar and no rabbi and not much hope of being written up in the Book of Life. A new year in a new world, he thought, though this world wasn't really new for anyone besides him.

He missed the round challot the baker and his plumply wife put out for the holiday every year, spirals set with dried fruit and nuts, laced with honey. He hadn't thought about home in so long, it was strange that the bread was what he recalled the most; the smell of it was so strong in his memory he could have sworn he was waiting in the bakery. Elena's expression had gone very far away when he'd mentioned it, and then she'd said, "They were on the ship to Pengoa, the bakers. I wonder if they've opened another shop there."

There was no way to rest without risking death. Elena had made some very thin argument that the horses were working and not them, so somehow it did not count as a violation of the holiday. "Do you actually believe that?" he'd asked.

"Of course not," she'd said, and handed him an apple that tasted precisely like an overgrown lentil.

In truth they ought to have kept going even after sundown, but they'd had to stop again, because the horses were tired and Barsilay was having trouble staying upright in the saddle.

"This isn't good," the old woman had muttered to Elena, after they'd finished their meager Rosh Hashanah dinner—apples and some sort of cholent that also tasted exactly like lentils, served in a tureen Barsilay had made out of an acorn that lent the stew a somewhat acrid aroma. "At this rate we'll still be in Sefarad at midwinter. Don't you have some spell for making the horses go faster?"

"I have," Elena said, taking a moment to rebraid her hair, "but I can only cast it on the horse I'm on, which doesn't help us." They'd stopped at the crest of a hill, and she nodded at the road ahead. "There's fresh water that way, I can hear it."

Naftaly strained and heard the sounds of a stream close by. He helped Barsilay off the horse; his legs were healed now, but his balance was still poor. "You should take the opportunity to clean yourself up a bit more," he suggested.

Barsilay only nodded and allowed himself to be led down the hill.

"Can you …?" Naftaly said, when they were mostly alone.

"I can undress myself," Barsilay said. "Better if I get used to doing small things for myself before something important comes up." He pulled his shirt over his head, revealing the cauterized wound on his shoulder covered with silver scar tissue. He splashed in the icy water, cupping it in his hand and pouring it onto his hair. Without looking up to Naftaly, he said, "Am I so hideous as all that?"

Naftaly felt himself coloring. "Of course not. I was only thinking it would be better if you weren't bathing in water so cold."

"No choice, I'm afraid," he said. "I don't have the magic right now to heat the water. Probably just as well. I'd end up killing anything living here, and I hardly need the guilt." He looked up. "I can't get my hair clean like this."

Naftaly took off his own shirt and came to stand behind him, finger-combing the snarls out of the other man's hair while doing his best to rinse the dried blood and road dust away. "Is your magic any stronger yet?"

Barsilay leaned back against Naftaly's legs, soaking his trousers. "My mind is focused on trying to move an arm that's not there, and then I'm startled when nothing happens. It's making it harder to concentrate on anything else. I'm sure that's part of the problem. I do wonder..." He drew a breath and turned his head to look at the place his arm had been. The outline of an arm glimmered in the air, and then was made solid.

"You said that wouldn't happen," Naftaly said, putting out his hand to touch, and then pulling back before he made contact.

"It's not real," Barsilay said, flexing and unflexing the new fingers. "It's a phantom only, mostly air with some of my shoulder mixed in."

"Does it work?"

Barsilay scooped a handful of water and let it run through his fingers. "A bit. But there's no sensation, so there's not much I can do with it beside look pretty."

"Still, it might be helpful if you need to disguise it. I don't imagine there are many one-armed Maziks."

"There aren't," Barsilay agreed, "but I'm not sure how many will know that Barsilay b'Droer only has one arm. The only one who knows is the Courser, and I don't think she'll let that slip unless she needs to. Otherwise Tarses will want to know why she took my arm, and that conversation won't end well for her. Still, it does make me more memorable, and that's a problem by itself."

"Does it cost much magic to maintain the illusion?"

Barsilay used the phantom to splash icy water at Naftaly. "Ordinarily, I'd say not. But I've so little right now, it's bothering me a bit to have to keep it up." He let go of the illusion and scowled at the stump of his upper arm. "I won't get used to this quickly."

"Does it hurt?"

"It's fine," he said, unconvincingly.

"Would you lie to me, after everything?"

"Does it help for you to know what can only hurt you? Yes, it still hurts. It feels as if she's still stabbing me."

"There might be medicine for that," Naftaly suggested. "Elena had quite the store of amapola at one point."

Barsilay snorted. "Amapola's addictive, even for Maziks, and I'd need enough to fell a horse just to take the edge off. I'll have to get used to it, or hope it goes away, or distract myself from it. Surely you've gotten all the tangles out?" This last part was because Naftaly was still combing his hair, which had been smooth as silk for some time now.

"Sorry," Naftaly said. "I don't mean to fuss, it's just that you almost died, and—"

"Fuss. Please." Barsilay reached up and ran his wet hand down Naftaly's arm. "Tell me how utterly devastated you'd have been if I'd died."

Naftaly sputtered a bit in response.

"Would you have wept for me?"

At that, Naftaly abruptly walked out of the stream, a hand pressed to his mouth. "You're cruel," he said, thickly, "to make this a joke."

"What am I making a joke?"

Naftaly struggled to put his shirt back on over his wet chest. "Your death. My feelings."

"Neither of those is funny to me. I'm sorry, little one. I was only fishing for a few kind words."

Naftaly turned back. "What words are there? You nearly died in my arms and I— I— I'm not like you. You drop words like flowers from your mouth like it's nothing. I've never had anyone to— to— to *say* things to. What do I say? That when I saw you dying it was worse than if the whole world was ending? That I can't quite believe you're here and not inside some dream I'm not sure is real? Because you're the exact sort of thing my mind might have created if it was looking to invent some fantasy?"

Barsilay looked a bit taken aback by this outburst before letting a smile settle on his face. "That's what you say."

From further downstream, the old woman called, "If you've finished your declarations, I feel you should know this horse is looking at me very hard in a way I don't like, and we should probably keep going before it gets peckish."

FOUR

THE OLD WOMAN was not sure how she felt about any of this.

She was very old and very tired, and had little energy left with which to worry, and yet that was what she did. Naftaly was in love with a Mazik man. A Mazik man who seemed to be quite old, much more powerful than he was letting on, and who was likely to get them all killed.

She'd lived on the streets long enough to know how the world operated, so Barsilay's gender did not much concern her. The rest, though . . . it was bad. Naftaly was young, and Barsilay was not, and he was an innocent, and Barsilay most certainly was not, and Naftaly was a fool.

The old woman did not know if Barsilay was a fool or not, and which option was better. Either he was, and they were all doomed, or he wasn't, in which case what the devil was he doing with Naftaly?

She muttered as much to Elena while they rode. Elena only raised an eyebrow while meeting the old woman's gaze over her shoulder, as if to say all this had occurred to her, too. They dismounted for Rosh Hashanah, and she watched Barsilay watch Naftaly pray, and wondered what was going on behind those lovely orange eyes.

They had not quite enough food, because Barsilay's magic was not strong enough to make more than a little. So every evening Naftaly would sneak some of his food to Barsilay, and the old woman would sneak some of hers to Naftaly when he wasn't looking, because he was too thin, and too in love to look after himself.

She had been in love before, more than once. And more than once, it had ended badly. In her long experience with men, she'd learned there were two options: either they left you or they died, and usually they died.

The men went off to bathe, and the old woman took advantage of the light that remained to put a few paces between herself and the others, so that she might think a little. Rosh Hashanah seemed a good time for a think. Consider her regrets, and so forth, if she had any.

She asked herself, should she have gone back through the gate at the last moon, to mortal Rimon?

No. She'd probably have died in the wilderness, and she'd have been alone, besides.

Should she speak to Naftaly about Barsilay?

She'd seen enough infatuation to know that wouldn't help.

What should she do then?

She wished she could hear a shofar, to knock some of the cobwebs loose in her mind. Her body ached from riding and sleeping on the ground, and this was likely to be the easiest time they would have. It would get colder the further they rode, unless they were caught first. At some point they would run out of food, or else that palomino mare would take a bite out of one of them and that would be that.

If they were very, very lucky, they would get to Zayit. At which point she rather suspected Barsilay would abandon them in favor of whatever Mazik friends he might have there, who could be of actual help to him. When that happened, she told herself, she would take Naftaly and go through the gate to mortal Zayit.

It was, she believed, not a bad place to be.

TOBA BET DREAMED she was in a wood that was nearly pitch dark. No stars whirled overhead; indeed the sky was as dark as ink, and the only light was from some source in the distance she could not see. Using magic to create a small light in her hand, she looked around and saw that the trees were all fruiting—not only pomegranates, but olives and grapes, too. It was nearly as silent as the void. Toba Bet made her way carefully to the source of the light, which she found came from a pair of sconces set in a stone wall with no visible seam. She stepped closer, looking for some markings on the stone, and found the dimly illuminated outlines of three leaves: pomegranate, olive, grape. Taking her finger, she traced lines connecting them, crisscrossing the space as Asmel had shown her.

The stone swung open, and Toba Bet stepped inside, into a chamber very much like Asmel's observatory. The room was octagonal and overhead were not the usual spinning stars of the dream-world but some magic-made facsimile of the Mazik night sky. The walls were lined with books and scrolls and various pieces of equipment: astrolabes and weights and measures, together with things Toba Bet had never seen before. Throughout the room, in twos and threes, were some fifty or sixty Maziks, too engaged in their discussions to have seen her come in. They were arguing, mainly, some illustrating points with the aid of illusions they cast in midair, showing diagrams or mathematical equations or star charts. The closest of these groups was in a discussion led by a very animated man, short for a Mazik, with curly hair, who had created an image of a transparent Mazik and was explaining something to do with the circulation of magic within his extremities. He noticed her watching and abruptly stopped speaking while those with him looked at her with overt fear.

Toba Bet bowed a little and said, "I'm sorry to have disturbed your discussion. I am here on behalf of Adon Sof'rim, who seeks your help."

One of the other Maziks, a woman with hair as red as pomegranates, said, "Adon Sof'rim has been beyond the giving or accepting of help for this entire age. Who are you to come here and trade on his name?"

The entirety of the Colloquium stopped their conversations at this, and all eyes were on her. They were afraid, all of them, of who she might be, and they came in a circle around her. Someone whispered, "We should wake now, this can't be safe," and someone else whispered, "Adon Sof'rim would not have sent someone here," and then another, "I heard Adon Sof'rim was dead."

"I am Adon Sof'rim's ward," Toba Bet said, continuing the fiction they'd concocted when she'd first come through the gate to Rimon.

"Adon Sof'rim's ward was to be the bride of the Lymer of Rimon!" someone said.

"No!" Toba Bet protested. "I refused that!"

"Then you would be dead!"

"Please!" Toba Bet cried. "We do need your help, if you would only listen! I need to find two astronomers—"

"This is a trick," said the man nearest her. "A Cacería trick." And he vanished, having woken. The Maziks who had been standing around him murmured to each other; it sounded like they agreed.

She was losing them, and there would be no second chance. If they thought she was a spy, she would never be allowed back in.

Asmel's name was not enough to trade on, here. She needed her own, no matter how dangerous a gambit it might be. Drawing herself up and hoping she had enough dream-magic to make herself seem taller, she shouted, "I am the heir of Marah N'Dar. And *I* need your help."

A great many exclamations went up around her, and more of the Maziks began to wink out like extinguishing lights. They were waking up. First a few, and then more.

"Wait!" Toba Bet called. "I am who I say!" Then, when that failed, she called out, "Molka To'ara!" *Monarchy is Abomination.*

The effect was immediate. Every Mazik in the Colloquium vanished at once, except one: the woman with red hair. She stood watching Toba in the sudden silence, her arms crossed over her chest. "You know," she told Toba Bet, "the Caçador himself used to say those words, long ago."

"I am not his," Toba Bet said. "I swear it."

The woman regarded Toba Bet a long time and said, "For you to come here invoking ha-Moh'to, you are either telling the truth or mad. So tell me, while I decide which you are, why does Adon Sof'rim need our help?"

Toba Bet explained as much as she dared, as quickly as she could; dreaming in this place seemed to be draining her magic. She was not sure how geography worked in the dream-world, but for Maziks to be dreaming in the same place from three different cities must have taken some particular magic, and she wasn't sure how long she could sustain it.

"Aravoth," the woman said, looking mystified. "I cannot help you. I'm not sure anyone can. Since the Fall it's been death to discuss it, even outside of Rimon. And even before, it was not a place anyone tried to go."

"But Marah hid the Ziz there," Toba Bet said. "She can't have been the only person to know how to get there."

The woman thought about this before shaking her head again. "If anyone living knows it, they've kept it secret indeed, but it's possible a very old Mazik with a very thorough understanding of the stars might have learned something. Most of the remaining Maziks of the First Age died in Luz—the only other person I can think of might be the Great Astronomer of Te'ena."

"Asmel thought so, too, but—"

The woman said, "You need to speak to Adona Maz'rotha."

From Asmel, Toba Bet knew that Maz'rotha was the dream-world name for Rahel, the Mazik who had stayed in Zayit after Asmel's university had been shut down. Toba Bet said, "Was she here tonight?"

"She stopped coming. Last I spoke with her, she was too close to the sea and it was interfering with her dreaming. But she told me, then, that she was working on a way to communicate with Te'ena across the sea. Whether she managed it or not, I don't know. But if you find her, there might be a way for her to get a message to him."

"Where is she?"

"She was in the process of building an observatory here." The woman drew a map of light with her finger and indicated a position on the coast, not far from where Barcino was on the mortal side. "You might try dreaming yourself to that area. If the salt is hampering her, she might simply be dreaming nearby."

"Thank you," Toba Bet said. "I'm sorry to have frightened the others."

"They are easily frightened," the woman said. "But for good reason."

"You were not frightened."

"I am older than most," she replied. "And Adon Sof'rim was a good friend to me for a very long time indeed."

This was Mir b'Cohain, Toba Bet knew. So her dream had not been a complete failure.

"Adon Sof'rim bade me find you," Toba Bet said. "He said you would help us. We're coming to Zayit now."

"I'm afraid I'm not there," she said. "I'm in Anab 'til the spring. I'll drop the wards on my house in Zayit. You can stay there at least, and be comfortable. Asmel will know where it is." Mir was fading a bit, in and out. Toba Bet herself was having trouble remaining there. "Be careful," she said, before she was gone. "You're invoking dangerous names."

AWAKE THE NEXT day, Toba Bet was beginning to worry about their lack of speed. Traveling off-road was even more difficult for the horse than she'd predicted, but staying on the road and being hunted by soldiers was no longer a reasonable option. *Bad choices and worse ones*, she thought. The trick was picking the least terrible, only Toba Bet guessed there was no way to know if you'd succeeded 'til you'd been left in the woods with a pack of wolves or else decapitated and consigned to the void.

And Rosh Hashanah had come and gone, as she'd dragged her horse through the wilderness. She thought of her grandfather's voice on every other Rosh Hashanah she'd ever known, blessing her name to be inscribed in the Book of Life.

She wondered if that were still possible, because the original Toba had died, and because she shared her name with her sister. She had never had her own name. Even now, she could not call herself Toba in her own mind.

But Asmel had stopped calling her Toba Bet some time ago.

"Asmel," she said, "you insist on calling me Toba."

"That is your name."

Toba Bet twisted her mouth to one side. The man was being deliberately obtuse. Or else he'd forgotten which Toba she was. "Asmel," she said again.

"The appellation was made because we needed to distinguish the two of you. That's no longer a concern."

"You were fairly adamant that I was not truly Toba," she said. "I don't see why that's changed, just because she died."

"I am not sure what you wish me to say," he said. "Are we to discuss your fullness as a person again?"

"No. I want to know if you call me Toba because it allows you to discount my origins."

Asmel said, "If you would prefer I continue to call you Toba Bet, than I shall do so. I recalled that you objected to the alteration of your name originally. Was that not so?"

"Asmel—"

"You wanted rather badly to be acknowledged as your counterpart's equal. I am puzzled that you object to it now."

"I suppose I don't object," she said. "It's only that I want to know what you mean when you call me that."

"What I mean?" he repeated.

"What is it you think I am?"

"I could ask the same," he said. "I am quite altered from what I was. Am I still Asmel? Will I be, once I no longer remember him?" He sighed heavily. "I cannot answer you. You will have to decide the significance of your origins for yourself. 'Til then, I'll call you whatever you like." Both of them were walking, because the ground was too unsure for the horse to be carrying a rider, and Asmel slowed his pace and tugged on the reins a bit. "Something is ahead of us."

Indeed, through the trees Toba Bet could see an encampment, which consisted of a pavilion and a pair of tied-up, saddled horses. No people were visible; Toba Bet assumed they must be inside the tent.

She said, "Should we turn back?"

"Just give it a wide berth," Asmel said. Asmel led them around clockwise, and then a man stepped out from behind a tree into their path.

The horse startled and nearly bolted, and Toba Bet was sure if she'd been the one holding it, it would have. But Asmel's hand was sure, and he brought the beast down before turning to the intruder blocking their progress: a middle-aged man with a covered head and clothes that were too clean to have been traveled in. He'd come from the pavilion.

"Good afternoon," he said placidly, to which Asmel muttered an equivalent greeting. "You've strayed from the road. Are you lost?"

"We've strayed no more than you have," Asmel replied. "We are only cutting through the woods to save a bit of time on the way to Vercia."

"Vercia is quite some ways," said the man in the very clean clothes, "and you appear to have traveled far. Won't you join me for a meal before you continue on?" Here he inclined his head toward the pavilion.

"Thank you, no," Asmel replied. "We still have quite a distance to cover today."

"Indeed," said the man. "But surely you didn't intend to walk all the way to Zayit before nightfall, Asmel."

Before Toba Bet could react, the man put out a hand, and their horse slumped to the ground, dead.

If she could have become birds again, if she'd been strong enough, she would have. Instead, she growled, "Leave us be."

"We would leave you be, birdling, had we a choice," the man said. "But we have orders and you have made yourself so very easy to catch." Here, his voice dropped into a register that was most definitely not human—nor Mazik. "And we do hate Asmel. We hate him so very much."

The man pulled back his hood, revealing a tonsured scalp. Taken with the ornate pavilion and the richly saddled horses bearing the crest of Mansanar, this was no ordinary monk or priest. This, Toba Bet knew, was the Queen's confessor.

Asmel took a step back, keeping Toba Bet behind him. "What is your quarrel with me?" he asked. "I don't recall a personal vendetta with any demon."

"Don't you? Don't you?" the confessor asked. "So much is your fault. Everything. Is everything your fault? If not for you, we would never have ended up under that mountain!" The demon's own voice mixed with the priest's screams, a horrible sound like breaking glass and torment.

"You can't be one of Rafeq's," Toba Bet said. "Those demons are beneath the mountain still."

"We are not one of anything! We were all together, one, all of us, 'til Asmel told the King about us. 'Til Asmel betrayed us!"

"I don't care what you think he did, you'll come no closer," Toba Bet said.

"You cannot stop us," the demon said. "We will kill him and scatter what's left from here to the sea!"

"You'll not touch him!"

"Toba," Asmel murmured, "have a care. You can't kill a demon."

"I can try," she snarled, and then, because she had nothing with which to defend herself, she made her arm into a blade.

It was more painful than she could have imagined, as the bone became sharp and the rest of her arm fell away, a pain so acute she thought she might faint. But she held up her arm and said, "I'll cut you to pieces."

The demon laughed. "For what purpose? What care is it of ours if you cut this priest? We can still take you as ourselves." And he lunged for Asmel, pulling a knife from his belt as he moved in a sickening way that must have broken some of the priest's bones. Toba Bet wheeled toward him, raising her blade, and sliced off the man's hand.

The demon let out a wail like breaking glass and fell to his knees, grasping at the bloody stump of his arm with his other hand. "Birdling!" he shrieked. "You are a fool!"

Toba Bet had raised her arm to strike again, meaning this time to take the demon's head, but Asmel gripped her by the elbow. "Don't," he said, and then they were running away into the trees.

"Why did you stop me?" she asked, once they were well away.

"You never listen," Asmel said. "You can't kill a demon. You'd just have killed the man it was possessing. My guess is the demon was ordered not to leave that body, which is the only reason I'm still alive." They had to pause to climb over a fallen tree; there was a path past it that looked like it was probably worn by deer. Toba Bet thought it would have been better not to take such an obvious route, but otherwise there was so much bracken the woods were impassable. "If the demon remains corporeal, we have a chance of escaping. Once it leaves the host, we have no hope of getting away from it. A demon can fly, replicate itself, come out of the ground, even."

"Should I be trying to cover our tracks?"

"No point to it," he said. "The path we're on is the only one we can take." He tsked as his boot caught in some bracken. "I'm very concerned about how easily he's found us. Remember I told you that with your magic unbound, La Cacería would be able to track you in the mortal world. It seems this demon has that ability as well. He'll catch up to us as soon as he's able, which won't be long."

"What do you suggest?"

"We need another horse," he said, "or two would be better. We can't move fast enough this way."

"That's something that's troubling me. How did he kill the horse?"

"I have no idea," Asmel admitted. "I don't know what Rafeq's demons might be capable of."

"And why hasn't he caught up to us yet?"

"I don't know! Maybe he's still bleeding, Toba, I don't know. What we need to be concerned with is getting another horse."

"Well, we don't have enough money for another horse," Toba Bet reminded him. "Unless you think we should steal one."

"I'm not above stealing one," he said. "But we'd have to find one first. Is there a pueblo near here?"

"Asmel, I barely know where we are. Our best bet is to loop back to the road; at least we'll eventually come to an inn or something, and there will be a horse to steal there. But then we have to worry about the soldiers."

"I'd rather worry about the soldiers than the demon," he said. "I agree, we should go west again." Taking her hand, he changed direction, heading in a path Toba Bet supposed was meant to put greater distance between them and the demon while eventually getting them back to the road.

They threaded their way through trees and brush for hours. It had not rained in weeks, and the leaves underfoot crackled so loudly that Toba Bet occasionally winced; there was no way to move quietly, and it made it more difficult to listen for anyone who might be following. She'd asked Asmel how long it might take the demon to staunch its bleeding arm, and he'd replied that he had absolutely no idea. The sun was growing low on the horizon. It would be dark before they got back to the road, and it would be impossible to keep going.

Coming around a copse of hollies, Asmel caught his foot on a root and went down on a knee. "Are you all right?" Toba Bet asked, as he rose again and limped a few paces on his left leg. "Is it your ankle?"

"It will right itself in a moment," he said.

"No," Toba Bet said, "it won't." She forced Asmel to sit and pulled his trouser leg out of his boot, and then pulled off the boot itself when she couldn't find the injury.

"There's no time—"

"Shut up," she said, setting her hand to the ankle, which was already swelling.

"You have no idea how to heal that."

"Not really," Toba Bet agreed. "So you might want to tell me."

"It's not the bone," he said. "If you can just get the swelling down—"

But Toba Bet was already feeling inside the injury with her magic, and she could see the problem: a soft-tissue injury. "Asmel," she said, "you're all spongy inside." She imagined her magic as something cold and soothing, and let it creep into the worst of the swelling.

"Ah," he said.

"Better or worse 'ah'?"

"Better," he said. "Give me my boot." He pulled it back on and rose again. "Now I really am wondering how he hasn't caught us yet. We're critically slow, and he has a horse." Testing the ankle and finding it passable, they began walking again, albeit at a slightly slower pace.

"You can't think he's given up?"

"Of course not," he said. "But none of this makes any sense. He could have killed me back there, and didn't, either with the knife or however he killed the horse."

"He thinks you're useful," Toba Bet said.

"No," Asmel answered. "He thinks keeping me alive is useful, and those are two very different things. But the time may come soon when keeping me alive is no longer useful to you. Prepare yourself for that moment, when it comes."

Toba Bet gave no answer. She could have mentioned that he had kept her alive in the Mazik world when killing her—or letting her die—would have saved his magic and Barsilay's arm. She could have mentioned that letting Asmel be killed to save herself would have made her no better than Tsifra. But Asmel would only have some counterargument, and that would cost them energy and focus, neither of which could be spared.

So for once, Toba Bet let Asmel think he'd won the argument.

+ +
+ · + + + +

THE CONSENSUS BETWEEN Naftaly and his companions was to travel on the road, because all that mattered now was speed. Elena's ability to speak La'az Sefardi was now at least mostly fluent; probably, Barsilay posited, because her Mazik lineage had gifted her with accelerated healing. She took advantage of the improvement by trying her speed litany on the Mazik horse. This only succeeded in making the palomino mare even more skittish than usual, and she tried to take a bite out of Elena's foot for her trouble. She tried teaching the litany to Naftaly, but he only succeeded in making the horse turn around and stare at him, which was so unnerving he was not keen on trying again. Teaching it to Barsilay was out of the question for now; the man had nearly no magic left in him at all.

Naftaly found himself continually peeking behind him, looking for dust rising from the road or any other sign that someone might be coming after them, but there was nothing so far as he could see. They'd slowed their pace for a bit, to avoid overtaxing the horses, and Barsilay had begun experimenting with the phantom arm, trying to use it to hold the reins. He was forced to abandon the effort after the third time he veered too close to the other horse—and the two women—which was the direction the mare most wanted to go.

"I can't tell how hard I'm pulling the reins," Barsilay admitted. "I'm sorry."

"Do you want to switch places for a bit? I can hold the reins and you can rest a while."

"No," he said. "I'd like to keep trying. It will be better in the long run if I can make this useful."

"How long will it take us to get to Zayit, at this pace?"

"If we can't find a way to go faster, I fear it will be too long." Barsilay sighed. "When I encouraged you not to steal the fastest horses, this is not quite what I had in mind."

"Then we should stop, have something to eat. If you exhaust yourself past being able to sit in the saddle, it will be worse than a half-hour's rest by far."

"No, we've not come far enough to rest yet. Wait. You, woman, why are you stopping?"

This, of course, was directed at Elena, who had halted her bay gelding and was in the process of sliding down its back. "I can't bear the complaints any longer," she said, jerking her head toward the old woman. "She's exhausted, and you need to eat and drink to replace all the blood you lost."

Barsilay grumbled that this was a mistake, but pulled his horse alongside theirs all the same and allowed Naftaly to help him down. The old woman was clutching her backside and moaning. "Leave me here," she said. "I'd rather die than sit another hour on that animal. I swear its back is made of iron. May as well be riding a bouncing frying pan."

"Should we stop so close to the road?" Naftaly asked.

"It'll make it easier to see anyone else coming behind us," Barsilay said. "I'd like to keep my eye on things so long as we're stopped. I won't feel comfortable 'til we're past the mountains."

"I'm still not sure staying on the road is best," Elena said. "We're awfully visible this way, and we don't have speed as an advantage, riding two abreast. We may as well have stealth."

"We're too slow," Barsilay agreed. They led the horses far enough from the road so as not to be directly on it but close enough that they could still look back and see anyone approaching. As they sat down, Naftaly handed Barsilay a spare handful of lentils, which he turned into some kind of lukewarm stew and passed around. "Sorry it's not properly hot," he said, leaning back and setting his bowl on the grass half-finished, because he still had no appetite. "But there's no other way than the road. I wish I could dream of someone who knew about horses."

"You still have no dreams?" Elena asked.

"Not since you freed me from prison," he said. "I don't know when that's likely to resolve. You still haven't been able to find Toba?" he asked Naftaly.

"No." Naftaly's dreams, since he'd come to the Mazik world, had mainly consisted of him hiding in the city somewhere, afraid of meeting Tsidon again. So far, however, he'd seen no one, and though he'd tried very hard, he could not manage to dream his way to Toba.

"Keep trying," Barsilay said. "She could be sleeping odd hours. I'm sure you'll find her eventually."

Some hours later, they'd ridden a bit further. By then they'd left the foothills behind, and below them lay a valley. To the right were fields of low green plants; a little farther down the road was a stone building. From the other horse the old woman said, "I thought you said it was uninhabited between Rimon and Zayit. So what is that?"

"Ah," Barsilay said. "That is a lentil farm. I suppose it speaks ill of me that I didn't think of those. There are several; the land's decent here, relatively. The ground's too rocky closer to Rimon. It's the main reason the city's not larger." He drew rein for a moment. "In the old days, they paid mortals to send lentils across the strait from Tamar. You know, let the humans ship them, and then send them through the gate. But after La Cacería took over, that stopped, and now, lo ..." He gestured. "Suboptimal farming."

"Wouldn't it be better to have the farms where the good land is?" Naftaly asked. "What's the point in keeping everyone near the gate if it's hardly used anyway?"

"You're asking me to ascribe logic to this?" Barsilay said. "Of course it would make more sense, but Maziks like cities, and baths, and markets. No one wants to live in the wilderness." He peered out at the fields below them. "We'll have missed the harvest, just. Too bad. We could have used more food."

"Doesn't appear they've finished harvesting," Naftaly said. "Do you see? The plants are still drying in the fields."

"That can't be," Barsilay said. "It's already mid-autumn, isn't it? I'm a bit muddled on the time."

"It is," Naftaly said. "But I can see the plants. They've been cut, but that's all."

"They still have the pods attached?"

"That's what I'm telling you," Naftaly said.

"Would the farmers be in the city, dealing with the new Queen?" Elena asked.

"No," Barsilay replied. "The farmers wouldn't be in a position to have to make nice with a new queen."

Elena said, "Look," and pointed toward the main building beside the fields. A pair of Maziks was coming out of it, carrying something between them. They were dressed in blue, in livery Naftaly recognized as belonging to La Cacería.

Barsilay's face went white. "We have to hide," he said. "Right now. And hope they haven't already seen us."

When Naftaly had come through the gate the first time, he'd nearly been captured by blue-clad Maziks, led by Tsidon the Lymer. He'd frozen Naftaly's muscles to prevent him escaping, and the sensation came back to him now, of being unable to run away. He reminded himself he was under no spell this time. The men hadn't seen him.

Still, his head began to ache at the sight of them, and he thought, *Not now*.

"Get down," Elena said, sliding off the side of her horse. "You're too visible up in the saddle, and the horses will kick up too much dust if we start riding fast... Did you hear me?" Naftaly had already gotten down, but Barsilay was frozen in place, and so Naftaly had to haul him down from the saddle; he seemed mostly unable to move. This was a problem because Naftaly could not lead the horse and drag the other man at the same time.

"Barsilay," he said, "I won't let them take you again."

Barsilay was shivering. "You think you'd be able to stop them?"

"He won't need to," the old woman said, "if we hide quickly enough. Move your feet."

That seemed to jostle him a bit. "Keep your hand on the saddle," Naftaly said. "I'll lead the horse."

The problem was that there was no decent cover in the valley. The land was flat, and the trees far between. Four people with a pair of horses were hard to conceal. They turned west, off the road, to put as much distance between themselves and the farm as possible and made for the tallest trees they could find.

"Glamour your eyes," Barsilay told Naftaly. "Maybe they'll only take me and not you."

"Don't be foolish," Naftaly said, but he'd already done his eyes, and he looked to Elena, who was muttering something and patting vigorously at her own face and the old woman's, until the two of them looked . . . not young, but less obviously wrinkled and with square-pupiled eyes.

"You still look like an old cow," the old woman said. "Could you take off another ten years?"

"I'm trying," Elena said through gritted teeth. "It was easier to make you look like an old man than a young woman."

"How long will that hold?" Barsilay asked.

"Not more than a quarter hour," Elena said. She did look younger now, perhaps forty, but Naftaly wasn't sure it would fool anyone, and the old woman, more wizened to start with, was still visibly wrinkled.

"They're here to take over the lentil farms?" the old woman asked. "What would that get them, if all those lentils are going to Rimon anyway? I don't understand Maziks. Do you even have money?"

Barsilay was too preoccupied with moving forward to answer. Naftaly's mind caught on the word *lentils*, though, and it spun around inside his imagination 'til it made him dizzy. He wondered why it should trouble him so, that word. "Was it always lentils?" he muttered, feeling the words grow heavy in his mouth, and his body followed. He slumped forward into Barsilay, who glanced over his shoulder with a concerned eye.

"Little one?"

But Naftaly's vision was already cutting out, and he felt himself slide sideways. Barsilay caught his shirt just in time to keep his head from hitting the ground.

In his mind, he flew, circling up to the sky and then south, past Rimon, past the sea, to what he knew must be Tamar.

Tamar was a walled city, he'd heard before, and many of the Jews who had fled Rimon had gone there. It was closer than Anab or Te'ena; it seemed a likely refuge. Only what Naftaly saw was people dead outside the walls, the gates shut tight, as refugees died in the desert of exposure and thirst. He felt himself in one person, and then another, and then another, as the pain of dehydration took them past reason, and then when he could bear it no longer, he felt something shift inside him, the horizon turned upside down, the stars whirled overhead, and he was in a different walled city.

Tamar, still, but Mazik Tamar. And in this city, likewise, people were dying. Not refugees, and not because of cruelty, but of hunger. *Blight.* He heard the word inside his mind. *The crop is diseased.* He had another sense, too, some sort of latent understanding: the blight was spreading.

Naftaly gasped and opened his eyes to Barsilay's, close above him. He was on the ground, the horse nearby. "Can we do nothing for him?" he was asking the women.

"He'll come back in a moment," the old woman said. "Is this some Mazik affliction?"

Then Barsilay realized Naftaly had returned to himself, and cupped his hand behind the other man's head. "Are you well?" he asked.

Naftaly would have answered, but instead the horror of it all gripped him. He'd seen so many terrible things, and now here was more. He began to weep, and then wept more because he was ashamed of his own tears. He could do nothing for anyone in Tamar. They were dying. He could feel a trickle down his upper lip: His nose was bleeding.

Barsilay pulled Naftaly's forehead against his shoulder. "I'm sorry," he said. "Can you tell us?"

"It's Tamar," Naftaly said. "They locked the gates. They wouldn't allow the Jews inside and they died outside the walls, thousands of them."

Elena put her hand to her mouth, and the old woman turned away.

"There's more," he croaked. "In Mazik Tamar, there's famine.

The lentil crop was blighted, and they're dying in the streets. And the blight is spreading."

Barsilay let out a long breath and pulled Naftaly closer. "You saw all this? Both worlds?"

"Yes. Though . . . I think what happened in Tamar—in mortal Tamar—must have already happened some time ago. The expulsion was months ago; there wouldn't be so many going there now."

Barsilay sat back and said, "I wish Asmel were here. There's so much about this I never learned. But it seems to me you've seen the effect of the Mirror."

Naftaly rubbed at his aching forehead and took some water from Elena. He felt somewhat worse than he usually did after a vision; a dull ache was throbbing behind his left ear. "You mean the Jews were left outside the walls to starve in Tamar, so in Mazik Tamar the crop has failed?"

"Something like that."

"But what's the point of my seeing it, if there's nothing I can do?" Naftaly felt himself on the verge of tears again. "There's never anything I can do. Not for Tamar. Not for Pengoa. Nothing I see is ever any use; it's like it's all there to torture me, so I know precisely every shade the world is ugly, but without any hope of ever saving anyone."

"You've never been able to control what you see?"

"No," he said. "It seems to be completely random." He clutched at his hair. "I hate it, Barsilay. I wish it could be taken from me." He looked up. "Can you help me?"

Barsilay said, "If I could, I surely would."

"Never mind, then," Naftaly said. "I'm all right now, and we still need to get farther away from the farm." He struggled to get his rubbery legs under him.

"We should put him on a horse," the old woman said. "He'll be weak for a bit now."

"All right," Barsilay agreed, and was in the process of helping Naftaly up when the old woman let out a strangled noise.

A man stood behind her, clad in blue, with his sword to her throat. None of them had heard him approach. They'd been too preoccupied with Naftaly's vision, and now he'd gotten them all captured.

"Barsilay b'Droer," the soldier said, "what are you doing so far from Rimon with three strangers and only one arm?"

TOBA BET KEPT turning back to look for the demon, and did not know if she felt better or worse that there was no sign of him at all. They were on foot, and he'd had a horse; they shouldn't have been able to escape so easily, even with his hand cut off.

Asmel seemed to have come to the same conclusion, as he'd watched her turn her head, listen, and turn back yet again. "This entire situation feels strange," he said. "What you did back there, with the demon's arm. I keep thinking of Barsilay, and what your sister did to him."

Toba felt a wave of shame and tamped it down. "I did it to save you. I wasn't torturing him."

"I know you weren't. It was just the way it happened. She took your companion's arm. You took her companion's arm. It . . . It felt like the Mirror, a bit."

"But that happened there first, and here second. Isn't that backward?"

"Yes, that's what I'm wondering." He shook his head. "Or maybe it's not the Mirror at all and I'm seeing what's not there, I don't know." He held up a hand when she moved to pass him some magic. "Save it, I'm not addled. I've studied the Mirror all my life, and I still barely understand how it works. Why some things are reflected and others aren't, no one has ever been able to say. We aren't meant to understand it, and I keep wondering if the rules aren't consistent."

"That doesn't make any sense," Toba Bet said. "Laws are always consistent; that's why they're laws. If they seem to shift, it's because you haven't pinned them down."

"Possibly," he said. "But I do wonder if the reason I can't pin this particular law down is that there isn't one. It's not as if every person in the mortal world has a counterpart in the Mazik one. It's not even possible: There are too many humans and too few of us. It's more… trends, I don't know."

"I won't believe the universe runs on chaos," Toba Bet said. "Probably this felt like the Mirror to you because you've studied it for so long. You see what you look for. Here." She passed Asmel a bubble of her magic, the size of an olive. They'd figured out some days ago that he could inhale these, which was easier than having Toba Bet press the magic into him. This one he looked at regretfully, if Toba Bet read him correctly, before slowly breathing it in.

After a moment, he exhaled. "Thank you," he said, "for letting me keep my mind a little longer."

"Well, we do need it," she said, "even if you are a failure at understanding universal laws. Do you hear water?"

"I don't think—" Asmel was saying, and then they came out of the thickest part of the trees and came up short, because what lay before them was a river. "What river is this?"

It was not a wide river—too narrow to be the Tagus, which was still miles away, or the Garro, which they'd crossed three days prior. Toba Bet had never been this far north and had little idea of the local landscape beyond what she'd seen on her grandfather's maps. Asmel, she suspected, should have known a river of any size so near to Rimon after living there as long as he had, but his memory was so unreliable these days that it made it hard for him to navigate.

"Do you not know where we are?"

Asmel considered. "I know we're in mortal Sefarad somewhere between Rimon and Barcino, but I don't know what river this might be. Which means I don't know how we can get around it."

"Here," Toba Bet said, passing him a bit of her magic.

"It's too much," he said. "You just gave me some."

"See if it helps," she insisted, and he reluctantly breathed it in. Then he let out a disgusted grunt.

"Still no idea?"

"None," he said. "But if we get back to the road, there's bound to be a bridge." They altered their course, giving up their northern vector to head due west. Only a few minutes later they found themselves confronted again by the same river. "Did it loop behind us?" Asmel muttered. "We'd have crossed it already ..." Turning to Toba Bet, he said, "Can you send up a bird?"

Toba Bet threw her hand skyward, sending a lark up, which circled three times before flying along the eastern course of the river. "It keeps going that way for as far as I can see. We must have just missed the bridge when we came off the road in the first place."

"Meaning we'd have to go back to where we met the demon in order to cross it," Asmel said. "How very convenient. Bring yourself back." While Toba Bet's bird flew back and landed on her outstretched palm, Asmel made his way down the riverbank.

"What are you doing?" she called after him. "Look at the current!" But Asmel knelt down near the edge of the water, frowning, and then he plunged his hand in.

"It's as I thought," he called back, pulling his hand back and showing it to her, completely dry. "Artifice, all of it."

"The whole thing's a glamour? Is that even possible?"

"It's so well done I can't even see the edges of it," he said. "I can't tell if it's a dry riverbed he's used or if the entire thing's been made from scratch. It must be costing him nearly all his magic to maintain."

"But surely he must have known we'd see through it eventually. All we had to do was touch the water."

"We've already wasted more than an hour because of it," he said. "I imagine it's done its job. Come." He motioned for Toba Bet to join him, straightened, and continued across.

Crossing the false river was a strange feeling. The current looked real, the water sounded real, and yet their feet only went down an inch into what looked like water before hitting the ground. "It'll be like this the whole way across," Asmel said.

"Are you sure? Because it would be unfortunate to get halfway across and find the demon's glamoured a false river on top of a real one, and we only realize it when we're both drowning."

"It's a fair point," Asmel said, stooping to pick up a handful of pebbles from the ground. He tossed one out several feet in front of him; when it hit solid ground, they continued, stopping every few feet to make sure there wasn't water or something worse underneath.

When they'd crossed to the other side, Toba Bet said, "You know, this still strikes me as odd. What a massive use of magic for a glamour he must have known we'd see through, only to slow us down for an hour."

"If you hadn't sent up a bird, it might have been longer. We could have been following that all day, getting farther from the road all the time. Come, it can't be much farther now."

Toba Bet hoped he was right. She hadn't slept in days, and with all the walking and the terror of nearly losing Asmel to the demon, her energy was starting to flag. The moon had risen overhead, a waxing crescent. What day was it? Toba Bet could not even remember, she was so exhausted. She wanted to stop and rest at the other side of the river, but Asmel was right—if they were still within the range of the demon's glamour, it was a bad idea.

"Soon," he said, setting a hand on her shoulder. "Then when you dream you can find Barsilay and tell him—"

"Asmel," she said, turning to face him, then running a hand down the left side of his hair to the ends. A lock of it had been cut. "When did that happen?"

Asmel looked unhappy indeed and had just opened his mouth to answer when his words were cut off by the sound of a horn blowing in the fog.

A hunter's horn. And it came not from behind them, but ahead.

FIVE

"WHAT HAVE WE stumbled into?" Asmel asked Toba Bet, as from somewhere nearby hounds began to bay. Behind them, the river vanished.

"Your hair," Toba Bet said. "Asmel—" The horn sounded again, and everything came into focus. "You're the hart."

Gripping her hand, he said, "Can you put the river back?"

"Not like it was—"

"Put up anything, even if it buys us ten minutes," he ordered, and together they charged back into the area where the water had been. Toba Bet cast a weak version of the river that had been there a moment ago and they dashed into it, not stopping until they'd come out the other side. When they looked back, they could see the silhouettes of several mounted hunters on the shore, with baying hounds scenting the air at their heels. "Those are mortals," Asmel said. "They won't think to test the water. We're safe as long as it lasts."

"And what will they think when it does fade?" Toba Bet asked.

"I imagine they'll be telling tales of that for a while," he said. "We don't have long, and we can't get back to the road."

"Which way do we go, then?"

"The demon was close enough to conjure the river and give my scent to the hunters," Asmel said. "He's somewhere nearby. If we go the wrong way, we'll run directly into him again."

"My bird saw no sign," she said. "If he only just gave your scent to those hunters, that puts him on the other side of the river." She sent a second lark into the sky and put it in the oak nearest the water. "At least we'll know when the river's gone, or if one of those hunters is reckless enough to try fording it."

This seemed to Asmel as good an idea as any, and they needed to move in any direction that was away from the river before Toba Bet's third-rate glamour came down. So Toba Bet grabbed Asmel's hand in hers and together they ran east.

"How many hunters did you see?" he asked.

"I saw five horses," she said. "I'm assuming there are more on foot, and I don't know how many dogs, but by the sound there were plenty. The demon would have had to gather all of them here long before we arrived."

"The pavilion was set up some time ago as well," Asmel agreed. "He's prepared for us, and he wants to make sure we know it."

"But why?"

Toba Bet thought of her sister, who had given her a worthless warning. Asmel would have known the man was possessed by a demon the instant he saw him. So why bother? To encourage Toba Bet's trust? There was no point; Toba Bet would never trust her sister. Her mind picked at the loose threads. There must have been some reason beyond the obvious.

"This is all tied to my sister. She wants me to know the demon is working for Tarses, and that he's one of Rafeq's. And she wants me to believe the demon means to kill you and capture me. Except, it doesn't seem to be trying very hard."

"You think she's trying to obscure the demon's real purpose? Stalling us within range of the gate 'til she can get here?"

"But that just circles around again," Toba Bet said. "What's the point of the warning? I don't understand this at all." There was some element of misdirection here that she could not see.

"Toba," Asmel said. "You must leave me. They aren't hunting you. The demon's entire plan hinges on you staying at my side."

"You don't know that," she said. "My leaving may be exactly what he expects. He thinks you'll convince me to abandon you and run north, and he'll be waiting to catch me alone the second I do."

"No. There's no advantage to him catching you alone because I can't protect you. I am nothing but a liability to you and you know it. I'm a drain on your magic and I'm slowing you down. You must leave me."

"You are not a liability," she said. "I wouldn't have even realized that was a demon if you hadn't told me. There's too much I don't understand still, and I need you."

"If you stay, you'll be captured!"

She put her hands on either side of his face. "I won't. I don't care how much Mazik magic that creature's eaten, I'm still cleverer. I outwitted Tsidon, I outwitted Tarses, and I'll outwit whatever's out there. And if there's something else, I'll have to be smarter than that, too."

"Truly, your false confidence is remarkable."

"It's not false," she said. "I've thought about this, you know. Why does Tarses want me as his heir so badly, when he has one already? I'm not stronger than she is, or faster, or more loyal, so what have I that she does not?" She tapped her temple. "I was raised to be a scholar, Asmel. I saved you once, and I'll do it again. Now, let's decide what our assets are, shall we?"

BY HER RECKONING, Toba Bet and Asmel were blessed with the following assets: the hunters likely did not know Asmel was not a real hart, she and Asmel could tolerate salt where the demon could not, and the demon would not want to risk further harm to its human host.

"I'm not sure any of that helps us much," Asmel said. "I may as well be a real hart, out here in the wilderness; it's not as if I can go inside and bar the door. There's no salt at hand. And I've already explained why we can't kill the human host."

Toba Bet was crouched in the dirt, listening to Asmel's harangue. "I'm trying to concentrate," she said. "Could you sulk more quietly?"

"I'm hardly sulking, I'm trying to explain—"

"Shh!" she hissed. "I'm making something."

What she was making was a doe, out of earth. She'd have liked to make one larger, but they were running low on drinking water already and she didn't want to use all that was left on mud that might fall apart when it stood up.

"Are you hoping they'll hunt that instead?" Asmel asked.

"No," Toba Bet said, and then she licked her thumb and ran it down her creation's forehead, willing her spit to smell like the most delectable doe in creation. That was another asset she'd forgotten to list for Asmel: It was mating season. Then she blew a stream of air across the creature's face and into the wind, and waited.

She did not need to wait long before a stag arrived, then two, then three. She'd been hoping for more. Five or six would have been nice, but she didn't dare wait any longer. Asmel was right; they'd stayed still too long already. "How can I make them be still?" she asked Asmel.

"Will their eyes to see only darkness, and they'll be still a moment," he said. "Probably not much longer."

"Good," she said. "Take your knife and cut off some of your hair."

"I see what you're thinking," he said, taking out the knife, "but that won't have enough of my scent." He handed her three locks of hair, and she took each and rubbed it across his neck, wet with perspiration, and willed the scent stronger, then she used a bit of magic to affix each to the antlers of a different stag.

She turned toward her mud creation, far too small to be a real deer, but pungent enough to confuse a stag at a distance in the dark. "Now go," she said, and it took off into the trees. A moment later, the stags gave chase.

"It'll fall apart in a few minutes and the stags will scatter," she said. "Let's go."

"You're assuming they'll hunt those three stags and not me?"

"I am. Because you'll be going where a real deer would not. Toward the sea."

+ +
+ · + +   +
+

ELENA WATCHED BARSILAY go ashen, but he kept his expression steady as he told the Cacería soldier, "I'm afraid I don't know you, sir."

"Don't you? Well, I suppose I don't have so much free time as you, to sit in the baths and lounge around Asmel's alcalá. Some of us have things to do, you know, for the good of Rimon."

"Indeed," Barsilay said. "Then let us not keep you."

The soldier chuckled. "I'm afraid I'm under orders that concern you. Dealing with the lentils will have to wait."

"The lentils?" Barsilay said. "My, that does sound important. I do think you should continue . . . moving them, was it?"

"Something along those lines. But you haven't said what you are doing here."

"Having an orgy," Barsilay said flatly.

"With these three?" the soldier asked.

"My tastes," Barsilay said, "are eclectic."

"I should say so." The soldier lowered his sword from the old woman's throat. "Well, I'm sorry to cut your diversion short."

"Are you? Because we'd be happy to welcome you."

"I'm afraid it goes against my creed to make love to a man and then kill him after," the soldier said, gesturing with his sword. "You understand."

"Of course," Barsilay said. "But certainly you don't have orders to kill these three, so why not let them go?"

"My orders were to kill you and anyone I find with you. But first, if you wouldn't mind, I believe you are in possession of a page of a certain book?"

At that moment, Elena's glamour—poor as it was to begin with— began to fade. She still looked reasonable at first glance, but the old woman was bad off indeed. Only her eyes stayed square.

The Mazik at her elbow had not yet noticed, but he would in a moment, and Elena's eyes were not far from turning back, too. She had little time to think. She clutched her side, cried out, and doubled over.

"Stop that," barked the Hound. "I don't care if you writhe on the ground, it's no matter to me."

"What have you done to us?" Elena cried. "Have you blighted us both?"

"What?" he said stupidly, and then the old woman, finally catching on, the great cow, clutched at her wrinkled face and let out a very convincing scream.

The Hound turned to see the old woman's ancient complexion and jumped back from her. "Mother of monsters," he cried, and Elena took advantage of his eyes on her, pulling the small knife from her belt and slicing off her own braided hair.

"What have you done?" Elena wailed.

The Hound, now utterly baffled, staggered back a few feet. "You've taken poison," he said. "Or you've been cursed. Stay away—"

Elena took that opportunity to launch herself at the man, throwing her arms around his neck. "Save me," she whispered, and then she took her severed braid and shoved it down the front of his tunic, and then she pushed the man directly in front of the palomino mare.

He was a tall man, nearly as tall as the horse; when the mare snapped his neck, it was so quick he did not even have time to cry out. Then there was a great deal of blood.

Elena flung herself away from the mare, who was in a frenzy, seemingly unaware that her prey was a Mazik and not a mortal. Elena grabbed the old woman by the arms and pulled them both well clear of the scene. The old woman was retching, and Elena would have been, too, if she hadn't been frightened to numbness.

"It..." the old woman said. "It's eating him."

"Yes, I know."

"I rode that horse, and now it's eating someone. It's...It's..." And then she nearly fainted.

Naftaly caught the old woman and lowered her to the ground before checking on Barsilay, who had lost his phantom arm somewhere in the fray—probably when the horse took it upon itself to eat the soldier. "Shouldn't we stop it?" Naftaly asked.

"Well," Barsilay said, "if it keeps going, we don't have to worry about someone identifying him later."

Elena pointed a finger at him in agreement. "I don't think we can keep that horse, though," she said. "There's no trusting it now."

"We'll trade it with his," Barsilay agreed, as if his face wasn't the color of parchment. He was very good, Elena had noticed, at pretending to be perfectly fine when he so clearly was not. It was a useful skill, particularly for a king. Maybe she'd underestimated him.

NAFTALY WAS STILL half-dead on his feet, so Barsilay took him a bit away from the horror of the horse and set him down with a cup of wine he'd made from their water. "To settle your nerves," he said.

"I think you need that more than I do," Naftaly said.

"True," Barsilay replied. "Give it back, then."

Naftaly smiled and took a drink of the wine before handing it back.

"We were very lucky today," Barsilay said. "If there'd been more than one Hound, we'd have been caught, and no trick of Elena's would have saved us. We have to do something different."

"Stay off the road," Naftaly said. "But I'm worried for the horses."

"So am I. I was a fool; it never occurred to me to look for soldiers anywhere but behind us. I never dreamed they'd be out here already. Apparently my imagination has insufficient scope."

"How could you have known?"

"I should have assumed they could be anywhere," Barsilay said. "I won't make that mistake again. There's more afoot than I'd guessed. They're stealing horses and lentils. It's a bad combination."

Naftaly had been through the siege of Rimon recently enough that the stockpiling of food and horses hinted at one major possibility. "You think they're preparing for war? But with whom?"

"I don't know," Barsilay said. "Tamar would be easy pickings with the lentil crop blighted, but it's on the other side of the strait."

"Zayit, then?"

"The supply line would be awfully hard to maintain. I don't see how it could be done. But Tarses is planning something, that's certain. It will be an unpleasant task to contain him, now he's Consort."

Naftaly said, "I'm sorry."

Barsilay looked perplexed. "You're sorry?"

"I know this isn't the path you wanted, and it will be difficult, but—"

"Stop," Barsilay said quickly. "Don't finish the thought."

"But—"

"This isn't a conversation I can have with you now. Please. It isn't a safe topic."

"Meaning you don't want to think about what comes next, or about who you are?"

"Meaning it's *unsafe*," Barsilay snapped. "And I'm no one."

So he kept insisting. But Naftaly couldn't resist pressing a little, so he asked, "Unsafe for whom?"

Barsilay's eyes were scanning the trees behind Naftaly, and he said, "For all of us."

SIX

AS THE DAY dawned, Toba Bet and Asmel continued their journey to the sea, and the weather grew progressively worse. At first, Toba Bet was glad for the rain, since it would wash away their tracks and slow down the hunters, but it brought their progress nearly to a halt. The ground was a slippery mess, and her feet were growing numb in her wet shoes, and she was fairly sure Asmel was going to get sick if she didn't get him warm. She managed to make him a shawl out of a leafy twig, but it was quickly as wet as the rest of him.

Worse, with the rain they couldn't see the sky, so Toba Bet had to pray they were going east, toward the sea. Asmel eventually suggested she make a compass, and she put something together out of a small stone and half an acorn filled with water, which revealed that they'd been heading south for some time. It took all of Toba Bet's will not to smash the thing into the ground when she realized.

"Let's stop for a few minutes and eat," Asmel suggested gently. "We haven't heard the hounds recently. I think it's safe, and we're both exhausted."

Toba Bet knew it wouldn't matter how tired they were if the hunters caught up to them, but stopped anyway. They'd lost most of their provisions along with their horse and only had the small bag of lentils Toba Bet had been carrying on her hip, probably not much more than another week's worth. She took two lentils and made them into bread, which they ate in the rain, crouched under the shelter of the largest tree they could find.

"I think it's letting up," Toba Bet said. "I hope we can recover some of the ground we lost."

Asmel was too tired to answer. She used a little magic to try to dry his hair, and then her own, and then passed him a bit of magic when she thought he looked more lost than usual. By then the sun was descending, and the rain had broken enough that they could see the waxing moon beginning to ascend.

They began walking again, and after another hour the stars were visible along with the moon, which bolstered Asmel's spirits. "I can find a clearer direction with the stars than with your compass," he said. "If we're making for Murcia we need to change our course a bit north to account for the ground we lost." He pointed at the sky. "We need to keep after that star."

"Are you certain?" Toba Bet asked.

"My issues this far have all been with my more recent memories," he said. "I'm not having any trouble reading the sky."

So they followed Asmel's stars another hour, then two, and into the night, because they did not want to risk stopping to rest. And then, they came to another river.

"I don't understand this," Toba Bet said. "Surely this isn't the same river?"

She took out her compass and filled the bowl with water again, and let out a cry when it stopped spinning. Again, they'd been going south instead of east. "You said you were sure!" she said. "You said—"

"I am sure! It's your compass that's wrong."

"My compass is not wrong," she said. "If we'd been going east, we wouldn't have come back to the river!"

"You don't know this is the same river," he said.

"There's no river between where we were yesterday and the coast!" She turned to face the water, reflecting the moonlight. "Unless this is a glamour."

"Toba—"

"It has to be," she said. "There is no river in this part of Sefarad. See?" And she strode straight into the water, only to find that the river was very real, and there was a very deep drop-off where she'd put her feet.

The water went all the way to her chest and, before she could think how to get out of it, the current caught her and pulled her off her feet. Asmel came splashing in after her and grabbed her by the waist as the water went up over her head. It took him several minutes to get them both out, Toba Bet coughing all the time since she'd breathed in the river. They were soaked all the way through, and muddy, and Toba Bet could not stop shaking.

"You never listen," Asmel said. "If you'd stopped for three seconds we could have checked to see if the river was real without jumping into it."

Toba Bet knew he was right, but she said, "It isn't my fault you can't read the sky!"

Asmel said, "You sound like a child."

"It isn't my fault you haven't any magic!" she cried. "It isn't my fault we're being hunted!"

"Dearest—" Asmel began, but Toba Bet shot back, "I am not your dearest! I'm not Marah, and I'm not the real Toba. I am the buchuk you soundly rejected, so don't try to soften me with pet names now."

Quietly, Asmel said, "I know who you are."

"Are you sure?" she asked, to which he gave no answer. She wept loudly as she wrung river water out of her clothes and hair, which was when she realized the pouch that held what was left of their lentils had washed away. She'd run them both into the river, and now she was abusing Asmel for it, and she felt wretched because she knew what was happening to him.

She'd gone into the void quickly and all at once; Asmel was on his way there slowly, watching the atoms of his mind wink out one by one, knowing the inevitability of it. Eventually, he would forget everything about himself. He would live out what remained of his lifespan as a mortal, and then he would be extinguished, and he was in the middle of it, of watching it, watching the void consume him, bite by excruciating bite. Toba Bet could prolong the process with her own magic, but she could not prevent it.

"Asmel," she asked, "what happens to mortals after they die?"

"I haven't the faintest idea," he said. "Whatever happens to them happens out of the sight of Maziks. Are you asking if they go to the void?"

She had been, but didn't much want to phrase it so bluntly.

He said, "I don't know. Maziks aren't much concerned with such things."

Toba Bet cried a little more before saying, "The lentils are gone."

"I assumed," Asmel said.

"I'm sorry," she said. "What will we do?"

He finished wringing the water out of his own hair and said, "We'll eat something else, and we'll keep going east."

"But how do we know which way is east?"

"We'll wait for the sun to rise," he said, "and start walking toward it."

IT WAS YOM Kippur, and Elena and her companions marked the occasion by forgoing the day's lentils—beside Barsilay, who could not afford to go hungry. Somewhere Alasar would be fasting and praying and believing, most likely, that his entire family had died.

She felt twisted up about it, but there had been no choice. Well, there had been, but if you were forced to choose between anything and a child, you chose the child, even if what you were leaving behind was a husband. That was how things were done, and Alasar, she knew, would have done the same.

She did not expect ever to see him again. If she were very lucky, she might see Toba—or what was left of her—in Zayit. Elena did not much mind that she was a buchuk. She was still hers, the child she'd cared for since her own child had died. She'd convinced Alasar to leave the girl unmarried, lest her Mazik powers pass to her children, and Elena maintained she'd followed the best available course. Only now Toba was having to move through the world in a way Elena had not prepared her for, as a Mazik or as a woman, and about that Elena could not help being sorry—especially seeing Naftaly, whose father had made similar choices and raised a son too innocent to survive a world that wanted him dead twice over.

It was probably more than twice, now that he was allied with Barsilay.

Elena and the old woman rode the bay gelding while Naftaly and Barsilay took the Hound's horse, and together they picked their way across the countryside parallel to the road. After a day traveling this way, Barsilay insisted they get back on the road. "We're too slow," he said. "This can't work, and once we get much farther north, we'll have to get back on the road anyway. The only alternative is to go through the mountains."

"Is that so terrible?" Naftaly had asked.

"There are things in those mountains I wouldn't like to meet," he said. "The road is safer and faster. We'll just have to be more careful."

Elena was not sure how that would be possible, especially given the fact that she was fairly certain they were being followed.

They camped some distance from the road a few nights after the incident with the Hound, eating some quite nice stuffed eggplants Barsilay had made them—he seemed to be recovering his strength a bit—and she was cross because she'd knelt down to tend to the fire and torn her skirt at the knee.

"We'll get you another in Zayit," Barsilay told her. "That one won't serve there, in any case. All your clothes will have to be replaced."

"I liked this skirt," Elena grumped. "The wool's so thick I can't feel the cold so much. Alasar gave it to me last winter." She smoothed the moss-green fabric across her legs.

"It's my father's," Naftaly said absently, while Elena looked up from her skirt in surprise. "He made it."

"You recognize a plain skirt he sewed a year ago?" the old woman asked.

"I'm the one who bought the fabric," Naftaly said, "and I got in rather a lot of trouble for it—it was too heavy and too hard to sew, and the color was out of fashion." He fingered the back of his ear. "I bought a whole bolt of it, and he had to sew it all himself, since I couldn't stitch through it well enough. He was so angry." He sighed. "I'd mend it for you, but I haven't got a needle or thread."

"I can help you," Barsilay said, plucking a blade of grass from the ground, and handing it to Naftaly. "Put it over the hole."

"I can't mend with an illusion," Naftaly protested, but Barsilay said, "Just act as if you are mending it." And then he put his finger over Naftaly's thumb on the grass, and it blended itself into the fabric and was whole again.

"How did you—"

"I gave you a little magic," Barsilay said. "Don't worry, it was a very little. But the work was yours, you see?"

And indeed, when Naftaly took his hand away from the fabric, the hole was filled in, but it shimmered in the moonlight; he'd changed the color, only slightly, and now it had a golden undertone. Elena fingered the repair and said, "It's lovely."

As she watched the others drift off to sleep, she wondered how Barsilay could pass his magic to another person, and what else Naftaly might be able to do with it, and what *she* might be able to do with it. And then she put it to the back of her mind, which was occupied with a far more pressing issue that had been troubling her for several days.

Elena slept only a few minutes, and the rest of the night kept watch on the trees at their backs, listening and waiting. Beside her, the old woman snored under a blanket Naftaly had made from dried leaves—an illusion which only lasted a few hours, and then she was grumbling in her sleep about the cold.

The next morning Elena stretched her aching back, splashed a little water on her face, and confirmed that none of her companions had their throats slit in their sleep. Her stomach grumbling, she walked away from their small camp, leaving their horses and pet Mazik behind, until she was well out of ear and eyeshot.

Then she sat down and absentmindedly drew a circle in the dirt around herself and said, to no one in particular, "How much longer do you intend to follow us?"

She was not surprised when no answer came, so she went on, "What are you hoping will happen?"

"She's waiting." This from Barsilay, walking up the path behind her. She'd heard him coming. He wasn't good at being quiet, but he'd moved faster than she'd realized he could. Well, good. He must be feeling better. "Your little circle wouldn't stop her killing you, by the way. Though I'm sure she thinks it's adorable."

Scowling, Elena said, "How long have you realized we're being followed?"

"Since you fed that Hound to our horse."

That was longer than Elena had been aware of it. "Do you know who it is?"

"Yes," he said. "And if she wants us dead, there's nothing any of us can do about it, so try not to worry too much."

"Who would worry about that?" she muttered. "Doesn't she want you dead?"

Barsilay pondered this. "Oh, almost certainly, but I'm guessing curiosity has stayed her hand." Here, he cast his eyes on his empty sleeve, as if to say that whoever was watching was probably wondering how he'd lost his arm or, more to the point, why it had been taken. "It's certainly not that we were friends at one time."

"Friends," Elena mused, "or lovers?"

"Is there a difference?" he asked with a smile. "But that was long ago."

Probably this conversation was for the benefit of the unnamed Mazik concealed nearby. Elena had not seen her, but she'd seen signs of her—a movement at the corner of her eye a handful of times, enough to tell her it was not an animal she sensed, and that the person must be relatively small to stay so well hidden. Elena guessed she'd been listening to their conversations for some time. Elena hadn't brought it up before because she assumed that if the boy found out he would flail around so much it would force their tracker into action. And she couldn't quite trust the old woman not to alert the boy to the danger.

"Why doesn't she ask you directly?"

"She probably thinks I'd lie. I'm a very good liar."

"Have you lied to her specifically?"

"Of course."

Of course, exasperating man. "So you propose we just let her continue following us?"

"I don't think we have a choice," Barsilay said, staring out into nothing. "She can't very well pretend she hasn't seen us and go back to Rimon. Either I let her go on following us, or I demand she kill me now. Would that be better?"

At that, Elena got up from the rough ground. "Damnable thing," she said. "No wonder she wants to kill you."

"But she hasn't!"

"If she doesn't, maybe I will!"

"You would never," he said.

"I would. That horse looks very hungry, and of the two of you I prefer him. So stop with your false charm and wake up the others so we can get to Zayit, and at least we'll be someplace civilized when that woman decides it's time to kill us." In this time, she had stalked back to the camp, but when she turned around, Barsilay was holding out a small cake he'd made from one of their few remaining lentils with an unfortunate grin.

A honey cake. "Am I a child?"

"To me? Yes."

"You're upset because you think I don't like you. Must everyone like you? Does it affront your dignity to think someone finds you insufferable?"

"I like you," he said. "A great deal."

"Lies," she scoffed. "No one does."

"I never lie about matters of affection. Also you remind me of someone."

Toba, he likely meant, though he wouldn't mention her in front of his friend in the woods. She felt herself thaw, just a bit. He'd been Toba's friend. She'd said as much. And Toba had never been much for friendship. "This changes nothing," she grumped, and then took the cake and shoved it in her mouth.

TOBA BET MANAGED to close her eyes for a few minutes that night, thinking of the place on Mir's map where Rahel was supposed to be.

In the dream-world, she found herself on a hillside, looking down to the coast. Rising from the shore was a stone tower, its spire reaching into the whirling stars. Toba Bet made her way down the hill to the base of the tower and pushed open a door that, were it in the waking world, would have been heavy.

The inside of the tower was completely empty and mostly dark, but a staircase spiraled up, so Toba Bet followed it to the upper rooms. There was no sign anyone had ever been there. She ran her hand along the interior wall, searching—for what she did not know. This was not the real tower; it was only a dream. And Toba Bet did not know what it meant for it to be empty. She went to look out the window, which offered a view of the darkened coast. A filmy bauble, like those Asmel used to keep samples of air, hovered just outside. Toba Bet reached for it and looked at it carefully. It was empty. She supposed it could have held air, but what use was keeping samples in the dream-world, which had no air anyway? She brought it close to her face, looking for something within it. Beneath her hand, it quivered.

As her surprised breath hit the filmy exterior, the bauble burst, and out of it came a woman's voice, which said, "What is Tarses doing in the Gal'in?"

Toba Bet wiped the residue of the bauble onto her dress. She knew little of the Gal'in; in the mortal realm, the mountains north of Sefarad were empty, so far as she knew, except for wolves or bears. You couldn't farm them, or trade across them.

Had the bauble been Rahel's?

A person dropped down from the ceiling, startling Toba Bet so badly she nearly woke, and then righted herself on the floor. She was no taller than Toba Bet herself, with dark skin and a canny expression. From Asmel's description, this was not Rahel.

"No one ever comes here," the woman said, friendly as anything, as if she hadn't just descended from the ceiling like a bat. "Are you looking for someone?"

"Yes," Toba Bet said, because an obvious lie seemed more dangerous. She would tread with care, now; she could always wake herself up later.

"For the woman who built this tower? She's long gone," the woman said.

"Where did she go?" Toba Bet asked.

"The void, I'd assume," the other woman replied.

Toba Bet felt the chill of it creep into her limbs again.

The woman said, "Are you all right?"

"I'm quite fine," Toba Bet said. "But since she's not here, I may as well go."

"Don't," said the other woman, running a hand along the windowsill as if looking for dust. There was none, of course.

"Why?"

"Because I've been here all night by myself, and now I'm bored, and you look a little like someone I know, around the eyes, I think, and she's always such fun in dreams. Stay and tell me a story. Or take off your clothes, I don't care which." The woman manifested a pair of silver cups, filled with what might have been red wine, before offering one to Toba Bet.

"No, thank you," she said, but the Mazik replied, "Then I shall be insulted."

Toba Bet tried to wake then, and found that she could not.

"Who are you?" she asked.

The woman laughed and said, "Drink your wine, lest I take offense."

Toba Bet thought this was probably a bad idea. But this Mazik was more than a little dangerous, and Toba Bet seemed to be trapped here with her, so she sipped the wine, which was stronger than anything Barsilay had ever given her.

"Now, why did you say you were here again?" the Mazik asked.

Toba Bet's vision was growing cloudy around the edges. "I already told you."

"Right, you were looking for the woman who made this tower. Why?"

"We were lovers," Toba Bet said, relieved she'd retained the ability to lie.

"You seem awfully undistressed by her death, then."

"I have others," Toba Bet said.

"Any you'd shed a tear for, if *they* passed into the void?"

"I'll let you know. Why are *you* here?"

"Me? Oh, the same reason," the Mazik said, downing her wine in a single draught. "We were lovers."

"Did you kill her?"

"No, I didn't."

"Do you know who did?"

"Could have been any number of people. What is your appellation, here?"

"My appellation?"

"What do they call you, dreamer?"

No one in dreams had ever called Toba Bet anything. "I have no dream appellation."

"None! So all your lovers—"

"We don't talk much," Toba Bet said flatly.

"Sounds delightful. A relief, really, spending half your life with no name at all! Ah, it sounds lovely. I suppose I don't like my own name much. I can't imagine why I chose it."

Toba Bet was not sure where this conversation was going, but she assumed it ended with her being tricked into revealing her name. Better, she thought, to lead away from that line of questions. "You could choose a new one, under the right circumstances."

The woman snorted a little. "And what circumstances would those be?"

"The Queen of Luz could change a name," Toba Bet said.

The Mazik looked quite startled and said, "Who told you that?"

Toba Bet was feeling very strange. The wine was not poison, but neither was it wine. She was very hot and very dizzy. "It was part of some old story. She had the power, because of the mandate of Luz."

"The power to change a name?"

When Toba the Elder had been young—not more than twelve or thirteen—she'd gotten it into her mind to sneak extra Shabbat wine into her cup when her grandmother's back was turned, and she'd enjoyed it so much she'd refilled it again three times before anyone caught on.

She did not recall much of what happened later that evening, beyond a sense that Elena had yelled for the better part of an hour, while Toba had been sick repeatedly, and she'd been made to spend the next month scrubbing the floors instead of studying with her grandfather.

Toba Bet, in this dream, was far drunker than she had been that night, either because it was dream-wine, or because of some intention the other woman had laid on top of it. She felt strange in a way she decided she enjoyed, and found that she liked the feel of words against her heavy tongue. She said, "That's what . . . I said. So I guess that power also passes to the heir of Luz."

The woman drew very close to Toba Bet and said, "And who is that?"

Toba Bet was just sober enough to realize what she was about to do, and wavered on her feet a little before whispering into the other woman's face, "Damned if I know." And then she leaned in and kissed the other woman on the nose, who whipped her head back in surprise.

Toba Bet took advantage of the moment and woke to find Asmel awake and looking like he'd lost himself again. She passed him some magic, and when his expression cleared, she told him simply, "Rahel is dead."

NAFTALY FINALLY DREAMT outside of the city of Rimon, in the wilds of Sefarad. Barsilay was with him, standing on top of a hill, looking down to the sea, and the wind blew through the grass and his hair. Naftaly was still overawed by the man, whose eyes were particularly golden in the starlight. He'd been oddly quiet since they'd encountered the Hound at the lentil farm, and it worried Naftaly. There was strain in the lines around Barsilay's eyes, too, that Naftaly could never quite erase, not with clever asides, not with furtive touches.

Barsilay looked down at Naftaly and sighed. "I was afraid I'd never dream again," he said, and he kissed him.

It was the first time they'd been alone since Barsilay had been imprisoned, and they'd shared so many dreams inside his tower cell. Only Barsilay did not seem to feel much like talking, and then they were in the long grass, and the wind was blowing on Naftaly's bare skin, and Barsilay was shading out the stars overhead.

Sometime later, when they'd been quiet so long Naftaly thought Barsilay might have fallen asleep—before realizing that wasn't possible—Naftaly asked, "Is this different here, than in the waking world?"

Barsilay said, "Yes, it's different." He rolled over on his side, propping his head up on his arm. He hadn't bothered with the phantom, and Naftaly was a little glad he felt he didn't need to. "I hadn't intended for this to happen here."

"No?"

"I don't mean I regret it. It's only that I thought it would be better waking, first."

Naftaly looked up at the dizzying stars and said, "Only you realized we might not live long enough to make that happen."

Barsilay laughed sadly. "Not without an audience, anyway."

Naftaly said, "There's always an audience. I haven't had a waking moment to myself in . . . Not since I left Rimon." He thought about this. "Aside from that time Elena nailed me inside a coffin. I have some old woman or other with me nearly every moment, can you imagine?"

"I very much can," Barsilay chuckled. "May I admit something to you? Something I'd never admit awake?"

"Of course."

"I enjoy them." He laughed. "Is that mad?"

"You were locked away alone a long time. I can see how their voices in your ear might be . . ."

"Soothing?"

"Are they?"

"They are. Very. It's like, every time my mind wanders someplace dark, one of them's yelling about some nonsense or complaining about some little peccadillo of mine, and then I forget to finish my fugue."

"You think they're doing it on purpose?"

"Actually, I do."

"I only wish I could be as helpful."

"Oh, little one, I don't mean it that way. Come here." He put his arm around Naftaly and pulled him close. "What you give me is more than help, you know that, don't you? If there's any part of me you find worthwhile, it persists because of you." He exhaled into Naftaly's hair. "And if we ever make it to Zayit, I am looking forward to being alone with you awake."

"In a room with a door," Naftaly said. He plucked a blade of grass and ran it down Barsilay's profile, which made him smile.

"I think that will do very nicely," Barsilay said. "I guess we'd better hurry up, then."

TOBA BET'S MAGIC had grown erratic from too little sleep and too much strain, and she was having trouble creating enough to give

Asmel, whose memories were growing more unreliable. The rate at which he needed magic had increased; she was having to give him some every few hours now, and she could not admit the toll it was taking on her.

They also had no food. She'd tried making bread from acorns, but it tasted so bitter it made Asmel retch, and while she'd choked some down, her stomach had hurt for hours. She was hoping to find some berries or mushrooms, but it was too near to winter, and they found nothing.

They'd stopped to rest a few minutes. Toba Bet's feet were bleeding again, and she suspected Asmel's were, too. Asmel had closed his eyes, and she was about to pass him more magic when he said, "Don't. I don't need it now."

"I'm only trying to help you," she said.

Without opening his eyes, Asmel said, "I will ask this once, because I must know. Why did you bring us here? Why did you not simply take us to Barsilay?"

"If you've been wondering all this time, why ask now?" Toba Bet asked.

"I thought it kinder to let it be. But now I must know. Why have you done this? You knew they could track you here. The demon aside, Tarses will send soldiers through the gate at the next moon."

"Yes, I know. But they can't track *you*."

"Toba—"

"I just needed to find someplace safe for you."

"And then?"

"And then I don't know," Toba Bet said. "I had no great plan in mind, all right? I'd just felt myself die, in case you're forgetting, and the person who killed me also tortured my friend and cut off his arm, and mainly I was thinking I'd like to get as far away from her as possible before she kills what's left of me and probably you, too, while she's at it. I'm sorry I had no plan. I'm sorry I didn't carry you up a mountain to Barsilay, who may not even be alive anymore. I'm tired, Asmel. I'm so tired, and I don't want to die again."

She wept from exhaustion as much as fear. But Asmel, rather than offering words of comfort, simply said, "Stop."

"Would a kind word kill you? After everything?"

"What kind word would you have? Shall I lie to you? You've never appreciated falseness before. We will grow steadily weaker until the demon catches us, and it won't be much longer. We can't trick him away from tracking you. We'll never make it to Murcia, let alone Zayit."

"Then we must go where he can't," Toba Bet said. "Into the sea, to Te'ena."

Asmel looked thoroughly taken aback. "No," he said. "If Barsilay does have a mirror here, it may well be you. You're both hidden heirs. You're both escaping Rimon. You both have companions without magic or obvious utility. And if you are also Barsilay's mirror, it becomes doubly important for us to be careful. Mistakes we make here could play out there in terrible ways for him."

Toba Bet could not discount this argument, but wasn't sure it mattered. "What about Aravoth? Our only hope is to somehow speak with Omer. Rahel is dead; the only way to talk to him is to go ourselves to Te'ena."

"Rahel is dead?" Asmel rubbed at his eyes. "Rahel is dead. I'd forgotten. But the fact remains: If we flee into the sea, what happens to Barsilay, who cannot go there?"

"Is protecting Barsilay our only concern?"

"He's our immediate concern."

"No, our immediate concern is not being caught by that demon. Anyway, you said yourself the Mirror is not so specific," she said. "Maybe he'll flee west instead? Listen, if we have no idea how the Mirror works, there's no point in worrying about how it might reflect our actions. And anyway, it's not only our actions being reflected. Did you consider it might not be safe for Barsilay to go north, either, because he may be contending with his own set of villains? There are more people hunting him than chasing us."

Asmel sighed an old man's sigh.

"I don't see we have a better option," Toba Bet said. "La Cacería can't have anyone coming at us from Te'ena—it's impossible to get to in the Mazik world since it was made an island. It's completely cut off from any Maziks who weren't already there at the Fall. But from mortal Te'ena, we can get a ship to Zayit."

"This is a bad idea," he told her.

"Do you have a better one?" she snapped. "Right now our only choice is to flee to where the demon can't follow, and that's Te'ena."

Asmel looked deeply miserable and said, "I have no better plan."

TOBA BET AND Asmel walked all night toward the sea, under a moon that was growing increasingly full. They were running out of time to get away from Rimon before the moon made them a target for more than just the demon. If his mission was only to keep them nearby, he'd succeeded. Every few hours, they heard the hounds in the distance, chasing one of her enchanted stags, but Toba Bet harbored no illusions they would save them in the end.

"He's created a pincer," Asmel said. "The demon to the west, the hunt to the north, and the Courser will be coming up from Rimon to the south. There's no place to go but into the sea. I don't like this."

They'd stopped to eat a few pine nuts she'd turned into sour bread, because she couldn't spare the magic to make anything more complex. Her clothes swamped her; she'd lost any weight she'd put on living with Asmel and Barsilay, and more besides. If they couldn't find a way to escape, the demon would simply run them down. She was nearly at the end of her strength and magic both.

Since she had not answered, Asmel continued, "Has it occurred to you that Te'ena might not be safe, either?"

Toba Bet said, "What can you mean?"

"I mean the demon seems to be herding us exactly there, and the Courser is as capable of crossing the sea as you are."

"But for her to get to Te'ena on the Mazik side would be nearly impossible," she said. "Maziks have no ships or sailors; they can't sail across saltwater at all. She'd have to find a way to get there alone."

Asmel said, "The question to ask is whether your sister has the wherewithal to get to Te'ena on her own, and we can assume her abilities are similar to yours. Presumably she can cross saltwater and has a reliable source of magic."

"But can she build a ship and sail it?" Toba Bet shook her head. "There's technical knowledge there, and who would she learn from? No Mazik."

"I don't like it," he insisted.

"We'll have to leave before the moon, is all. Once we're in Te'ena, I should be able to dream my way to Omer, and after that we can get a ship to Zayit. Anyway"—she waved an arm at the sky—"the moon is still days away from full."

"Three days," he said, squinting up at the sky. "That doesn't give us much time to get a ship out of Te'ena."

"We'll have to hurry," she agreed. "But at least we know she won't be there waiting for us."

It took Toba Bet and Asmel 'til the hour before dawn to reach the coast, by which time Toba Bet found she could go no farther. The hours of running, the massive drain on her magic, and the sleepless night had taken what strength she'd been gifted by her sturdy mother and Mazik father and wrung it from her. Her legs gave out, and she looked up to Asmel and simply said, "I'm sorry."

Asmel's strain was only slightly less than hers, and there were lines showing in his face that had not been there three days ago. "Come on," he said, kneeling in front of her. "You've done enough."

"We'll be too slow this way," she said, looping her arms around his neck, because the alternative was to stay sprawled out in the dirt, which served no one. "You're hardly better off than I am."

"I'm leagues better off than you are, and you're barely more than air these days." He rose and settled her weight on his back. "Barsilay will be so angry when he sees all his hard work gone. You're nothing but bones."

"If Barsilay wants to fatten me up again, I won't complain," she said into Asmel's shoulder, because it was too difficult even to lift her head. "He can stuff me with all the pheasants he wants."

Asmel set a pace which Toba Bet thought not quick enough, but it was probably better to make consistent progress than collapse a mile closer to Murcia, so she held her tongue. "Was it pheasants he was stuffing you with?"

"Always," she said. "So many pheasants. Must be a favorite of his."

Asmel said, "Barsilay hates fowl. Never eats it at all."

Toba Bet coughed into his neck. "Perverse man. I hope he's all right."

"You never were able to dream of him?"

"No. But considering how little I've slept, that doesn't mean much. Asmel, I'm so tired."

"If you think you can sleep like that, you should. Your magic will recover faster."

"You'll drop me if I fall asleep. You're exhausted, too."

His eye met hers over his shoulder. "I would never drop you. Don't you trust me at all?"

Toba Bet was barely awake and said, "You know precisely how I feel about you."

She felt his back stiffen a little, and he grumbled. "Any feelings you might have are solely because I was a friend to you when you had none."

"What I feel for Barsilay is friendship," Toba Bet said. "My feelings for you go beyond that."

"What reason could you possibly have to love me? I've given you none."

"You've tried very hard not to," Toba Bet agreed. "We're both exhausted, Asmel. Must we litigate this to within an inch of our lives? I know you feel nothing in return. You don't need to tell me this."

Asmel was so quiet that Toba Bet thought his memory might be fading again, and then he said, "I never said I felt nothing in return."

Toba Bet said, "Asmel—"

"Would you like to litigate this too?" he said softly. "Go to sleep, Toba."

TOBA BET COULD not quite believe she'd managed to sleep on Asmel's back, but fatigue must have won out because when she opened her eyes again the sun had hit the horizon. She's been so exhausted she hadn't even dreamt.

It was not the sun that had woken her, however—it was the hounds. And she and Asmel didn't appear to have covered much distance, either. Murcia was still much too far away; this despite the fact that Asmel's pace had doubled.

Asmel must have sensed her waking, because he said, "We have a problem."

"I hear the problem," she said.

"We won't make it to Murcia before they catch up."

"Make for the shore," she said. "At least we can retreat into the water."

She could hear Asmel grinding his teeth. Of course, neither of them could swim.

"It's still all we can do," she said. "Put me down."

"We can't afford to waste your strength running," he said. "We'll need it when they catch us."

They only made it another few minutes before Asmel had to relent and set Toba Bet down. They fled down to the beach, Asmel looking more uneasy by the moment, as if waiting for the salt in the air and the sand to burn him alive. "Is that a boat?" he asked, indicating a shape in the water, though even Toba Bet, who had lived all her life in the mountains, knew it was. It had a single short mast, and was big enough for no more than two people who liked each other a great deal. It seemed too small to be seaworthy.

"It's tied up," she said. "Must belong to a local fisherman? It's small enough for that."

It seemed entirely too convenient.

"I think we should continue up to Murcia," Toba Bet said. "I don't trust gifts from strangers."

"Nor do I," Asmel said, but then they paused to listen to the hounds. "They're close now."

Toba Bet felt a flash of anger. What kind of hunters would follow a scent to the beach? No deer would ever run that way, where there was no cover at all. Hunters should know that much, and should have realized something was amiss. Were they insensible?

They were working for a demon, so probably they *were* insensible. If the demon could glamour a river out of nothing, they might not even know this was a beach. They might well believe they were still in the forest. They might well believe Asmel was a stag, when they saw him. There was no choice but the fisherman's boat.

The hounds were on the beach now.

Toba Bet could see the men arming themselves with bows, their eyes focused on Asmel. They did not seem able to see her at all. The sun was pink on the horizon, and they loosed their arrows; Toba Bet held up a hand to knock them aside with magic, only panicking at the last moment when she realized she had no idea how.

She tackled Asmel to the sand instead, knocking the wind from both of them. When they'd stopped rolling, his eyes had gone glassy and far away. "Asmel?" she asked. Her hand on his shoulder came away wet with blood, and she realized she'd been a step behind. An arrow had caught the edge of his upper arm, tearing his coat and the skin underneath; a silver wisp of her own magic evaporated from the wound. Up the beach, she heard the huntsmen sound the mort, a horrible noise that echoed in her chest. They believed Asmel was dead.

There was no place to go but into the water, and shortly that wouldn't be possible either. She pulled Asmel up by his unhurt arm and shoved him back toward the boat. He was too muddled to argue, and in the dawn light, she could see that his arm was bleeding freely.

They needed cover. Toba Bet threw up a fog behind her, hoping it would mask them long enough to get away from shore and wondering what the hunters would think of a hart escaping into the sea, when she heard one of the men say, "Dear God, that's no stag."

So the demon's glamour had worn off. Then she heard a scream, and another, and the sounds of the horses in terror. Someone was killing the hunters.

There was no way to see who it was in the fog, but it could only have been the demon, killing his men either in a rage or because they served no further purpose. She'd managed to get Asmel to the boat and shoved him into it, cut the rope, and pushed it away from shore with all the strength left in her half-Mazik body. Asmel had enough sense left to say, "There's a sail," and then he was unconscious.

Toba Bet had no idea how to hoist a sail, but she unfurled it as best she could and sent wind into it from the palm of her hand, which only succeeded in tangling it She was barely able to get it pointed the right way when, through the cleared fog, she saw the demon on the beach, mounted and with bloodied sword in hand.

He was riding Asmel's horse.

Toba Bet managed to hold the mast still this time, as she forced enough air into the sail to blow them out into the water, toward the open sea.

Seven

ELENA FOUND BARSILAY'S reaction to their tail to be wholly unacceptable. She understood his position perfectly: Whoever this woman was, they could not hope to fight her. But to do nothing at all, besides wait for her to get bored and kill them all? It was unendurable.

They'd stopped to eat a few lentils made over into meatballs and rest the horses when Naftaly said, "I was thinking again about your speed litany."

She didn't like him bringing it up so openly, but there was no point trying to quiet him about it now, so she said, "What about it? I tried it before and it didn't work."

"But maybe it would work for Barsilay, now that his magic is stronger. That's what I was wondering."

"A mortal spell?" Barsilay asked. "How does it work?"

Elena did not precisely know how it worked. There was a litany she'd learned from her grandmother, long ago, to make an animal go faster. You whispered it to your horse or mule or what have you, and then . . . things happened, as if the horse suddenly remembered how to knit spaces together under its feet, and then one gallop covered ten paces instead of five. It was not that the horse went faster so much as that it covered more ground when it moved. "I don't know how it works, only that it does. At least, it did in the mortal world."

Barsilay said, "I've never tried to work mortal magic before; I'm not sure I even could. Can you show me?"

Elena hesitated, because the Mazik woman would be listening to all of this, and she definitely did not want to teach it to her. "Come closer," she said, and she very softly whispered the litany into Barsilay's ear.

"Goodness," he said. "That's complicated. No wonder it won't work here."

"My glamour worked."

"You cast that on yourself and the old woman. If you tried to glamour me, I don't think you could. The magic is too different. It doesn't work the same." He took another lentil and changed it into a meatball, then handed it to Naftaly. "The lentil changes because I mean for it to. That spell . . . It has nothing to do with intention. That's about mastery. I think it probably took you a very long time to learn it properly?"

"Years," she admitted. All her grandmother's spells took years to learn right. There were very specific words in a very specific order, and if your pronunciation was anything apart from perfect they did nothing at all. Where her grandmother had learned them was a mystery Elena had never solved. They were little things, mainly: glamours that held a few minutes, the speed litany, spells for locating lost items or people, casting a demon from a house without using salt, that sort of thing. Housewives' charms, she'd always thought of them. Most people could not work them because most people did not have the wherewithal to practice the same spell without effect for years on end. Barsilay, she suspected, would be a quicker study. "Couldn't you use your own magic the same way?"

"If intention were enough to speed up a horse, we'd have been in Zayit days ago," he said.

"What if you mixed them together, your magic, your intent, and the litany? Might that work?"

He thought on this a minute. "It's possible," he said. Then, eyeing the other two, who were still eating, he added, "Let's discuss it closer to the horses."

Elena rose and followed him back to where they'd left them. They didn't stop to eat in view of the horses lest the animals get ideas, but they weren't so far off, either. Checking to make sure the others were too far away to hear, Barsilay leaned forward and murmured directly into Elena's ear. "I don't wish to speak about the litany just yet. There's something more urgent that requires your particular brand of magic. Mine's still too weak and I don't trust it."

"What do you want me to do?"

He placed his hand over his tunic, where she knew he kept the missing page of Naftaly's book, folded and wrapped in a piece of cloth. "Can you cast something that will tie the fate of this to my own?"

She hesitated for a moment—why was he asking what was impossible? Only then she remembered: Naftaly's book had been made by mortals. It might well respond to one of her enchantments. But which of her little spells might work? She'd have to modify something she knew already, and that was difficult, and there'd be no way to test it. Elena met his gaze; he was being deliberately cagey.

"No," he said. "It's not enough. Can you tie its fate to all of ours?"

Now Elena was unsure. "You may not want to do that," she said. "I had a stroke not long ago. I could have another. And the old woman could go any day."

Barsilay exhaled heavily. "I didn't account for mortality," he said. "Something else?"

It would take two spells: one to bind the group and a second to trigger some kind of ward in case of violence, not only sudden death.

In his ear, she whispered, "What kind of violence do I need to account for?"

Barsilay said, "Anything you can think of that is quick and impossible to see coming."

The spell would have to be broad then; she'd never be able to come up with every possibility. She said, "Are you sure you want to do this? If something goes wrong for us, no one will ever be able to put the gate back."

"I'm hoping she won't be willing to risk it," he said. "Can you do it?"

The wording would be tricky, but she nodded. "It won't last very long. My magic is limited."

He pressed his mouth to her temple. "I'll give you what I can." And Elena felt the warmth of his magic enter her with a jolt. Even that small amount was more than she'd ever imagined with her own threadbare powers. What few spells she knew were based on taking an impossibly small quantity of magic and spinning it cleverly to do what she wanted; it was mastery built on precision, so that nothing would be wasted. How different Mazik magic must be, she thought, when they were practically made of the stuff.

With what he'd given her, she could weave a spell that would last days or weeks, not hours. She carefully whispered the command to the paper, told it what she wanted it to do, firmly and carefully. "It's done," she whispered. "But how will she know?"

Barsilay's eyes were somewhere far away, looking at something she could not see. "She knows already," he said.

"But if that's true, why would she let me do it? Why not kill me before I could enchant it?"

Barsilay's arm had been looped behind Elena's shoulders this entire time, but now he pulled it between them to reveal a small ball of blue flame in his palm. He'd been holding it behind her back since they'd started speaking, to kill them both and destroy the page at the first sign of trouble. Elena nodded her understanding and approval both. "Well done."

NAFTALY WAS DELIGHTED to find that his suggestion had been a good one: it turned out that Barsilay was able to use Elena's speed litany quite effectively. They made excellent time 'til the sun went down, and the next morning Barsilay was strong enough to turn several of their ranch-stolen lentils into a breakfast that satisfied even the old woman. They'd managed to come all the way north to where Barcino would have been, if they'd been in the mortal world. Here, there was nothing but wilderness and a rocky coastline that Naftaly could see sloping down from the hills.

Barsilay was washing his face and hands with a few drops of water while the old woman grumbled and stretched her back, and then said, "So you'll recall you told us there were no Maziks between Rimon and Zayit."

"Apart from the farmers, yes."

"Right, apart from the farmers." The old woman pointed at the valley below them, very near the sea. "Does that seem like a farm to you?"

Naftaly and Barsilay both drew close and looked down where she'd indicated. "That's a tower," Barsilay said. It had been too dark the night before to see such a thing, and Naftaly might have missed it, anyway; it was the same color as the earth it sprouted from. "Why is there a tower?"

"I take it those are not naturally occurring here," Elena said. "They don't just pop out of the ground?"

"Of course not."

"Then it seems that someone has built a tower. Here, in the absolute middle of nowhere at all."

Naftaly squinted at it, rising on his toes. "Is it an outpost? For observation, maybe?"

"There's nothing to observe," Barsilay said. "Rimon and Zayit don't have border disputes; no one cares about all the empty land in between them. And there's no use looking out to the sea. Nothing could possibly come from that direction besides storm clouds."

"It does look like a watchtower," Elena said. "Are you sure?"

Barsilay let out a sharp exhale of frustration. "I would very much like to know who built it," he said, "but not enough to risk our lives."

"Could you send a sentry of some kind?" Naftaly asked. "Like Toba, with her birds?"

"I think I have enough magic now," Barsilay said, "but it would be dangerous if it were caught ... Whoever is in that tower would know there was another Mazik nearby, and they might be interested in finding out who it was."

"Well, pick something there's a lot of," the old woman suggested. "And just make something that looks the same, so it doesn't stand out."

Barsilay extended his real arm, and at the end appeared a gull, which he tossed into the air. The gull circled toward the flock of seabirds that were perched on the rocky coast, then closer to the building. Naftaly lost sight of it as it approached the tower; it was simply too small and too far away.

"I'm checking the windows," Barsilay said.

"And?" Elena put forth.

He scowled and said, "Hmm," and then made a gesture that Naftaly guessed was meant to dispel the bird. "It looks totally abandoned, from what I can tell."

"Can you see what it was, before they abandoned it?" Naftaly asked.

"Based on what I could see through the windows, it looks like an observatory."

Naftaly's eyes went up to the top of the tower, as Elena said, "It looks more like a lighthouse to me. Why put an observatory down at sea level?"

"Maziks don't use lighthouses," Barsilay said. "Maziks don't use *ships*."

"Maziks don't seem to know where to put their telescopes, either," Elena was saying, but Naftaly's eyes were still on the top of the tower. It must have had a very fine view of the coast. He felt the breeze on his face, and then realized he was inside the tower, looking out at the coast below, as a fleet of ships sailed past—more ships than he could count.

Naftaly leaned out further, trying to count, and then, amid the ships, there was a shimmering light illuminating a winged figure: four wings, like one of the cherubim.

He opened his eyes from the ground, where Barsilay was smoothing the hair out of his face. The ache behind his left ear had progressed into a sharp pain; he set his hand against it and came away with blood.

"Are you all right?" Barsilay asked, to which the old woman barked, "Does he look all right to you?"

Naftaly said, "I wanted to see the view, and I did," and then he closed his eyes again.

Barsilay was able to ease the worst of Naftaly's pain with some gentle application of magic, and Naftaly told them about the fleet and the winged being, which Barsilay found utterly perplexing. "It must have been something in the mortal world," he said. "But I can't account for the figure you saw."

Naftaly, on the other hand, was more intrigued by the fact that he'd seen what he'd wanted: the view from the tower. Barsilay gave him some food he barely tasted, and when he'd recovered his strength, he said, "I'd like to go inside."

TOBA BET KNEW that the voyage from the mainland to Te'ena took the better part of a day, depending on the wind and assuming you knew which way you were going. She hoped heading due east would be good enough. Te'ena would be too big to miss, she hoped. If only she had a compass.

She'd managed to stop Asmel's bleeding and pass him enough magic to bring back his mind after he'd forgotten he'd lost his own magic and panicked over the presence of so much saltwater. He remained oddly quiet, though, and she wasn't sure if the issue was that he was on the dreaded sea, the fact that he'd been brought down by mortal hunters like an animal, or something worse than all the rest. She looked away from the sail long enough to see him taking in the entire scene, murmuring, "Extraordinary."

"The sea, you mean?" But Asmel had returned to his reverie. After a while longer, Toba said, "I wish you would speak."

"What's there to say?" Asmel said. He'd not bothered to sit up since she'd bandaged his arm with a torn piece of her own coat.

"You could give me some advice on how to make sure I'm still going east," she said.

"We're still in sight of land, little fool. Just keep moving away from it. By the time we've lost sight of that, we should be near enough to Te'ena to see it."

That much should have occurred to her; it was a blessedly clear day, the only luck they'd had in ages. Well, not the only luck. They'd found a random unattended boat. "You still think this boat was planted there?"

"Unless you plan to double back to shore and take our chances with the demon, it doesn't matter." He shook his head weakly. "We've committed to this course now." He finally managed to sit up. "You should sleep, if you can. I'll mind the sail."

"Do you have any idea how to sail a boat?"

"As much as you," he said. "If we need more wind, I'll wake you. But we seem to have enough for now. I doubt you'll dream, though. There's too much salt here."

So Toba Bet lay down in the bottom of the boat and slept, and just as Asmel said, she was as dreamless as she'd been all the years she'd worn her amulet.

The sun was growing low on the horizon when they finally pulled their boat onto the shore of the isle of Te'ena. Toba Bet had slept long enough to restore her mood. There was no way the demon could follow them, and no one else from La Cacería could have gotten there in advance of the moon. They were completely, blessedly safe, a sensation Toba Bet had not experienced since she'd last been playing with maps in her grandfather's study—before the Queen had cast the Jews from Rimon, and before Toba had ever heard of La Cacería. How long ago that had been.

They pulled the boat onto shore together, Asmel still favoring his injured arm. "We still have two days until the moon," Toba Bet said. "I'll find us enough for passage on to Zayit, and we'll be with Barsilay by the end of the week."

"Assuming he's already made it there."

"If not, we'll wait for him. Someplace warm and dry, in a nice, fluffy bed with plenty of food. Doesn't that sound delightful? We can visit the university. You must have friends there, don't you?"

"I do," he said. "I haven't been there in years. Didn't want to leave the alcalá unattended." He huffed a bit. "I suppose Tarses has already leveled the place by now."

"He's probably too busy searching it for hidden treasures," Toba Bet said.

"I'm not sure that's better. Why are we dragging this damnable thing out of the water?"

Toba Bet stopped and looked down at the boat. "I don't know. I suppose it might be of use to someone, though. Seems a waste to let it float out into the open sea."

"I think we've pulled it far enough," he said. "We should find our way into the city. What is your plan for funds?"

"I could do some translations," she said.

"That's far too slow; you'll never earn enough that way."

"Of course, I wasn't thinking. I could sell my body at the docks." When Asmel looked like he might have objected, she said, "You're right, I'll never earn enough that way, either. I could sell *your* body at the docks. There's an idea."

"You're in awfully high spirits under the circumstances."

"What circumstances? There's no demon here; he can't have followed us into the saltwater. There are no hunters, there's no way anyone from La Cacería could be waiting here, my sister couldn't possibly get here before the next moon, and we can dream of Omer and be gone before then anyway." She prodded Asmel in the chest. "I'd call that a major victory. Apart from your getting shot, I mean."

"Yes, but we still have to come up with enough money to book passage to Zayit—"

"The boat!" Toba Bet said triumphantly. "We can sell the boat. Why didn't I think of that? I'm sure some fisherman or other will pay us for it. We just need to get to the port." She stopped and looked around. "Which way do you suppose that is?"

"I haven't been to Te'ena since the Fall, and I haven't been in mortal Te'ena ever," Asmel said. "You could send up a lark."

Toba Bet shook her head. "I'm too tired. I don't think I could maintain one." Squinting into the setting sun, she asked, "What is this place?"

The place in question was a roundish building not far from the shore. It was too squat to be called a tower and looked a bit like a barrel with aspirations. It was made of sand-colored stone, had windows on the upper section that looked out at the water, and was surrounded on the coastal side by a low wall.

Asmel looked up at the edifice that caught the evening light before them. "I don't know," he said. "But it was made by Maziks, and after the Fall, too."

Toba Bet startled. "How can you tell?"

"No visible mortar," he said, "and the stone was polished by magic. You can tell by the grain. As for the time frame . . ." He indicated the low wall that separated the building from the coast. "That's a seawall. There was no sea here before the Fall. This was built after, and based on the vegetation, I'd say it was used until recently."

"It's likely mortals took it over," Toba Bet suggested. "It's a perfectly good building, and there are plenty of people living on Te'ena on this side of the gate."

"It's as good an explanation as any," he replied. "But I'd still like to know which Mazik came through the gate and built this place." He craned his neck back. "Must have taken ages, working one night a month. And for what?"

"Let's go and look, then," Toba Bet said. "It's not as if there are any Maziks there now, and if it's full of mortals we'll just leave."

Asmel let Toba Bet take the lead as they made their way around the wall, which was not so tall from the other side, as it was built into the side of a dune. "Odd again," he said. "Why build it that way?"

"Maybe the dune shifted over time," she said. "Come on, there's the door."

The door in question was made of dark wood that had been badly damaged by the sea air, and Toba Bet wondered how a Mazik could have even entered such a place without poisoning themselves. A strong wind from the surf could have been enough to sicken a Mazik for weeks, if not worse; Toba Bet herself was nauseated from their voyage and the air so close to the coast was not making it better. She pushed the door and found it unlocked. It swung inward on salt-corroded hinges.

The building had not, in fact, been maintained by mortals or anyone else. Piles of sand, which must have blown in with a storm, had gathered in the corners, and many sand crabs scuttled for cover at Toba Bet and Asmel's approach. "I don't understand any of this," Toba Bet said. "Why would a Mazik put up a building here? Even without the sea so close, it's not as if they could sleep in the place. They'd barely get a dozen hours a month out of it."

The great room on the main floor had a table under the window covered with papers, but they were all so black with mold that whatever had been written on them was indecipherable. Asmel rifled through them and found one folded and sealed with wax.

"Do you know the seal?" Toba Bet asked.

"I can't make it out," he said. He dropped the paper. Together, they made their way up the stairs to the second floor, where they found a window that stretched the length of the building, over a table littered with more moldy paper. Atop it were several items Toba Bet recognized as cartography equipment.

"They must have been mapping the coastline after the Fall," Asmel said. "Trying to determine the size of their prison."

"Why do that here, and not on the Mazik side?"

"I can't imagine. But look, there's nothing else they could have been doing with all this." He took a pair of calipers, the mechanism rusted in place, and let them clatter down to the table again. "Maybe there are more answers on the Mazik side, but we don't dare wait for the moon. There's no way to check."

Toba Bet picked up a pot of dried-out ink and held it to the light. She did not like mysteries. But staying for the moon to explore Mazik

Te'ena was not a viable option. Outside, the sun was nearly down. "We should be on our way," she told Asmel. "It'll be too dark to see where we're going soon, and I'm not sure how far we are from the city."

"We should stay and rest until tomorrow morning," he said. "We won't get a ship before then anyway, and I can see you're exhausted. You've used too much magic and breathed too much salt."

"I'll be all right."

"You won't," he said. "I can see it. You're fading already." He looked back from the window to the mostly empty room. "It's not beautiful, but it's safe, and that's more than we've had in days." He smiled sadly. "At least one of us needs to stay reliably lucid."

Toba Bet conceded the point. They found a small jar of very old lentils in a cupboard, and Toba Bet took a few and made them into bread for dinner. After they'd eaten, they stretched out on the hard floor; Toba Bet had too little magic left to make anything into a cushion or a blanket. "I'm sorry," she told Asmel. "This is horrible."

"It's not horrible," he said, then added, "It's just very bad."

"Is that a distinction?"

He breathed loudly in the dark. "'Horrible' is starving while several mortals hunt you because they think you're a stag, as a demon urges them on. 'Very bad' is sleeping on cold stone after having eaten bread that tastes like stale pulses."

She laughed softly. "I'm sorry. I did try to take the stale flavor out."

"You failed."

"Oh, I know. I still taste it."

Asmel chuckled a little. Outside, the waves were close enough to hear. Toba Bet had never seen the sea before yesterday, and hadn't had much time to enjoy it. She wondered how Asmel felt, sailing over the saltwater with a face full of briny air. "I hope my grandmother and Barsilay are all right," she said sleepily. "I miss them."

Asmel was already asleep, by his breathing. Toba Bet, free now to look at the little of his face she could see in the dark, watched him—

his silver hair curling around his temple, his silver eyelashes against his cheeks—and within a few moments she was asleep, too.

She woke not long after, a sense of unease in the pit of her stomach. Sitting up slowly, Toba Bet took in the dark room. Everything was the same, and Asmel still slept at her side, but something was off. "Asmel?" she said quietly.

"Don't wake him," said a voice she would know anyplace. "What we have to discuss is better between us, anyway."

Toba Bet was already on her feet as her sister unfurled herself from the shadows. Through the window, she could see the moon had risen: the full moon. They'd counted the days wrong.

But we saw the moon, she wanted to shout. And it was still days off full. And it wasn't fair.

It was cloudy, and you saw a glamour, said a voice that sounded oddly like that of the original Toba. *And you're an idiot.*

Toba Bet barely had enough magic to make her arm a blade, but she did, and she threw herself at her sister, ready to kill her.

EIGHT

IT SEEMED TO Naftaly that the observatory had been abandoned long ago, based on the state of decay. The land surrounding it was overgrown and, according to Barsilay, the interior rooms were thick with dust and cobwebs.

The old woman said, "You were bleeding from your nose and ear both. I think you should rest. And anyway, oughtn't we let it be?"

Naftaly said, "It was only a little blood and it's stopped." To Barsilay he said, "You said you wanted to know who built it and what was inside."

Barsilay frowned. "I would like to know what was happening here. Asmel will want to know."

"Is it really worth slowing us down?" Elena asked. "I understand your curiosity, but we do have good reason to keep moving, and whatever ships Naftaly saw aren't here."

"No, you're right," Barsilay said. "We shouldn't linger."

Naftaly said, "But what if it's something important?"

"What could be important in an abandoned tower?" the old woman asked. "Probably the haunt of some old Mazik who got bored and went belly up. That's what your lot do, isn't it? Die of ennui or whatnot?"

"Something like that," Barsilay said. Then, to Elena, "I won't force this on anyone, but is an hour too much?"

"I think that's reasonable," she said. "May I go in with you?"

The old woman stayed behind to rest her back, while the others found the door at the bottom securely locked. "Can't you magic it open?" Naftaly asked.

"It's not working," Barsilay said with a hand on the door. "Either there's magic warding it or it's blocked on the other side."

"Is there some other way in?"

"Doesn't seem so," he replied.

"Could we climb up?" Naftaly asked. "There's a window not far up that looks large enough to slip through. It's probably no more than twenty feet, and there are vines growing all the way up the tower on that side."

"High enough to break your neck," Elena said. "You've only just been unconscious. And you expect Barsilay to do it with one arm?"

"I believe I can do it," Barsilay said, replacing his phantom arm and wiggling its fingers experimentally. "This should work well enough to climb a short distance. You should stay down here."

"No," Naftaly said. "I'm coming, too. It's not so far a climb, and whatever you did seems to have resolved my headache."

The old woman said, "Just let Barsilay go. He'll tell you what he sees."

"I don't need to be coddled," Naftaly said testily, rising to test the strength of the vine they intended to climb.

"It's not coddling when you've just been ill," Barsilay told him. "No one wants you to get hurt over nothing."

Naftaly, by this point, had already begun climbing, which forced Barsilay to come up after him.

"How is it nothing? You were the one who said you would very much like to know who built it and what was happening here. You said it might be important."

Barsilay, by then, had climbed up alongside him. "I'm hardly the final authority on what's important."

"Are you angry with me for agreeing with you?"

"No," Barsilay said. "I'm a bit worried about why."

"Why I'm agreeing with you? What, you think it's the whole . . .

thing we don't talk about? Of course not. What do I care about that?"

"Are you sure?"

"Barsilay, I'm completely ignorant here. If you say something's important, what choice do I have but to take you at your word? Should I disagree with you just to be spiteful?"

"Not spiteful," Barsilay said, catching himself when his false hand caught air instead of vine, and Naftaly's arm quickly went to brace him against the wall. "I'm fine," he said. "Thank you. It's not spite I'm after. It's just ... I want you to have a realistic view of who I am."

"I think I do," Naftaly said.

"Little one," Barsilay said, "I've made some very bad choices in my life."

"You've told me. I know. So have I, by the way. Anyway, I wanted to see as much as you."

"You thought there might be ships out there?"

"Of course not," Naftaly said. "I just ..." He hesitated; his reasons would probably sound foolish to Barsilay. Of course there would be no ships. But he wanted to see if the coast really looked the way it had in his vision. And he wanted to be the one to climb up, and not be left on the ground.

They were within grasp of the windowsill, and Naftaly waited while Barsilay climbed over the edge and landed rather gracelessly on the floor. "Ugh," he said.

Naftaly, at the windowsill now, could see what Barsilay meant: the amount of filth was hard to qualify. He swung a leg over and pulled himself inside the room, a large chamber that took up most of the tower, with bookshelves lining the outer wall.

"A library?" Naftaly asked.

"Seems so," Barsilay said. "I saw more interesting things in the chamber at the top. Let's go up."

At the far end of the room was a doorway leading to a spiral staircase they followed up, finding another room of books immediately above them, and then, at the top, the observatory Barsilay had seen earlier.

A telescope was situated in the window. On the worktable that took up a third of the room were several large maps, annotated in Mazik writing that Naftaly had no hope of making out. "It looks like whoever made these was mapping the coast," he said, because that much at least was obvious.

"Yes. I wonder why," Barsilay said absently. "It's the same bit of coast mapped three times. Why bother?"

"This is the tower?" Naftaly asked, touching the mark that looked like their current position.

"It must be. Look, there are dates on these. This was fifty years ago, this a hundred, and this was just last year."

Naftaly arranged them all in order. "The tower's closer to the sea now," he said.

"That's not possible." But it was what the maps showed ... A hundred years prior, the tower was drawn several quarters of an inch farther from the coast. Naftaly could not make out the scale of the maps, but he guessed the difference must have amounted to ten or twenty feet in real terms. Revisiting the oldest map, he realized it wasn't the tower that had changed position; the distance from the mountains was always the same. It was the coastline that was moving inland. "It must be a drafting error."

Barsilay left the table and started examining the shelves, most of which were filled with glass orbs empty of any visible matter.

"I saw those in Asmel's observatory as well," Naftaly said.

"Yes, he had some ideas about salinity in the air," Barsilay said. "This person may have been doing something similar. But who was it?"

Naftaly had found a stack of papers mixed in with some books on one of the shelves and was flipping through them, feeling increasingly useless because he could not read the Mazik writing. They could have been anything: notes, or scientific treatises, or a grocery list. Halfway through the stack, he found a folded piece of paper with a broken wax seal across the fold. "Is this a letter?" he called.

"Yes," Barsilay said, taking it from him and examining the seal. "This was from Te'ena, but ... how?"

"Could it be that old?"

"Not by the paper," Barsilay said, unfolding the letter and reading it. "Mother of Monsters," he muttered. "This observatory. It was Rahel's."

RAHEL, BARSILAY EXPLAINED, had been a master in Asmel's university, until it had been shut down over Asmel's teachings about Aravoth. The rest of the faculty had their memories of Asmel's heretical lecture tampered with and continued living in Rimon, though they recalled enough to give Asmel a wide berth so as not to attract attention from La Cacería.

Rahel had not been there the day La Cacería had stormed the great hall of the university. She'd been away in Zayit, and by the time Asmel and Barsilay had been released from prison, the rumor was that she'd decided to stay there: a logical course of action. How she'd ended up in a tower in the middle of nowhere was a mystery, but she seemed to have been in somewhat regular contact with a scholar in Te'ena, and the subject of the letter Naftaly found was a disaster occurring within the Dimah Sea. It was rising.

Barsilay went back to the table and stared soberly at the map, running his finger along the receding coastline. "If this trend continues," he said, "in another hundred years this tower will be underwater."

"What could be causing it? Did either of them know?"

"I know," Barsilay said. "When the Luz gate was torn out, it tore a hole in the firmament. That's what caused the flood. That's where the Dimah Sea came from." He met Naftaly's eyes. "The tear is still open."

"Does that mean the water will keep rising forever?"

Barsilay said, "I don't know. It might."

"Is there any way to stop it?"

"Put back the gate," Barsilay said. "And soon, by the looks of it, or this tower won't be the only thing underwater."

"Zayit and P'ri Hadar are both on the coast in the mortal realm."

"Here, too. And so are Anab, Habush, and Katlav. They'll all be lost in a human lifetime. I wonder if Tarses knows. Or if he cares."

"Do you think Rahel could have been working this close to Rimon without him knowing?"

Barsilay tossed the letter down. "I don't know, but she was one of Asmel's scholars, and Tarses would have had people keeping tabs on her. I think he must have known."

"Then what do you think happened to her? There hasn't been anyone here in ages. Do you think she went back to Zayit?"

"Possibly," Barsilay said, staring at the paper on the table.

"What aren't you saying?"

"No point burdening you with conjecture. I think we've had our hour. The ladies will be wondering about us. I don't think we'll learn more here, anyway."

"Barsilay!"

"If it's all the same to you, I'd rather try the stairs than go back out the window. The door should open from this direction."

It did not escape Naftaly that Barsilay's anxiety had spiked. Something very bad had occurred to him, bad enough that he didn't want to share it, because if it had been some little guess or other he would have said. He wondered dimly if Barsilay would have told Elena, if she'd been there.

Heading back to the stairs, they continued down past the library, and then found themselves blocked by a wall in the middle of the staircase.

"This makes no sense," Naftaly said. "Surely Rahel didn't always come and go through the window?"

"This has been added recently," Barsilay said. "See, the stones don't match the walls. There's a patina on the old ones this wall doesn't have."

"Why would anyone wall off the bottom half of the tower?"

"I can't imagine," Barsilay said. "But I guess it's the window again for us."

They climbed down—which, unfortunately, was a great deal harder than climbing up. Naftaly was very worried Barsilay might not make it and so he climbed half the way one-handed himself, leaving a hand free to rest on Barsilay's arm, until the other man finally looked over and said, "If you're planning to catch me one-handed, why don't we save ourselves the trouble of climbing and just fall to our deaths now?"

Once they got to the bottom, they found Elena and the old woman in front of the door, which now stood open, both of them looking a little smug.

"Turns out Mazik locks can still be picked, given enough persistence," the old woman said. "Come and see."

Naftaly followed Barsilay inside the base of the tower. The first thing he noticed was a distinct lack of dust. The second was that the stairs were gone; it was one giant room, with a ceiling that extended all the way to the new wall they'd discovered earlier. The room itself was stacked with crates that extended into the darkness above. "Do you know what's in the crates?" Barsilay asked Elena.

"I was afraid to open one. Something horrible might have come out and eaten me."

"Not if it's what I'm thinking," Barsilay said, turning to Naftaly. "Help me?"

The two pried the top off one of the smaller crates: it was filled with smaller ceramic pyramids, stacked in opposite directions to make better use of the space. Barsilay lifted one of those on the top row and turned it right-side up, then removed a wax seal from the top. It was filled with lentils.

"That's what I thought," Barsilay said. "I'm surprised you all don't smell them."

"Surely it's not all lentils?" Naftaly asked. "There's enough here to last all of Rimon for … I don't know. Months, I'd say."

"I think it is," he said. "It's been converted into a storehouse. Or a silo."

"A silo," Naftaly said. "For whom?"

Barsilay let the lid of the crate fall back into place. "For Tarses's army, on their way to Zayit. You asked about the supply line ... Well, we're on it."

Naftaly found himself and the women being ushered back to their horses with a sense of urgency he hadn't noticed from Barsilay since they'd left Rimon. "Isn't it odd they left all this unguarded?" the old woman asked.

Elena and Barsilay exchanged an uneasy look that conveyed a shared understanding of some dark piece of information.

"What is it?" Naftaly asked. "You think it's not strange? Or you think ... you think it is guarded?"

"I think we should go," Elena said.

"Quickly," Barsilay said. "We should go quickly."

"What aren't you saying?" Naftaly asked. "Barsilay?"

"Hashem's sake," the old woman blurted at Naftaly. "One of them wasn't bad enough? You had to bring us another schemer?"

"No one's scheming," Barsilay said. "Calm yourself."

"That's exactly the sort of thing *she's* prone to say," she barked back.

To Naftaly, Barsilay said, "Go untie the horses."

Naftaly hesitated. The old woman was right, and Barsilay and Elena were both behaving in a distinctly Elena-like fashion he did not like. But ... it was Barsilay. He untied the horses.

They'd been riding a few minutes when Barsilay, riding in front, leaned back against Naftaly's chest. "I didn't want to alarm you, that's all. I don't think we're in immediate danger. It's just that there's someone following us, and I think the reason the lentils weren't guarded is that she told whoever was there to allow us to pass."

Naftaly let this settle on him. "If she has the authority to tell Cacería guards to let us pass, she must be very important."

"Extremely."

So many questions cycled through Naftaly's mind, the foremost of which was: Why weren't they all dead? But what he led with was: "And Elena knew?"

Barsilay nodded. "I didn't choose to tell her. Elena noticed on her own, and I didn't tell you because I thought you might have trouble ignoring the person following us."

"But you decided Elena was more trustworthy with this than I was?"

"No, of course not. I had no intention of telling her, either. Are you angry?"

"Yes. Yes, I am angry. I don't like you not telling me things. I know it's been your habit since . . . always, but after everything, I think I deserve to know what's going on."

"I'm sorry," he said. "I'm not used to having a companion. Not one like you."

"Don't try to manipulate me out of being angry," Naftaly said. "I should be angry."

"Little one—"

"Must you call me that? Am I a child to you?"

"No," he said, but Naftaly knew it was a lie. "No, of course not. I'm sorry."

"Would you stop being so conciliatory?"

Barsilay scoffed. "It seems everything I say makes you angrier. What would you have me do?"

"I would have you stop placating me with what you think I'd like to hear! Ah, there's no time for this. What is your plan for dealing with this woman?"

"I'm working on that," he admitted.

"That's why you need to tell me things! I can help. I, too, want her not to kill us. Who is this woman, anyway?"

"She's called the Peregrine. She's probably the deadliest assassin in this world or any other, and she's almost certainly listening to this conversation right now and having a good laugh about it."

Naftaly said, "Oh."

A bit later Barsilay asked, "So do you have an idea for keeping her from killing us?"

Naftaly said, "No, I don't."

NINE

TSIFRA HAD TO work very hard not to kill Toba by accident, as what Toba lacked in skill she made up for in sheer murderous rage. Tsifra found herself dodging repeated attempts to stab her in the neck, and then, when that didn't work, in the chest, and when that didn't work, the neck again.

The Peregrine had told Tsifra once that her fighting technique was all substance and no style. Toba had neither; she hacked as artlessly as a woodsman with an axe.

Asmel was trying to determine some way to help, but it was dark and the two women were roughly the same size. A good thing, too, because it would have been even harder not to kill both of them, and if Asmel died, Tsifra's plan fell apart. "Stop," she told her sister. "I'm not here to kill you."

"I'm here to kill you," Toba answered, and this time managed to catch Tsifra in the shoulder before she could parry it.

"Would you just listen? I'm trying to reason—" She had to stop, because now Toba was trying to force her back across the table through the open window. A better solution, really, since it only required brute strength and no finesse, but Tsifra had her beaten in strength, too. She managed to get a foot up to Toba's chest and kicked her back across the room, giving herself enough time to get away from the window. She was low on magic, and didn't dare waste any.

"I have no interest in your reason," Toba said.

"Listen to me! You've had no combat training, you don't know how to wield that blade, and I could have killed you ten times in the last minute if I'd wanted to."

"I know you don't want to. Your orders are to bring me to Tarses."

"If I declined to give you to him before, why do you think I mean to do it now?" She dropped her blade and took a step back. "If you'll leave off trying to stab me for a minute, I have a proposition I'd like to discuss that would benefit both of us. A trade."

"You have nothing I want," Toba said.

"Are you sure?" Tsifra made her arm flesh again. Toba, not trusting her in the least, did not follow suit. "I think you'll want this." She reached down the front of her tunic and pulled on the chain that hung around her neck, displaying the blue jewel at the end. She paused long enough to make sure Toba recognized it before saying, "You don't want this back for him? I'd have thought you would."

"There's nothing to be done with it," Toba said. "It can't be put back. It's not worth trading for."

"That's what I thought, too, but I've recently heard differently. There *is* a way to put it back."

Toba eyed Asmel over her shoulder. "Is that possible? Rafeq said it wasn't."

"Rafeq?" Tsifra asked. "The man under the mountain?"

Asmel said, "Yes, and so far as I know he was right. I've never heard of a safira being put back."

"According to my source of information, Rafeq was the one who figured out how to do it," Tsifra said. "Seems he didn't want you knowing that."

"Why would we trust you more than him?"

"You haven't even heard what I want in exchange," Tsifra said. "I want the killstone of ha-Moh'to. I know you lied to me before. I know you have it."

There was a very long pause while Toba and Asmel exchanged

meaningful eye contact and no actual words. Then Asmel said, "And what will you do when you have it?"

Tsifra said, "Kill Tarses."

TOBA BET AND Asmel had pulled back from the Courser, who perched on her heels on the windowsill. Toba Bet lowered her arm but kept her blade. "We can't trust her at all," she told Asmel.

"Of course not, but she is consistent at least. She killed you before because she didn't trust Tarses, and that hasn't changed. Remember who she is; she has very good reason to want to kill him."

What he meant was that Tsifra was an alternate version of Toba. Toba was a free individual because her grandmother had tricked Tarses into thinking she'd died as a baby. She'd been raised in relative comfort by her grandparents, translating texts and listening to old stories in her grandfather's study. Tsifra had been forced to give up her name and autonomy at birth, and had spent every day since in fear for her life from the man who'd raised her to be his monster.

"Our interests align for the moment, but you're forgetting the most pressing issue," Toba Bet reminded Asmel, in case he had forgotten in his present state that they did not actually *have* the killstone, and at some point Tsifra would figure that out.

Asmel said, "We're at an extreme disadvantage here."

"Now who's taking pleasure in stating what's patently obvious?" she said.

From her perch, some distance away, Tsifra said, "Have you decided which of you is going to tell me you haven't got it anymore?" She stood up. "Don't deny it. If you had it you'd have traded it to me by now. So where did it go? Tarses hasn't got it. I suppose that leaves Barsilay?"

"No," Toba Bet said, a little too quickly. "Barsilay hasn't got it. I told you the truth before: It was stolen by Rafeq, after we liberated him from the mountain."

Tsifra looked like she might have laughed, if she had been a different sort of person. "You're telling me that he lied to you about being able to get the magic out of a safira, and then he stole your second safira and the killstone with it?"

"We have only your word he was lying," Toba Bet said.

"The person who gave me this information had no reason to lie," Tsifra said. "In fact, it would be highly against his interest to do so." She let out a huff. "All right, I'll make you a different deal: Help me find Rafeq and get the killstone back, and I'll give you Asmel's safira."

Toba Bet disliked the sound of that very much. Even if she knew how to find Rafeq, having to track him down together with her sister sounded like the next thing to suicide. But Tsifra added, "Your other option is I kill Asmel and take you back to Rimon, so think carefully before you decline."

"I could still kill her," Toba Bet murmured to Asmel.

"If you weren't completely exhausted and nearly out of magic, maybe," He said, and then called to Tsifra, "Before we agree to anything, I want to know who gave you the information about the safiras."

Tsifra cocked her head to one side. "Haven't you figured that out yet? You've met him. It was Atalef. The demon."

"The demon!"

"You still haven't realized we've been working together?" Tsifra said, a little proudly. "I needed to meet you in person somewhere I could be sure Tarses wouldn't have anyone listening. I'm the only one in La Cacería who can come here. And if I'd invited you, you'd never have come. So he made it so you'd have no place else to go."

Toba Bet was a little irked that she hadn't pieced that together. She asked, "And you expect us to believe that once you have the killstone, you'll leave us in peace?"

"Once Tarses is dead, I can't think of a single reason you and I would ever have to meet again. You and Asmel can live your lives as you see fit, and I'll do the same."

"And what will happen to La Cacería?" Asmel asked.

"Once I'm no longer in it," she said, "I don't care what happens to it. My will belongs to Tarses, not the order. Do we have a deal or not? The moon won't wait."

"There's one other thing we want," Asmel said. "The book."

Tsifra said, "I don't have the book. Tarses has the book, except for the page you stole." Toba Bet did not think it worth mentioning that she didn't have that page, either... Probably the less Tsifra knew about their assets, the better. "But if we manage to kill Tarses, you can have the book. I don't care what you do with it, so long as you promise to leave me alone."

Toba Bet looked miserably at Asmel, because it was looking very much like she had no choice. "You said yourself we can't trust her," she said.

Asmel looked equally troubled, but he said, "There's only one element of her story that needs to be true: that she wants Tarses dead. Do you trust that? Implicitly?"

Toba Bet said, "Yes."

Asmel nodded. "Then make the deal."

"All right," Toba Bet told the Courser. "Let's go."

Tsifra nodded sharply. "Get yourself ready then," she said, because Toba Bet was still undressed and barefoot. While Asmel began sliding his boots on, Tsifra held out a hand. "No. We can't bring you. You can't help us, and you'll slow us down. You have no magic and you're injured besides."

"I'm not leaving him," Toba Bet insisted. "It's either both of us or none."

"Toba," Asmel said, "she's right. I can't help you."

"But if I leave you, what will you do for magic? I may be gone for weeks."

"Leave me a supply," he said. "Enough to last me until the next moon. I'll book passage to Zayit and you can meet me there."

"What if I'm delayed?"

"Then I'll find Barsilay. Toba, if I go with you, I'll increase the odds this whole arrangement fails. I cannot go."

"I'm not sure I can pull out a month's worth of magic at once."

"Then I'll give you some of mine," Tsifra said. "Will that do?"

Toba Bet felt a wave of revulsion and spat, "No!"

Tsifra scoffed. "I'm not offering to bed your lover."

"It will serve," Asmel said. "Toba, you mustn't be sentimental about this. You'll go to Sebah. I'll rest 'til my arm heals and go to Zayit." Then he pulled Toba Bet into an embrace and said into her ear, "I'll wait a bit, then follow. I will find Omer." He kissed the top of her cheekbone, and added, "The moon won't wait."

"Has this just now occurred to you?" Tsifra said crossly.

So Toba Bet and Tsifra pulled out a month's worth of magic between them, storing each ration in a glass-like bauble—twenty-nine, because Toba Bet had insisted on one extra. She was leaving him with all their food, and whatever money he'd be able to get selling the boat, and he walked with them to the center of Te'ena's fig grove, where the gate was a pillar of light stretching into the sky. "I have no pretty words to give you," he said, taking both her hands. "Go and do your work."

"Right," she said. "So I'm off to kill my father, then."

"The gate won't hold much longer," Tsifra said.

"We have hours!" Toba Bet countered.

"Do you intend to drag your feet through this entire mission?"

"Toba," Asmel said. "You must go."

Toba Bet exhaled some of her anger. Stalling would not make leaving Asmel easier, and it would not make her alliance with her sister more bearable. "I'll see you in Zayit," she told him.

"Yes, you will."

"This is agonizing," Tsifra said, and she grabbed Toba Bet's arm and shoved her through the gate.

NAFTALY TURNED THINGS over in his mind, mulling over whether Barsilay had been right not to tell him, whether he really was dull enough to have triggered their tail in a panic. He was a foolish man, who hadn't even realized Barsilay had been lying to him for several days, hadn't noticed there was a dangerous Mazik following them, and was probably not good for much but inspiring his companions to pat him fondly on the head.

On the other hand, he found he was rather angry about it, and the more he ruminated, the angrier he became.

Their rest that evening was uneasy, though at least now they had ample food, since the old woman had made off with a bag of lentils large enough to last them weeks. The speed litany had gotten them well away from the tower, and the trees were thicker this far north, but they were still near enough to the coast to hear the sea. Naftaly thought it was a mistake to be so close to the ocean; if the woman following them decided to act, it would be easy to pin them against the saltwater. Though if Barsilay was right, maybe she wouldn't even need to do that. No one knew if Elena's charm on the page was still active or not, and Naftaly guessed that at some point the Mazik would take her chances with it rather than risk them either trying to renew it or vanishing into Zayit with it.

That night, as they sat around the fire Naftaly had built—as there was no longer any reason to try to conceal their location—Elena stared into the embers and said, "I saw the shadow of the mountains today."

"The Gal'in?" Barsilay said. The ground was cold, and he'd made the four of them mats to sit on from fallen pine branches. Their breaths were visible in the firelight. "Yes, we'll be closer to them tomorrow. They come nearly to the coast."

Elena sat quiet long enough to let Naftaly know she was thinking about her next words very hard before she said, "My uncle used to tell me there were lions in those mountains at one time."

"Yes, that's true. But they've been gone here as long as in your world."

"They were hunted?"

Barsilay watched her for a long time, the firelight flickering on his face. They were two of a sort, he and Elena, speaking in silences as much as with words, and Naftaly found himself at a loss trying to fill in what wasn't being said. Elena wanted to know what was in the mountains. Probably she wanted to know if there was something there that could be used against the woman stalking them. Barsilay said, "Not hunted. Displaced."

"What could displace lions?"

Barsilay smiled a bit, looking slightly feral in the dark as he considered his words. "I've mentioned to you that Zayit is the richest of all the gate cities. After the Fall, they took over the mortal trade route. The wealth they pull in is vast."

"What is wealth, for a Mazik who can make anything?" the old woman asked.

"Only what we can't make ourselves," he said. "Lentils, for the cities with poorer farming. Horses. Fine human-produced goods our magic won't copy, like spices. And the one thing no Mazik may touch but many covet: salt."

"Salt?"

"A poison and deterrent," Barsilay said. "A thimbleful will kill your worst enemy, if you can get it into his food. Salt on a blade will leave an enemy with a wound that can never heal. You can imagine possessing it is highly illegal."

"So only the most powerful Maziks have any," Elena said.

"Of course. And all the salt in the world is brought in through the gate at Zayit, making the Maziks who import it the wealthiest men and women you will ever find in any world. Richer than the spice merchants, or the silk merchants, or the Queen of Rimon herself. So bearing this in mind, you'll understand why the adonate of Zayit decided they could not risk any harm to their enterprise, any agents of chaos thrown into their finely wrought economic machinery."

"By agents of chaos," Elena said, "I assume you mean demons."

"You assume rightly," Barsilay said. "They cast out every demon within a hundred leagues of Zayit. Most of them ended up in the Gal'in." He pointed toward the mountains to the north and west. "Those mountains are absolutely infested with demons."

Don't think of going into them, he said with his eyes.

Elena's mouth tugged down at the corners, but she said nothing more on the subject. Naftaly lay down in his usual spot by Barsilay's side, thinking of what an infestation of demons would look like—a hundred, or a thousand, or more—and what the woman listening to them in the dark would make of this conversation, and how much longer she would wait to act.

That night, Naftaly opened his eyes again in the dream-world, apparently alone.

The space he found himself in was so much like the waking world that at first Naftaly thought he was awake again; the mountains were at his back and the sea before him, only the fire was gone, and the horses, and the women. The stars whirled overhead as they only did in the dream-world, and sitting on the hill looking down to the sea was Barsilay.

Barsilay's face was turned toward the sky. "I missed the stars," he breathed. "I thought I'd never see them again."

Naftaly sat down beside him. "Are we alone?"

"We are. If *she* were here, I'd sense her. And I don't think she'd risk sleeping, anyway." He let out an impossibly long breath and rested his head against Naftaly's shoulder. "I'm so tired of watching every word. It's almost like being in prison again."

Naftaly said, "I'm sorry. If you'd told me earlier, I might have helped, somehow."

Barsilay tensed against him. Naftaly, still peeved, went on, "You asked me if I had an idea. And I do have one."

"Do you?"

Naftaly hesitated. Then he said, "Will you agree to hear me out 'til the end?"

Barsilay chuckled. "Is it so terrible? Fine, I agree."

Naftaly pulled a blade of grass and twisted it between his fingers. "You are the heir of Luz."

Barsilay scoffed, earning him a reproachful glare. "I'm sorry," he said. "I don't want to be, you know this."

"It changes nothing. You are the heir, and right now that may be the only advantage we have." He exhaled. "I think we should go into the mountains."

"If you think the demons will care whether I'm the heir of anything—"

"So you make them care!"

"Are you suggesting I make a bargain? With demons?"

"I'm suggesting you do something to save yourself, yes."

"I have nothing they want."

"Yes," Naftaly said, "you do. These demons have been displaced. What they'll want is a guarantee they won't be displaced a second time."

"You want me to offer them the Gal'in?"

"Why not? It's uninhabited anyway. The demons will do no harm to anyone there. Give them the mountains. It's in your power."

"It isn't."

"It will be."

"It will be if I take up the throne," Barsilay said, rising. "Which I have no intention of doing, so you're suggesting I make a false promise to demons. I may as well pour salt in my eyes." He stalked down the hill toward the sea, and Naftaly followed.

"Isn't that what we're doing out here? Trying to find some way to put the gate back in Luz and restore the throne?"

"Putting the gate back and restoring the throne are two entirely different things!"

"Are they?"

"Yes! One improves the state of the world. The other decidedly does not, and I've no desire to discuss this further."

"You agreed to hear me out 'til the end," Naftaly reminded him.

"What more could there possibly be? You want me to make a promise that presupposes I've agreed to be King. Well, I've seen kings, little one, and I have no intention of ever being one. My entire life has been a fight against kingship. I see what you are thinking, and no. I might start off very well, the best king the earth had ever known. But eventually, inevitably, I would be corrupted by my own power. It is unavoidable. It is what monarchy is: corruption by design. And still you object? All right. Perhaps I am all that you believe me to be. I will never falter, not a single day as King. Someday, my throne will pass from me. Can you vouch for my heir as well? Or the one after that? Because if I resurrect this throne, I am very much responsible for what they might become, too: great parasites that control everything around them in exchange for some illusory feeling of security. I have more than enough blood on my hands already, you know this."

"It would not have to be that way!"

"It would be that way! You are asking me to become what I find most loathsome on earth." He paused. "And even if I thought differently, what in the world do you want from the demons in exchange?"

"I hadn't gotten to that part yet," Naftaly said. "You offer them permanent residence in the Gal'in. In exchange, they take care of our hunter."

Barsilay looked startled. "Give them the Peregrine?"

"If what you've said is true, she won't be able to resist following us into the mountains. She'll want to know why we're going."

Barsilay's eyes were wide. Naftaly said, "Is there any other chance of escaping her?"

"You're asking me to hand someone over to demons to be killed," Barsilay said.

"You didn't complain when it was Elena feeding one of your enemies to a horse."

"Well, she hadn't asked me in advance."

"Would you have objected?"

Barsilay said, "I don't know. What you're suggesting is horrible on all possible fronts. I don't want to make a deal with demons. I don't want to even begin to entertain the idea of becoming King. Naftaly, you do not understand what you ask of me."

"So what is our only other option? Continue as we've been doing, and let this woman kill us all?"

Barsilay grasped him by the shoulder and said, "I will not be King.

I warned you. I warned all of you to go back through the gate. I told you staying here would end badly. Is it my fault you refused to listen? I won't compromise myself this way. Not even for my own life."

"Not for mine, either?"

Barsilay turned sharply away. "None of you are a threat to the Peregrine or her master. I may still be able to save the rest of you. There's a gate in Zayit. I may yet be able to see you through it."

"So we all go back to the mortal realm and you stay here and die? I won't accept that."

"You should never have come here to begin with! I never wanted anyone to risk themselves on my behalf. I never asked for it."

Naftaly said, "For all your objections, you certainly sound just like a king."

"How dare you! How dare you say that!"

"It's the truth. There are four of us with our lives in the balance, and you would make the choice for all of us. Just like a king."

Barsilay's mouth worked, unable to respond. "You don't know what you're asking of me," he said again.

"I'm asking you to save us all. Life rules over everything, Barsilay, even your ambitions."

"My ambitions? It's precisely because I haven't any that this is a problem! It's my values you object to."

"Fine," Naftaly said. "I object to them. I don't want you to die. The rest is noise. But you are too much above me to value my opinion."

Barsilay's eyes were on the stars again, and Naftaly watched horrified as they filled with tears. "Fine," he said. "If this is what you want, fine. We will ask the women, and we will choose, the four of us. If the others agree with you, I will do it. I'll go into the mountains, and I'll make a bargain with the demons. I won't force my choice on you, if you won't have it." Naftaly reached a hand toward Barsilay's arm, but he pulled away. "You've asked me to take the first step toward becoming a monster. Don't ask more of me tonight."

TEN

TOBA BET LANDED in Mazik Te'ena on her rump. "Was that necessary?" she asked her sister incredulously. The fig grove was identical to the one they'd just left. The moon was hidden behind a bank of clouds, so the only real light was from the gate.

"I was sparing you what little dignity you have left," she said. "You should be thanking me. All that blubbering... Unbelievable."

"It isn't my fault your life has been devoid of emotional attachments."

"Isn't it?" Tsifra asked, as they turned their backs on the gate. "I do believe you made me a promise once. To steal me away from my wicked father, and then I'd come and live with you, and your grandmother would feed me sweets all day."

"I was a child."

"I know. So was I." She scanned the sky. "The sun will be up soon, and my boat's north of here. Let's be on the move."

"How did you get a boat here? I'd wondered about that. Maziks don't know how to build boats."

"I made the boat," Tsifra said. "And I sailed it... Why do you look so surprised? You sailed here yourself, and I can't believe that you know more about it than I do."

"I didn't build the boat! Wait. Did you arrange for that boat to be left there?"

"Of course. How else were you going to get here?"

Toba Bet felt incalculably stupid. She'd believed herself the cleverer of the two, but Tsifra had outsmarted her at every turn.

"Am I less stupid than you'd believed?" Tsifra asked.

"I never believed you were stupid," Toba Bet said.

"Only stupider than you. Remember this: while you were eating sweets on your grandmother's lap, I was keeping myself alive. Don't assume there was any luck involved in my survival."

Toba Bet thought of several arguments in response to this claim—that learning to please one very unpleasant person was a specific type of cleverness not applicable to most situations, and that she'd had to be clever, too, to keep her grandparents from hating her for killing their daughter—but decided Asmel would tell her to be silent. It was funny, she thought, how his counsel lived in her mind. Don't antagonize her unnecessarily, he would say. It's to your advantage for her to think she's wiser than you are.

All right, then. She would let her sister have that victory. "Fine," she said. "Let's see this fine boat you've made."

They made their way through the dark olive grove, Tsifra pulling a light-stone from her bag, and then down to the beach, passing what Toba Bet could only describe as a herd of tiny flame-eyed dragons, each the length of her forearm. It was hard to see their color in the dark; they could have been silver or yellow.

"They aren't dangerous," Tsifra told her. "I assume they eat vermin—there are plenty in the city."

"You've been to the city?"

"Only once. Our father ordered me to kill someone there when I was young."

Toba Bet took her eyes from the dragonettes. "Who?"

"An old astronomer," Tsifra said, "called Omer."

Toba Bet did her best to keep her face blank, and was glad when Tsifra turned her back, giving her a chance to draw a deep breath.

Omer was dead, and Asmel was on his way to find him.

Toba Bet didn't dare ask her sister what Asmel was likely to find there—some horrible scene—or if he would just wander around Te'ena looking for him 'til he forgot what he was doing.

Better not to think like that. Asmel had plenty of magic, between hers and Tsifra's. He would remember not to stay in Mazik Te'ena past the moon, and that he needed to pass back to mortal Te'ena to get a ship to Zayit. He would not forget.

What to do about Aravoth, though . . . That was a problem for a later time.

IT HAD BEEN Naftaly's idea to go through the mountains, and he maintained this was the best course right up until they found themselves *in* the mountains. The ground was rocky and difficult for the horses, and the trees were so close they made their way almost impassable and blocked out most of the sky.

They'd had a quiet conversation that morning; there was no way to discuss the specifics of Naftaly's plan with the Peregrine listening, and the women had been initially perplexed by the suggested change in route. But Naftaly had made a pointed comment about the mountains being the better bargain for a man like Barsilay. Elena had said, "Ah," and the old woman, looking out to the trees, had said, "He's too injured to travel this close to the sea, isn't he?" And so they had chosen the mountain road.

Barsilay was alarmingly quiet, either because he was angry his humans had betrayed him by electing to go this way—with all it implied—or because he was frightened. The speed litany was too dangerous to use on the uneven terrain so they went slowly, and had traveled most of the day, nearly 'til sunset, when Naftaly suddenly felt a creeping dread he could not qualify.

"Barsilay," he whispered, but the other man held up a hand to quiet him. He was wearing his false arm; whether it was to better control the horse or to present an uninjured image to the demons, Naftaly was not sure.

The air was filled with the sound of hissing, like wind in the leaves, only everything was still. "Stop," Barsilay whispered to Elena, who pulled her horse up. Both the animals' ears were pricked and swiveling, listening intently. The bay gelding, under Elena's hand, pawed the ground until she told it something and patted its shoulder, and it stilled.

"What is that?" the old woman asked.

"I don't know," Naftaly said. "Do you hear language in it?"

They listened for a bit. Elena said, "I hear it. I can't make it out."

Naftaly had a sudden urge to turn around and go back. This must have been a mistake. Riding directly into a nest of demons? And none of them even knew how many there were. A plural organism, Barsilay had called them. Maybe their numbers were unimportant; there could be twenty or two thousand just as easily. What had Naftaly been thinking?

From her horse, Elena hissed, "Uncover your shoulder," and Barsilay said tightly, "Not yet."

A hundred plumes of smoke swirled down from the trees and circled around them, causing the horses to rear and the old woman to nearly fall from the saddle. The hisses took on a crackled edge, and then as one they whispered, "Barsilay."

"Demons," Elena spat.

Barsilay said, "Are we old friends, then, that you know my name?"

"Barsilay of Luz," they said. "Your home is beneath the sea."

"That's right," he said. "So you do know."

"Did you come to die? These mountains are ours."

"No," he said. "They are not. But I could make them so."

"They are ours," the demons insisted. "None claim them. And who are you, Barsilay of Luz, to make such a claim?"

"None claim them yet, but soon there will be Maziks who do. War is coming between Rimon and Zayit, and these mountains will be crawling with Mazik soldiers. You'll be cast out again; it's only a matter of time. I am the only one who can prevent it."

"How?" they hissed.

Barsilay hesitated long enough that Naftaly thought he'd changed his mind, but the demons said, "There is another here, Barsilay of Luz, who means to kill you if she can."

"I know," he said. "And if you prevent it, you have my word these mountains will remain in the care of the demons for all time."

"Who are you to make such a promise?"

"I am Barsilay b'Droer, the heir of Luz. And when the time is right, I shall be King."

"King," they said. "We think not."

"I bear the mark," he said.

"Show us," they wheedled.

"I need assurances first. Will you kill the one who hunts me?"

"You ask us to fight the Peregrine?" The whispers echoed *Peregrine* all through the forest.

"She is but one, and you are many."

"She is the Peregrine!" the demons said.

"None may kill you. She is no exception."

"She can hurt us badly, badly, badly. Do you know what it is she carries, Barsilay of Luz? Poison! We smell it on her, even from here, poison meant for you, but she will use it on us if we go against her."

"If you don't, she will use it against me, and everything I've offered you dies with me. If I become King, these hills are yours forever."

The demons became very agitated indeed. "War," they whispered. "War," and then "soldiers" and "cast out."

"Show us," they demanded. "Show us the mark."

"Will you agree, if I show you?"

"Show us!"

"Agree first," he said, because he knew the Peregrine would be watching, and it was only the chance he was lying that stayed her hand.

"Show us! If you show us, we agree. We agree!"

Barsilay tore open his tunic at the neck, revealing his chest, where the mark had appeared after the Courser had severed his shoulder in the prison tower in Rimon.

"Truth," the demons said. And there was a roar of hisses like water, and the plumes of smoke burst from the clearing, rushing through the forest, breaking branches. There was a horrible sound like steel on glass.

"Go," Barsilay told Elena, kicking his horse into motion. "Go!"

Naftaly had to cling to Barsilay's back, branches whipping his face and the horse almost stumbling in its panic to get away. He could hear Elena's horse behind him, and the shriek of the demons, so many demons.

"They're killing her," he said into Barsilay's back.

"Isn't that what you wanted?" Barsilay replied angrily. "Did you think it would be pretty?"

Naftaly found himself weeping into Barsilay's shoulder, the sound of the demons loud in his ears, until they reached the crest of the hill below them. They were descending again, and over the tops of the trees below them they could see all the way to the sea.

Barsilay stopped the horse, his breath shaking, and dropped the illusion of his left arm. His face was scratched all over, more than Naftaly's, even. "Are you all right?" Elena asked him.

His eyes were still on the sea below, the sun nearly down. In the last light of the day, Barsilay pointed down toward the coast, where on the far horizon a city clung to the land above the shore. "Zayit," he said.

ELEVEN

TOBA BET FOUND that Tsifra's boat was very much like the one Toba Bet and Asmel had sailed in, except that it had obviously been made with magic. The hull had no visible seams, and Toba Bet guessed that the Courser had made it out of a single piece of wood—a fallen log, probably—that she'd hollowed and expanded. Its mast that grew up from the bottom like a sapling, and its sail was made of the same cloth as Tsifra's clothing.

So foolish, that Toba Bet had believed her sister wouldn't be able to find a way to Te'ena. Toba Bet had never seen a boat before two days ago, but Tsifra had lived her life in the wider world.

Still, Toba Bet knew the reason it had never occurred to her to try making a boat was not the lack of technical knowledge about boatbuilding, it was that it seldom occurred to her to use magic at all. Asmel was always the one reminding her what she could do, and now he wasn't here. Her magic wasn't as weak as it had been, but she still had trouble remembering that she was a Mazik. She wondered how long it would be before that thought would occur to her without surprise.

They sailed with the dawn, back toward Mount Sebah and the demons that were still trapped there, that had been left trapped by Toba Bet herself, and not even by her buchuk. The demons would know who had done it. "There may be a problem," she told Tsifra. "Those demons are not going to be pleased to see me." She explained their last encounter, when she and Asmel had gone to learn how to make a safira from Rafeq, and Toba Bet had tricked the demons and left them stranded under the mountain.

"So you are telling me they're likely to kill you on sight," Tsifra said.

"It may make more sense for you to go into the mountain alone."

"Oh no, I'm not doing that," Tsifra said. "They might well kill me on sight as well. We're two half-Maziks with the same name, who knows what they'll assume?" She pondered this and lowered her hand, which she'd been using to make wind for the sail. "You'll have to take a turn with this; I'm too tired from giving magic to your lover."

Toba Bet took her place behind the mast and blew out a weak puff of air before giving up.

"Are you ill?"

"I was chased halfway across Sefarad by your demon, then I had to sail to Te'ena under my own power, then I had to donate two weeks' magic to Asmel, and on top of that I haven't slept. I feel awful."

"I'm no better," Tsifra admitted.

"I suppose we'll just have to float for a while," Toba Bet said.

"I'll lower the sail, then. The wind will blow us back toward Te'ena."

They floated like that for some time, neither speaking. Then Toba Bet said, "How do you plan to keep the demons from killing us?"

Tsifra said, "Leave that to me."

ASMEL WAITED THE space of half an hour before following Toba through the gate to Mazik Te'ena.

Before the Fall, he'd visited often enough. The city had been a vibrant center for learning, and its loss had been nearly as severe as Luz's when it had been cut off in the flood: two great cities lost in the space of a single day. He'd had most of his education on Te'ena, studying astronomy with Omer, back when he and the world had been much younger. He'd been offered a place there, too, but instead he'd insisted on returning to Rimon. He'd wanted to create his own university, the great work of his heart.

Following the trail Toba had left in the dry soil, he made his way through the gate to Mazik Te'ena, and then north, into the old city itself. He had, he guessed, fewer than three hours until the moon set. If he allowed himself to be marooned on the Mazik side of the gate, there would be no ship to take him to Zayit before the next moon, and he would run out of Toba's donated magic. He would find himself trapped while he slowly forgot himself and then likely starved.

If he'd had magic, he would have made himself a time-counter, or he'd have conjured wings to glide from the hilltop into the city. He'd have been quicker, and had more time. But as it was, by the time he managed to walk into the silent city, he wagered he had less than an hour before he'd have to leave again.

It would not be enough time for all he wished to do, but it would be the only chance he would get to find Omer's library, one of the grandest in Mazikdom.

Omer was an ancient Mazik, much older even than Asmel, one of only a handful of those born in the first age that Asmel had ever met. He'd also been a member of ha-Moh'to, making him one of Marah's confidants. Asmel did not know if he yet lived, somewhere in Te'ena, or if he'd entered the endless dream. The Maziks in the greater world had tried to dream their way to those in Te'ena, but failed. The sea seemed to make it impossible, even the saltless sea of the dream-world.

ASMEL MADE HIS way into the heart of the city, hearing nothing but occasional birdsong and his own heavy steps; it seemed there were few Maziks left living. In the main square, the buildings were all bare, overgrown with native vegetation.

The house Asmel had been searching for had been reduced to

ash. He approached it, kneeling down, and ran a hand through the blackened dirt where Omer had kept some of the oldest books known to Maziks. Even without magic, Asmel had a fairly good notion of what had happened: the Courser had burned this place, and not recently, from the state of things. No one else could have done it, and the fire had been too contained to have been naturally occurring.

Had she killed Omer, too?

From within the scrub that had grown over the area, a few sets of beady red eyes looked out at Asmel, cocking their heads collectively to one side, and then the other: the Te'ena sand-dragons, each the size of a small weasel. They lived down on the beach and in the wilderness; he'd never seen them in the city before.

Certainly not so many.

They began to creep out, their orange scales shining in the moonlight. There were ten, then twenty, and they grew ever closer, scenting the air with their snouts and tongues. One took flight on its translucent wings and flew in a circle around Asmel, sniffing at him. "Begone," he said, waving a hand around it, and then realized he had no magic with which to banish the things.

One lighted on his bicep, looked him directly in the eye, and sank its teeth into his arm.

Asmel shouted, and beat at the creature with this other hand, and the others swarmed forward. He felt teeth in his calves, his shoulder, his neck.

And then there was a flash of light, and the dragons shrieked and flew away, their wings brushing against Asmel's face as they retreated. He turned to see the form of a tall man, his hair concealed under a hood, which he pushed back to reveal an angular face. "Asmel of Rimon, as I live and breathe. What have you done to yourself?"

The face and voice were altered—he'd likely disguised himself, but not beyond recognition: Omer, the Great Astronomer of Te'ena.

Omer, the man who had taught Asmel everything he knew about the stars.

He was no less than a living treasure to Asmel. In his estimation, one of the wisest Maziks ever to live. Without Omer, there would have been no university in Rimon. In essence, without Omer, there was no Asmel at all.

Asmel rose and went to take the man's hands and kissed his cheek. "I saw this and thought the worst."

"The worst nearly found me," Omer agreed, laying his hands over the nastiest of Asmel's bites and healing them, one after another. "Fortunately, I had warning."

"Warning?"

Omer glanced around the empty plaza. "Why don't we continue this conversation off the street?"

"I'm afraid I have no time," Asmel said. "I must leave before the moon sets."

"This will take no time," Omer said, and taking Asmel by the hand, led him to the fig tree in the center of the plaza, where he set his hand to the trunk, whispered a few words, and then he and Asmel were inside a grand library topped with a glass dome.

Books lined every surface, shelves crisscrossing the room in all directions like a labyrinth. The light filtering from the dome was green, some effect of being hidden within the tree.

Were they inside the tree? Or was the tree a portal? Asmel marveled at all he saw. "You saved your library."

"Not all of it," Omer admitted. "Just the important books. I had to let that woman believe she'd carried out her task, or she'd have come back. Until recently, I had a correspondence with Rahel. She mentioned that Tarses the Betrayer was working with a woman with a reputation for popping up in strange places."

"I've met her," Asmel said. "She killed one of my dependents."

"I'm sorry to hear it. She killed my buchuk," Omer said, "and I'm still angry about it, too."

"Are you all alone in this place?"

Omer looked a bit consternated, as if not sure he could still trust his old friend with these new eyes. He said, "There are some of us left. Fourteen, all told."

"Only fourteen, of the whole city?"

"When it became clear there was no way off, most of us entered the endless dream. Those left are the ones who still had something to do. I still have my work."

"And that's been enough?"

"I haven't been completely cut off until recently. We trained four birds and sent them out, one to Rimon, one to Zayit, one to Tamar, and one to Erez. The one to Zayit was the only one that returned. Rahel moved from Zayit to a spot near the border so we could communicate more easily, but then I stopped hearing from her. I suspect she's dead."

Asmel ran a thumb over his lip. "I've heard the same elsewhere. Times are grim, and that's not new. But the moon won't wait for me, and I must ask the question I've come for. I need you to tell me all you can about Aravoth."

"About Aravoth?" Omer said. "For what purpose? If you think there's help to be had there, there isn't."

"It isn't help I'm seeking," Asmel said. "It's what Marah hid there, long ago, which needs finding."

"She hid something in Aravoth?"

"To keep the Ziz from Tarses, she hid it there. To mend the firmament, we're going to have to retrieve it."

"You can't," Omer said. "It's impossible. You can't go into Aravoth. You'll die."

"How can you know that?"

"Because," he said, "we tried it, and we failed."

ZAYIT WAS ANOTHER two days' ride, during which time Elena took the opportunity to beat a primer on the politics of Mazik Zayit out of Barsilay. "What's it matter?" he'd asked her. "It's a city with a government."

She'd wanted to point out that as the heir to the entire known Mazik world, it should matter to him a great deal, but elected not to press the issue, which seemed to be something of a sensitive topic. Still, he'd explained things enough to give her a grasp of the situation: Zayit had grown wealthy after the Fall of Luz, and wealthier still when the mortals of Zayit had launched a crusade against the city of Habush some three hundred years prior. The Maziks, it seemed, had used the event as an excuse to divest Habush of some of its riches, and made off with several tons of iron, a material Maziks could not make with magic, along with silks and spices and other items they promptly sold to the other Mazik cities at inflated prices. So, the very wealthy city of Zayit had become even wealthier.

The city itself, Barsilay explained, was ruled in the main by a council of adons, who themselves elected a prince who ruled with a rather circumscribed set of powers.

"Why elect a prince at all, then?" Elena had asked.

"How should I know?" Barsilay said. "I suppose they like keeping one around in case things go sour, then they can kill him and pick someone new. Are you done asking questions?"

So Zayit had a king, sort of, and a group of extraordinarily powerful lords who pulled the strings, but at its core the city operated on the influx of hot-and-cold-running money.

And information. The Zayiti spy network was regarded as more successful even than Tarses's, because they were not known to have ever killed anyone, implying either that they'd never needed to resort to violent methods, or that they were sufficiently subtle that they'd never been caught. In either case, there were entire business enterprises in Zayit that ran on the currency of well-kept secrets.

"So they use them for blackmail," Elena had surmised.

"Sometimes. There's a lot you can do with a valuable secret if you've a creative mind."

"Sounds like your natural habitat," the old woman told Elena. "You can put out a shingle. Between the poisoning and the scheming, I'm sure you'll do excellently."

That had been the extent of Barsilay's tutelage on the subject. How the Zayitis would feel about playing host to the heir of Luz was not a question she'd bothered to ask. The city had done well out of the shadow of the Empire. Why would they want to put themselves back under someone else's boot?

And would Barsilay be willing to become the person wearing that boot? Elena could not imagine the man as king of anything—he didn't have the instincts for it. He was a genial person who liked conversation and making people feel at ease. A man like that wouldn't last a week as Emperor. She suspected Barsilay was clever enough to have figured that out.

Would Tarses really kill him for being the heir to the throne of some long-lost city that hadn't existed since before the Temple? A throne the man clearly did not even want?

She wondered how many heirs there had been before Barsilay, who had lived and died in obscurity. With Mazik longevity, it was impossible to tell, there could have been two or a thousand, and Barsilay likely did not know either. And if Barsilay died, how many were left after him?

None of it made much sense as far as Elena was concerned; not Barsilay as King, not Barsilay killed for being heir, not Zayit pretending it could run an economy on poison forever. But Elena supposed no one had asked her opinion.

In any case, she reminded herself, she was not in Zayit to affect any kind of political change; she was there to meet Toba and bring her home, and let the Maziks worry about themselves.

NAFTALY HAD NEVER traveled farther from Rimon than Merja, and here he was, in the heart of Zayit. He tried not to gawp like a bumpkin, and failed.

They were disguised as well as they could be: Barsilay with his false arm, Naftaly with his false eyes, and the women safely hidden behind veils, with only their glamoured eyes visible.

Mortal Zayit was built on an island in the lagoon, but the Mazik city was walled and clung to the coast, a maze of brightly painted buildings fronting on freshwater canals the Maziks had modeled after their human counterparts'.

"Were they compelled to dig those out by the Mirror or do they just like the aesthetics?" Elena asked, as they crossed a stone bridge and looked down into the clear water.

"I doubt even they know," Barsilay said. "But it's pretty enough, isn't it? Still, Maziks on boats . . ." He shook his head. "In Rimon, they say the Zayitis are crazy."

"Better not say it so loudly," Naftaly said, because there were plenty of Maziks around. The others ignored them mainly, but occasionally an inquiring glance landed on them, either drawn by the two veiled women or else by Barsilay's handsome face.

"Oh, they love it," Barsilay said. "Eccentricity is prized here, you'll see."

It did seem so. None of the buildings matched any other; some had classical façades and others were made with the red-and-white brickwork common in Rimon, and still others were painted the blue of the Dimah Sea. Crisscrossing the canals were a series of stone bridges, decorated with olive-tree finials atop the railings, grander or smaller depending on the width of the canal beneath.

The Maziks themselves seemed no different than those Naftaly had seen in his dreams, every color and gender possible. Occasionally a curious set of eyes met his, and he looked away quickly, unsure if he were accidentally showing interest, or if they knew, somehow, that he was foreign by his dress or his manners.

Elena, at least, would be able to speak to them. Barsilay had been right: He should have learned Zayiti. Of course, he wasn't exactly sure who he was planning on speaking to, and that was a bigger problem: Barsilay had never said exactly what he intended to do when they got there, because it had seemed so improbable they'd ever get there at all. "Barsilay?" he murmured.

"I am taking us someplace," he answered. "We're not wandering, if that's your worry." He stepped around a puddle in the uneven cobbles. "Asmel had friends at the university here, once. I'm hoping one of them might be willing to put us up until we figure out what to do next."

"And what are we going to do next?" Naftaly insisted.

"I don't know," Barsilay said tightly. "Which is why we need to find a safe place to stay while we figure it out, or else wait for Asmel to get here."

"Are you relying on him telling you?"

Barsilay stopped short. "I did not say that. But if you're concerned about my lack of judgment—"

"Would you mind holding this quarrel 'til we're inside? A loud argument on the street in a foreign tongue does nothing to keep us inconspicuous," said Elena.

Naftaly, about to say more, snapped his mouth shut. "I didn't mean to quarrel," he said softly. "I'm only worried."

"I know," Barsilay said. "So am I."

The four of them crossed two more bridges and a central garden filled with olive trees—not, Barsilay said, the real grove where the gate would be found, but an expensive replica maintained by the Prince to remind everyone of the source of the city's wealth and power. Several more turns, another bridge, and then they stopped at the threshold of a faded, dark house with a peeling façade.

"A ruined alcalá, a ruined tower, and now this," the old woman said. "I think you Maziks have quite a time keeping up your buildings."

"Regime change is hell on infrastructure," Barsilay said, lifting a hand to knock on the door. When there was no answer, he sighed. "She's not been here in some time, which means she probably warded the house when she left. It will take me hours to get those down. We should—"

The old woman pushed at the door experimentally, and it opened with a creak. She put her arm over the threshold, waved it around a bit, and then stepped into the house.

"No wards?" Naftaly asked. "Is that strange?"

"Very strange," Barsilay said, casting a ball of light in his palm, since the house was utterly dark inside. "But we so seldom have any luck, I don't want to question it too much."

"Whose house is this?" Naftaly asked, taking in the front room while Elena went to pull back the curtains from the windows. The room was mostly bare, besides a table and chair. Further in was a sitting room with a dining table and beyond that must have been a kitchen. The entire place smelled as if it had not been aired in some time.

"Mir b'Cohain," Naftaly replied. "An astronomer, like Asmel."

"Hasn't been home in a while indeed," the old woman pointed out, while Barsilay rifled through the papers left on the table, and said, "Ah! She's not dead." He held up the paper. "She's in Anab 'til spring. Visiting her son."

"You seem oddly pleased by this. Weren't you counting on her to help us?"

"Yes, but at this point finding one of Asmel's contacts is still alive is good enough. Anyway, she won't mind us using her house. And if she does mind, she won't know. At least not until April. Is there food?" he called to the old woman, who had gone on into the kitchen and begun opening cabinets.

"Not a crumb," she said.

"She must have cleared it all out before she left to keep the vermin out," Barsilay said, pulling the last of their lentils out of his purse and making a meal of garbanzo stew, which the old woman grumbled about, muttering that it hardly mattered since everything he made tasted the same, anyway, and it was all bland as wood shavings. "Can't you add something to it?" she asked. "I know you can't salt it, but some pepper?"

"We haven't money for pepper," Barsilay said. "You'll be eating wood shavings for a while, I'm afraid." He finished the last of his dinner and said, "Since I have to go talk to the Zayiti Prince tomorrow, I'm going to bed now."

"The Prince?" Naftaly asked.

"I suppose we'd better warn him about Tarses, hadn't we?" He got up from the table, leaving the rest of the food, and stumbled up the stairs, at which point Naftaly realized that he would be sleeping in a bed for the first time in weeks, in a room with a door.

After making an awkward show of finishing his own dinner, Naftaly followed upstairs, washed in a tub of hot water Barsilay had left out for him, and realized he'd been wrong to be preoccupied with the door, because Barsilay could not bear to have it closed.

"Do you mind it terribly?" Barsilay asked, opening it again after Naftaly had shut it. "It's just that I don't think I'll be able to sleep all closed in. I suppose I've become used to sleeping outside under the stars."

Naftaly knew it was not that at all, and that Barsilay might well never be comfortable in a closed room again, but he said, "Of course. Though we'll probably be able to hear the old woman's snoring with it open."

Barsilay smiled in the dark. "I find I've come to enjoy the lullaby of other people. Even if it's snoring." He held out his hand to Naftaly, who crossed the room and sank down to the bed.

"Zayiti beds are so high up," Naftaly said, for want of anything else, because they were mostly alone and he knew what should come next.

"I won't let you fall out," Barsilay said, reaching for him, and then, feeling Naftaly's muscles go stiff, letting him go. "Is it the door?"

"It's not the door."

"I can close the door."

"Don't close the door."

"I don't mind."

"Barsilay, don't close the door." Naftaly rolled onto his back, looking up at the dusty ceiling. "I don't know what's wrong with me. My mind keeps turning, like a wheel with a broken axle. It just goes and never gets anywhere. Tomorrow morning we're going to try to talk to the Prince of Zayit . . . Do you know who I am?"

"I do."

"No, you don't. I'm the addled son of a tailor who can barely sew. And you're going to be the King of . . . of everything! Barsilay, what can I possibly be to you?"

"Everything," Barsilay said. "And stop belittling yourself. You think kindness and loyalty are things easily come by in this world or any other? I've lived long enough to tell you they are not."

Naftaly said, "You'll need a wife."

"I've somehow managed this long without one."

"You'll need an heir!"

Barsilay laughed, draping his arm over his eyes. "I don't even want to be King, and you have me building a dynasty? I won't need a wife, nor an heir, nor whatever else you're about to say next. I have no intention of ever being anything but myself, the wastrel you saved from a tower. And I really don't care whether you can sew. It's a useless skill anyway."

Naftaly rolled back over and kissed him, not because he believed anything Barsilay had said, but because he'd said it and that was enough. "I love you," he said between breaths, once he'd found that the antidote to a turning mind was Barsilay's mouth and Barsilay's hand on his neck, and shoulder, and back. "And whatever you say next had better not be any kind of joke."

"Say you love me again, and I'll never joke for the rest of my life," Barsilay said into Naftaly's collarbone.

"I love you," Naftaly said again.

"Say you don't care I'm the heir of anything."

"I don't care," Naftaly said. "I don't care at all. But you could say you love me, too, a little."

"Haven't I said so?"

"You've said a lot, but not that."

"I'm sorry then, Naftaly, my love, who I will love until I die." And he kissed him again, and again, and then Naftaly forgot that the door was still open, or that there were a lot of people who wanted both of them dead, or anything else besides Barsilay.

+
+   +
+ · + +   +

TSIFRA N'DAR, THE Courser of Rimon, had sailed all the way to the coast of Sefarad in a boat made of magic and a dead tree, and as soon as she put her feet on solid ground realized she could go no further. Her sister was similarly exhausted, and so the two of them managed to put together a lean-to Tsidon would have laughed at, if he'd been there. *Looks like it's been assembled by a drunk mortal in the dark,* he'd have said, and he'd have been right.

But the two of them were nearly unable to stand, and had almost been unable to get off the beach before they'd collapsed, exhausted, and passed out under their badly assembled nest of branches.

Tsifra was afraid to sleep, because she might be called by Tarses, who might realize she was not where she was meant to be. If he found out she was with Toba, it would be worse, because then there would be no excuse not to bring her immediately to him. Her life ran very much on luck now. If Tarses called her, she would have to go. If he asked her where Toba was, she would have to tell him.

She hadn't accounted for Toba not having the killstone. Probably she should have jettisoned the plan at that moment, killed Asmel and brought Toba to Tarses as ordered, but she'd imagined the life she'd have if she could use the killstone, and she wanted it badly.

Fortunately, as she'd hoped, she dreamed again of Atalef instead.

"You have her?" he asked, without preamble.

"Of course," Tsifra said. "But I need your help." She explained how Atalef's old master had been the one to steal the killstone, how they planned to use the other demons to track him down.

"The birdling tricked them," Atalef said. "She is right, they won't trust her twice."

"And if I go alone?"

"They'll be very angry, very hungry. They've had no magic since their master abandoned them." Atalef swirled, thinking it over. "They will likely kill you, too, and eat your magic. They won't stop to think what they are doing. They will not be quite like us. They have been imprisoned too long. They will be more like demons than Maziks. And they will be very angry."

THE REPUBLIC OF SALT 157

"How do I prevent them killing me? How did the Caçador steal you away?"

"The Caçador had a trap. But even if it still exists, you cannot risk looking for it."

"Then give me something I can use," Tsifra said. "A message from you?"

"You won't have time to give it," Atalef said. He was becoming increasingly agitated. "It won't work. It won't work!"

"It *will* work," Tsifra said. "There must be something. Your name. Give me your name."

Atalef exploded. "No! Never!"

"Then give me another way!"

"I will never give my name. We can't trust you with that."

"I can use it to get the rest of you out from under the mountain," Tsifra said. "Do you understand? This is better than we'd hoped. You can reunite with the rest of yourself, and Tarses will be dead. He won't be alive to abuse your name any longer."

"But *you* will know it."

That was true, and Tsifra hoped that Atalef wouldn't come to the very obvious conclusion … That he would need to kill her, too, once this was over. "If you cannot do this, then I will have no choice but to give my sister to the Caçador. He'll kill me, and you'll be in his service for the rest of your life."

"Forever," Atalef said unhappily.

"Forever," she said. "You know I am your only ally. There is no choice."

"My name," Atalef said unhappily. "My beautiful name."

"Tell me," Tsifra urged, "and I will share it with no one."

"You will not hurt us? Not bind us? And never share it?"

"Never," she said.

"Then give us yours, and we will give you ours. A fair trade."

Tsifra hesitated. It was a fair trade, but that didn't make it a safe trade. To give her real name to a demon? It was unthinkable.

It did occur to her that giving her name to Atalef also meant handing over her sister's.

On the other hand, Toba was not there to object.

"You ask for trust but give none," Atalef said, which was of course the absolute truth, but Tsifra had taken too many steps down this particular path already, so she said, "I am Tsifra N'Dar."

Atalef spun delightedly. "Of course! A bird name for a birdling. How did I not see, little bird? I smelled it, but did not taste it. Lovely, lovely."

"Your part of the deal," she reminded him.

"Kaspit Rokedet," Atalef whispered solemnly. "Is it not a lovely name?"

Tsifra repeated the name three times in her own mind, lest it fade from memory when she woke. "The most beautiful name in all the worlds," she said.

TWELVE

ASMEL FELT A familiar fog begin to descend upon him, and a rising panic to go along with it. He was in Te'ena, with Omer, and the information he was getting must be delivered safely to Marah.

That last part was wrong; he knew it was wrong. Marah was dead. Marah was gone, and not recently, either. It was Toba, Toba who needed his help. He pictured her face in his mind: dark eyes, canny expression that seemed to say, *I know exactly who you are, and I'm not impressed*. He loved that expression.

Toba, he reminded himself, and opened the bag that contained the baubles filled with her magic. He'd told her that it did not matter to him that some of them were Tsifra's, but that had been a lie; he did not much want to use those, and had pushed them all to the bottom of the satchel behind the women's backs. Before he could breathe in the magic, Omer stayed his hand. "Save that for later," he said. "You can have some of mine."

"Are you sure?"

Omer passed him a small amount of magic, and Asmel inhaled it. It felt different than Toba's, older and somehow more relaxed. Toba's magic felt like drinking fire, a bit—there was a certain taste of urgency in it, perhaps because of her youth or else because she'd been under so much strain.

The fog lifted in Asmel's mind. "Thank you," he told Omer.

"Consuming magic won't hold you forever," Omer said.

"I know," Asmel said, then recalled what they'd been discussing. "Did you say you went into Aravoth?"

Omer's troubled expression had not faded, but he answered, "Indeed I didn't, but I was among the scholars that studied how to get inside it. Getting into Aravoth requires a mathematical calculation; you can't simply wander in. You do understand that a gate is not a singular entity. There are two separate gates, one in the mortal side, one on the Mazik, and Aravoth in between."

"I've surmised as much," Asmel said.

"Right," he said. "Right. They were made so that when you step through one, you step into the other and instantly traverse the space between them, unless you go through at the correct angle." He conjured a brush and painted a line on the floor, and a semicircle abutting it. "There are one hundred eighty degrees you can use to enter a gate. If you enter anywhere through this arc, you end up on the other side. But if you enter at between five and eight degrees on either edge, you can slip into Aravoth."

"That's a narrow window indeed. And if you enter at less than five degrees?"

"You'd be bisected by the edge of the gate."

Asmel winced, not least because there was only one way Omer could know that, and he wondered how many people had been bisected confirming the measurements.

"But that was only the lesser problem," Omer said. "Once we calculated the angle of entry, we sent through an expedition of three people: one Mazik, one mortal, and one who was both." Here he paused. "The mortal returned carrying the Mazik's body, so mad we could not even understand what had happened, beyond the fact that she'd died instantly."

"And the half-Mazik?"

"That she survived was the only piece of information we could glean from the mortal who'd gone mad. But the half-Mazik never came back out. We don't know if she couldn't or didn't want to.

After that, we suspended any further inquiries. Whatever is in Aravoth, it isn't for us, Asmel. You can't go there."

"I'm afraid we have no choice."

"I'm sure you think so," Omer said. "I can't imagine what Marah was thinking, sending the Ziz there. You've already given up your magic and your immortality, and I suppose you think your sanity is simply one more sacrifice, but you can't find the Ziz in that state, let alone bring her back. It's a suicide mission."

"For me, it might be," Asmel said. "I'm not the one who will be going."

"You intend to send another half-Mazik? But you don't know what will become of them once they're inside."

"We have no choice! The firmament must be mended, and this is the only way. Surely there's some other knowledge you have that might help."

Omer thought about that for a long moment. He said, "If I had to guess, whatever killed the Mazik is the same force that kills a Mazik in the mortal realm outside of the full moon."

"There's no moon in Aravoth."

"That's my theory," he said. "Based on my study of the mortal who went mad, it seemed like whatever she perceived simply overwhelmed her mind. I think magic might have shielded against that."

"In that case, why didn't the half-mortal return?"

"That's the issue—I don't know, and we were never willing to risk sending someone else to find out. It's possible the gates move inside Aravoth, as they do in the mortal world. She may not have been able to find her way again. Since you have no choice now, what I would say is to spend as little time there as possible. Still, there's a great deal of risk, Asmel. Do not delude yourself. Aravoth is not safe."

OMER RETURNED ASMEL to the gate by stepping through a different fig tree. The moon was at the horizon, and Asmel cursed the lack of time. "There's more you haven't told me," he said.

"I know there's no time left," Omer said, "but repairing the Luz gate is more important than you know. When the mortals tore the gate out, the rent they left behind remained open. The waters are still coming, Asmel, even now. The Dimah Sea is rising, and in another hundred years most of the cities will be against the sea. In a thousand, we'll have lost everything except Rimon, Erez, and the outlier cities."

Asmel nodded. "We will find a way to mend what was broken, Omer. Do not give up hope. If we are able to raise Luz—"

"Then what? You can't use the same technique to save Te'ena. We're too remote. There's no way for you to create a bridge from here to Zayit. It's impossible. Asmel, we cannot be saved. The only way off Te'ena is to do as you've done, and for what? To lose all that we were, in exchange for forty years of unencumbered life as a mortal, ended with a dreamless death?"

Asmel fixed his eyes on the stars, dimming in the coming dawn, and said nothing.

"I'm sorry," Omer said.

"No, your assessment is entirely correct. By any measure, my life has no value. Only there is still work for me to do, so I will continue as long as I can. I'll train a new bird to get to you as soon as I'm able. Please remember, you're not forgotten."

Omer's eyes crinkled as if he meant to smile, and Asmel thought at first his words had pleased him. It was only after, when he was stepping back through the gate, that he realized the idiocy of what he'd told him: he was the only one to remember them, and the life of Asmel's memory was rapidly drawing to a close. He'd forget them all, and then there would be no one.

There would be Toba, still. Yet another reason to get himself to Zayit before the next moon. He would tell her about Aravoth, and about the Maziks that remained in Te'ena, and he would make sure someone sent a letter to Omer. Wishful thinking, that he'd hold out long enough to do any of it. But for now, he set his path toward the mortal city of Te'ena.

ELENA WOKE THE next morning in her cozy bedroom, the old woman snoring gently beside her. The room needed a good cleaning, but it was warm and dry and the bed was soft, and at first Elena considered staying in it 'til dinnertime. But then she heard the men speaking downstairs, so down she went, and found that Barsilay and Naftaly were already dressed and stepping into their shoes. "We're off," said Barsilay, tossing her a small silk purse. "I found this upstairs. It should buy us enough lentils to last 'til the next moon, if you bargain well."

"Why are you taking the boy?" the old woman asked, following Elena down the steps. "Isn't there a chance you might run into trouble?"

"I can't see how," Barsilay said. "Zayit isn't Rimon; the government isn't inclined toward harming its citizens."

"But you aren't a citizen," the old woman pointed out, to which Barsilay only replied, "Do you think it might rain later?"

"Shouldn't I be the one to go with you?" Elena asked. "The boy doesn't speak a word of Zayiti."

"Let me worry about that," Barsilay replied. "You know quite well I can't take you to see anyone from the government. They'd want to see your face, and then where would we be?"

Elena took the purse and pocketed it. "Fine," she said. "But where am I to buy lentils?"

Barsilay shrugged. "Ask around, you shouldn't have much trouble. We'll return before dark, I think."

"You think?"

"Well, I hope. And feel free to tidy, if you're inclined. The dust is dreadful."

"I beg your pardon!" Elena said indignantly.

"No need," Barsilay replied. "Not your fault it's filthy." He smiled over his shoulder, Naftaly looking slightly sheepish, and then they were gone.

The old woman came the rest of the way down the stairs, saying, "I can't believe after everything those two have gone off and left us to clean the damned house."

"I have no intention of cleaning anything," Elena said. "Get your clothes on."

The two dressed, ate a little breakfast that Barsilay had left for them, and stepped out the door into a chilled fog that made Elena's bones ache. It was probably worse for the old woman, though she only rubbed at her shoulders and did not complain. The Mazik-made cloaks Barsilay had found them in an upstairs cupboard were fairly good at keeping out the cold, though, so she wrapped hers tighter around herself and made a note that she should find another one they could make a skirt from, and one for the old woman, too. "Are you sure this is a good idea?" the old woman asked.

She was not, but they did need food. So Elena asked a Mazik woman in a blue cloak, who directed them to a shop across the bridge that Elena could not find, so she asked a man in green, who directed her to cross a second bridge to a shop Elena still could not find. And then, purely by chance they came upon a pair of Mazik children—the first Elena had ever seen, anywhere—who took them across another bridge and to the front door of a shop in exchange for Elena's smallest coin, which they then took into the shop themselves.

The shop itself was not what Elena would have expected. She had hoped to buy the lentils direct from a farmer and save some money that way, but as it wasn't a market day she assumed the next best thing would be some kind of dry goods shop, which is what she'd asked the children for. A foolish request, she'd realized, because what sort of dry goods did Maziks buy, apart from lentils?

Mortal-made goods would seem to have been the answer. The shop was bustling with a trio of shades, sweeping and tidying and adjusting the merchandise. Brightly colored silks that looked like they'd come from the east lined one wall, and on the other side of the store was a wooden chest with some twenty drawers labeled in Mazik writing; Elena could smell it from where she stood, redolent with spices, enough to buy half a kingdom in the mortal world. On the third wall, the one with the door they'd come through, there was a shelf piled high with trinkets made from the same metal as her coins.

The only visible Maziks were the children they'd followed inside, who pointed at some sparkling confection, handed Elena's coin to a shade, and then departed with a small parcel.

"This doesn't seem the type of place to sell lentils," the old woman said in her ear. "It all looks like luxury goods to me."

Elena agreed, but approached the nearest shade and asked about lentils nonetheless. The shade disappeared into the back of the shop and was replaced by a Mazik woman in a dress the color of grass, her hair tied back in length of silk. "You want lentils?" she asked, cocking her head to one side. "I don't normally sell those."

Elena felt her energy flag a bit. "We're newly arrived from Rimon and missed the market," she said, taking the purse out of her pocket. "Even if I could just buy enough to last 'til next week—"

"From Rimon?" the shopkeeper asked. From beneath the silk wrapping her hair, Elena could see the sparkle of an emerald set in her left ear, an earring shaped like a wing that began in the lobe and swept halfway up her ear. "What news do you bring from Rimon?"

Elena was not sure of the best way to answer this. There was no benefit in lying, but she also didn't want to draw more attention to herself than necessary. She said, "There is a new queen in Rimon."

The other woman's eyebrows lifted. "A queen? I'd believed Relam had only sons."

"He did," Elena said. "The succession was changed. I'm afraid I can't tell you more than that."

"Hm," the shopkeeper said. "Well, that's interesting, anyway. I wonder what became of the sons. Nothing good, in Rimon. How many lentils do you want?"

At this point Elena had the unpleasant realization that she had not much idea what lentils cost in Zayit. Barsilay had told her the purse should buy enough lentils for a month, but how many lentils was that? Sometimes he used only two or three lentils to make a meal, and other times a handful. And worse, she wasn't sure what sort of system of measurement Zayiti Maziks used. She mentally cursed Barsilay for not telling her these things before he'd left. She felt in the purse for her coins: two of the large ones and six of the smaller ones. One of the small ones had been enough for two children to buy candy.

She handed one of the larger coins to the shopkeeper. "What will this buy me?"

The woman snorted a bit. "Ten."

Ten? Ten lentils? Ten pounds of lentils? Elena did not dare even ask. She briefly made eye contact with the old woman, who also had no idea how to proceed. At least this way she would not spend all her money. She said, "Fine." The woman made a motion to one of the shades who vanished into the back and reappeared with a small sack, which it exchanged for Elena's coin. The sack was mostly empty, leaving Elena with the distinct impression she'd just been swindled. "Thank you," she said sharply, and then took the old woman by the elbow and pulled her out of the shop.

"Did she just sell you ten lentils?" the old woman asked incredulously.

Elena had already opened the bag and looked inside. "Yes," she said. "That's exactly what happened."

"Aren't you meant to be the clever one?"

"Apparently not clever enough," she said.

"That won't last us a week."

"No, I'm aware of that."

"Should you go back in and buy more?"

"I won't give that woman any more of our money," Elena said. "We have enough to last a day. We should return to the house."

The old woman grunted an agreement. As tired as Elena was, she was probably worse off. They were hungry and it was cold, and until Barsilay came back there was no way for them to get anything else to eat.

For the first time in weeks, all Elena could think about was how much she missed her warm house in Rimon, and Alasar snoozing in front of his books, and Toba poring over some translation as if she might become a scholar, too.

Toba would be coming, she reminded herself. Elena only needed to keep herself alive until she got there.

"Come on," she said, linking the old woman's arm in hers. "Let's go back and wait for the others."

They went back through the cobbled streets, past Maziks dressed in purple and gold with jewels in their ears and hair, past shops selling food that smelled like spices Elena had never tasted, and from somewhere unseen, she could have sworn she heard singing and the strains of a flute, playing a melody so sweet she had to stop a while to listen.

TOBA BET HAD NEVER expected to return to Mount Sebah, least of all accompanied by her own murderer.

They'd woken that morning, both of them still groggy and low on magic, and eaten some bread Tsifra had made from what remained of her supply of lentils. It had been better than the bread Toba Bet was able to make, which irritated her, and she wanted to ask how Tsifra's magic was so much stronger when their ancestry was so much the same.

"It's only practice," Tsifra had said, which irritated her more, because Toba Bet had not asked the question aloud. It was almost like having the original Toba back, reading her thoughts. "I've been making my own bread since I had teeth to chew it. No one fed me otherwise. Tarses would have killed them for it."

"You don't need to remind me our father is horrible," Toba Bet said. "I already know it."

"No," Tsifra said, chewing thoughtfully. "I don't think you do know it. You suspect it. But you haven't seen it."

"I saw him cast Prince Relam and an innocent child into the flames," Toba Bet said. "In the Plaça del Rey."

"Were you there that day?"

"I was."

Tsifra said, "I didn't know that. Did they scream?"

Toba Bet looked at her in horror. "What sort of question is that? They were burned alive!"

"Well, did they?"

"No," Toba Bet said. "They didn't."

"They died too quickly," Tsifra said, as matter-of-factly as one might say, "The soup is boiling," or "It looks like rain."

"I imagine so," Toba Bet said.

"Then you don't know the extent of what Tarses is at all." Tsifra ate the last bite of her bread and dusted her hands together. "You should know that usually when he kills people, they scream a great deal."

Toba Bet said, "And when you kill people?"

Tsifra smiled grimly. "You should know the answer to that, shouldn't you?" She stood. "Let's go. We have to pass Rimon to get to the mountain, and we can't risk being seen. Tarses thinks I'm on the mortal side and I'd rather not have to answer questions about why we're here instead."

"Doesn't Tarses always know where you are?"

"If he had to track everyone in La Cacería, he'd never have the time or magic to do anything else," Tsifra said. "He counts on fear or loyalty to keep us in line."

"And how many in La Cacería are loyal in truth, then, and not only afraid?"

"That I can't answer. Any who aren't loyal are too clever to make it known."

"What about the Lymer?"

"Tsidon? Loyal," Tsifra said. "Extremely, I think. He's nearly as deluded as our father himself."

"Deluded about Tarses's motives? Or his character?"

"His character—what a question. You must understand, Tarses believes himself the savior of the world. He thinks whatever he does is justified. If he kills a thousand people, or ten thousand, it doesn't matter. In his mind is an equation, and on one side lies . . . infinity, I guess. There is nothing he can do that is so terrible it's worse than the alternative. The numbers in his head always render him the hero, to himself and Tsidon both, I think."

Toba Bet had never fought against Elena's firm hand; she'd been too afraid, and too weak. Aside from the time she'd drunk all the Shabbat wine, there had been few times when she hadn't done as she was told.

Even so, she knew rebellion when she smelled it, and here it sat. Tsifra did not only fear Tarses, she found him contemptible. Toba Bet wondered how she could make use of it. "Are you so much better? You weigh your life against that of others, and set the value of yours higher."

Tsifra scoffed. "Of course I do. Every living creature does exactly that. You count yourself superior only because you've never had to make that choice. Although I do recall you coming at me with a sword not long ago."

"That was different," Toba Bet protested.

"Was it? Did you not intend to kill me with that blade?"

"You were threatening Asmel."

"Asmel will die on his own. You came at me because you were afraid I would kill *you*, and I don't blame you for it, if that's what you're thinking. I'm only saying you can't fault me for wishing to continue living. That's what life is: a wish to continue. Anyway, I harbor no illusions. I am not the champion of some greater good no one can see but me. I am only myself, and I serve myself because no one else will."

That was the end of the conversation, and Toba Bet found herself following Tsifra through the wilds of Rimon for several hours without speaking again. But she wondered: At what point had Tarses gone from being Marah's friend to the Caçador, and had she seen the sort of person he was becoming? Or had he been that man all along, and just kept it hidden within himself? She did not suppose she would ever learn the answer.

+
+   +   +
+   · + +   ·   +

IT TOOK THREE days for Toba Bet and Tsifra to arrive at Mount Sebah, despite their haste. They'd had to take a detour south of the city to avoid any chance of being seen, and by the time they were able to draw close to the mountain, the sun had descended, leaving long shadows that fell across the rocky ground.

It was so much colder than it had been last time. Tsifra had managed to thicken their clothes, but not enough, leaving Toba Bet to wonder if her sister wanted her to suffer. She also wondered how the change in temperature would affect the density of the rock they might have to pass through. Colder water was denser than warm. Perhaps they would be unable to pass through it. Perhaps they'd end up trapped inside, like Rafeq had been.

Toba Bet told herself to stop being absurd. Rock was not liquid. The temperature could not affect the density. At least, she was fairly sure it couldn't. She wished she had taken a bit more time with the works of Aristotle in Asmel's library, to be sure.

She and Tsifra made themselves transparent, as Asmel had taught her. Toba Bet said, "Are you certain you can control them?"

"I can," Tsifra said.

"They why do I need to go with you?"

"I don't want to risk them feeling betrayed when they come out of the mountain and find you standing there like a scarecrow. Better they know you are with me from the beginning."

"Still," Toba Bet said, "they are going to try to kill me as soon as I pass through."

"That's why I'm going first," Tsifra said. "You'll have at least two seconds to get ready." Tsifra held out her hand for Toba Bet, which she stared at in response. "In case one of us gets turned around in the rock," Tsifra said. "This will be safer."

"I won't get turned around," Toba Bet said. "And I don't much care if you do."

"You would leave me stuck in the rock with Asmel's safira? I don't think so."

Toba Bet reluctantly took her sister's hand, and Tsifra passed into the rock, pulling Toba Bet behind her. Toba Bet felt the grit against her skin, and tasted the bitterness of the salt in her nose and mouth. Then she was through, into the center of the mountain, and she felt herself flung to the ground and a thousand talons tearing into her skin, and the hiss of many voices screaming, "False, false, false!"

Toba Bet flailed her arms at the demons and found it hopeless. They were insubstantial to her touch, but had no trouble touching her. She felt the sharpness of their claws or teeth or scales against her skin, and then, an instant later, Tsifra's voice, rising about the sound of shadow-wings. "Kaspit Rokedet, do not touch her."

A hundred wails rose up in response. "How do you know our name, our beautiful name? Rafeq, Rafeq gave it to you, and we shall kill him."

Tsifra said, "It was not Rafeq who gave it, but your other self. He bade me tell you that you must help us. In exchange, we shall take you from this place and reunite you."

There were a number of inarticulate whispers after that, which went on for some time, and Toba Bet was able to get herself up and inspect the damage to her skin. Scratches, mainly; the demons had not been trying to kill her quickly. She had one significant cut on her left forearm, which Tsifra set her hand on. When Toba Bet flinched, she said, "Just hold still," and then the skin knit together, leaving only a silver scar to show the spot.

Meanwhile, the demons continued to whirl around the room. "Our other self?" they kept repeating. And then, "Our other self was stolen."

"I know," Tsifra said. "The man who stole him is our enemy, too."

"Where is our other self?"

"In the mortal realm, but you cannot go to him yet. There is something you must promise to do for us, first."

"But we cannot trust you, birdling, because the other with you is so very false."

"I could order you," Tsifra said. "But I would rather not."

"She is false," they repeated.

"Then don't trust her. Trust me."

"But you are the same, birdling."

"We are not the same," Tsifra said. "Not at all."

The demons went quiet for a minute, thinking, and then said, "What is it you wish?"

"I will take you from this mountain, and then you must help us find Rafeq."

"Rafeq, who abandoned us?"

"Yes, Rafeq who abandoned you. He has taken something that we need returned, but we don't know where he's gone. You, who have shared so much of his magic, surely you can find him. Do you know which way he's gone?"

"We cannot tell, from inside this mountain. The salt blocks us, birdling." The demons considered. "But once we are outside, then yes, we can find him. We can find the traitor Rafeq, who made us and left us here to die in the salt. We will find him quickly."

"Good," said Tsifra. "Good. So I have your word?"

"You have our name, you do not need our word. But yes, you have that too, if it pleases you. We wish to find Rafeq, birdling. We wish it very dearly." The demons extended a clawed hand to Tsifra. "Take us out."

Tsifra said, "Very well." She extended one hand to the demons and the other to Toba Bet, who had noticed there had been nothing said about what the demons would do after they found Rafeq.

Later, she would wonder why she did not ask about this. But not until much later. She took her sister's hand, and let herself be led back into the rock, and then, once they were free, the demons shrieked so loudly she was sure they must have heard them all the way to Rimon.

Toba Bet doubled over, nauseated from the salt, and watched the demons whirling overhead. "Are they abandoning us?" she asked.

"I think they're scenting the air," Tsifra answered.

"Rafeq may have gone a great distance by now," Toba Bet said. "You think they will be able to find him?"

"North," the demons whispered as they flew. "He's gone to the north, and then east."

"How far north?" Tsifra asked. "How far east?"

The demons whispered and then some of them broke off from the rest of the mass, rising higher into the sky, past the point where Toba Bet could see, circling the mountain so fast they left a wind in their wake. "Zayit," the demons whispered. "Rafeq the Traitor hides his face in Zayit."

Thirteen

NAFTALY FOLLOWED BARSILAY out of the house at dawn, in a set of borrowed clothes he rather thought made him look like an adon gone slightly eccentric; his long coat was a shade of gray that leaned purple, and his trousers were blue and his stockings green. Barsilay had presumed the clothes belonged to Mir's son, the one in Habush. "Does this all really go?" Naftaly asked, as Barsilay secured the door.

"It goes in Zayit," Barsilay replied. "The tastes are a bit different here."

"And remind me who we are going to see?" Naftaly asked.

"Whomever will speak to us," Barsilay said. "I'm hoping for the Council of Ten, but I have no great hopes. I'm not that important."

Naftaly looked at him out of the corner of his eye, but only asked, "And if the Council of Ten won't talk to you?"

"Then I'll talk to whomever they shunt me off to."

"And if they don't believe you? What then?"

Barsilay said, "I'll have to convince them, that's all." They turned down another narrow street and crossed an arched stone bridge over one of the canals. In the daylight, Naftaly could see that there were fish swimming in them, the length of his forearm in all sorts of colors from white to red to black, some spotted, others striped.

"There are fish!" Naftaly exclaimed.

Barsilay stopped short and said, "Fish?"

"Yes, in the canals, look. Are they magic?"

"Ah," Barsilay said, and began to laugh. "I was worried you'd— Never mind. Toba had a thing with fish. And a thing with birds, come to think of it. Hm. But those, no, they're just ordinary fish."

"What happens to them when the water freezes?" Naftaly asked.

"In the winter the stones are enchanted to keep the water warm," Barsilay said. "Pretty, aren't they? Though I always thought it was a bit grotesque to have fish living in the city's water source."

Naftaly made a sour face, and Barsilay laughed. "They do filter the water before it's drunk. Or so I've heard."

"Where does it come from, the water?"

"There's an underground aquifer it's piped in from," Barsilay said. "At least that's what Asmel told me the last time we were here. That was ages ago now. I was scarcely more than a boy then." They crossed the bridge and down another street, lined with shops that were opening for the day. "I keep wondering what he would do, if he were here. He'd know the right thing to say to the Zayitis, I'm sure."

"I still don't understand why you're taking me with you," Naftaly said. "I don't even speak Zayiti. It would have made more sense to take Elena."

"Elena's face won't bear up under scrutiny," Barsilay said. "And I don't need you to talk, I just need you to be there. A man is more trustworthy when he appears with a companion."

"So I'm there to ensure you don't look like a lone madman."

"Mainly," Barsilay agreed. They came around another corner, and into the olive piazza they'd passed by the night before, cast in fog. Several shades were sweeping up leaves, others were pruning a tree that had suffered a dead branch. Mist clung to the leaves, dripping off onto their heads as they walked underneath. On the far side was a great building Naftaly could only describe as a palace. Only the front façade was visible from where they stood, but it was several stories tall, with a set of arched wooden doors fifteen feet high and flanked on either side by a guard dressed in green. Craning his neck back, Naftaly could see a pair of bronze statues on top of the roof, overlooking the doors: two Zizim crouched as if to pounce. Their front halves were eagles, with wings pinned back and taloned feet gripping the edge of the wall. Behind, they were lions, with tails curled around their strange bodies. "Stolen from Habush," Barsilay said in Naftaly's ear. "Among other things. Assume the walls have ears in this place."

This palace, Barsilay had explained, was the seat of the Zayiti government, a system which seemed so Byzantine Naftaly could scarcely understand it. In mortal Rimon, there had been a Caliph, and after the Caliph there was the Queen, and the Queen had advisors and courtiers, but none of them could actually do much; the Queen was the authority, and everyone else served at her pleasure. Zayit was a different animal altogether, with its elected Prince and its councils for this and that, some of which no one quite knew the purpose of. The foremost ministers were known as the Savii, wise Maziks who presided over things like the city's finances or trade or defense.

Of course, Mazik Rimon had another power besides its Queen, too: La Cacería, which did not exist in Zayit. They were too heavily dependent on trade with mortals to eliminate contact, so they'd regulated it instead. Every Mazik who traveled through the gate was registered with the city, and tracked via some magical means Barsilay could not explain, except to say that every Mazik with authority to use the gate was fitted with an earring of some kind that could not be removed and kept a record of whatever they did.

Naftaly had seen a few such people while they walked—men and women with a silver cuff that ran from the top of the ear to the earlobe, which it pierced, the bottom piece set with what might have been an emerald. Barsilay had explained that typically these were important people in the merchant classes: not the heads of wealthy families, but their most trusted aides and their bodyguards.

Inside the building, Maziks came and went quickly, speaking in quietly urgent tones with one another. Barsilay flexed his false hand several times, which Naftaly recognized as a nervous habit he'd developed. Probably he was trying to make sure he didn't forget to maintain the illusion. He stopped and spoke quietly to a man in a velvet cape, who indicated a door on the other side of the hall before going off in another direction. "That will be the petitioner's office," Barsilay said. "He'll decide with whom we can speak."

Naftaly expected the petitioner to be on an elevated seat, offering judgments from some high place, but instead the Mazik was behind a desk, sorting through a stack of paper and looking slightly harried. When they approached, he looked up, frowned, and then went back to work. Barsilay cleared his throat, and spoke in Zayiti, and the petitioner glared at him with some measure of incredulity. Barsilay repeated himself. The man said something that might have been, "And who are you?" because Barsilay replied with his name, and Naftaly's, and the man said something that might have been, "And should I know those names?" because Barsilay said, "No," and that much Naftaly understood.

There was more discussion, and a lot of headshaking on the part of the petitioner that led Naftaly to believe Barsilay had been right and they would not be speaking to the Council of Ten, but then Barsilay said, "Tarses b'Shemhazai," and the other man's expression changed. He asked a question, and another, and then he turned to Naftaly and asked a question he could not understand, and Barsilay set a hand on his shoulder and said what was probably something like, "My young friend is too provincial to speak Zayiti," because after that the petitioner spoke in Rimoni.

"How long ago did Tarses become King Consort?" he asked.

Naftaly stammered a bit before saying, "I don't know, exactly. Oneca became Queen at the last moon, and we learned of the marriage a few days after."

The petitioner tapped his lips with his fingers, then said, "I'll let you speak with the Savia della Mura."

"But the Council—" Barsilay began.

"If the Savia think it's merited, she can send you to the Council."

"Fine," Barsilay said. "Thank you."

The petitioner nodded curtly and wrote something on a piece of paper that he sealed and handed to Barsilay. "Take this upstairs. Then burn it. Then wait."

Barsilay bowed slightly and took Naftaly by the elbow. "Why did he ask me about Tarses?" Naftaly asked.

"He wanted to see if we'd really come from Rimon," Barsilay answered. "Probably most people in Zayit don't know about the marriage yet."

"But he knew?"

"Yes. He knew. Or he wanted me to think he did. Come on, let's go upstairs and find someplace to burn this."

THE SAVIA DELLA Mura, Barsilay explained, was in charge of the city's defense—Naftaly understood enough Zayiti to know she was called the Wise Woman of the Wall. When she appeared, her face looked like it would have had lines on it, if that were possible. She strode to the center of the room, stood in front of them, and said, "I am Efra b'Vashti." She cast her steel-colored eyes at Naftaly. "The petitioner told me that one only speaks Rimoni."

"Yes," said Barsilay. "You— You alone are in charge of the city's defense?"

"Of course not," she said curtly. "But I am all you are getting today. Tell me what you've come to say."

"All … All right," Barsilay said. "Tarses b'Shemhazai is no longer only the Caçador of Rimon."

"He is the King Consort, we know. Continue."

"We have reason to believe he's planning an invasion of Zayit."

"We know this, too," said Efra b'Vashti.

"You do?"

"Yes."

"But … forgive me, we entered the city yesterday, and it did not seem that you have taken any protective stance."

"Measures have been taken."

Barsilay frowned. "What measures?"

"You can't possibly believe I would tell you that."

"We walked in as easily as a knife through a pear."

"Are you an army?"

"No," Barsilay said. "We are not an army, but—"

"Do you think we don't know our business in Zayit?"

"Madam—"

"Have you anything else to tell me?"

Barsilay exhaled loudly. "Tarses has commandeered horses and is stockpiling food near the border," he said, "if that is news to you."

She looked at him a long time. "Horses?"

"Horses. I'm not sure how many, but more than a few."

Efra tilted her head to one side, considering. After a minute, she said, "Wait here," and crisply turning, she left the room.

"Is this a good sign or a bad sign?" Naftaly asked.

"Good, I think. She's at least interested enough to ask someone else's opinion."

"But don't you think they'd be more apt to listen if you told them who—" Barsilay shot him a quelling look, and Naftaly said, "Never mind."

Efra did not return for several hours, during which time Barsilay managed to make a pair of chairs out of a pile of wood stacked by the fireplace. Naftaly fell asleep in one of them, in fits and starts.

When Efra returned, she said, "The Ten will see you now."

"The Ten?" Barsilay repeated.

"I believe you heard me," she said, and then her eye caught the fact that Barsilay's left sleeve was empty. He'd been resting too long.

Barsilay quickly brought back the illusion, to which she replied, "Why bother now?"

But he kept the phantom arm, and he and Naftaly followed Efra down a different set of stairs than the ones they'd come up, across a marble floor set with the olive crest of Zayit, to a room with a set of doors cast from bronze that showed a fleet of ships sailing through a gate. "Answer what they ask of you. But don't expect answers in return." She opened the door and let them step inside, shutting the door behind them.

The room was nearly dark, but it was large enough to hold a horseshoe-shaped table with a chair at the center. Around the table were ten Maziks, men and women, their faces mostly invisible in the low light. "Sit," one of the Maziks said, indicating the chair. Barsilay complied, while Naftaly hovered nervously by the door.

"Either stand with your companion or leave," the same Mazik said. "Don't skulk."

So Naftaly came and stood behind Barsilay's shoulder, and the Maziks asked Barsilay several questions in Zayiti before switching again to Rimoni. "How many horses?"

"That I don't know," Barsilay admitted. "We know they seized the ranch of Adon Ruven, and he was known to have some hundred mounts, but there could well be others who had their horses taken."

"And the lentils?"

"The same—we don't know. But the storehouse we found near the border had at least a thousand isaron's worth."

The Maziks exchanged glances. "And why are you telling us this?"

"I have seen what Tarses has done in my own city. I've no wish to see him do it here as well."

"Do you bear Tarses personal ill will?"

Barsilay said, "Yes, I do."

"And your companion?"

Naftaly looked up. "What?"

"Where does your loyalty lie?"

He had no idea how to answer such a question, so he said, "My loyalty lies with Barsilay."

This satisfied them, for good or ill, because they asked no more questions. "You may go," the Mazik said.

"I beg your pardon," Barsilay said, "but what is it you plan to do?"

"We plan to protect our city," he replied. "You may go."

"But how, precisely?"

"Your presumption is noted. Now go out or be taken."

Barsilay rose from his chair, then said, "There is one other thing I think you should know."

"Barsilay b'Droer," the Mazik said, "I know precisely who you are. You are a Rimoni outcast. You live in a ruined university with your disgraced uncle. You could not possibly know more than we do about what Tarses is planning."

Barsilay went a little red in the face. "Nevertheless, I shall tell you. Tarses's Courser is not a full Mazik."

The Mazik did not even look up. "We are aware." But then something did occur to him, because he asked, "Where is Asmel?"

Barsilay replied, honestly, "I don't know."

The Mazik nodded and flung a hand at the doors, which opened. Giving a perfunctory bow, Barsilay turned and went. Naftaly mimed the gesture and followed. The doors closed rather firmly behind them, leaving them alone in the hallway. Naftaly was not sure if Efra b'Vashti had been in the room with the others; it had been too poorly lit to tell. Outside the bronze doors, he asked, "Do they always sit in the dark?"

"They didn't want us to see their faces," Barsilay said.

"They seemed to know a great deal."

"Yes."

"Do you think it will be enough to save the city?"

Barsilay said, "Who can say? The Zayitis know their business better than I do. Or weren't you paying attention?"

Naftaly would have asked more, but the look in Barsilay's eyes told him to be quiet. "So what do we do now?"

Barsilay rubbed his eyes. "We go home."

IT WAS LONG after they'd left the shop with the lentils, and the old woman was watching Elena doubtfully as they turned onto yet another narrow street, only to come upon another unfamiliar canal. The old woman said, "Admit it. We're wandering."

They'd been wandering for some time, truth be told. They'd left the house in the fog and it was still foggy, and Elena had been relying on landmarks that she could no longer find. "If we could find the large stone bridge again, I can find our way from there," she said.

Elena had expected to feel more at ease in Zayit, where she could speak without translating inside her head. Instead, she was overwhelmed by the place: the winding streets that connected to each other with small bridges, the vivid colors, so many shops and so much noise. Rimon had been a maze, too, but there you could navigate a bit by elevation. Here, everything was flat. Worse, it was growing dark, so the brightly colored buildings blended together, making one street look much like another.

Elena wondered where Toba was. It was possible she might have already come to the city. It was also possible she was still in Rimon, trying to escape her murderous father.

In either case, Zayit was the only place she had some hope of finding her. What Elena would do after that was another consideration. She wanted to take Toba home to Alasar in Petgal. But she suspected Toba might have other plans and would require a great deal of convincing.

She was not sure what she would do if Toba elected to stay with the Maziks. She did not like to think about it, and the effort of not thinking about it was giving her a headache.

"We've been looking for that bridge for hours and haven't seen it," the old woman said. "We must have come to the other side of the city completely. Can't you ask one of these Maziks for help?"

After her experience in the lentil shop, Elena was reluctant to approach any more Maziks. Still, she was forced to agree with the old woman that there was little option, so she approached what may or may not have been a young woman and asked for directions to the great stone bridge with the olive finials. The Mazik, who did not look altogether surprised to be approached by foreigners, gave them a set of directions that would have confused anyone, and then continued on her way.

"That sounded complicated," the old woman said.

Elena set her jaw and said, "Come on." They took the five turns the woman had given her, and then the sixth, and then: a great stone bridge.

"It's the wrong one," the old woman said.

"I can see it's the wrong one," Elena replied. There must be two such bridges in Zayit, and the woman had directed them to the one that was closer. She tried to remember if there had been some specific identifying feature on the other bridge, but could not recall. Probably it had a name, which she should have asked Barsilay.

"Do you notice there are an awful lot of people out here?" the old woman asked.

Of course Elena had noticed, and she'd wondered about it. The later it got, the more people there were out on the street, as if the Maziks were making last-minute preparations for some holiday. They were excited, she could see that much. She strained to hear snippets of conversation, people talking about meeting friends or where they would go. "I think they're preparing to celebrate something," she said. "I don't know what."

As the sky went dark, light-stones winked on, suspended from the eaves of buildings and floating over walkways, and Elena saw a pair of Maziks emerge from a house with faces painted so brightly it startled her: a woman with scarlet feathers painted around her eyes and another with gilded lips and eyelids. Their hands clasped, they brushed past Elena and the old woman, talking about some lover one of them hoped to see, and whether he would be alone or with friends of his own. Then another trio, all painted to look like their faces had been coated in diamonds, came the other way.

"I think it's a festival," Elena said.

"Is there any danger?" the old woman asked.

"I doubt it's the old-woman-eating festival," Elena replied. A woman with her hair braided to look like golden vines twined around her head came the other way, and since she was alone Elena stopped her and asked, "We've only just arrived in Zayit. What is all this for?"

The woman smiled broadly. Her square-pupiled eyes were so light blue they stood out even in the darkness, and Elena suspected they were more artifice than anything. The Mazik woman said, "But even abroad, you must know this is the Zayit Moon."

"But the full moon was days ago," Elena said.

"Oh, of course, but here in Zayit we celebrate the moon for three nights," she said.

"But, why?"

"Why not?" the woman asked, and kissed Elena on the mouth, right through her veil, and then laughed and walked on.

Elena was left sputtering while the old woman said, "I thought the Rimoni Maziks were odd. We should get off the street before we're pulled into this bacchanal . . . I don't want any of them kissing *me*."

"I am trying to get us off the street," Elena said, but there were so many Maziks out now that she found herself carried away with the group, and couldn't have changed course even if she'd had any idea which way to go. They were rushed along like flotsam caught in a current, shorter than everyone else, and older, and certainly more confused.

Music was playing somewhere, some combination of instruments that Elena could not see, but which made her head start to throb. The old woman clutched at her hand, and she squeezed back—if they were separated, she did not think she'd ever find her again, and she was entirely likely to be crushed.

Overhead, there was a flash of light, which exploded out into the shape of a large flower, and then another nearby, and a sound like cannon fire far away. The Maziks clapped their hands and cheered, and then more flashes lit the sky, so much that the streets were bright as day down to the cobbles.

As they were swept along, Elena saw that they were passing a side street with fewer Maziks, so she pulled the old woman in that direction until they were clear of the crowd.

"I hate Maziks," the old woman said, gasping, once they were relatively free.

Elena was equally breathless. The sky overhead was still filled with bright explosions and the air smelled of gunpowder. She hadn't eaten all day and between her hunger and the crowd, she'd grown nauseated to the point she thought she might faint. She needed to get them home, but had no idea how to do it.

Finally, a thought sprang to mind. "I've been thinking about this wrong. I should be looking for Naftaly." They only needed to find someplace private so she could cast her looking spell. She scanned the area. Zayit was very urban indeed, and there were few spaces one could think of as private; even the alleys that connected the main streets were so short they were still visible. They would have to go indoors. Spotting a dark house, Elena took the old woman by the hand and pulled her to the door, which she found unlocked.

"Ought we be going into a strange house?" the old woman asked.

"I only need two minutes," Elena said, stepping through. "No one's here now."

The house was nearly pitch black inside, and Elena found that she was unable to turn on the light-stone she'd taken from the house that morning.

"What are you going to do here in the dark?" the old woman whispered.

"Do you have a candle?"

"No, I haven't got a candle! Where would I have found one?"

She would just have to manage. Squatting down on the floor, she realized she could not draw a map of the area in the dust; she had no idea where she was. The best she could do was pinpoint a cardinal direction, which was not very helpful in a city this size with so many buildings. Still, it was better than ricocheting around in the dark, which was what they'd be doing otherwise. Taking the stone with Naftaly's name from her pocket, she muttered her spell and began to swing it around.

"Do you have a stone with my name on it?" the old woman asked.

"Of course not, you're always here. Now shut up." She swung the stone in a spiral, hoping to get any sort of pull that might tell them at least if they needed to go north or south, but felt absolutely nothing. "He can't have gone through the gate. The moon was days ago."

"He has to be here somewhere," the old woman said. "Maybe you're doing it wrong."

"Would you like to try?" Elena asked, swinging the stone in the other direction. This time, she felt something. "I have him," she said, a little triumphantly, and then the stone snapped up and smacked her in the forehead, knocking her backward.

She rubbed the sore spot above her eyes, blinking a few times to clear her head. "I don't understand," she said, and then saw that the old woman was looking into the darkness with a horrified expression, and then she saw the outline of a man appear in the doorway.

The man stepped through. The room was so dark she could barely see him, but then the moonlight hit the window and his blue eyes caught the light. "Tracking spells don't work in Zayit," he said. "But I suppose two mortals wouldn't know that, would they?"

FOURTEEN

NAFTALY AND BARSILAY left through the enormous doors of the palazzo and went back into the olive piazza only to find it had already grown dark. Naftaly hoped that Elena had managed to buy lentils somewhere, because he hadn't eaten since that morning. "Are you well?" Barsilay asked him as they walked down the steps of the palazzo, through the shadows of the golden Zizim on top of the façade.

"I'm only hungry," Naftaly said. "And confused."

"Confused?"

"You could have demanded their plans," he said. "Made them tell you."

"Not this again," Barsilay said. "If I did declare myself, what do you suppose would happen? I have nothing but a title, and if I start acting like I'm preparing to take the throne, it does nothing but earn me a very large number of enemies I can't contend with. I did what I needed to do. I warned them what was coming. Now it's up to them to do whatever they think is best."

"And you plan to sit here and watch?"

"I plan to eat my dinner and take a bath," Barsilay said.

"Have you really no plans beyond that?"

"No," Barsilay said. "I don't." He cocked his head to one side. "Do you hear that?"

"What's happening?" Naftaly asked, because what he heard was people in the streets, and he'd been relieved that Barsilay had asked the question, because he'd been worried this was the start of a vision. The last time he'd seen so many people outside at once was the day the Edict of Expulsion was issued in Rimon, and they'd all been weeping.

Barsilay touched his elbow. "There's nothing wrong," he said. "It's the festival of the Zayit Moon; I'd forgotten this would be the last day."

"A festival? Is that safe for us?"

Barsilay laughed. "Of course it's safe. Come, we'll have to pass through on our way home. Take my hand so we won't be separated."

"But—"

"Be easy. You'll enjoy this, and I won't let you get lost."

"I'm so tired, Barsilay."

"I know," he said. "We'll only pass through." Barsilay led Naftaly out of the piazza and down one of the wider streets, which had filled with Maziks dressed in colorful costumes. Music was playing somewhere. Naftaly leaned in toward Barsilay's ear and shouted, "Where is that coming from?"

Barsilay smiled and pointed upward, to the second-floor windows above the shops lining the streets, which had been thrown open. In the windows were shades playing all sorts of instruments: strange flutes and pipes and small harps shaped like birdwings. Naftaly stopped moving to listen, only to be jostled from behind. How did the shades all play together, when there were so many?

A man handed Barsilay a goblet made of purple glass, which he downed in one gulp. Then he laughed and said something to the Mazik, who filled it again so that he could hand it to Naftaly, who eyed it a little suspiciously. "It's good!" Barsilay shouted, so Naftaly drank it. It was like wine, but stronger and sweeter, and it tasted like berries rather than grapes. The man with the glasses kissed both of their cheeks before taking the glass back. Barsilay's face had gone slightly pink, and Naftaly wondered if it was the alcohol or the fact that the Mazik had been tall and handsome.

They continued down the street, since there seemed to be little other choice, and someone passed them sweets that tasted like honeyed strawberries, and someone else gave them more tiny goblets of some spirit that cleared the head like mint leaves, taking a kiss in payment. Everyone seemed eager to kiss Barsilay.

The shades playing above the street shifted to a livelier melody and the Maziks in the street began to dance, some in pairs, some all together, so drunk they were laughing. Barsilay pulled Naftaly into his arms and spun him in a circle, despite the crowd, and kissed the space under his ear.

Naftaly was so drunk it seemed the whole street was spinning, and he was afraid he might lose Barsilay and never find him again. But Barsilay held him fast, and they danced all the way down, 'til Barsilay moved them to another side street, where there was more wine passed to them. The Maziks around them were growing bolder every moment—kisses on the cheek became kisses on the mouth, and a woman bare halfway down her bosom kissed Naftaly so hard he nearly stopped breathing.

Then, overhead, came bursts of flowers made of light in the sky and the scent of cannons, and Naftaly began to tremble, because surely this was a vision. Barsilay, noticing his distress, pulled him against a building, bracing himself with his arms against the wall and shielding Naftaly from the crowd. "It's only fireworks," Barsilay told him. "They bring them through the gate. They're only meant to be pretty."

Naftaly said, "They all kissed you."

"They kissed you, too."

"They didn't want ..." Naftaly huffed a little. "They didn't want to be rude to me."

Barsilay laughed again. "No, dearest, that's not why," and the heir of Luz kissed Naftaly the Tailor against the wall on the street while every Mazik in Zayit danced past. Then he leaned back and said, "Let's find our way home now, shall we?" and all Naftaly could do was nod.

They somehow crossed the bridge and left the merrymakers behind, though the strains of the music could be heard anywhere within the walls of the city. Naftaly stumbled after Barsilay up to the door of their house, and then inside. The light-stones they'd left had turned themselves back on at their approach, but there was no sign of the women.

"Where do you suppose—" Naftaly began, and then Barsilay was flung across the room by a shape that shot out of the shadows and landed, straddling his chest, with a blade at his throat: a woman, small, dressed entirely in dark gray with her face hidden in a hood.

"Give me the page," the Mazik said, "and I'll forget I saw your companion."

From the floor, Barsilay said, "Naftaly, go back outside."

Naftaly found himself unable to move. He would not run and leave Barsilay, but if he tried to help him, the woman would cut his throat.

"Naftaly," Barsilay said. "Please."

The woman said, "I have only one question before I kill you. Is it true? What you told the demons, is it true?"

Softly, because of the knife, Barsilay said, "Is what true?"

"Are you the heir of Luz?"

ELENA MOVED TO stand in front of the old woman, watching as the Mazik pulled a light-stone from his pocket and lit it in his outstretched hand. "You may as well dispense with the veils; whatever glamour you have on your eyes isn't strong enough." He crossed to where Elena stood, stunned, and picked up the stone she'd managed to hit herself in the face with. "Naftaly, eh?" He tapped the name with his finger and handed the stone back to her. "You needn't look so alarmed. I have no quarrel with mortals. Though I would like to know what you are doing in here."

"It was unlocked," the old woman put forth.

"A locked door," the Mazik said, "invites questions."

"And an unlocked one invites visitors," Elena said, taking off her veil, since it was no longer performing its duties, and allowing herself a better look around the room. It was similar to the house of Mir b'Cohain: a large downstairs room with a few doorways—probably leading to a kitchen and sitting room—and stairs leading up. It was cleaner than Mir's house, but there was little in the way of furniture, and the windows had all been covered, as if someone had recently died.

The Mazik sighed. "Yes, I failed to account for wandering mortals. Wandering *old* mortals, my goodness," he said, getting a look at their faces, as the old woman had now removed her veil, too.

"We seem to be a bit turned around," Elena said. "If you could offer us some directions, we'll be on our way."

"But it's dark out," he said, holding up a hand. "Stay the night, and be off in the morning."

"Thank you, no," she told him.

"I really do think you should stay," he insisted.

Elena was across the room in a moment and had him pinned to the wall in two. "If you think I am too old or too mortal to take on the likes of you, you are very much mistaken."

But of course she was, on both counts. Up close, the man towered over her. That he hadn't turned her into a slug or worse probably had something to do with the bemused expression he wore. "Is this your usual response to hospitality?" he asked. "I will admit I haven't spent much time around mortals recently, but your aggression seems excessive."

The old woman said, "Don't mind her. Also, we're not strictly together."

Elena backed up several paces. "I don't wish to be confined."

At that, the Mazik smiled sadly. "I have no love for it, either. Won't you stay and have supper with me, and you can tell me why you're here? I give you my word, I won't keep you a moment longer than you wish. But I think you might be of help to me, and I believe we may know someone in common."

Elena did not trust this man at all, but her tracking spell had not worked, and the alternative was wandering in the cold all night. So she said, "What is your name, sir?"

The Mazik said, "You may call me Rafeq."

ELENA AND THE old woman sat around a high table eating a meal made from the lentils they'd bought earlier in the day, which Rafeq had made into a beef stew heavy with dried fruit.

"Tastes less like lentils than usual," the old woman said approvingly, which Elena thought was true, but wouldn't have pointed out. She knew precisely who Rafeq was. Toba had told her about him, and she knew that he was probably not trustworthy and certainly very powerful. What was interesting to him about a pair of old mortal women was a mystery, though, and Elena had never been very good at leaving those alone.

Also, she really did not want to be wandering around in the cold any longer. A month of travel had her feeling her age for the first time, and she could swear she felt the bones in her hips rubbing together when she walked.

Rafeq himself was very quiet, reminding her of the awkward students Alasar had brought home for dinner, newly away from their own families and unable to make eye contact with strangers. Too many years under a mountain would do that to a person.

It did not help that she was unsure what conversation she might safely make; how and why they were in Zayit, who their companions were, and *what* they were, in terms of potential status, all seemed very unwise to bring up. What could she tell him?

The old woman said, "Were you really under a damn mountain? Or was that a different Rafeq?"

Rafeq set down his tumbler of wine. Elena considered kicking her, and swore under her breath. The old woman said, "Listen, I can hear the gears turning in your brain from this side of the table, trying to figure out what to tell him about us. But if he's who we both know he is, he's probably already figured out two Rimoni mortals didn't just wander through the Zayit gate, which means we must have been traveling for some time on the Mazik side, which means we probably heard stories about him, as we were wandering, alone and in disguise."

She'd said it so pointedly there was no way Rafeq could believe it, but he only picked up his wine again and said, "And how was it you came to be in Mazik Rimon, alone and in disguise?"

"We saw the gate and walked through," the old woman said.

"And the wolves did not molest you?"

The old woman sputtered a bit, and said, "Wolves?"

To Elena, he said, "I can see the Mazik in your eyes, but I would not have thought you had enough blood to fool the wolves."

"Yes," Elena said. "I suppose they weren't hungry enough to test it."

"And instead of going back through the gate, you walked all the way to Zayit? For what purpose?"

"Well," Elena said, "better here than there."

"And I suppose you intend to find a way back through the gate here in Zayit at the next moon?"

"That is our hope," Elena said.

Rafeq chuckled a little, clearly believing all this about as much as Elena had expected. At least he hadn't known to ask about Barsilay. After a few more bites, he said, "I'm thinking that you may be able to help me with a puzzle I've been working."

Elena said, "What puzzle is that?"

He took hold of the chain around his neck and brought out a blue jewel he'd had down the front of his shirt. "It's this," he said. "Though I don't imagine you know what it is."

Elena recognized the jewel at once: It had hung around her granddaughter's neck nearly all her life, a gift from Elena's own mother meant to keep Toba safe in the mortal world. At that time, the stone had been in the center of a hamsa, but the setting had been destroyed some time before. What was left was the safira of Marah N'Dar, and inside that was the killstone of ha-Moh'to.

"Your eyes have already betrayed you," Rafeq said. "I think it would be best if we proceeded from a place of honesty, don't you?"

"All right," Elena said. "I honestly know that you stole that jewel."

"I don't deny it," he said. "Then I assume you are acquainted with the person I stole it from?"

"My granddaughter," Elena said.

"Ah," he said. "It grows ever clearer. Your granddaughter threw in with a lost cause. This is why I stole the jewel."

"Not lost," Elena said. "Only delayed. She's coming here now."

"Is she? And Asmel? He survives?"

"I believe he is with her."

"They presented Tsidon with a false stone and lived," Rafeq said. "I am curious to learn how."

"We don't know the details ourselves," Elena said. "The point is, I know what you have. I assume you mean to use it, somehow?"

"I do," he said. "But I can't do it alone. I need someone who can handle salt. And I suspect you will do nicely."

TSIFRA KNEW THERE was no way to get to Zayit with the provisions she and Toba had; they had nearly no food left, their clothes were much too thin, and Tsifra had declined the demons' dubious offer to carry the two of them there through the sky. Tsifra wished the demons would be willing to make themselves less conspicuous ... Either their time under the mountain had left them with poor coping skills or else they'd always been more chaotic than normal demons, because they were so noisy they frightened the birds away wherever they went, leaving a direct trail to their location for anyone watching the sky.

"We'll need horses," she told Toba, once the demons had scattered, looking for their own food. "Even with their name, I don't trust them enough to let them carry me into the sky."

"Agreed," Toba said. "But you can't very well walk into Rimon asking for horses without being seen."

"All the horses in Rimon will be gathered to the north of the city. If two go missing, it will be a while before anyone notices."

"Why are all the horses gathered in one place?" Toba asked.

"Tarses is making preparations for war," Tsifra said. "He plans to attack Zayit in the spring."

Toba gasped and said, "Zayit? You couldn't have mentioned that before I sent Asmel there?"

"There was no place else to send him," Tsifra said, "and this is months away. If we succeed, Tarses will be dead by then. The horses will be kept by the northern garrison, that's where Tsidon sent the horses that were confiscated after the King died. But I can't take the demons any closer without getting us caught. I had no idea they'd be like this."

"Can't you order them to quiet down?"

"I did, this morning. Lasted an hour before they started up again."

"I think they're agitated we're moving so slowly. Maybe they're trying to force us into letting them carry us north."

Now there was a thought, but Tsifra wasn't sure these demons could make plans like that. "I don't think they have the self-mastery for that sort of thing."

"They're cleverer than you give them credit for," Toba said. "Are they not the same manner of creature as your friend Atalef?"

"Atalef spent years training to serve Tarses. These just spent half an age locked under a mountain. I think they're probably a rougher sort of being. Atalef always maintained he was Mazik."

"These say the same. Careful they aren't manipulating you—it's in their interest for you to think they're unsophisticated."

Tsifra nodded.

"Still," Toba continued, "you're right. If they're looking to be rid of us, getting us caught by the garrison would do it. Don't take them any closer. We'll have to come back for them."

"If what you say is true, they can't be left alone. You'll need to stay and watch over them," Tsifra said.

Toba winced. "You'll recall they tried to kill me yesterday?"

"I ordered them not to touch you. You should be safe enough."

"You could give me their name," Toba suggested.

Tsifra hesitated. This would be the logical thing, of course, but if she gave Toba the name, the next thing Toba would do was order the demons to take Asmel's safira, and the thing after that would be to kill her.

Or so Tsifra would have done, in Toba's place. She said, "I promised Atalef I wouldn't give the name to anyone else."

"You promised Atalef," Toba Bet said. "Do you have some plan to find him again?"

Tsifra said, "His movement is limited. He'll have been ordered not to leave the Queen's confessor, in mortal Rimon."

Toba Bet said, "The confessor was injured. What happens if he dies?"

Tsifra was vaguely amused by the wording, *The confessor was injured*, which conveniently left out the issue of who had injured him. It was unlikely to have been Asmel, in his present state. She wondered what exactly Toba had done to him. Not a fatal wound, by Toba's phrasing, but a serious one. She decided not to ask, let Toba think she hadn't noticed. "If the body dies? It depends what orders Tarses has given him. But if I know Atalef, his greatest desire is to be united with the other demons."

"So he would come through the gate back in Rimon?"

"No," Tsifra said. "Demons don't need the gate. They are able to cross between worlds through the dream-world."

Toba said, "So he would come to them directly."

"Yes. Are you worried he'll hold a grudge for whatever you did to him? Don't bother. If you kill the host, you are only doing him a favor."

The demons, by then, had returned from hunting and settled in the trees nearby. "Well," said Toba, "I suppose we'll see."

TOBA BET WISHED there had been some alternative to watching over the demons, who were already inclined to despise her. She was also distressed because there seemed to be many fewer of them than there had been earlier, and she did not like that she'd lost track of them.

"There were more of you," she said. "Are the others hunting?"

"Those are dreaming," they told her. "They will come back. We do not dream all at once."

"Dreaming? Do you sleep?"

"We dream," they said. "We are Mazik."

"Yes, I recall," she said, sorry she had even asked.

"Birdling," they hissed at her, from their perches in the trees, "what do you dream of?"

"It's better if we wait in silence," she said. "I don't wish to expend all my energy in conversation, since we have so far to go."

They laughed. "You believe you are so very clever, just like Rafeq. Just like your father."

Toba Bet knew they were baiting her, so she said nothing in response.

"So clever," they went on, "and us locked away so long, learning nothing. Tell us, in all your travels, have you come across the others?"

Toba Bet meant to ignore them, truly, but she said, "The other what?"

"Our brothers," the demons said. "Our sisters."

"We told you about Atalef," she said.

"No, no, not those. The older brothers. The older sisters."

"I don't understand. You mean ordinary demons?"

"No!" they said. "*The others*. The originals. Did you think Rafeq began with us? With magic?"

"Speak plainly," Toba Bet said, a little more crossly than she'd intended, and they laughed gleefully.

"You don't know! You don't know about the others, and you think you are so clever!"

"No, I don't know, so tell me if you like or else be quiet."

"She doesn't know!" they mocked, and they spun down from the trees all around her, coming close enough that she could feel them against her.

Toba Bet went very still and said nothing. "Poor birdling," they said. "Poor buchuk. Yes, we know what you are. You wonder what it means. Would you like us to tell you?"

Toba Bet said, "No."

"No," they mocked. "We shall tell you anyway." And here their voices dropped to a hundred whispers, and they said, "It means you are dead."

TSIFRA LEFT THE demons in the care of Toba and made her way to the northern garrison alone, keeping her face shielded by her hood, sticking to the shade, and knowing that if anyone were to look closely enough, she'd be caught anyway. Maybe she should have let the demons carry them to Zayit, but if the question was whether she trusted herself not to be caught, or the demons not to drop her from the sky, she landed firmly in her own camp. But when she arrived at the garrison, there was no horse in sight.

It was manned, barely, by a skeleton crew of lesser Hounds. Upon closer inspection, she realized these were the remnants of Tsidon's men—those not killed or driven mad by Toba when she'd escaped through the gate. These men were too brittle to have been left in charge of the garrison. They'd been left behind.

Tsifra had a dark feeling indeed as she scented the air and examined the soil, and then found it was all unnecessary—she could see where the horses had been taken, the cold ground having been beaten smooth by their hooves. They'd gone north, all of them.

She could have gone back to Toba right then and told her there were no horses to be had there, but she wanted to confirm what she suspected.

The offices of the garrison commander were empty, and Tsifra swung in through the window, finding everything had been left orderly. On the table was a layer of ash: he'd burned correspondence recently, which was protocol, but the Peregrine had long ago taught her a trick to reconstitute burned paper. It was not foolproof—even at her best, she could not bring back more than half of the original page—but it might be enough, since she already knew what she was looking for. She swept the ashes into her hand and smoothed them against the table, once, twice, three times, revealing a letter in Tsidon's hand: the man's orders.

As the paper had been burned recently, Tsifra was able to reconstitute more of it than she'd expected—nearly three-quarters. And, more significantly, it was the important three-quarters.

They'd caught Zayiti spies in Rimon.

One of them had broken under torture.

He'd revealed that the Zayitis knew about the invasion, which was no surprise; Zayit's spies were as good as any in the world, as good, even, as Tarses's Falcons. But what was more noteworthy was this: The Zayitis had bought gunpowder from the mortals, and they'd put cannons on their walls, and they'd increased their salt stores by a factor of at least three.

The next section of text was garbled, but then came the last point, and what Tsifra had suspected. Tarses had moved up the timeline of the invasion. He was taking his troops to Zayit now, in the winter.

Who would move an entire mounted army in the winter? It was madness. Tarses was panicking, beginning the invasion before Zayit could make further preparations. Before they could ask for help. If Tarses had taken the army already, they might be there in a matter of weeks and Zayit would not be expecting them for months. Even if they decided to call to P'ri Hadar for aid, the army would never get there in time, which meant their only defense would be their salt.

It should have been enough to defend the city, but if Tarses was moving his army, he must have found a way to contend with it. He would take the city, and it would not be possible to dig him out. He'd have access to the largest stockpile of salt in Mazikdom. He'd be the most feared Mazik in the history of the world.

Tsifra passed her hand over the letter, returning it to ash, went back out the window, and returned to Toba.

"There are no horses left in Rimon," she told her. "And it's worse. The army marched three days ago."

"To Zayit?"

"To Zayit. And if they get there before we do, we'll never find Rafeq."

"But that's impossible. How can we arrive ahead of a mounted army with three days' lead?"

Tsifra said, "We'll have to let the demons carry us."

THE PEREGRINE ADJUSTED her weight and pressed the knife closer to Barsilay's throat. Naftaly had no doubt she would kill him; there was no hesitation in her face, only resolve. "Do you mean to restore the throne?" she asked. "Give me the truth."

Naftaly took in the shape of the woman with the knife: small, with dark skin and hair mostly concealed under a hood. Her eyes were so dark she might have passed for mortal, her pupils indistinguishable from her irises. She turned her head toward Naftaly long enough to let him know she considered him no threat, and then returned her gaze to Barsilay on the floor beneath her.

Barsilay said, "Does it matter so much to you?"

"Yes, it matters!"

Barsilay said, "Why? You'll kill me either way. Just let my friend go. He's no one to you, and if you hurt him you'll feel bad after."

"Will I?" she said. "Perhaps I will. Perhaps I'll cry about it, after I recall how you tried to distract me by changing the subject."

Barsilay laughed a little. "Always so clever."

"Answer the question!"

"Answer mine first. Why do you wish to know?"

"Because the King of Luz could break my contract!"

From the floor, Barsilay said, "What?"

"You heard me," she said.

"Weren't you ordered to kill me?"

"My orders don't concern you," she said.

"Meaning they aren't my business, or that they aren't—"

"My patience grows thin."

Naftaly said, "Tell her, Barsilay."

Barsilay shouted, "I told you to get out!"

"Do you mean to take up the throne of Luz?" she asked again. When Barsilay did not instantly answer, she said, "Once upon a time, a lord of Luz lost his name to his mistress. He went to the Queen, who changed his name in exchange for a hundred years of his favors."

"That's an old story," Barsilay said. "Where did you hear it?"

"From a little bird," the Peregrine said. "And I already confirmed it: the Queen of Luz could give someone a new name. You could change *my* name. Then Tarses would have no hold on me."

Barsilay breathed a few times before saying, "Do you understand what must happen for me to do that? It isn't enough for me to declare myself. I would have to find a way to raise Luz from the sea, somehow claim the book which your master already has in his possession, and restore the gate. The chances of any of this are—"

"Terrible," she said. "They are terrible."

"You were never one for lost causes," Barsilay said.

"That's true," she agreed. "But the way I see it, I have two choices: I can take a one-in-a-thousand chance on you, or I can continue to serve Tarses for the rest of my life."

"I think one in a thousand may be overstating it..."

The Peregrine pressed the knife a little more. Since his eyes had adjusted to the darkness, Naftaly could see silver scars on her forearms, probably from the demons in the Gal'in—the demons he himself had set on her. She said, "Do you not understand what is happening? Do you think he means to stop at Zayit? Tarses is reconstructing the Empire—an empire based from Rimon. We will have another king, Barsilay. The question is whether that will be you, or it will be Tarses."

"I don't want to be King," Barsilay said. "I would rather die."

The Peregrine nodded, once. "And that is why it must be you."

Barsilay was breathing so hard Naftaly could hear him from the other side of the room.

The Peregrine said, "Swear to me, then. Swear you mean to do this."

He'd managed to avoid this very moment with the demons; Barsilay had only promised them the Gal'in should he become King. The oath the Peregrine was forcing was not so open-ended. If he swore this, Naftaly knew, there would be no going back. He either became, truly, the heir of Luz, the future King of Luz, or else the Peregrine would kill him. And Naftaly would watch him die.

There passed several long moments as the two men watched each other over the Peregrine's blade. Naftaly said, "Barsilay, please."

Barsilay reached up and pulled open the collar of his shirt, revealing the mark to the Peregrine. "Fine. Fine! I am the heir. And I will try to take the throne, though I tell you now that I will almost certainly fail and die in the attempt." He closed his eyes and turned his face away from Naftaly and the Peregrine both.

The Peregrine pulled the knife from Barsilay's throat. "In that case," she said, "I will almost certainly fail and die helping you."

FIFTEEN

TSIFRA MADE A little food, and she and Toba ate while they sent the demons off to hunt in the forest for an hour as the sun was rising.

She'd been uneasy about trusting Atalef. And now look where it had led her: trusting her sister, trusting demons to carry her into the sky. She wondered what the Peregrine would say about any of this, but it wasn't as if she could tell her. It seemed almost amusing, that the person most like a friend to her had to be kept so much in the dark. Tsifra supposed this was as much for the Peregrine's protection as her own.

She watched Toba eat the middling bread she'd made, and then, once the two of them were sure they were alone, they worked on revising a list of rules meant to keep them both alive as the demons carried them north.

The demons would not lift them more than ten feet above the ground. The demons would not carry them over water. The demons would not carry them into trees, or buildings, or rocks. The list was very, very long. At the end, Toba made another suggestion: the demons would not carry them except when the sun was out.

"But that will extend the trip by days," Tsifra protested. "And we have little enough time as it is."

"If they carry us in the dark, we'll have no way of knowing what's beneath us," Toba said. "Or in front of us. It makes it much too easy for them to find some way to kill us that we haven't thought of. I know it will take longer, but they want to kill you for knowing their name and me for betraying them. We can give them no opening, and traveling in the dark does that."

Tsifra grunted. She was angry about the lost time, but more than that, she was angry she hadn't thought of it. She'd lived under Tarses's rules all her life . . . She should be the sort of person who thought that way. More than Toba, who'd been so coddled she'd probably never even slept in a bed without a pillow before she'd had to flee from Tsidon.

"Fine," Tsifra said, and then Toba said, "There is one more thing. The demons spoke of others—apart from Atalef. Do you know what they meant?"

Tsifra said, "No, I don't, but are you sure they weren't only playing with you?"

"I don't think they were. They said something about magic not being the first thing Rafeq used in his experiments, something about older brothers and sisters. I thought maybe you'd heard a rumor, at least."

"I haven't," Tsifra said. Older brothers and sisters—a terrifying thought. But truly, the demons might just have been taunting Toba. She made a note to ask Atalef about it, the next time she saw him.

Together, Tsifra and Toba presented their conditions to the terrifyingly delighted demons, who lifted the two sisters in their shadowy claws as high as their agreement would allow, and carried them north so quickly Tsifra could barely see for the wind in her eyes.

THE PEREGRINE HAD sheathed her knife, sworn up and down she hadn't killed the two women—and, in fact, had no idea where they'd gotten to—and then Naftaly had been sent to bed by Barsilay. He spent several hours staring into the darkness, imagining the old woman somewhere out in the cold. At one point he got up and opened the door, only to be greeted by the Peregrine's eyes shining just outside his bedroom. "Do you think you can possibly find them wandering around a strange city in the dark?" she asked.

"I can hardly just sit here," he responded, and she said, "Then I shall go. I can't sleep anyway."

"I shall go with you," Naftaly said, and she replied, "No," and then she was gone.

He went back to bed and must have slept then, because when next he opened his eyes the sun was up and Barsilay and the Peregrine were sitting in the main room over a table full of exotic-looking fruits.

"Are the women here?" Naftaly asked. "Did they come back with the lentils?"

The Peregrine said, "No sign. I was out until dawn; I only returned an hour ago."

"You must be tired," Barsilay said, to which she replied, "If I sleep, I risk getting new orders from Tarses in the dream-world."

"Yes, about that," Barsilay said. "Had he not ordered you to kill me already?"

The Peregrine smiled thinly. "You know, that's a bit funny."

"Is it?"

"What Tarses ordered me to do—with regards to you, anyway— was to hunt you down and take back the page of the book in your possession. Which I have done."

Here Barsilay put a hand to his breast. The Peregrine said, "I took it last night, you fool. It's safe. Now as to whether hunting you down included killing you . . . that's the funny bit."

"One could argue it was implied," Barsilay said.

"Would you like to make that argument?"

"No," he said. "But I think Tarses will make it, so what happens to you if he finds out?"

"Nothing good," she said. "So for now, let's make sure he doesn't find out."

"Agreed," Barsilay said. "Back to the matter of the women—how is it you couldn't find them? Isn't tracking people down your special forte?"

She looked thoroughly peeved. "Tracking spells don't work in Zayit, even for me. Wherever they are, they're indoors, and they've concealed themselves, or else someone else is concealing them."

"For what purpose? They're just two old women."

"Right," she agreed. "They're just two old women, and so we ought to concern ourselves more with the fact that Tarses is planning to invade Zayit in a few months, which means we have little time."

"Little time to do what, exactly?" Barsilay said. "I already tried to warn the Zayitis. They wouldn't listen, and I don't think they'll be more apt to listen to me if I show up with a Cacería spy on my arm."

"No, of course not. They'll execute you on the spot," she said. "Do you not understand why I've decided to let you live?"

Barsilay looked a little uneasy. "Because I can break your contract with Tarses, once I—"

"You idiot," she said. "It's because I think there's a real chance for you to take up the throne. I don't need you to be the heir of Luz, I need you to be King of Luz. And I only think you might be able to do that because you are walking around with the greatest asset in Mazikdom, but for some reason it hasn't occurred to you to try to exploit it."

Barsilay looked at her darkly. "No," he said.

"Ah, so it has occurred to you."

Naftaly said, "What does she mean? What is your asset?"

Sitting back in her chair, she said, "Does he really not know?" Barsilay shook his head at her, and she said, "He's right, you know. You do treat him like a child."

Barsilay swore and looked away. Then, looking back at Naftaly, he said, "She means you."

Naftaly sat dumbfounded, then concluded Barsilay was making a joke, then realized he wasn't.

"I've watched you have visions twice now," said the Peregrine. "One of Tamar, which was entirely true, and one of the Rimoni fleet, which will become true. Neither of which you could have known. The only other person I've ever met with true prescience is Tarses." She turned to Barsilay. "You've known Tarses even longer than I have. I'm sure you know the extent of his gifts."

"His prescience? Of course. He's hardly been discreet about it. But

I also know it has limits. He only sees possible futures at a distance. He can't see what's directly in front of him."

"So you do know," the Peregrine said. "And up 'til now, that's been enough. But Tarses's plans *are* directly in front of him. If he is to make a mistake, it will be now. And this is the first time in all my years as Peregrine that I've heard of someone with the power to counter him. Elena said your visions are never wrong."

"You can't have heard that," Naftaly said.

"Of course I heard it, and it was one of the more interesting things I heard, beyond all that blubbering about undying love—I did consider killing you just to make you stop. Anyway, is that true, what she said? Does what you see always happen?"

Naftaly said, "So far, yes. But I don't think that means it will always be true forever. And really, I have no control over the visions; I could fall over right now and see something happening in P'ri Hadar that's no use to us at all, or I might not see anything for months."

"That isn't what you said when you saw the ships."

Naftaly did not remember exactly what he'd said about that.

The Peregrine said, "You said you were thinking about the view from the window, and then you saw a future version of it. So apparently you have control of it sometimes." She looked at Barsilay very hard. "Strange that he can't control when he has them, though. Why do you think that is?"

Barsilay said, "I don't know."

"You're telling me you haven't even examined him?"

"Of course I haven't. What could I do, even if I found something? I have no idea how to fix something so complicated as a mind, even if I knew how to diagnose the problem, which I don't." He threw up his hand. "I don't even know if there is a problem. Maybe this is just how his mind works."

"Hang on, there's a chance you could fix this?" Naftaly asked.

"No," Barsilay said earnestly. "There's not. I was a bad student a very long time ago, and besides that, you're mostly mortal. I wouldn't have the slightest idea where to begin."

"You fixed Toba," Naftaly said.

"And I nearly killed her in the process!" Restoring his tone, he added, "She had a much simpler problem. It was only a bit of scarring. I wouldn't dare trust myself with something so precious as your mind. Even the smallest error could destroy you."

"But if you can't do it, isn't there still a chance someone else could?" Naftaly asked.

"A fully trained doctor, you mean? I— It's possible, but I'm not sure of the reception you'd receive from a Mazik doctor."

"You said there's no Cacería here," Naftaly pointed out.

"And there's not, but that doesn't mean the Zayitis like mortals running around their city. Everything to do with mortals is regulated to the teeth, and they might assume you're trying to make deals outside of the auspices of the trade guilds or that you're a spy sent from mortal Zayit. It's too dangerous by far."

"No," the Peregrine agreed, "you couldn't take him to a Mazik doctor. But that doesn't mean *you* couldn't consult with one."

"You're suggesting I go to the university and run this by one of the professors as a hypothetical?" Barsilay asked.

"You were a student, once. Surely you know how it's done."

Barsilay's eyebrows were drawn up as he considered this. He said, "Well, that's all fine, but even if they suggest something I might try, I'm still the one stuck doing the work with no experience and no oversight. It's too risky for Naftaly."

"You don't know that," she said. "They might well suggest giving him some sort of drug."

"They aren't going to suggest a drug!"

"You have no idea! Are you so afraid you won't even ask the question? We have an opportunity to get ahead of Tarses. What are you doing?"

"This is not your choice to make," Barsilay snapped. "Just because you've been listening to our conversations for the past month doesn't give you license to pop in and act as if you have equal say."

"Don't *I* have a say?" Naftaly asked. "It is my mind we're discussing, and I don't appreciate you acting like it's your tool to manipulate, or yours to protect."

"Naftaly," said the Peregrine, "do you understand—"

"Yes, I understand perfectly. I'm not stupid." He went to Barsilay and laid his hand on his shoulder. "I want you to go to the university. Please do this for me."

Barsilay reached up and took his hand. "All right," he said. "I'll go." Then he left the room to ready himself for the day. Naftaly would have followed, but the Peregrine held him back, saying, "You should go with him. If he learns something he doesn't want you to know, he's too likely to lie about it."

"There's no point," Naftaly said. "I barely understand twenty words of Zayiti."

"Is that the problem?" she said. "That's easily fixed." She cast a bit of shadow from the tip of her finger and said, "Let me have your ear."

"What is that?" he objected.

"A translator shade," she said. "It's only a tiny bit of magic. It won't hurt you."

"You want to put some of your magic inside my ear?"

"It knows Zayiti," she said. "It will whisper the translation to you."

"You want to put some of your magic *inside my ear*?" he repeated.

"It doesn't do anything but translate! And it only lasts half a day at most, and only if you stay within range, so don't plan to go more than a mile from here. Don't you want to understand what they're talking about?"

"But," he said, "if this is yours, won't it mean you'll hear all our conversations, too?"

The Peregrine looked a bit like she hadn't expected him to figure that out, which rankled. Why did everyone think he was so stupid? But she said, "Weren't you planning to tell me anyway?"

Naftaly did not quite know how to answer that. She said, "There's really no other way to help you besides going myself and whispering in your ear, and I have my own tasks to attend to. Do you want this or not?"

The question, really, was whether he trusted Barsilay to tell him the truth more than he trusted the Peregrine to put her own magic inside his head, and with any information she might learn from inside his ear. He trusted the Peregrine not at all. It made him very uncomfortable to realize that when it came to sharing difficult information, he did not trust Barsilay any more than that. Finally, he said, "Do I have your word it will go away in half a day, and leave nothing behind?"

"Yes, on both counts. You have my word."

He leaned down toward the Peregrine. With one hand she held his earlobe, and with the other she slid the shade into place. He found, to his surprise, that he could not feel it at all.

"How do I know it's working?" he asked, and the Peregrine replied in Zayiti, which he was about to protest meant it wasn't working, but then he heard a whisper in that ear in Rimoni that said, "Do you think I would give you something that didn't work?"

So when Barsilay stepped out the door to make his way to the university, Naftaly was at his heels.

Barsilay frowned when he realized what Naftaly intended. "She gave me something to translate the Zayiti," Naftaly said, tapping his ear. "I want to go hear what they have to say."

Barsilay looked troubled indeed. "You let her put a shade in your ear? Do you not trust me to do this?"

Naftaly did not know how to respond to this uncomfortable truth. It wasn't Barsilay's fault that he was so fearful, but he'd proved too quick to make decisions himself rather than present Naftaly with unpleasant choices. He said, "I have never seen the inside of a university."

"You have," Barsilay said, choosing to ignore Naftaly's nonanswer. "If you visited Asmel in Rimon, that entire edifice was a university."

"I would think the personnel that was more significant than the building," Naftaly said.

Barsilay gave a defeated sigh, and said, "Yes, well, of course. All right, come and see the great University of Zayit. And mind your eyes."

Sixteen

TOBA BET HAD believed herself accustomed to the act of flying, after all the days she'd spent as a flock of larks. She was used to the feeling of wind under her wings and against her face.

The reality of flying as a person was altogether different, and not at all pleasant. Her body caught against the cold wind like wet laundry left out to dry, the demons' talons were sharp against her skin, and she was acutely aware of gravity in a way that made her stomach lurch.

The demons stopped overnight somewhere south of Barcino, and Tsifra made a fire to prevent Toba Bet and herself from freezing in the cold. She'd taken lentils from the garrison, but there had been nothing in the way of warmer clothes. The army had taken everything with them, and their own clothes were so threadbare now they couldn't even be altered with magic; they kept changing back. All she'd managed was making a pair of hats out of dried leaves to wear under their hoods—which was better than nothing but only just—and those kept breaking apart, too.

The sisters sat as close to the fire as they dared, and once the demons returned from hunting, they couldn't even risk being that close, so they enjoyed the warmth while they could. They'd concluded it was not safe for them to sleep at the same time with the demons about, so they took turns, sleeping in shifts until the sun came up and the demons would lift them into the air again.

That night, Toba Bet dreamed herself into a wholly foreign landscape. She was not quite sure how the dream-world worked, but she'd never managed to dream outside of Sefarad. She assumed there was some rule or other that caused her dreaming location to be tied to wherever her physical body was, which explained why she wasn't regularly encountering people speaking Baobabi or Tamari in her dreams.

Which was why it was so odd that the place she dreamed now appeared so alien. The trees bore no resemblance to any she'd seen on either side of the gate, laden with fruit that looked like starbursts. The land itself was dry, the soil, in the starlight, might have been either red or orange, and as she came through the forest she found a tree that had been made to grow extremely wide; it would have taken ten of her, standing with arms outstretched, to encircle it. Carved into the tree was a door.

It was, she realized, an almond tree.

Toba Bet knocked on the door, and it opened.

Standing inside was the oddest Mazik Toba Bet had ever seen. His face and figure were reasonably normal—black hair, an angular nose—but there was something insubstantial about him. He wasn't transparent, exactly, but he somehow managed to give that impression. The light did not quite reflect on him as if he were solid.

"You're here," he said. "I think. Have I imagined you?"

Toba Bet took in the space behind the Mazik . . . It was a house, or some version of one. There was a large cushion on the floor and a low table, which was set with some large metal pitcher and two cunningly carved goblets.

"Were you expecting me?" she asked.

"Yes, and no. I thought you'd be more familiar. Taller. You ought to be taller, and your hair is the wrong color. But I guess the blood is dilute by now."

Toba Bet frowned at the man; she did not like talk of blood from Maziks, especially here. She said, "Why do you look like that?"

"Do I look strange to you? Yes, I probably do. Well, that's because I'm not dreaming, like you are."

"Not dreaming? But then you must be—"

"Dead," he said. "Quite. You should come inside. I've been hiding this place for ages, and I don't want anyone else to find it."

Toba Bet looked over her shoulder, looked back, and said, "Why should I trust you?"

"Now that part's familiar," he said. "You sounded just like her, for a moment."

"Like who?"

"Like Marah," he said. "Who else?" And then he went inside, turning back once to beckon Toba Bet after him.

Toba Bet followed the dead Mazik into the almond tree, which looked like a squat house once she was inside. "Did you call me here?" she asked, as he sat on one of the cushions and indicated he expected her to sit on the other. The top of the house, which should have been inside the tree, was a glass dome like Asmel's observatory, through which she could see the whirling stars.

"I did," he said. "I heard a rumor."

"From whom?"

"Better I not say," he said. "Suffice to say the rumor was that Marah produced a legacy, and that you are she." He looked at her a long time in the starlight, and she realized that his eyes, like Barsilay's, were orange.

"You are of Luz," she said. "Who are you?"

"An old friend," he said. "Of Marah's."

Toba Bet startled again at his use of her name—taboo in the dream-world—and the Mazik said, "I am not shy to use her name here, now she is dead. The rules of this place do not seem to extend past death, mine or hers—though hers, I'd wager, is so much nicer."

Toba Bet said, "Nicer? If you've been here all this time, you must know she's not dreaming with you."

"Of course I know. She's in the void."

He'd said this so plainly Toba Bet could hardly do more than stare at him. Did he even know what the void was? Could he not even bear to imagine it? Finally she said, "This place is infinitely better than the void."

"Is it?" he asked pointedly, and a little painfully. "Is it really?"

Toba Bet found she could not answer, but the Mazik went on, "In the void, there's nothing. Nothing! Blessed rest. Here, it's just endless days that stretch on for eternity, unrelenting, without even the release of sleep. There is nothing but what you see, day after day, with no hope of it ever ending. It's maddening. You have no idea how maddening. Anyone I ever loved is in the void. I am hopelessly alone, do you understand? I can't sleep, I can't die. I'm caught in infinity, and there is no escape."

Quietly, Toba Bet asked, "Could you not learn to love someone new?"

"No," he said. "No. For the dead in the dream-world, there is no moving on in that way. Especially for me. I must be so very careful. If any Mazik ever discovered who I was, rather than an eternity of nothing, my existence would become an infinity of torture. I can't risk it. I speak only to myself and to the shadows, which only sometimes whisper back."

"You risked calling me."

"Because I know you," he said. "I know what you mean to do, and I would help you if I can."

"Who are you?" Toba Bet insisted. "Apart from my foremother's dead friend."

"My name is Dawid ben Aron," he said. "Architect of the Fall."

TOBA BET STARED at the wine in her silver goblet, made to resemble a tree not unlike the house she sat in. This was Dawid the half-Mazik, the man Marah had been searching for after Luz had drowned, the man who had pulled the gate from the firmament, and also the man who had saved the book.

Marah had written of it in the journal Toba the Elder had found hidden away in Asmel's alcalá. From Marah, Toba knew that Dawid had spent some years after the Fall locked away in prison in P'ri Hadar, before escaping and making his way—with the Ziz—all the way to Rimon.

Toba Bet did not know how much time she would have before her sister woke her, and suspected she might never find Dawid again. She had so many questions: about the gate, about Marah, about being half-Mazik. She said, "Why did you do it?"

"Why did we pull the gate from the firmament? We were betrayed," Dawid said. "By Tarses. He'd been our friend, he'd been Marah's friend, so when he came and told us the Queen of Luz was sending Maziks through the gate to murder us all for using Mazik magic, we believed him. We had to. His suggestion was that we simply take the gate and hide it. Tarses would send word from P'ri Hadar once it was safe enough to restore it. But we hadn't realized what it would do, pulling it from the firmament. And then you know what happened after."

Toba Bet nodded at her wine. Barsilay had shown her an illusion of the Fall, of the water rushing in through the tear left in the firmament, drowning both the mortal and Mazik cities, creating the Dimah Sea and isolating Te'ena from the mainland.

"I saved the book, you'll have heard that much, and I'd almost returned it to Marah when Tarses betrayed her, too. I was there that night, on Mount Sebah, when he turned up with his blue-cloaked soldiers and demanded she give him the book and the Ziz. Marah ordered me to take the book and flee, and I did. I took it and hid. And when the moon set and Marah had not found me, I despaired. There was no other Mazik I could trust, and I could not risk Tarses getting the book, but neither could I bear to destroy it. I gave it to the least likely person I could find, someone whom Tarses would never suspect." Here, he nearly laughed. "I went into a brothel, and I asked for the ugliest whore in the place, and I gave her whatever money I had and told her the book was an ancient curse and she should burn it the next morning after I'd gone. Then I spent the night with her and died in her bed."

"But she didn't burn it," Toba Bet said. "She gave it to her child."

"That is what the whispers say," Dawid said. "And if they are true, I may be able to redeem some small measure of my honor. I can tell you what you need to know to find the book."

"But I know where the book is," she said. "It's with Caçador, in Rimon, save the last page, which I stole."

Dawid's face fell. "Then all this was for nothing," he said sadly.

"Maybe not," Toba Bet said. "Tell me anyway."

Dawid said, "Very well," and then he took his finger and traced a series of letters in the table, leaving trails of ash in the wood. "Do you see? Will you remember?"

Toba Bet nodded, and he wiped the ash away. "What is it?" she asked.

"The name," he said, "of the book."

"But how can that help?"

But Dawid had already set his hands on Toba Bet's shoulders, and she felt herself fading from the house, from the dream-world. He said, "Do not trust the book near the Queen of P'ri Hadar. Until it is time to replace it in the firmament, do not take it there, or she will seize it again, as she once seized it from me."

Toba Bet blinked a few times and found herself in front of her old house in Rimon. In her hand was a branch of almond blossoms, which turned to ash and blew away, and then came Dawid's voice, one last time: "If you see the heir of Luz, tell him I am sorry."

ASMEL'S JOURNEY FROM Te'ena to Zayit was unbearable.

He tried to take it in stride and document the experience—after all, what other Mazik had ever undertaken a sea voyage? But he was miserably seasick, and the smell of salt stuck in his throat, and the other passengers on the boat stank of unwashed mortals. If only there had been some way to travel on the Mazik side: a friendly Ziz to carry him across the sea, or something along those lines. He hated boats, he concluded, and hoped never to see one again.

Worse, the sea voyage seemed to be accelerating the degradation of his memory. Twice he'd been up on the deck, trying to focus his eyes on the horizon as an old sailor had suggested, when he'd realized he had no idea where he was going, or why, and he'd had to take some of Toba's donated magic earlier than planned or else risk forgetting to use it at all. He would have to space the doses out further than intended, otherwise he would not have enough to last 'til the moon.

As they approached Zayit, Asmel stared at the railing in confusion: the harbor was completely full of ships, so many it did not look like it would be possible for more to sail in. Admittedly, he did not know how harbors normally looked, but this seemed untenable.

Behind him, a sailor said, "These are all mercenary ships. Looks like every one in five hundred miles. There's no way through."

"They're expecting an attack?"

"What else? Not sure how they're paying them all just to sit there, though. Must be costing a fortune." He nodded to Asmel. "Just wait, the captain's sent someone to talk to the harbormaster. They'll let us through. We've got cargo they want."

"Right," Asmel said, curling his fingers over the railing. "Of course."

It took until the next day for the captain to get permission to dock from the harbormaster, and then Asmel took what was left of his magic supply and made his way into the city. He had two weeks left before the moon, and not quite enough magic, and he did not know the location of the gate that month.

This was probably the only mortal city on earth that might have a moon codex, but Asmel did not think it would be wise to go looking for the salt guild in his current condition . . . He was too suspicious, and the Zayitis were already expecting an attack. Fortunately for him, Asmel was an astronomer. Given enough time and the proper equipment, he could calculate the location of the gate himself.

He was not sure he had enough time. As for the equipment, it was only a matter of convincing the Zayiti astronomers to let him use theirs.

Asmel bought an overly salty breakfast and secretly took another dose of Toba's magic before setting out, recalling there was a time, not long ago, when he would have gone days without sleep or food while working. These days, his body felt the effects of months of hard travel, and his mind was never quite as sharp as he recalled, as if he were thinking all the time through a fog. The most clarity he had was immediately after ingesting Toba's magic, but even then, his mind was not as it had been, and likely never would be again.

He put on his best Anabi accent, and went to the man he'd learned was the third-best astronomer in Zayit, and told him he was a visiting scholar looking to analyze the local sky. In exchange for borrowing his equipment, he offered up some of his own calculations regarding the orbits of some of the outer planets. The man was delighted, of course, because he was not capable of having made such calculations himself, and the knowledge would catapult him into position as Zayit's second-greatest astronomer.

Asmel felt more at ease in the man's lackluster observatory than he had in months. The telescope was not as good as he'd have liked, and the sextant was calibrated off by half a degree, but it was good enough. It would do. He would make do. He would find the gate.

The next day, two men from the salt guild showed up and dragged him away.

THE UNIVERSITY OF ZAYIT was spread out across several buildings, not housed in a single massive structure like Asmel's school in Rimon. Barsilay explained to Naftaly that he would know the students by their robes: those in the sciences wore deep blue, the social arts wore green, and the medical students—of whom there were relatively few—wore scarlet.

"I had no idea there would be so many students," Naftaly said.

"Since the University in Rimon was shut, Zayit has grown quite a bit," he said. "You'll hear plenty of Rimoni, if you listen."

"Do they go back home, once they've studied?"

"Some of them do," Barsilay said. "Others stay, or go elsewhere."

Barsilay and Naftaly had colored their cloaks to resemble the medical students', and together they walked on one of the many covered walkways that connected the university's buildings. Students in blue cloaks were arguing about some point of philosophy that had to do with free will; Naftaly suspected that Toba would have been interested, had she been there. "We'll stand out as medical students, you know," Barsilay told him. "There aren't many Mazik doctors, because Maziks don't suffer disease."

"Then why have doctors at all?"

"They treat injuries, but not many of those, either, since they mainly heal on their own. Mostly Mazik doctors treat the aftereffects of malignant magic, or sometimes a congenital problem. In Luz the Mazik doctors would treat humans, too, but that hasn't been the case for ages."

"So you were trained in how to treat humans?"

Barsilay gave him a wary look. "I did not complete my training. You know this. And I was a terrible student."

"So you keep insisting," Naftaly said.

"All right. I know a little. I could set your bones or treat an infection, if it wasn't too serious. But don't go trying to get yourself sick or injured just to test me. I haven't used any of this knowledge in years."

"I wasn't about to test you," he said.

"Isn't that why you came?" Not waiting for an answer, Barsilay made his way to a small group of scarlet-robed Maziks and began peppering them with questions about the medical faculty. A few minutes later, when he was satisfied he'd found what he needed, he took Naftaly by the hand, past the central square with a carved statue of something that might have been an hourglass with a globe on either side, and into one of the smaller buildings. "There's a lecture that starts in a quarter hour with a professor who might suit our needs," he said.

The lecture hall was ovaloid, with arced benches sitting on steps leading upward, like an amphitheater. The stage was set with a lectern, which after a few minutes was taken up by a Mazik man in a black robe with a scarlet collar, who Barsilay had said was called Saba b'Mazlia. His curly hair was close-cropped, and he gave the impression of a man who was talking about one thing while thinking of something else. Probably he had given this lecture many times before. He conjured a model of a phantom Mazik, showing within his transparent skin how his magical pathways flowed inside his body.

He began—and Naftaly was very grateful for the Peregrine's shade whispering in his ear, or he'd have understood nothing—by giving an introduction to how to examine a patient in order to determine whether an issue was congenital or based on an injury, because an acquired problem required a different approach than one present from birth. Even with the Peregrine's translator, Naftaly understood little of what was said, but eventually the professor came to the subject of intervention in congenital cases, and what might be better treated or left alone.

"One must consider the dueling issues of safety and function," the professor said. "A congenital issue is much trickier to treat. On the other hand, one must consider the quality of the patient's life. For example, in my practice I do not intervene until a defect disrupts the control of magic by more than fifty percent of what one would expect."

Here, Barsilay stood up. "Fifty percent in a fully Mazik patient, correct?"

The professor paused a moment, surprised to have his rote lecture interrupted, because now he was going to have to think a little. "Obviously I do mean that, yes."

"What about in a part-mortal patient? There the threshold might be different."

"In a part-mortal patient, there is a great deal that is different," the professor said, then seemed to return to his script. "So if our assumed threshold is fifty percent, then when we encounter one more strongly afflicted—"

Barsilay said, "Such as?"

"This is beyond the scope of today's lecture," the professor said, "so unless you have a specific question—"

"Say you have a part-mortal patient with a low quantity of magic, but some congenital issue that affects that magic. What sorts of issues are you looking for that would be different than in a full Mazik?"

"This seems abundantly unlikely."

"It's a hypothetical," Barsilay said.

The professor sighed. "In a hybrid population, there's an equilibrium between the Mazik and mortal parts of the body. In other words, the strength of the physical structures is consistent with the amount of magic present. But in some cases, this equilibrium does not develop. The structures are too weak to accommodate the magic present, and this can present in strange ways, particularly if the subject has elected to reside in Mazikdom."

"Why should that make a difference?"

"Because even a part-Mazik in the mortal world will have his magic partially suppressed."

"Meaning if he stays in the mortal world, the problem may be less severe?"

"That is what I said, but such a subject would be so rare and so unlikely to survive early childhood, I can't say it's ever been tested. Why are you asking this?"

"It's a hypothetical," Barsilay insisted. "But if you had a patient who had managed to survive early childhood with such a condition, how would you treat it?"

"If a move to the mortal world were not possible, the safest way would be to remove any remaining magic," the professor said. "But as you can imagine, not many would consent to that."

"And a less safe way?"

"That would be to strengthen the structure at the point of failure—"

"How?"

"You are monopolizing my class."

"We haven't reached the end of the scenario. Unless the issue is that you don't know what to do for this patient?" At that, the other students began to murmur, and the instructor's face darkened.

"I am very close to putting you out," he warned.

"I apologize," Barsilay said smoothly. "I only want to play this out to the end. Your patient refuses to have his magic extracted. Then what? Can you treat the condition medically?"

The man seemed to be struggling not to strangle Barsilay with his bare hands, but he said, "What are the symptoms? He's having trouble with transfigurations?"

Barsilay hesitated before saying, "Not quite. He has— In this scenario, he has issues with his senses. Attacks, occasionally, followed by pain and weakness."

The doctor looked at Barsilay very hard and said, "This doesn't sound like a problem of magic."

"Say you've determined it is"—Barsilay waved a hand vaguely— "*somehow*. Could it be treated medically?"

"No," the doctor said. "No, there's no medication for that. You'd have no choice but to find a way to strengthen the underlying structure, but it's very risky. Presuming you were dealing with a weak and failing organ, you might well blow a hole in the person you were trying to save."

This had all gone in a direction Naftaly had not anticipated. He'd lived with his visions, well, not happily, but with a begrudging acceptance for most of his life, and it had never occurred to him they were more than a bit annoying. He'd come to the university in the hope of learning to control them, and now this doctor and Barsilay were discussing things like points of failure and blowing holes in his brain.

Naftaly felt himself stand up. "Weak and failing?" he asked.

The professor looked to him in surprise. "Yes, the organ in question would be in poor shape if this had been going on long enough to seek medical care."

"So you're saying if you do nothing, he dies, and if you intervene, he probably dies as well?" Naftaly asked.

"That is the likely outcome. In which case it would be better to let nature take its course than to let him die under your hand." He turned to Barsilay. "There, now we've played it out. May I continue my class?"

Barsilay, visibly shaken, sat down, and Naftaly sat next to him, and for the next hour they listened to the professor discuss how to treat unhealing burns without paying attention.

After the lecture, Naftaly was following Barsilay from the room when the professor stopped them both. "You are newly arrived from Rimon?"

Barsilay screwed his eyes shut, which was when Naftaly realized the extent of his own error... He'd asked his questions in Rimoni, of course. "Yes," Barsilay said.

"And how many part-mortal patients are you planning to encounter in a city that forbids their existence?"

Barsilay said, "I was only trying to push out the boundaries of my knowledge. I know it's a far-fetched scenario."

"Indeed," the professor said. "Well, I appreciate a man who lives life with a question on his tongue. But if you'd really like to help your part-mortal friend with the failing brain"—here he looked pointedly at Naftaly—"why don't you come with me to my office and we'll examine him together?"

ELENA HAD SPENT the morning trudging down to the sea and back by herself since the old woman had been snoozing and Rafeq, of course, could not go. Rafeq had given her a water flask large enough to hold nearly a gallon of seawater, which was heavy once it was full, thank you, and then she'd trudged it all the way back into town, and then she'd sat in the kitchen and boiled it until all the water was gone and she was left with several spoonfuls of sea salt.

Performing all these tasks left Elena with a great deal of time to think.

The old woman had wanted to go in search of Naftaly and Barsilay at dawn, and Elena had suggested staying a bit, because if they really could get the killstone, that would help more than anything else they could do. Elena had asked her for one day, to determine whether she really thought it was possible. After that, they would leave Rafeq behind and go back in search of the others.

Rafeq had offered the general scope of his plan: He hoped to break the safira down into small enough parts that it could be inhaled, and some person would have to volunteer to do this thing. That person, then, would absorb all of Marah's magic as well as her memories, and what would be left behind would be the killstone of ha-Moh'to, which they could then use to kill Tarses.

How convenient for Rafeq that two salt-immune mortals had wandered into his house.

How very, very convenient.

And how fortunate that one of the mortals who had wandered into his house carried a very deep grudge.

Elena knew she could trust Rafeq even less than the woman who had swindled her for ten lentils, but for the chance to kill the man who had killed her daughter and threatened Toba, she would make do, at least for now.

Moreover, if Tarses were dead, there would be one less impediment to her taking Toba back to Petgal.

By this time, the old woman had roused and poked her way into the kitchen, and she stirred the salt with her finger in the cooling pot. "It amazes me that it takes so little to scare them," she said. "Too bad we didn't think to bring any with us."

Indeed it was too bad, and Elena had thought so often. A few sacks of salt and she'd be running the place. As it was, if she boiled enough seawater she'd eventually have enough to take over the world. On the other hand, seawater was heavy and she'd already tweaked her knee carrying this much. Ruling the world was probably better left to those with younger joints.

"So what is your plan for breaking down the safira?" the old woman asked. "Are you just going to roll it around in the bowl?"

That was one idea. Truthfully, Elena wasn't sure exactly what to do, since she didn't know whether she would need to apply pressure, and she was a bit worried about losing the fragments of the safira as they broke off. "It might help to use the salt to make a rasp, but I'm not sure how I'd attach it to anything."

Through the door, Rafeq said, "I could make you an adhesive."

"You could just come into the room," Elena called to him. "The salt won't leap up and attack you."

"I spent enough of my years in a salt prison," he said. "I'll keep well away now. Do you have something to attach it to, if I gave you adhesive, or will you need the rasp, too?"

The old woman rifled through the drawers and came up with a dull knife, which she handed over. "I have something," Elena said.

There was silence on the other side of the door. The old woman said, "You think this will work?"

"It should, according to what he's told us."

"Do you think you'll need all of it?"

"The salt?"

"You think I could pinch a bit to add to my dinner?"

"No," Elena said. From the other side of the door, there was a soft thump, and then the door opened a crack. "For goodness' sake," she muttered, and pushed the door open to find a pot containing a whitish liquid had been placed on the floor. A few feet back, Rafeq eyed her warily.

"I'm not going to attack you," she told him, and then took the pot of adhesive and went back into the kitchen, hearing the door click shut behind her.

She applied a thin layer to the knife, and then poured the salt over it, and then, once it was dry, she sat down to file away at the safira. "I'm going to start," she told Rafeq.

"Do you have something setup to catch the fragments?"

"Am I an idiot?" Elena was sitting over a glazed ceramic bowl, which she had wedged carefully between her knees. "All right," she told the safira. "Time to give up your secrets."

She ran the rasp over the surface, in one long, slow swipe. A wisp of blue powder appeared in the bottom of her bowl. And then she was hit in the face with an acrid odor, and the old woman was coughing, and then Elena's eyes were on fire.

She dropped the rasp into the bowl and ran to the window, where she and the old woman both stuck their heads out, gulping air.

"What happened?" the old woman asked.

"I don't know," Elena said. She took the cloth she'd tied around her hair and secured it around her nose and mouth instead.

"What has happened?" came Rafeq's voice.

"I'm trying to determine that," she said. "Don't come in."

"I wasn't planning to."

Taking the rasp out of the bowl, she could see immediately that no salt remained. Had it completely disintegrated? She dipped her finger into the blue powder in the bottom of the bowl and lifted it to her eye to examine it.

"Is that wise?" the old woman asked.

"Probably not," Elena said. The blue powder had a sheen to it. That was the safira, of course. It had worked, mostly. But as she squinted, she could see something else . . . a second silver-white element mixed in. She pulled the cloth down below her nose and smelled it. Nothing. Carefully, she touched the powder to the tip of her tongue.

The old woman cried, "Are you mad?" and Elena sputtered, because it burned, and the old woman poured several glasses of water down her throat to dilute it. "What were you thinking?"

"I wanted to see if it was still salt," Elena said. "It isn't, by the way."

"Are you alive?" Rafeq asked. "What happened?"

"I'm not having this conversation through a door, and the salt's gone, so you may as well come in," Elena said, and he carefully crept into the room, keeping well away. "Come and look," she said, indicating the bowl.

When he got as close as he meant to, she showed him the sparse contents. "The good news is it worked. The safira was ground down into the powder you see here."

"So what made you so ill? I heard both of you coughing."

"The salt...decayed." Elena showed him the knife, still coated with adhesive but nothing else. "It's all gone. It seemed to break apart into some kind of miasma and then this second powder. Do you see it?"

"I see it," Rafeq said. "What is it?"

"Not salt," she said. "Some constituent element? I don't know. But it seems fairly corrosive, if not toxic, at least to me. Not sure what it would do to you."

"I have no intention of touching it," he said.

"She ate it," the old woman pointed out.

"Are you mad?" he asked.

"Can we return to the experiment?" Elena asked. "We do have something that works."

"It barely works," the old woman put in.

"Barely working is still working," Elena said. "The only problem is the miasma."

"It's not the only problem," Rafeq said. "You've lost the salt it took you all morning to prepare."

"Of course that occurred to me," she said. "I'll just have to make more."

"How much more?" he asked.

Elena looked at the almost imperceptible smattering of blue powder in the bowl. "Do you have a scale sensitive enough to measure this?"

"I do," Rafeq said, "but you'll have to filter out the decayed salt first."

"It could be water soluble," she mused.

"Recall what happened when you mixed it with the water on your tongue," the old woman pointed out. "You can't assume it will behave the same as salt."

Elena tapped her smarting lip with her clean forefinger. "Magnet?"

"Does it look like iron to you?" Rafeq said.

"Could you make a specialized magnet, with magic?" Then, "Could you make a magnet that would attract the safira fragments?"

Rafeq thought a moment. "I think so. Yes. Bring the bowl upstairs."

They followed Rafeq up to the room he slept in, which had a small bed pushed against the wall under the window and a table littered with pieces of metal equipment he must have been using in earlier attempts to get inside the safira. Shoving things aside, he came up with a balance.

"You can't have weights small enough to measure that amount of powder," the old woman said.

But he did. The weights were on pieces of metal thinner than a leaf of paper, the smallest of which were nearly transparent. Rafeq made a ball of his own magic, which he used to pull the safira bits loose from the decayed salt, and Elena carefully put it on the balance ... It was slightly lighter than his smallest weight. Then she weighed the safira. Then she frowned. "I need paper," she said. "And a pen."

After giving her both, Rafeq watched intently as Elena wrote out an equation, accounting for the weight of the safira, the powder, and the salt she'd used. "How do you know how to do this?" Rafeq asked. "These are complex equations."

"My husband was a translator," she said. "Do you think I never read any of his books?" She scribbled a few more lines. "Damn," she muttered.

"What have you figured?"

"The amount of salt we'll need," she said. "Twenty pounds."

✦ SEVENTEEN ✦

ZAYIT'S SECOND-BEST ASTRONOMER was a man with aspirations. Asmel had been clever enough not to have gone to the salt guild asking about the gate. He hadn't been clever enough to realize the mortal salt guild would have feelers out looking for people trying to find it themselves. They'd been warned, apparently, by the Maziks: Conceal the location of the gate at all costs. If anyone arrives and asks for the codex, kill them. If anyone arrives and begins an analysis of the stars, kill them. Trade through the gate had been suspended indefinitely.

The salt guild did not kill Asmel for one reason: the man instructed to pass on the order suffered a heart attack on his way to work that morning and died. So Asmel sat in a makeshift cell in the basement of the mortal salt guild, and the men set to guard him were left to wonder if they should kill him or just keep him.

If they killed him without a direct order, it would not go well for them, so they decided to wait. The salt guild replaced the dead man with one of his subordinates. This man was not happy about his professional prospects, now that the guild had lost its most lucrative market and the price of salt was sure to plummet, and voiced the opinion that he should have gone into the oil trade with his cousin, who was making a killing selling to Katlav. He was very grumpy, very often, and the men guarding Asmel would have brought up the subject, but really, the man was awful and no one wanted to tell him anything.

In the dim light of the guild's basement, a pair of guards searched Asmel's belongings and found the remaining spheres of Toba's and Tsifra's magic. "I don't like the look of that at all," the first guard said.

"Who do you suppose he is?"

"Forget that. Do you think we can sell these?"

"How would we go about finding a buyer? We don't even know what they are. Hey," the guard called to Asmel, "what are these baubles in your bag?"

Asmel looked up from his spot in his cell. "Can I have one of those, please?"

"Shut up, you," the guard said. "Maybe they blow up? Throw one against the wall."

"Are you stupid?"

"Right," the first one said. "Right, that's a bad idea."

"They don't explode," Asmel said. "Really, there's nothing you can do with them at all."

"Then why did you want one?"

Asmel could not think of a response to that, because he could not exactly remember.

The guards put the baubles back in the bag and left it sitting in the corner. "Ah," said one, "I hate this post. Smells like mouse shit down here, doesn't it?"

"If we kill him, we don't have to sit down here any longer," the other suggested.

"But if we sit down here, we don't have to do anything," the other said. "Otherwise we're hauling salt ten hours a day."

"I don't understand why we're moving so much of it when the gate's shut."

"They're storing it up, didn't you know? I heard they paid double."

"Double, for it to sit in a storeroom?"

"I don't understand what they're doing over there. What the devil do the goat-eyes want with a thousand pounds of salt?"

"Damned if I know, but if they expect me to understand, they'll need to pay me extra."

Both men laughed.

"Some mess between their guild and their government, I heard."

"Aren't those the same thing?"

"Not yet," one guard said. "But we'll see how it turns out, I guess."

So the men ate and drank and played cards. And Asmel sat in a cell underneath the salt guild, and slowly forgot first why he'd come to Zayit, and then who he was, and finally that he'd ever been a Mazik at all.

DOCTOR SABA B'MAZLIA kept a suite of rooms in a nearby building and used the sitting room as an office. Naftaly tamped down his desire to ask a thousand questions . . . He'd already revealed far too much without meaning to. A fool, 'til the end.

"So," Saba said, once the other two were seated and he'd served them a hot infusion of something that tasted slightly like burned almonds, "Two men from Rimon, one mainly mortal, if my eyes are correct, and the other with a false arm." When Barsilay's eyebrow lifted, he said, "It's a very good phantom, but if you want it to be realistic you'll have to learn to do more with it. The musculature is too good for as much as you're favoring it." To Naftaly, he said, "I probably wouldn't have noticed you if you hadn't been so panicked in your questions."

Naftaly thought there was little point denying it now. "Did you mean what you said? About my brain failing?"

"Hm? Well, it's difficult to say without an examination, but we're not quite there yet." To Barsilay, he said, "You've some medical training, by your speech, but if you're newly here from Rimon it must have been long ago. Was your training in Rimon or somewhere else?"

Barsilay's eyes took in the room and the Mazik doctor, whose eyes were so dark he might have walked among mortals without them noticing anything amiss. He was short for a Mazik, shorter than Naftaly even, and had a slender face with prominent cheekbones. Evidently content with whatever he saw, Barsilay said, "I was trained in Luz."

"Long ago indeed, then," said Saba. "But I think you still remember how to take a history?"

Barsilay thought this over for a moment, and then asked Naftaly, "Can you describe your condition?"

Naftaly's eyes darted to the doctor, unsure of how much he dared reveal, but Barsilay said, "It's all right. He won't tell anyone else."

Naftaly was not sure how Barsilay could know that, but seeing as he was likely to die anyway, he said, "I have fits. I lose consciousness and then I have hallucinations, and when I wake up I'm quite ill."

"Can you quantify 'ill'?" said Barsilay. "For him, he doesn't know."

"I— I have terrible headaches and I'm weak. And my mind is muddled. But lately, they've been a bit different."

"Lately," the doctor repeated. "Since you came through the gate, I'd wager. I assume you were raised in the mortal world? You haven't been careful enough to have grown up in Mazik Rimon."

There was no use in denying it, so he gave a nod. The doctor said, "Go on, then."

"With the last one, he bled from his ear and nose both," Barsilay said. "We were hoping there might be some way to determine the source of the problem."

"Hm, yes, that would be the starting place. How regularly does this happen?"

Naftaly said, "It's variable. It could be as often as every few days or as seldom as every few months. I've never been able to find a pattern to it."

"And how long ago did it start?"

"Since my childhood. I can't remember not having them."

"Ah," said Saba. "Interesting indeed. And have you examined him?"

"No," said Barsilay. "I was worried my examination might harm him."

"Well then," said Saba, "I suppose I had better take a look." He rose from his chair and lay his left hand on Naftaly's forehead and his right along the base of his skull. "I need to pass a bit of magic into you to see if I can feel what's wrong. It shouldn't hurt, but I need you to tell me if it does."

"Wait," said Barsilay. "If his brain is already weakened, isn't it ill-advised to pass more magic into it?"

"It's a very small amount," Saba said. Then, "Do tell me if you feel anything."

Naftaly did feel something, a slight warmth that passed through his forehead and moved around inside his mind. It was not painful, but it was strange. And then a spot behind his left eye began to ache, a twinge, and then a stab of pain. He gave an involuntary shout and Saba pulled his hands away, but he felt himself slumping forward in the chair, and then everything went very quiet. He was out in the piazza again, and everything was coated in a blanket of snow. There were men on horses, dressed in purple, the leader in a diadem set with green stones. But the man's horse slipped on the snowy cobbles and went down; Naftaly heard the snap of the horse's leg as a voice—Saba's voice—was saying "It's too early for snow."

Then black dust began to fall from the sky, settling on the white snow, melting little pits where it landed. Not dust, but ash.

Zayit was burning—the buildings all aflame with a fire so loud it hurt Naftaly's ears. The canals had boiled dry; the olive trees in the courtyard of the palace had burned black. And then, when it seemed things could grow no worse, a black rain began to fall that, rather than extinguishing the flames, fed them.

Naftaly saw no people anywhere. Whether they'd escaped or burned already, Naftaly could not tell, but then a voice—Barsilay's voice—said, "There is no saving it."

When he came to, Saba was pulling back his eyelids and staring into his pupils. "He's awake," he told Barsilay, letting go of his face. "That shouldn't have happened."

Naftaly took a shaky breath. His head ached, but with less ferocity than usual after an episode. "How long was I gone?"

"Only a few seconds," Barsilay said. "Are you all right?"

"Snow in the piazza, the prince's horse is lame," Naftaly said softly, closing his eyes again as Saba said, "It's too early for snow."

Quickly, Barsilay asked, "Did you learn anything in your exam?"

Saba had gotten up and poured another cup of tea, which he pressed into Naftaly's hands, saying, "It's as I suspected. You have slightly more magic than your body can handle. Based on the lack of scarring, I'd say the damage is all recent. In the mortal realm these fits were an annoyance more than a danger, but being on this side of the gate has increased the discrepancy. The easiest solution would be to go back where you came from."

"No," Naftaly said. He took a long sip of the bitter tea, which seemed to ease his headache, and he wondered if Saba had put something else into it. "Is it fixable?"

"Certainly. If you pull out the magic, it will be completely resolved."

"Pull out my magic?"

"You'll live and die as a mortal," Saba said. "But isn't that what you always expected? You'll lose the fits, and you won't dream."

Barsilay asked, "What would that mean for his death?"

"Would he enter the void?" Saba shook his head. "I don't know."

"What about the other method you brought up earlier? Strengthening the underlying structures? Is that a possibility?"

Saba said, "He's too reactive. I couldn't even do an examination without triggering an episode—anything more would likely kill him outright."

Barsilay swore under his breath. Then he said, "Hang on, if the issue is too much magic, can't he just siphon a bit of it off each day? Get rid of the excess?"

Saba pondered this. "It's an idea. But I'm not sure his magic is strong enough to extract it with the precision required. The balance is so fine it would have to be a minuscule amount indeed, and if you couldn't be consistent you'd end up with a biphasic effect that would make him even worse. I'm not sure how to accomplish it." He put down his own tea. "You must understand that this is causing damage. If you suppress your magic, you will live a normal mortal lifespan. But if you don't, each time you suffer an episode it makes things a bit weaker. This will probably be the thing that kills you, unless you return through the gate."

"When?" Naftaly asked. "When will it kill me? In a year? In ten years?"

"I can't say with any confidence," Saba said, "only that it will happen eventually." He rose and went to the door, opening it. "If you don't care for either of my solutions, let me give it more consideration, will you? Come back tomorrow. Something may have occurred to me by then."

Barsilay helped Naftaly off the table, quietly, and the two men walked out into the street in their crimson cloaks. As they made their way back to the house, Barsilay said, "You saw snow, here?"

Naftaly said, "Yes, the prince's horse fell. And then Zayit was burning."

Barsilay gripped his arm tighter, his face stony. "Did you see any indication of when?"

"No. But you told me there was no saving it."

SEVERAL DAYS INTO their flight to Zayit, Toba Bet closed her eyes for her meager allotment of sleep and found herself in a dense wood. The air was cold and the trees were mainly evergreen, and beneath her feet was a crust of snow.

She was in the mountains, she decided, and not the ones she was used to; it was too cold. Had she come all the way to the Gal'in? From behind her, she heard the flutter of wings, like a hundred birds, and then whispers and then hisses and then voices saying, "We want to show you something."

Demons, she knew. She recognized their voices, gritty as sand. "No, thank you," she replied, turning, and seeing nothing but shadows. "Where are you?"

One of the demons landed on her shoulder, a shadow that grew and contracted, and when she tried to knock it away it sprang talons and held fast. It felt different than the demons from under the mountain—smaller and darker in the night—though perhaps this was only because she was dreaming. It bit into her skin through her dress; its claws were like ice.

"Let go," she said.

"No," it whispered. "Come and watch and be silent."

The demons that had been in the tree took flight again and she reluctantly followed them. Ahead, in a clearing, there was something on the ground: a person, sitting quietly, with one hand out. The demon on Toba Bet's shoulder forced her to a crouch in the snow, behind a thicket of thorns that caught on her clothes. She looked at the dark shape of the man, dark hair pulled back, his face impassive in the starlight.

It was Tarses.

In his outstretched hand was a tiny dream-flame. As Toba watched, a demon from some other part of the wood approached, circling ever closer 'til it was hovering over his palm.

Tarses clapped his other hand down over the top of the demon, then vanished into the waking world. There was no sign of the demon.

"He took it!" Toba said. "But how? This place is just a dream."

"Fool, fool, fool, there is no difference between here and there, not for us. We go through whenever we wish, and now he is here, and taking us. The heir of Luz gave us these mountains," the demons said. "He gave them to us for always, and now look."

"I'm sure the heir of Luz would rather the Caçador not be here, either," Toba Bet said. "What is he doing with them?"

"He is taking us! Taking us away!"

"But why?"

"We don't know!" the demons crackled. "The younger ones cannot resist the flame, and he takes them!"

"Why don't you stop him, then? Why are you letting him take them?"

"We cannot touch him."

"You're touching me right now."

"You are weak," they said acidly.

"Why ask me to help you then?"

"Because you are of Luz," they said, and Toba woke.

Tsifra was looking at her strangely as she sat up. "You have a little longer," she said. "Why wake up now?"

"I'm done," Toba Bet said. "I had a dream I didn't much care for."

"The void again?"

Toba Bet thought about whether to share her latest insight. There were two possibilities: either Tsifra already knew what Tarses was doing, in which case telling her made no difference, or she didn't, in which case she might learn something from her reaction. She said, "Tarses is taking demons from the Gal'in. Do you know what he's doing with them?"

Tsifra looked deeply troubled and said, "I don't know."

"Is he trying to make more Mazik-demons? Like these?" She cocked her head in the direction the demons had taken to hunt.

"I don't think so. Doesn't feel like Tarses to retread ground like that."

"Doesn't it? He made both of us."

Tsifra screwed up her face. "Then I suppose it's possible, but I don't know why he'd need another Atalef. One seems plenty to me."

"Well, what else could he be doing?"

Tsifra said, "Nothing that serves either of us."

ELENA SAT AT the worktable in Rafeq's room, drawing with a pen and several sheets of paper from the stack he'd made for her earlier. Rafeq's various magical paraphernalia were in a heap in the corner to give her an empty surface, and she was working from an earlier draft she'd made that morning, which she'd propped up on a pile of books.

She'd never been taught to draw, but she found she enjoyed it. There was a certain satisfaction to keeping the lines straight, when they needed to be, or curving a precise number of degrees. It was a different type of mental exercise than she was used to.

The one-day pause she'd requested of the old woman had been extended again and then again, and the old woman was growing fretful without Naftaly around. Elena understood but was so focused on her designs that she told the other woman to go look for them herself; she was too busy and her work was too important.

The old woman had been angry, and left, and come back an hour later because she'd gotten lost. "It won't be much longer," Elena promised. "Then we can look together."

"Couldn't you spare a few hours?" the old woman said. "I can't even ask for directions."

So Rafeq, at Elena's request, made her a map—a very nice one, in Elena's opinion—that showed you how to get back to Rafeq's house from anywhere in the city. Elena gave the map to the old woman, who clearly did not trust it, but who disappeared for another hour with it nonetheless.

Earlier in the day, she'd asked Rafeq, "Why do you want to kill Tarses so much? Vengeance?"

"Vengeance and two lentils is worth the lentils," Rafeq had said. "I'm more worried about what he might do than what he's already done. That demon is not all he stole from me."

"What do you mean? What did he take?"

"You must know I was imprisoned for giving magic to demons, and you see, now, why I was doing it. But those experiments were only the latest in a series. Demons, you see, are not properly physical creatures, and before I started giving them my magic, I wanted to see what else they could hold. My earliest work was with the elements."

"Water, air, and so forth?"

"Indeed," Rafeq had said. "Most of those experiments did not work. You put earth into a demon, it just becomes a malevolent stone. Air and it blows apart. Water and it turns to poison. But fire—"

"You put fire into a malevolent spirit already inclined to use it?"

"It becomes a living flame, impossible to control, ravenous." He'd inclined his head. "I admit it was a mistake."

"And this living fire … Tarses stole it?"

"Yes, and I've worried every day since about what he might do with it."

It made it very hard for Elena to concentrate, thinking that her little ideas and sketches might be all that stood between the city and whatever Tarses might have planned for it. Rafeq came in when she was halfway through what she hoped was her final draft. "Still at work, I see," he said. "You've made a mess of my things."

"You made a mess of your things. I only moved the mess," she said.

Picking up the stack of discarded papers, he flipped through them. "Tell me what you're doing."

"Can't you tell? I'm designing a machine."

Rafeq pulled a drawing out of the middle of the stack: version six, which she'd aborted almost immediately and which showed an apparatus that looked like a spinning wheel with a bellows attached to one end, the idea being that it would blow the miasma away before it killed you. "This one looks rather dangerous."

"It was an early attempt," she said, setting down her pen.

"Yes," he said, examining the drawing she was currently working on. "Walk me through this one?"

Elena was rather proud of this latest version. "The safira goes here," she said, tapping the metal cylinder that was at the center of the drawing and that had a crank on one end. "The funnel at the other end is where the salt is added, a bit at a time, and then any pulverized bits fall through the bottom here—see, there's a sieve—and on top of that will be a piece of your magic too big to go through, which will attract the safira particles, and then the decayed salt all ends up in this basin at the bottom."

"And the miasma?"

"I haven't finished drawing that part yet, but there will be a bladder of some kind here…" She tapped the drawing near where the funnel was attached. "The miasma is contained there, until we can find some way to dispose of it."

"How large must the bladder be?"

"That's the weak point—I don't know. Better to err on the side of too big, I think. The miasma created by twenty pounds of decaying salt might kill anyone in the room."

"Or any adjacent rooms," he agreed. "Better to make it very big indeed. And what is this?" He pointed at the second drawing on the page.

"The same machine. Only it's the view from a different angle, so you can see what you'll need to build."

His eyes crinkled at the corners. "You want me to build this?"

"Of course, you're the only one with real magic. Can't you do it?"

He looked over the picture again. "Yes. Yes, I can make this. It is a good design. You did this all today?"

"I've been working it out in my mind since the earlier attempt with the rasp."

"I see," Rafeq said. "Still, it's a strong vision to have come up with so quickly."

Elena tried not to feel too puffed up.

He said, "I'm intrigued to see what you'll do once you're Mazik."

Elena's expression faltered a bit. She'd known, of course, that someone would have to take in all this magic—that was the point of the work, after all—but he hadn't ever come out and said it would be Elena.

"You're concerned about that?" he asked.

"Wouldn't you be? What will it do to me, exactly? All that magic?"

Rafeq conjured a second chair out of the floor and sat down facing her. "I really don't know. It's all been theoretical up 'til now."

"But in theory," Elena said, "will I still be myself? Marah's memories run quite a bit longer than my own. I worry—"

"They'll become the more significant part of your character? I don't think they will."

"To be fair," she said, "you do have a vested interest in getting me to agree to this."

"Of course I do," he agreed, "and you're wise to see it."

"You've been flattering me all morning. It doesn't make me feel better for trusting you."

"Should I insult you, then?"

"I would find that less concerning."

"All right," Rafeq said, sitting back in the chair. "Here is my honest assessment. You are very clever. But not nearly so clever as you believe."

Elena's eyebrows crept up.

"So you didn't want the honest insult after all? It's no more than your companion tells you all the time. Should it rankle more coming from me?"

Elena said, "Hardly."

"I can see it does. I think you are probably a very clever mortal who has been undervalued most of your life."

Elena was not sure whether the insult was more to herself or to Alasar, which riled her more than she might have expected. She said, "My husband respected me."

"I'm sure he did. He respected you very much while you cooked his dinner and mended his trousers." He held up a hand at her objections. "I'm sure he did. But what outlet has there been for all your cleverness these long years?"

"You would trivialize my very existence? The domestic is no less valuable than the public. Perhaps if you'd had a clever wife, you wouldn't have ended up under a mountain."

He smiled. "I'm sure you're right, but no clever woman would have had me. My point is this: your intellect has exceeded your circumstances, up until now. That is why you value my opinion, now your mind is able to expand, and the truth is, I'm impressed indeed. As to your question, I'm not concerned that Marah's memories will alter your personality. You've lived most of your lifespan already; your spirit is reasonably fixed, I think. If you were a young woman, then I'd worry. I think you will be able to look at those memories with a reasonable detachment, and I think you'll use them well."

Elena nodded curtly and tried not to let on that he'd embarrassed her, because his opinion did matter, and not only because of her present circumstances. He was old, and wise, and she valued both of those things. But he continued, "I would like you to stay with me, once you are Mazik."

Such a suggestion startled Elena enough that she repeated, "Stay with you?"

"I should not ask this of you yet, before you know how you will feel. But when you have this magic and Tarses is dead, I would like you to come with me to Luz."

"Luz is beneath the sea," Elena reminded him.

"I think your companions will find a way to raise it, Elena. I am hopeful. For the first time since my imprisonment, I am hopeful. I think Barsilay will raise Luz, and Barsilay will be King, and when that happens, he will want a university in his city."

This was beyond anything Elena could have imagined, and she asked, "You want me to help you found this university?"

Rafeq reached out and took her hand. "Think on it?"

What a thing. What he was proposing was ludicrous. Go off to Luz to become, what? Rafeq's academic partner, at least for the few years remaining in her lifespan? She was not so deluded to think he meant any more than that. Still, she had to admit the idea of spending her last years using her mind to great effect was intriguing.

Unless they would not be her waning years. Would she be immortal, too?

She was being absurd, of course. "Think on it?" She laughed. "You're thinking twenty steps ahead of where we are. Luz is beneath the sea, the safira is still whole, and we don't even know how to find the salt we need to break it open."

Rafeq's gaze went very far away as he thought on this, and Elena's own imagination was whirling as she considered all he'd told her.

EIGHTEEN

AS THE DEMONS carried Toba Bet and her sister, she became aware that they were not precisely flying; they were gliding on the wind. Earlier, she'd been able to feel their wings beating. Now, their flight was smooth. She decided she preferred this manner of flight, which resulted in fewer punctures from the demons' claws. She watched the ebb and flow of the air and realized the demons were not creating wind, as she'd done when she'd sailed to Te'ena. They were calling wind from elsewhere, pulling it toward themselves, and changing its direction.

That such a thing was possible had never occurred to her. How much magic she could have saved on that trip, if she'd known how to do it. She wondered if this same principal accounted for how Atalef managed to produce such vast and long-lasting glamours— glamouring even the night sky, the very moon, despite not being fully Mazik. They'd learned efficiency, somehow, or else all demons were naturally like this. They were very good at making use of what was already present: the wind, the light, a little fog.

It was still daylight when the demons set the women down again, beside a river Toba Bet did not know. It had snowed a bit, and the ground was coated in a thin layer that crunched beneath her feet as she touched the earth.

"Why have we stopped here?" Tsifra asked, once she'd caught her breath.

"We shall not carry you over water," the demons said. "Your rule, not ours."

That rule had been intended to keep them from being dropped in the sea, but Toba Bet supposed a river could be equally deadly, and this one was wide enough to be quite deep in the middle. "Can you make a bridge to cross this?" Toba Bet asked.

"It's too wide," Tsifra said. "It would take too long. Should we just tell them to make an exception?"

"And have them drop us in the middle?" Toba Bet asked. "We could make a boat."

"That sounds safest," Tsifra agreed. "But we'll need to look for a downed tree or a log close to the water. All this flying is exhausting me."

"Stupid birdlings," the demons grumbled. "No imagination. Everything so complicated."

"What would you suggest, then?" Toba Bet asked.

"The river is water," the demons said. "Maziks can make the water hot. Maziks can make the water cold."

"Freeze the entire river?" Toba Bet asked.

"Fool, fool, foolish girl, how are you alive?" they said. "You needn't freeze the entire river to cross it—you only have two feet!"

Toba Bet turned to Tsifra. "Would that work?"

"Sounds like a recipe to fall in the river to me," she replied, "but it also sounds a lot simpler than dragging a log to the shore." She removed her boots and hung them over her shoulder, then approached the river's edge. She gingerly placed the sole of one foot on the surface of the water, and Toba Bet saw the water freeze beneath it, leaving a circle of ice around her. Then the ice tipped over and she fell in up to her knees while the demons laughed.

"You have to make it wider if it's going to bear your weight," Toba Bet said. "It's just the surface that's frozen, right?" She took a step herself and made the ice half again as large as Tsifra had done, and then put her other foot out, and then began to run across the river on a skin of ice. Tsifra, after a few moments, followed her.

"Good," the demons crowed. "Good, then let's be in the sky again."

"Not yet," Tsifra said. "We need to eat a meal."

"You ate already."

"That was yesterday," Tsifra said. "And we're making better time today. We have a few minutes."

"All this eating makes you heavier," they complained. "And us slower."

"You'll just have to suffer," Toba Bet said. She'd gathered a few twigs and leaves, and handed them to Tsifra to make a small fire to warm their cold hands and frozen feet.

"You should know about making us suffer," the demons said, "Toba Bet."

Tsifra looked up from her pouch of lentils, which she'd just poured into her hand. "Why do they call you that? Because you were a buchuk?"

"A lesser name for a lesser creature," the demons said.

"That's not very kind of you," Tsifra said.

"But this is what she calls herself," the demons said. "Even in her own mind."

"How can you know what's in her mind?" Tsifra asked, and Toba Bet went numb, and not from the cold.

"Because she screams it," they said. "It is her way of torturing herself, because she feels guilty for living, when you killed her better self."

Toba Bet sat in silence, not wanting to discuss her inner world with either the demons or her sister. No one had ever suggested to her that demons could hear thoughts. They'd intuited enough about her name to know it had to do with birds, but not the name itself, or they'd have used it.

What else had they heard, that she'd thought private?

"If Atalef had been able to hear my thoughts, I would have seen a sign of it," Tsifra said, handing Toba Bet a bowl of the stew she'd made. "They're bluffing."

"We are not," the demons grumped. "If you shout loud enough, of course we hear."

"Then is that really what you call yourself?" Tsifra asked, and at Toba Bet's obvious discomfort, she said, "I wasn't raised by scholars. I know nothing of philosophy. But it seems to me that you were a buchuk in the past, and now you're just a person."

"I hadn't asked your opinion," Toba Bet said. "What do you know about me or how I was raised?"

"Only what you told me," Tsifra said. "When we were young, you used to tell me about your grandmother."

"Did I?"

"All the time. She was always telling you not to do things, you said. Or feeding you too much." She laughed a little. "You told me once she caught you eating an entire cone of sugar, and you weren't allowed any fairy stories for a week."

"I'm afraid my memories of the time before I had the amulet are a bit hazy," Toba Bet said.

"But you remember your grandmother, don't you?"

"Yes, of course."

"So tell me something else. You said she was very tall."

"Taller than me," Toba Bet said. "About the same as you, I think."

Tsifra looked strangely pleased by this. "And she was the one who tricked Tarses into leaving you behind," she said. "Did she know he was a Mazik?"

Toba Bet said, "She must have, somehow."

"But then she must have known you were Mazik, too. She could have given you to him, instead of telling him you were dead."

Toba Bet snapped, "Why are you asking about her? What can it matter to you?"

The demons hissed, "Jealous, she is jealous!"

Toba Bet wasn't sure which of them they meant.

Tsifra went very quiet. "Never mind it." Toba Bet got up and put out the fire and told the demons, "Let's go."

Toba Bet let the demons carry her skyward, and hated their taloned touch on her arms and legs, and hated the sound of their wings, and hated the sight of her sister flying next to her.

What right did she have to ask about Elena, or comment on her upbringing or her inner thoughts? And the demons . . . Had she ever thought of anything important while she'd been with them? How much did they know of what was inside her mind?

They could not know everything. Tsifra was right: If they knew her actual name, rather than a vague sense of it, they'd have used it. Screams, they'd said. She mentally shouted some particularly pointed insults in their direction, which upon further reflection, was probably not the best tack taken with creatures who were carrying you through the sky. *Go ahead and drop me*, she thought. *See how it turns out for you.*

They did not drop her, nor give any indication they'd heard this inner monologue, but her mind had turned to her true name, her Mazik name, Tsifra N'Dar. The name Marah had left her in her last act as a Mazik, the name she shared with her sister. *Toba* had been the use-name of the woman who had created her—the original Toba. It was another shared appellation. She hadn't wanted to be called Toba Bet; it was insulting to her, to be named as some sort of diminutive version of her older self, and she'd hated it badly.

And yet, still she used the name in her own mind, even after the other Toba had died. The demons were correct: she did it to torture herself. No one would force *Bet* upon her; Asmel had long ago stopped calling her so.

She could be only Toba.

There was a demon clinging to her shoulder and it whispered in her ear, "Do you know why you cannot call yourself so? Because it is an admission you are all that is left."

Toba Bet felt the wind whip her face, stinging her eyes.

Toba felt the wind whip her face, stinging her eyes.

THE OLD WOMAN was very annoyed with Elena and let her know as often as possible. While the witch was playing scientist with that slippery Mazik, Naftaly could be anyplace. He could be in a Zayiti prison, or worse, and still Elena spent her days drawing pictures of some infernal machine, and then, when she was done, drawing them over again.

The old woman had gone out a few times with the Mazik's map, but truthfully she did not trust it; what if it was meant to trick her away from the house, and Elena? The map showed her where she was and lit a pale-blue path back to the house. It worked when she tried it, but that did not mean it would always work, and she was afraid to go much out of sight of the house. She was frightened of Maziks, frightened of Zayitis, whom she could not understand, and frightened of the city that seemed to be designed specifically to make an old woman feel as lost as possible.

She had not felt so helpless since Savirra.

One morning, she and Elena had argued again about finding Naftaly, and Elena had told her the work with the safira was a higher priority.

"You've been seduced by that Mazik," the old woman had told her. "You can barely think for it all."

"I beg your pardon!"

"He's got you all turned on your head, saying all the things you like best, how clever your mind is and so forth. You haven't even stopped to think what sort of person he is, and if you should be joining yourself to him."

"I am not joining myself to him."

The old woman went on without pausing. "He just makes things without thinking of the consequences—sentient demons, living flame for Hashem's sake, horrible poisons and miasmas—and you're just going along with it, because he scratches some itch of yours. The man is a scourge!"

"He's not a scourge," Elena had said. "He's trying to save everyone from Tarses."

"At what cost? How many deadly plagues is he going to manufacture trying to counter the one he made before? Elena, he's making things worse."

Elena, at that point, had put the old woman out of the kitchen. So she took a few coins from Elena's purse, stole a small packet of salt, and marched out into the street, determined to find her way back to the other house and never to return to Elena at all. If only she could remember the name of the Mazik who lived there. Mir something? She could not recall the surname. Barsilay had only said it the one time.

So she wandered the street, unsure how she'd ever find her way since she couldn't ask the Zayitis, who peered at her curiously while she kept her veil close around her face. Taking out the map, she mentally divided it into twelve sections, as if it were the face of a clock, starting at six o'clock—near where Rafeq's house was—and then moving forward to seven, then eight. She thought she would recognize the bridge near the house Barsilay had put them in, if only she saw it again. She went up one street and down the next, peeking through alleys and listening for canals she might have overlooked. Everywhere she went were the wealthiest-looking people she'd ever seen, wearing colors that must have cost a fortune to dye—and Barsilay had said those colors weren't made by magic. They were all dressed in mortal-made silks with embroidery she suspected had likewise been done by hand, and she had the strange realization that not one time did she see anyone who might have been poor.

Where, she wondered, were the beggars? Maziks could make most anything truly necessary by magic, but the city still ran on money, and cities that ran on money had poverty, didn't they? Because what was the point of wearing all that finery if it didn't distinguish you from anyone else? And was it really worth dealing in poison, if all it got you was a nicer hat? The old woman went down another street, saw a bridge, and grew increasingly hopeful 'til she realized it was the wrong one again, and she had to stop and rest her legs.

If she put out a cup, would Maziks put coins in it, as people had done back in Rimon? What would they do if a beggar showed up?

Naftaly had said there was a lentil blight in the southern cities, and it was spreading. She wondered if such a thing had ever happened before: hunger, amongst the Maziks. It would only benefit La

Cacería if Maziks suddenly woke up with empty larders. It seemed to the old woman there were only two reasons a man might take up a weapon and fight for a cause he did not much believe in: either he was afraid, or else he was hungry. The Maziks in Rimon were being threatened by the Queen, the Maziks in Tamar were hungry, and it was in Tarses's best interest for those conditions to worsen.

She watched the great goldfish swim in the canal. In mortal Rimon, someone would have fished those out long ago and served them for dinner. What an absurd place this was. No wonder Naftaly had gotten lost in it. She missed him very badly.

Rising again on her swollen feet, she decided to proceed in searching a little longer, but noticed that below the bridge was a group of cats—strays, most likely, though they looked well fed. She'd always liked cats; she often had one or two around, when she'd been out on the street. Better company than most people, truth be told, and they kept the vermin away, which she supposed was why there were so many in Zayit. Probably the Zayitis kept all their lentils in one place, and whatever magic they used to keep out the mice was inferior to a pack of hungry cats.

Or else the cats were decorative, like the goldfish.

She tsk-tsked at the cats, and one of them, a small calico, looked up and cautiously stalked closer, then closer. Then she was sniffing at the old woman's skirts and then she was in her lap, and the old woman gingerly set her wizened hand on her back. "I'm sorry I haven't got any food for you," she said, but then she remembered the coin in her pocket, and nearby there was a small market stall, selling snacks and sweets to the Maziks who were coming and going. Gently moving the cat, she went to watch. The man who was running it was taking lentils from a basket, and changing them to various types of food, and then adding his own spices at the end.

She knew enough Zayiti to ask for fish, and he gave her some sort of fried fish on a wooden skewer, which smelled like the sorts of spices people with money used in Rimon. She took a bite and found it much nicer than most of the Mazik food she'd had until now.

Deciding she'd better not risk salting it as she'd planned, she went back to the small calico, and gave her half of it, which encouraged the rest of the little family of cats to swarm around her.

A man came from a nearby shop and began to upbraid her, pointing at the cats and saying only one word she could understand: "dirty." He was angry at her for feeding them in front of his shop. He wanted her to leave, and here was a scene she remembered. Her fish was gone now, anyway, so she turned on her heel, trying to look unafraid, and walked away.

She walked by the bridge, where one of the bloated goldfish had gone belly-up in the water. While the shopkeeper watched, she reached into the canal, fished it out, and threw it onto the ground by the bridge for the cats.

The shopkeeper looked at her with unbridled disgust. The old woman went off to look for Naftaly again.

She walked until her heels bled in her shoes, but still she did not find him.

SOMETIME AFTER THEIR visit to the university, Naftaly and Barsilay leaned against the railing of the stone bridge nearest their house and watched the Maziks go by. Shades in front of shops and houses cleaned up the remnants of the Zayit Moon festival, which had left shimmering slips of paper in the street that had yet to break down or make their way into the canals. At the base of the bridge, a small pride of stray cats had pulled a decaying fish out of the water and were alternately eating it and fighting with one another.

They had not yet had any luck finding Elena and the old woman.

The Peregrine had promised to look for them, but Naftaly knew it was not her priority, and he thought he should be looking for them himself. But several hours of wandering each day only left him lost and tired, and there was no trace of them anywhere he could see.

Barsilay was staring down at the canal, pulling at his lower lip, when he looked up at Naftaly and asked, "Does your head still hurt?"

This, because earlier in the morning, he'd been thinking of the old woman and had a vision of a dead fish, which he thought must be a bad omen except that it had been *this* particular dead fish, being feasted on by the cats of Zayit. It had cost him a nasty headache and a bleeding ear, too, and the old woman was decidedly not nearby. Still, they'd decided to wait to see if she made an appearance, and thus far she had not.

"No," Naftaly said. "It never hurts after an hour or two. Honestly, I think the doctor was overstating things. I'm no worse than I've always been."

"Do you truly believe that?" Barsilay asked, and Naftaly was quiet, because he did not.

"Saba said there might be some way to treat it."

"Doctors often say such things," Barsilay said. "The truth is, to treat the problem we need to understand the cause. If your mixed heritage were causing it, we should see some evidence elsewhere. But there isn't any. I don't understand."

Naftaly understood perfectly—his condition was deteriorating, and it was in his brain. The cause of it was mostly unimportant, and since Barsilay did not seem to appreciate his false optimism, he decided to forgo any further claims of denial. "So I suppose my choice is between a brief life and a dreaming death, or a longer life and the void." Naftaly pulled at the ends of his sleeves. "Doesn't seem like much of a choice, does it? Especially since I don't know how long I'll live anyway. The treatment's worse than the disease."

"Yes, but—"

"You'll still be able to see me, after I go," Naftaly said. "And really, what's the difference? We always knew I wouldn't live as long as you. What's a year or two, versus a few extra decades?"

"Please stop."

"I'm only sorry my visions can't be of more use to you. If there were some way to focus them, I could have helped you so much more than seeing bloated fish in the street."

"You help me enough," Barsilay said. "You are not a tool to me, no matter what the Peregrine might suggest." He sighed. "A better man than I would send you home at the next moon."

"What home would that be?" Naftaly said quietly.

"I could send you to mortal Zayit with enough silver to last you the rest of your days."

"I wouldn't go."

"I'm capable of forcing you," Barsilay said.

"Then I would come back again," Naftaly said. "Let's not think about this now. There's no gate tonight in any case . . . Are you listening?"

Barsilay's eyes were on the cats, which had picked the fish clean and were squabbling about the bones. Then he stood up a little straighter and bolted down the steps of the bridge. The cats scattered, but he managed to grab the slowest of the lot, a shaggy calico who complained loudly and tried to free herself.

"What are you doing?" asked Naftaly.

"Come on," Barsilay called. "We're going back to see Saba."

WHEN THEY RETURNED to Saba's house, there was no answer at the door.

"This is foolish," Naftaly said. "He's probably back at the university."

"Then we'll wait."

"On his doorstep? With a cat?"

"The cat is fine."

"Because you've enchanted it to sleep!"

"Well, what else was I to do with it?"

"This is absurd. Let's go back home, we'll come back tomorrow."

"We'll wait," Barsilay insisted.

"Why are you—" And here the door opened, and the pair went quiet indeed, because the person standing there was not Saba but Efra b'Vashti, the Savia della Mura.

"I thought I heard Rimoni," she said. "I did not expect it to be you. With a cat. Why did you bring a cat?"

Naftaly and Barsilay looked at one another. Naftaly had no idea how to answer, because he, too, failed to understand the cat, and Barsilay seemed disinclined to comment. From inside, Saba called, "Is it the Luzite and his Rimoni companion?" He came up behind Efra. "Oh, and they've brought a pet."

Quickly, Naftaly said, "We don't mean to disturb you when you're with your…"

"Sister," Saba said. "You should come inside. My, isn't that a chill? Almost as if there might be snow."

"It's too early for snow," said Efra.

"We shall see," he countered. "My sister was just leaving."

"Hm," she said. "Yes, well, I suppose I was." She exchanged a long glance with Saba and left.

Inside, Barsilay tossed the cat onto the doctor's table; she immediately jumped down and hid underneath, hissing and spitting.

"Why have you brought me this… creature?" Saba asked.

Barsilay pointed a finger at the creature in question. "Why does it look like that?"

Saba said, "It is a cat. Does it seem unusual to you in some way?"

"I'm referring to the coloring," Barsilay said. "Why is it like that?"

"Three-colored cats are common enough," Saba said. "I'm not sure what you're getting at."

"But why?" Barsilay insisted. "Don't kittens resemble their parents?"

"I think you should speak plainly. What are you saying?"

"I'm saying that the cat's body isn't a complete enmeshment of its parents. It's more like… a mosaic. The black parts come from one parent, the ginger the other."

"And the white? Has the cat three parents?"

"No, but you often see cats that are white and black or white and ginger … I think that could have come from either." He pointed at Naftaly. "What if he's the same? What if his body is the same? He has one parent of mixed heritage, and one fully mortal, so far as we know. You assume that the problem is localized to his brain. I'm thinking it may be more localized even than that, which is why he has no other symptoms. And if the problem is so limited in scope, then the treatment can also be localized, without suppressing all his magic."

Naftaly, who was only barely following the conversation, said, "How?"

Barsilay turned to him. "We keep the magic from building up in the weaker spot."

"I'm not sure how that would be possible," Saba said. "Siphoning it off once or twice a day would not be enough. You would need to constantly be pulling the magic out of that area."

Barsilay smiled broadly, pleased with the workings of his own mind. "Do you have any al'qot at hand?"

Saba looked puzzled for only a moment, and then delighted. "I don't. But I know where to lay hands on some."

He returned sometime later with a round silver box the size of Naftaly's palm. Opening it, he revealed what Naftaly had feared: a septet of slimy black leeches, the size of his smallest fingernail.

"Oh," Naftaly said, his stomach turning. "No."

"Don't be so squeamish," Saba said. "If your friend's assessment of your condition is correct—and I think it is—you and these creatures will become the best of friends."

"I don't see how treating me with leeches is going to help anything."

"Mortal leeches feed on blood," Barsilay explained. "Al'qot feed on magic."

"We use them sometimes for injuries," Saba went on. "They seem to be able to repair magical pathways a bit, if they're applied before scarring sets in."

"But I'm not injured," Naftaly said. "Isn't that what you just established?"

"That's not how we'll be using them," Saba explained. "The idea is that the portion of your brain that's responsible for your fainting and headaches is sustaining damage from the magic made elsewhere in your body. The al'qa is meant to siphon that magic out of the area before it can cause any problems."

"Like sucking the poison out of a snakebite," Barsilay said. "Only it's more of a long-term solution."

"You're saying I'm going to have one of these disgusting things attached to me for the rest of my life?" Naftaly asked.

"It is likely that the structure will strengthen once it's no longer being continually injured, but only time will tell for certain," Saba said.

"How long?" Naftaly insisted.

"Could be three months, or a hundred years, or not at all," Saba said. To Barsilay, he added, "I'm truly impressed. Honestly, well done. Assuming it works."

"And if it doesn't?" Naftaly asked.

"Then you'll likely faint after a while," Saba admitted.

"But then we'll just remove the al'qa," Barsilay assured him. "It doesn't take enough magic to be a real threat to your health."

"It's a slow feeder," Saba agreed. "Come here, I want to mark the placement." Very reluctantly indeed, Naftaly stepped forward, letting Saba probe the area behind his left ear. "Aha," he said, and then pierced the skin with what felt like a needle, and then—and here Naftaly thought he would faint straightaway—he quickly placed one of the al'qot.

"There we are," said Saba. "Well done, you."

"You mean in not passing out?" Naftaly asked miserably.

"I was speaking to the leech. It's attached. But don't touch it yet, let it get settled."

"I have no intention of touching it at all. Ever. Under any circumstances." To Barsilay, Naftaly said, "Can you take it off?"

Barsilay ignored this plaintive request and asked, "How do you feel?"

"Like there is something disgusting near my face."

"Yes, yes, apart from that?"

"I feel perfectly normal. But I usually feel normal! I don't feel bad most of the time, you know."

"All right," said Saba, "I'm going to try an experiment."

"Is that wise?"

"It will almost certainly work," he said. "I'm very excited about this."

"Yes," Naftaly said, "but that doesn't seem to be a good reason to—"

"Quiet, I'm doing it." And Saba touched the area near the leech with a finger, and Naftaly felt a faint buzzing warmth, and then … nothing.

"Well?" Naftaly asked.

"It's glowing, do you see?" Barsilay said excitedly.

"I see," Saba said.

"How is your head?" Barsilay asked.

"It's fine."

"No vision? No headache?"

"Actually, I do have a bit of one—could you stop crowding around my ear and shouting at each other?" The pair backed off, both looking more than a little smug. "Well?"

"I pushed a bit of magic into the area. No more than I did yesterday, which triggered the attack. But this time, it was all absorbed by the leech before it did any damage."

"But …" said Naftaly, because this meant he would no longer have any visions at all. Hadn't they gone to Saba in the first place to make his visions more useful? Everything seemed to have gotten all turned around. The Peregrine had called him Barsilay's greatest asset. Now he was just a mortal with a leech behind his ear.

"So here is what you must know," said Saba, blazing past Naftaly's existential distress. "They won't work if they aren't hungry, and al'qot only feed for a day before they fall off. So once a day, at the same time, you'll have to replace the one behind your ear with a fresh one. Cycle them."

Cycle them? They all looked alike. "How do I tell them apart?"

"Here," said Saba, "let me show you." He pulled the leech from behind Naftaly's ear and showed it to him. It seemed to glow from within. "That glow will fade over time. So long as the fresh one you apply is completely black, it will feed. Oh! And you'll have to keep it moist. If it dries out, it will die. Oh, and do be careful when you're removing it at the end of the day. If you squeeze it, it may regurgitate the magic back into your brain."

"How am I to remove it without squeezing it?"

"Just coax it gently," Saba said. "I'm sure you'll get the hang of it with practice. Come back again in a month and I'll reexamine you. Or sooner, if you notice a change."

Naftaly had many other questions he could not ask, but instead he followed Barsilay out into the street, dazed.

"You looked peeved," Barsilay said. "Is the leech troubling you?"

It was, but that was not really the problem. "The entire purpose of our seeing him was for me to be more useful, to find some way to make my visions less random, and instead we've just rendered them inert."

Barsilay stopped and set his hands on Naftaly's shoulders. "It helps keep your mind from sustaining further damage, and that's more important."

"Is it? Have you forgotten all that's at stake here?"

"Of course I haven't, but you can't do anyone any good if this kills you, and Saba says it will."

"He doesn't know everything," Naftaly said.

"We can't risk it," Barsilay said. "Listen, he's given you a treatment that can't make you worse. If the leech isn't doing right by you, you can simply remove it. But won't it be better for you, not collapsing and seeing horrible things you can't control?"

Truthfully, it did sound better, and six months ago if some mortal doctor had suggested such a treatment, Naftaly would have leapt at it. But now it seemed like he was giving up something essential . . . And in the back of his mind he also wondered if he was giving up his ability to find Toba, too. Would this affect his dreams? He had not had a chance to ask.

"Let's find something to eat," Barsilay said, taking him by the hand.

THE OLD WOMAN had thrice tried to find Barsilay's house, and thrice failed. "It's almost as if it doesn't want to be found," she said. "I can't understand it. The city's not so large."

This concerned Elena a great deal, because if the house somehow didn't want to be found, it could indicate that Naftaly was in trouble. Really, she ought to have gone herself and not left it to the old woman, but her work with Rafeq seemed the higher priority. If the men were in danger, the best she could do for them was make sure they had a way to deal with Tarses ... Or so she told herself. The truth was, she enjoyed puttering about Rafeq's small laboratory, with its endless supply of paper and Mazik gadgets he was always happy to explain to her—not as if she were some foolish cow of a mortal, but simply as if she were someone from abroad unused to local customs.

"Don't go back out tomorrow," Elena told the old woman. "You'll only exhaust yourself."

"I won't give up trying to find them," she protested. "I think you're so focused on the safira, you've forgotten why we came."

"We came because we were fleeing Tarses!"

"We came because we were protecting the boy!" The old woman got up, pushing her chair back. "And now we've lost him."

"He's not a boy any longer, and he's not alone. You think Barsilay will let anything happen to him?" Elena asked.

"We don't even know they're still together! Barsilay is a Mazik. Who knows what he's really thinking?"

Rafeq peeked around the doorframe.

"You can't have been hiding from an old woman's temper," Elena told him.

"I wasn't," he said. "I was making sure you didn't have any salt out." To the old woman, he said, "I keep my ear to the ground. If something had happened to two Rimonis, I'd have heard about it."

"So why can't I find them?"

"Perhaps you aren't looking hard enough," he suggested.

"Damned Maziks," she muttered, and slumped down on her chair again in the corner.

"You've been in here all day," Rafeq told Elena. "I wanted to know what you were doing, and have you come look at the machine."

"Have you finished it already?"

"Not yet," he said. "I wanted you to check what I have so far before I continue. Is that the decayed salt you have there?"

It was. She had the safira in front of her, plus several grains of the decayed salt she was handling with tweezers Rafeq had made for her. "I tried to determine if the decayed salt would still work to break down the safira. But it didn't."

"Does that mean it's inert?" Rafeq asked.

"It implies it," she said. "But it's certainly toxic to mortals, which doesn't sound so inert."

"Toxic to mortals doesn't necessarily imply toxic to Maziks," he said.

"I know it doesn't. But does it matter? All we're trying to do is break down the safira, and it clearly doesn't do that."

"You're right," he said. "But if our work is leaving some kind of by-product, I'd like to know what it is, wouldn't you?"

"Well, if you'd like to eat some of the decayed salt and see what happens, then by all means, go ahead."

He smiled a little. "I think we can try something a little less dramatic." He made a knife from the pen on the desk and cut two small pieces from the flesh on the inside of his elbow while Elena winced, and the old woman said, "Is this really the only way to do this?"

Rafeq said, "I would prefer to test the poison on a demon, but we haven't got one, so I'll have to do." He set the flesh on a metal plate and handed Elena a glass dome he kept on the table. "This will magnify the image so you can see what is happening better."

"You want me to look?"

"Yes, because first you'll be applying salt, so you can compare the reactions. I assume you have some left over?"

"A bit," she said, taking Rafeq's precision scale and measuring a grain of the salt that remained from her earlier experiment. She carefully placed it onto the sample, and watched through the lens. "Nothing's happening yet," she said.

"It may not be enough," he said. "It takes a fingertip's worth of salt to kill a full-grown Mazik. I'm not sure how much it will take to affect a small piece of skin."

So she added a grain, then another, then another, then at seven grains the sample began to shrivel, then turn black. She shuddered. "All right," she said, taking the phial of decayed salt she'd carefully retrieved from the kitchen. The grains were far finer than normal salt and difficult to measure, but she managed to get enough to equal a single grain of salt, and applied that to the sample. Instantly, the skin sizzled, and shriveled, and blackened.

Rafeq took a pace back, holding his sleeve over his nose and mouth. Elena took both samples and swept them into a ceramic pot.

"I suppose congratulations are in order," he said grimly. "You've just discovered a poison at least seven times deadlier than salt."

The old woman got up from the chair and examined the piece of burned skin in the bowl. "And if you do manage to get enough salt to break down the safira, how much of this toxin will you create in the process?"

Elena said, "I haven't calculated that yet. I'm not sure."

"But you said twenty pounds of salt, so you'll have quite a bit of this when you're finished," she insisted. "Do you really think it's worth it? To get the killstone, if it means creating so much of this toxin? What in the world will you do with it all? Bury it in the ground? And that's to say nothing of the miasma."

"I don't know," Elena said. "But what choice do we have?"

"To leave the safira alone," the old woman said.

"And let Tarses kill everyone in Zayit?"

"You don't know that he means to do that. Why would he want to kill everyone?"

"Do you think he intends to kiss them on the cheek? You're not so ignorant as that. You've seen too much."

The old woman frowned. "I'm sure he intends to do terrible

things. I just want to make sure you can control what you're about to create."

"Well," Elena said, sitting back, "it's a moot point, anyway, unless we have some way to get our hands on twenty pounds of salt, which we don't."

But Rafeq said, "There may be some way to do that, after all."

"And how dangerous is this way?" asked the old woman.

"When it comes to dealing with the salt guild, everything is dangerous."

NAFTALY VERY QUICKLY found that he did not like having a leech behind his ear. Saba had explained that the al'qot secreted some kind of numbing agent that rendered them painless once attached, but this didn't account for the fact that the blasted thing itched like the devil.

And that was to say nothing of the fact they were inhibiting his magic and visions both. He'd been able, however briefly, to imagine a future in which he could be something like Barsilay's equal—a king's equal, no less. He'd been a bit deluded—he knew it was fantasy—but even so, he'd gone off to see Saba with the idea of becoming a man who could counter the Caçador himself. Now he was not sure he could even dream.

"I'm not going to be able to tolerate this," he told Barsilay. "I can't even think about anything else."

"It's only been a quarter hour," Barsilay said. "You'll have forgotten it by the end of the day." He reached out to tug on Naftaly's hand, which had crept up and was scratching at the skin behind the leech. "Stop that. What you need is a distraction."

"Like contemplating the fact that this city is about to fall to a blood-soaked monster?"

"I was thinking of getting lunch, but I suppose your way works, too."

"Barsilay."

"That's many months off," Barsilay said. "It will keep another day.

Look: the sun is out, the air is crisp, and I have money in my pocket to buy my sweetheart a fine meal." He clapped Naftaly on the shoulder. Naftaly could feel the leech jounce against his skin. But he'd never been anyone's sweetheart before, so he said, "Buy me lunch, then."

The spot Barsilay found for them was some cross between a tavern and an inn, a bright space with a view of the olive grove in front of the palacio. Fancy Maziks were eating meals Naftaly could identify as smelling like fish or lamb, with spices he had never encountered before, never having had enough money to buy such things. The room was lit with light-stone chandeliers, despite the fact that it was the middle of the day and bright enough already, and several of the fancier ladies had light-stones set in their ears, as if it were some novel trend. There were so many dishes being served Naftaly could not believe there was even a set menu, but then, why would a Mazik inn have such a thing? Lentils were lentils, at least until some clever Mazik cook made them into something else with the wave of a hand. He wondered, vaguely, what was the point of eating in such a place at all, when any Mazik child could make whatever food he wanted without even lighting a fire.

"The value of the food," Barsilay explained, "is all in the spices."

Among people who could not salt their food, spices would seem to be doubly important, Naftaly thought. Everything he had eaten up 'til then had been unbearably bland. "I suppose that must be where Maziks would be most likely to spend their money," he said.

"Indeed. I was forever in trouble with Asmel for spending too much. 'We have no income. What can you be thinking?' But what is life, without flavor? Now, what do you want?"

One of the shades had come to hover by their table, awaiting some instructions. "I have no idea," Naftaly said. "Is the meat kosher?"

Barsilay laughed, once.

"Is it a silly question?"

"Only because Toba asked the same thing. The beef was never a cow in the first place, so I think it is."

"Is that how it works?"

"You tell me."

"But wouldn't that imply that Mazik-made pork would likewise be kosher?" Naftaly asked.

Barsilay tilted his head to one side. "We don't make pork."

"Don't you? Why?"

"It never occurred to me to wonder about it. Why don't you eat cats?"

"Cats certainly aren't kosher," Naftaly said.

"Is that the only reason?"

"Why? Do Maziks eat them?"

"Don't be absurd."

"Why is it absurd?"

To the shade, Barsilay said, "He wants chicken. Something with saffron, I think. Make it rich, he's too thin."

"I'm not."

"I will have fish," Barsilay said. "Unless the smell will trouble you?"

"Eat what you like," Naftaly said, and once the shade was gone, "You're bickery today."

"Because I asked for fish?"

"Just in general!"

"I suppose I'm in high spirits."

A shade—it may have been the same one, or a different one—deposited a bowl of olives on the table together with two small glasses of wine. Barsilay lifted his and sniffed it and drank.

"Is the wine mortal-made, too?" Naftaly asked.

"You know, I can't tell. I suppose we'll find out when the bill comes."

Naftaly ate an olive, finding that it had no pit and, of course, no salt, and he wondered how in the world it was possible even to cure olives without salt. It had a peculiar taste, but he was hungry, so he ate another, then another. At the next table, the Maziks were being presented with some sweet-smelling concoction that a shade set aflame, filling the room with the scent of burning sugar. The smell must have done something strange to the leech, because he felt a strange sensation of warmth behind his ear, which subsided after a minute. Naftaly asked, "Is it because the doctor called you clever?"

Barsilay's expression faltered. "What can you mean?"

"That your spirits are high. Is it because you had a compliment from a man you respect?"

"I am not a child."

"It isn't childish to enjoy compliments."

Barsilay finished his wine. "Chasing them is."

Naftaly drank his own wine. It was strange enough that he suspected it was not mortal, but then, his own experience was so provincial he may not have been capable of recognizing a Zayiti table wine. "Barsilay," he said, "you cannot be a doctor."

"I'm well aware," Barsilay said. "You needn't explain my limitations to me."

"They aren't your limitations," Naftaly said. "It's just that you have another path."

Their own shade returned, bearing a dish of heavily sauced chicken and another of fish, which it set down before producing two additional glasses of wine and then leaving again. Barsilay said, "I wish to discuss my path as much as you wish to discuss the parasite behind your ear." He cut off a piece of pink-fleshed fish and stuffed it into his mouth rather gracelessly. "Both are necessary and disgusting."

"So you admit it's necessary?"

"I've promised the Peregrine," Barsilay said. "So even if I disagree, I have no choice now, unless she gets herself killed, which seems unlikely. Eat your chicken."

The sauce was flavored with white wine and some spice that had a flavor Naftaly could not describe as tasting like anything other than itself. Perhaps, he thought, this was why Maziks could not replicate it; it was too peculiar and nebulous a thing to make from nothing. He was not sure if he liked it or not. It did not taste much like something his mother would have made. But he did not want to disappoint Barsilay, so he said, "I've never eaten saffron before."

"No? It's made from flowers, you know. More expensive than gold in the mortal world. Doubly so here."

"Doubly? How do you intend to pay for this?"

"Don't worry about such things."

"Spoken like a man who has never had to worry about such things."

A chair materialized between them, and the Peregrine sort of melted into it, as if one second there had been nothing, and the next there was a small woman, saying, "He means for me to pay for it."

Naftaly startled. "How did you—"

"She's been there ten minutes," Barsilay said. "Did you really not notice?"

"She has not been there ten minutes! Have you?"

"I was here when he expressed that I was unlikely to get myself killed," the Peregrine said. "Thank you for that."

"But I was looking right there when he said that, and you were definitely not ... Never mind it."

"You are paying, though, aren't you?" Barsilay asked.

"Wretched creature," she said. "I ought to just leave you here with your overpriced fish."

"But then I'd be arrested," he said. "And where would you be?"

"I despise you."

"You adore me," he said, and the way he said it—with absolute charming certainty—turned something over in Naftaly's insides. It sounded to Naftaly something like, *Yes, I recall we were lovers, but let's not say it outright.*

"It's a miracle you're still alive." She took the fork from Barsilay's hand and began eating his meal. "If I'm paying for it, I'm eating it. Is this cumin? With fish?" Which sounded something like, *Yes, wasn't that a good time? What are you doing with this mortal child?*

"I knew it was a mistake as soon as I ordered it," Barsilay said.

"It's disgusting," the Peregrine said.

"Then stop eating it."

"No."

To Naftaly, Barsilay said, "Eat fast, she'll come for you next."

Naftaly said, "What?"

"I won't," she said. "He's skin and bones; I won't be responsible for him keeling over. Hashem's sake, you have an al'qa behind your ear." She pulled a dagger—from where?—and pointed it in the direction of Naftaly's earlobe.

"It's fine," Naftaly said. "Leave it, please."

"You want me to leave that? Beside your face?"

"It's … medicinal."

She put the dagger away and glanced over at Barsilay. "Ah, is that what Saba suggested?"

"It was my idea," said Barsilay.

"Your idea?"

"Saba concurred."

"And they're going to help him see more clearly?"

Barsilay made no response.

"Isn't that why you went to see him? What aren't you saying?"

Barsilay shoved his plate at the Peregrine. "Just finish it so we can leave. We were having a lovely time until you showed up."

"With your empty pockets?" She laughed. "You only came in here because you knew I'd follow you."

"Yes, and about that, you could have just come and said hello like a normal person. One doesn't generally watch their allies from the shadows, you know. It isn't normal."

"Old habits," she said. "Rather like making your companions pay for your lunch."

"Wretched woman."

She stuck the last piece of fish into her mouth. Still chewing, she said, "Are you done, or did you want one of those flaming-sugar confections you were eyeing earlier?"

"Let him finish," Barsilay said.

"I was going to!"

"Finish your meal," Barsilay told Naftaly, who did not much want to eat the strange chicken with a pair of Maziks glaring at him. But he seemed to have little choice. He put a bit in his mouth. He chewed. They stared. He wanted, very much, to leave.

"Did the old mortals show up yet?" the Peregrine asked, when she was tired of watching him masticate.

"No," Barsilay said. "And I'm growing concerned. You saw no sign of them?"

"Nowhere," she said. "But I don't think they've gotten into any trouble with the Zayitis. That, I would have seen signs of."

The chicken was very dry in Naftaly's mouth, and he set down his fork.

"That's all?" Barsilay asked.

"My stomach isn't used to eating this much," he said, and the Peregrine went off to pay the bill, which Naftaly suspected was more money than he'd ever seen in his life.

Outside, Barsilay stretched his arms over his head—the real and false both—and said, "The food is so much better here than in Rimon, I'd forgotten."

"It ought to be better, for what those two plates cost," the Peregrine said.

"Are you so squeamish about spending Tarses's money?"

"No," she said. "Only there's a finite quantity, see, and we may need it for something else later, like getting you safely to P'ri Hadar, which I think we should probably do before Tarses arrives with his army."

He tsked. "The two of you will be fast friends, I see. Tarses won't attack in the middle of winter. Who launches an invasion when the mountains are full of snow? Tarses isn't stupid."

The Peregrine's head whipped around.

"What is it?" Barsilay asked.

"Stay here," she said, and took off at a run, and then she vanished. Whether it was around a corner or up the side of a building, Naftaly could not tell.

"What was that?" Naftaly asked.

"I don't know," Barsilay said. "Nothing good, I think. We should go."

"She told us to stay here, didn't she?"

"I think it was more like 'Don't follow me,'" he said.

"She was fairly clear."

"She knows I've never taken direction well," he said. "Let's go back to the house."

They walked quietly down the cobbled streets, Naftaly listening to distant conversation from some adjacent road or alley, and ruminated. Barsilay glanced over at him once, then twice, then, "Just ask it."

"You were lovers," Naftaly said.

If Barsilay was surprised to hear Naftaly had reached this conclusion, his face did not show it. He said, "Long ago. Before she handed me to La Cacería to pressure my uncle."

"Are you still angry about that?"

"I still remember it, if that's what you mean."

"Do you trust her?" Naftaly asked.

"I trust she wants to be free of Tarses."

"Were you in love?"

Barsilay stopped. "I was . . . young. I believed myself in love with many people then. If you're going to be jealous of everyone I might have loved in my youth, I'd advise you not to bother. You'll exhaust yourself over nothing." They rounded the next corner, and stepped into the path of the thoroughly annoyed Peregrine, who said, "What are you doing? I told you to stay there! Have you no care for your life?"

"What can you mean?" Naftaly asked.

"Did you see the woman I was following?"

"No," Barsilay said. "I saw no one."

"And what does that tell you?"

Barsilay said, "I have no idea."

The Peregrine rubbed at her forehead. "There was a woman, in the piazza. I only saw her face for half an instant. But she was one of mine."

"A Falcon?" Barsilay asked.

"Yes, a Falcon."

"How can you not know if one of your own people is here?"

"That is my point," she said. "I should know."

"Did she see you?"

"I don't think so," she said. "But I can't say for sure, and if she saw you—or worse, me with you—it would be very, very bad."

"Well, where did she go?"

"I lost her," she admitted.

"You lost her?"

"I was the one who trained her," she said. "I was thorough. Listen, if I didn't send her here—and I didn't—the only other person with the authority to dispatch a Falcon is Tarses. Which means he has plans here I don't know about."

Barsilay said, "That's not good."

"It's not."

"You really don't know?"

"Tarses likes to keep his plans modular," the Peregrine said. "Lots of parts moving independently. It prevents things all going bad at once if one person is compromised. But he's never kept me out of anything before."

"Do you think he suspects you've betrayed him?"

"No," she said. "I'd be dead then. It's not that. But whatever he's planning, I don't know the extent of it. I need to find her."

"Will she tell you what she's here for?"

"If I ask nicely," she said, and then cast her eyes to the sky, which had gone very gray. In the distance, there was a rumble of thunder, and then another, just as the first snowflakes began to fall in the city.

✦ ✦ NINETEEN ✦ ✦

TSIFRA WAS SO worried about Toba and the demons—who were growing more restless the closer they got to Zayit—that she was reluctant to sleep when it was her turn. Her mind had snagged on the tale of Elena thwarting Tarses. An old woman, of no particular power, and she'd tricked the Caçador of Rimon out of his heir! And for what? She hadn't turned Toba into a tool of her own. She'd put an amulet on her to bind her powers and raised her as if she'd been a mortal child, with bedtime stories and sweets.

Why had she done such a thing? It couldn't have been only for sentiment. Elena might have loved her daughter, but Toba had been the instrument used to kill her, bursting forth from her like a parasite. Who could love such a thing?

And yet, she'd kept Toba alive and in comfort all these years, and safe from Tarses besides.

Tsifra rubbed hard at her eyes, because her mind was caught in a loop and the exhaustion was making it worse. Toba, who had already slept, said, "It will be worse if you fall asleep while they're carrying you. Sleep now, I'm awake."

"Are you sure?" Tsifra said.

"I am. And here." Toba passed her a parcel of what turned out to be white cheese wrapped in a leaf. "I made this earlier when you were checking your map. I meant to give it to you before."

Tsifra took it without comment, and ate it, and slept.

She opened her dreaming eyes to the seashore, and thought at first she'd been summoned by Tarses, but then realized that her companion that night was the Peregrine, who stood looking out at the sea. She wondered briefly if she'd called to her, or if it was Tsifra herself who had pulled her in.

"I did not know you had an affinity for the sea," Tsifra said.

"Hm? I don't. I shouldn't even be sleeping now. This is your dream."

"Is it? How can you tell?"

She smiled. "I never come to the sea on my own. So I assume."

"Right," Tsifra said. "I heard you were on the way to Zayit."

"Did you? From whom?"

"Can't recall," Tsifra said.

"Hm."

"I heard you were chasing that girl around mortal Rimon," the Peregrine said.

"From whom?"

"Can't recall," the Peregrine said, and pulled Tsifra close, and kissed her mouth.

They only met like this in dreams. Whatever attachment they had—if one could even call it so—could not exist in the waking world without risking them both. And the Peregrine had other lovers, Tsifra was sure. She was too skillful not to, always knowing exactly what was needed, a level of precision that could only have come from a great deal of enthusiastic practice. That Tsifra had no such experience was obvious. Even now, she fumbled. She would never be subtle, not even in an intimate moment with the only partner she had ever had, or likely would ever have.

She was sure it meant little to the Peregrine: a release, probably. Pity, more than likely. Tsifra was not sure how she felt about it. She resented the Peregrine her nimble touch and complete control. But she was desperate, and that won out.

Some time later, with the stars whirling overhead, Tsifra found herself asking, "Will you stay in Zayit, even after the invasion?"

"I go where he sends me," the Peregrine told the stars. "Who knows where I shall be, in three months' time?"

Tsifra's face must have given her away, because the Peregrine leaned up on her elbow and said, "Tell me."

"I can't," Tsifra said. "I shouldn't know it myself."

"Then how is it you do? Asking questions you should not? I warned you about that."

"I'm too cloddish to heed such a warning. Did you not know?"

"Quiet," the Peregrine said.

"Fine."

"You'll tell me."

"You just ordered me to be quiet again."

"You never do anything I say."

Tsifra breathed the sea air that had no salt. "The invasion isn't set for three months' time. It's now."

"It's now?"

She really hadn't known and that concerned Tsifra a great deal, because the Peregrine, of all people, should have known this. Whether this indicated that Tarses was trusting the Peregrine less, or trusting less in general was a question for later pondering. "They broke a Zayiti spy, and learned the army was expected, and moved things up."

The Peregrine rolled onto her back. "I see."

She wanted to ask, *Should Tarses not have told you?*

She wanted to ask, *What does it mean that he didn't?*

She wanted to ask, *What are you doing in Zayit?*

But all she said was, "Be careful."

"Always," the Peregrine said, and kissed Tsifra's shoulder, once, then twice, then she said, "How do you feel about your name?"

"My name? I have no feelings about it at all."

"No? You never thought you might like a new one?"

Tsifra did not understand what she was getting at. "That isn't possible. A name can't be changed."

"Not for you or me," the Peregrine said. "I would ask a favor of you."

She had never before asked this, neither waking nor dreaming. Tsifra did not think the Peregrine had ever asked a favor of anyone; it was too dangerous for her to owe something to someone, and for the other party, too. But Tsifra was raw, and tired, and soon she'd either have the killstone or she would be dead, so she said, "Name it."

"So quickly?" The Peregrine laughed.

"Before I change my mind," Tsifra said. "Please."

"Please? Oh, I have missed you." Her face went serious. "Last time I saw you, you were interrogating a Luzite."

Barsilay? "I was."

"You took his arm."

"How do you know that?" Tsifra asked.

"So you know who he is? What he is?"

Tsifra said, a little uneasily, "How is it that *you* know?"

"Never mind how I know," the Peregrine said. "My favor is this: If you see him again, don't kill him."

"Don't kill him? But isn't your main mission to kill all the heirs?"

"Do I have my favor, yes or no?"

Tsifra sputtered a bit. It was a lot to ask, and it might mean disobeying orders somehow. Could the heir of Luz change a name? Tsifra did not think so.

But could the King?

"All right," Tsifra said. "I won't kill him."

TOBA HAD BEEN Trying for several minutes to rouse her sister. The demons had been out hunting and by the moon's position it hadn't been long; something had caused them to return early. Toba, who was meant to sleep second, had not yet slept at all. "Somethings happening," she said. "I've been trying to wake you."

Tsifra sat up and threw a handful of pebbles up at the demons. "Why are you like this?"

"Birdlings," they said. "Tarses's soldiers are in front of us. They are very close."

Tsifra got to her feet. "How close?"

"If we fly farther, we will reach them before the sun sets."

"That's close indeed," Toba said. "I'm actually surprised we haven't overtaken them before now; they must be riding fast."

"If we keep this way, they shall see us," the demons said. "We must go through the mountains."

Tsifra looked very dubious about this. "No," she said. "We can't go that way."

"Why not?" Toba asked softly.

"It will take too long, and the Gal'in are full of demons. Our arrangements are with *these* demons. I wouldn't like to think about what those others might do with us." To the demons, she said, "We'll have to wait until dark and fly higher."

"We cannot fly higher," the demons mocked. "You've given us rules."

"Fine," Tsifra said, as Toba hissed at her to be careful. "While we are visible to Tarses's soldiers, you may fly us higher than twenty feet."

"Good," they said. "Good!" And then they took hold of Toba and Tsifra, while Toba screamed curses because the other woman had set no upper limit, and they took them up, up into the sky, so high and so fast that Toba felt her fingers go numb.

As they flew, the demons as one began to cry out, screaming and making such a noise that Toba thought they were preparing to drop them to the ground.

But these were sounds of joy, not rage, and then as one they called out, "We are here! We are here at last!" And a new shadow appeared among them, shaped like a great, taloned bird.

"Atalef," Tsifra said, and he turned to her, his wings giving way to a hundred arms, and he used them to grasp her and lift her higher, and Toba went with them, into the cold, thin air. Her last thought, before she lost consciousness, was how much it felt just like the void.

+ + +
+ · + + +

"ARE YOU SUGGESTING we steal the salt?" Elena asked Rafeq, because such a thing seemed completely impossible and not even worth considering. The Zayitis would guard their salt ten times over, or more. The three of them were not getting near it.

"No," Rafeq said. "The salt stores are impenetrable. We'd never be able to break into them."

"Well, what then? We can't make this amount of salt from seawater, and we don't have enough money to buy it."

"Couldn't we just give the safira to the Zayitis?" the old woman suggested. "They have enough salt, and I'm sure they'd be happy to kill Tarses for you."

Rafeq mused on this for a while before he said, "If the Zayitis have the killstone, there is a risk of them using it on people other than Tarses."

"I thought everyone else whose name was in it was dead," Elena said.

"Not everyone," he said. "My name is in it. And more to the point, your friend Barsilay's name is in it. What do you think they'll do if they learn they have the means to kill the heir of Luz?"

If they were smart, they'd kill him straightaway, before he could take power. Elena said, "Then what is your intention?"

Rafeq said, "I really didn't want to go this route, but I don't believe there's a choice. We don't have enough money to deal with the salt merchants. But we may be able to barter for something they'll want even more than normal salt."

"The decayed salt?" Elena said. "You want to give it to the salt merchants? But—"

"I know. But we have nothing else."

Elena had misgivings, and the old woman protested outright, but he was correct: either they bargain with the decayed salt or give up entirely. There was too much at stake not to proceed. So Rafeq went off to make the deal with the salt guild: twenty pounds of raw salt, to be used in scientific experimentation on methods to create decayed salt—a product Rafeq claimed to have discovered by accident—in exchange for whatever decayed salt they produced. They would not reveal the safira or the killstone, nor would they cede ownership of their process.

Rafeq had explained, "You must understand how dangerous it would be if they were to discover we have a way to manipulate safiras. When I developed this theory, all I wanted was a way to get at the memories that had been lost over the years, all that knowledge that sat in boxes or on shelves. But that may not be what the salt guild does. They would be able to force their enemies to pull out their magic, and then transfer it into their mortal allies."

Elena understood. The Zayitis, for all they were better than Tarses, were still powerful Maziks. And powerful Maziks were not to be trusted any more than powerful men.

And here she was, about to give those powerful Maziks a lot of very potent poison. She told herself it was still the best course.

Rafeq returned that evening, looking grim, a leather satchel slung over one shoulder. The old woman was out searching again, and Elena was glad not to have her underfoot and arguing. It wasn't that Elena disagreed with the old woman's positions on principle, but she seemed to be suffering from an acute failure of imagination.

"Did they not agree?" Elena asked Rafeq, once he'd come into the kitchen. He'd made them both the hot, spiced wine he preferred; Elena did not ask where he'd gotten the money for the spices.

"Oh, they agreed," he said. "Twenty pounds of salt for our experiments. In exchange, all of the decayed salt goes to the salt merchants."

"And the miasma?" Elena asked.

"I didn't mention the miasma," he said. "It was bad enough giving them this."

"Are you having second thoughts?"

"Always," he said. Then, "There's more. I told them they were investing in our research."

"Our research, which we're keeping secret," she said. "Rafeq—"

Rafeq's dark expression became still darker, and he closed his eyes.

"On that point, they could not be dissuaded." He reached into his satchel and pulled out a large purse, which he tossed onto the table.

"What's the money for?" Elena asked.

"Our research," he said. "They wouldn't give me the salt unless I agreed to give it to them. So I let them think I'd accept payment for it."

"But if you give them our research, they'll have to know about the safiras!"

"By the time they come to collect our notes, Tarses will be dead," Rafeq said. "We'll be long gone."

"Your plan is to double-deal the salt guild. And you think that will end well for us?"

"It was the best plan I could come up with," he said. "I'm sorry you think poorly of it, but it gets us the salt and time we need to carry this off. You may tell me how angry you are about it once you're a Mazik." And he left the room.

Elena sat back down, feeling ill at ease, and understanding how it was Rafeq ended up under the mountain in the first place. On the table was a purse full of Mazik currency.

She decided not to count it.

TWENTY

IT WAS WELL after midnight, and Naftaly was watching as Barsilay paced, his agitation wearing a hole in the floor. The Peregrine had woken them in the middle of the night to tell them what she'd learned from some unnamed Cacería dream companion: that the invasion was imminent. Tarses's soldiers had already left Rimon and were riding to Zayit at that exact moment.

"How long, would you guess?" Barsilay stopped to ask her.

"Depends on the weather," the Peregrine said. "And whether he plans some alternate route to avoid being seen. The coastal route is being watched, and he knows it."

"But won't he have to pass that way, if that's where the food is being stored?" Naftaly asked.

"The silo you found? It was one of many. If he felt he had to bypass that one, he could."

"Where are the others? He can't mean to take his army through the mountains," said Barsilay.

"I don't think he does," she said. "There are other towers between the sea and the mountain that the Zayitis won't be able to find. The tower you found was repurposed. The ones we built just look like trees. They're very hard to spot, unless you see someone going into one."

"Give me a time frame," Barsilay said. "Weeks? A month?"

"Could be anywhere from days to weeks, if I had to guess."

"That's not long at all," said Naftaly. "But when we tried to warn the Zayitis last time, they didn't seem concerned."

"They lack imagination," the Peregrine said. "This city has never been attacked."

"Why the cannons, then?" Naftaly asked.

"They've been worried about Rimon for some time," she said. "And the Zayitis like to borrow things from mortals. When mortal Anab fell to the Ulimans, the Zayitis got the idea for mounting cannons on the walls and using exploding balls of salt as munitions. They've haven't been there long. Tarses was very angry when he found out."

"He hadn't foreseen them?" Barsilay asked.

"No. And he's worried about what else he hasn't seen."

"Will the cannons be enough to stop him?" Naftaly asked.

"The cannons work, if that's what you mean. It's just that they're limited in what they can do."

"Are they difficult to aim?"

"There's that," she agreed. "But the main problem is that the salt is just as poisonous to the people inside Zayit as it is to whoever they are trying to blow up outside. The cannons have been calibrated to fire at targets a large distance from the city. Once you get inside that radius, they're essentially useless."

"Still," Naftaly said, "it seems like a good defense, so long as you saw the other army coming. But surely there must be some other defenses as well?"

The Peregrine said, "They're planning to use the Mirror, I know that much, but I don't know how." Her head swiveled to the door. "I think you have your way in. Straighten your hair."

Barsilay said, "What?"

But the Peregrine had suddenly vanished, and then there was a loud knock on the door.

When Naftaly answered it, it was Efra, with Saba looking rather chagrined over her left shoulder. The entire street had been blanketed by snow overnight.

Efra cocked her head to one side and said, "My brother was

summoned in the middle of the night to heal the Prince's favorite horse. Now, tell me how you knew it would snow."

FOR SEVERAL DAYS Elena sat with Rafeq as he crafted the device from her drawings, while she made various suggestions. The vessel in which the safira would be ground needed to have steeper sides; the bladder for containing the miasma needed to be higher, to prevent a buildup inside the machine; the lever he made was too short, and then too long.

Rafeq, to his credit, never let on that her constant alterations were irritating, but he did insist on an explanation for each of them. "I'm going to be turning this handle for a very long time," she explained. "If I tear something in my shoulder, it will be a problem."

"I've been thinking about that," he said. "If you're the one adding the salt, we could have a shade turn the handle."

"I thought you said that wouldn't work, because of the salt?"

"Yes, but the apparatus is more sealed than I'd thought. It would free you up to make sure everything else is running smoothly. I'm afraid if you've exhausted yourself turning a crank you may not notice if there's a problem somewhere."

"All right," she agreed. "But I still think we need to address the ergonomics of the handle—if the shade fails, I'll need to take over anyway."

"Very well," he said, and made the handle again.

On the fifth day, Elena announced the machine was as close to her ideal as could reasonably be made. Rafeq sent a message to the salt guild, and an hour later four shades arrived carrying a litter between them, which they offloaded into the kitchen. Inside the litter was a locked wooden chest, which one of the shades opened with a shadowy finger, and then inside the chest was an oblong of glass, which the shades carefully placed on the table. Inside the sealed glass was the salt. The shade that had opened the chest handed Rafeq a sealed letter, and then all four shades vanished into a wisp of smoke.

"What does it say?" the old woman asked, as Rafeq broke the seal on the letter and began to read.

"They will return in twenty-four hours to claim the decayed salt, which we're to have sealed up in the same crate. And there was a brief reminder that if we haven't delivered it, we'll all be killed, et cetera."

"So nothing new," the old woman said.

"Nothing new," he said. "I think we should get started."

Elena ran a hand over the glass container that held the salt; it had a razor-thin seam around the top, and she lifted the lid and examined the contents. Twenty pounds of salt—enough to kill most every Mazik in the city. Despite what she'd told the old woman, she was not sure she was doing the right thing. She was not even sure who she'd be, once all this was done and she'd allowed herself to become a receptacle for Marah's memories.

Elena divided her life into distinct epochs in her own mind—her childhood, the early days of her marriage, her daughter's life, and then her granddaughter's—all defined by the person to whom she was beholden: her parents, Alasar, Penina, and then Toba. She was not sure to whom she would be beholden once this was done. She asked Rafeq, "What was your relationship with Marah?"

He seemed unsurprised by the question. "We were friends and confidants of very long standing. She was the greatest Mazik I have ever known."

"Are you hoping I will become that friend to you again?"

Rafeq said, "I believe you are so already, Elena."

THE SAVIA MADE Naftaly tell her seven different times how he'd seen the Prince of Zayit fall in the snow before she seemed to accept the reality of his visions. He'd also explained about the lentil blight in Tamar, the news of which was embargoed and had only just reached Zayit anyway. She escorted the men back to the palace, and shut them into a room which Naftaly thought was probably where the Zayitis asked questions politely before moving you downstairs to where the real interrogations were held. The room was empty except for the three chairs she'd brought forth from the wooden floor, and had no window, which was what made Naftaly suspect this was not where the Council of Ten brought people they liked.

Barsilay was perturbed that Saba had so freely shared Naftaly's abilities with what amounted to the government, but Naftaly supposed he could not blame the man.

"My brother says he gave you an al'qa to stop the visions," she said. "I want you to remove it."

Barsilay said, "No. The visions are damaging him."

"I would like to know what else he sees," she insisted.

"It doesn't work like that," Naftaly said. "I can't control when I have a vision, and I can't always control what I see when I do."

"If your visions are random, how can you know they are accurate?"

"They aren't precisely random," Barsilay replied. "They always involve the near future. And he's never wrong. The snow is the least of it. We know this city will fall to Tarses, and we know it happens soon."

"But isn't it possible he's seeing only one possible future?" Efra said. "This city is as secure as it can be."

"Because of the cannons?"

Here, Efra paused. She walked in a circle around Barsilay's chair, and then came to stand in front of him, stooped, and blew a stream of air into his face. While he looked up, bemused, she asked, "How did you lose your arm?"

Barsilay flexed his phantom hand and said, "I lost it in a Cacería prison. And you needn't have bothered with your truth spell first, I'd have told you that straightaway if you'd asked."

"What were you doing in a Cacería prison?"

"Tarses was using me as a pawn."

"So you are Tarses's pawn?"

"You misunderstand," Barsilay said. "Tarses was attempting to trade me for something he wanted."

"Did it work?"

286 ARIEL KAPLAN

"No," he said, "it didn't. And I imagine Tarses will probably kill me straightaway if he ever lays eyes on me again. Does that satisfy you?"

"For now," Efra said. "As to your question, we've had spies in Rimon for months; we know precisely what Tarses is going to do. His plan is to come at us via the Mirror—and we are countering him, using the Mirror. Tarses has a single mortal Courser. We have legions of agents in the mortal world—mortals who have been working with us for generations, and not only in Zayit. They know their business, and Tarses altering his timeline won't change that."

"What do you mean?" Barsilay asked. "What are they planning?"

"There is no need to tell you this," she said. "But trust me, there is more than one plan in place. Zayit has many layers of safety."

"But," said Naftaly, "it won't matter. The city falls; I've seen it."

This brought the Savia up short, and her mouth went very flat. Tapping her fingers on the arm of her chair, she got up and made a circuit of the room, coming to a stop before Naftaly again. "So you would have us surrender?" she said. "You're sounding more like one of Tarses's agents all the time."

"Believe me," Barsilay said, "we're not working with Tarses. But you must make a plan for what happens if your defenses fall. You have to secure the salt stockpile, and you have to secure the gate, and you must find some way to get your people out of the city before he burns it."

Efra huffed. "If we secure the salt as you're suggesting, we won't be able to use it to defend the city, and what you've told me becomes a forgone conclusion. Have you considered the city falls because you've told me to lock up all the salt?"

"But—" Naftaly began, and Barsilay held up a hand.

"She's right," he said. "They can't lock up the salt. But the gate is the larger issue. If the city falls to Tarses, he gains control of not just the salt here, but your resources in mortal Zayit. It must be secured."

"It *is* secured," Efra said. "We've anticipated his meddling with the gate. The entire Second Division is in the olive grove right now, and they've shielded it from the outside. Anyone coming into the grove will immediately be transported to the opposite side. It can't be penetrated. The grove can only be accessed from inside the city."

"From the tunnels," Barsilay said. Then explained to Naftaly, "Even I know about those—they go through the wall and take you to various points outside the city. They use them to import the salt directly from the grove inside the wall. But the wards on the grove won't hold forever. Either he'll find a way to get through from the city, or else the wards will break."

"Unless you're suggesting we rip the gate out entirely, I'm not sure what you'd have us do," Efra said. "We can't supply the men in the grove without that tunnel, and the men of the Second are our strongest. We've done all we can." There was a knock on the door, and a man came in and began speaking into Efra's ear.

The man stepped back out. Turning back to Barsilay, Efra said, "Our luck is better than you realize: we've just arrested a Rimoni spy. A fairly significant one, too."

Barsilay said, "Significant enough that you know who it is? How is that possible, if it's a spy?"

"Well, if we're to believe what she's told us, the spy we've captured is La Cacería's Peregrine."

ASMEL'S EARLIEST MEMORIES stretched back about ten days, and he played them out in his mind over and over, wondering if he would lose those, too—if maybe his mind only held space for ten days' worth of events, and as each day moved forward, he'd lose one at the other end. But eventually, he found that he had eleven days' worth of memories, and then twelve, as he sat in a cell in the basement of the mortal salt guild.

"Did I hit my head?" he asked his guard one day.

"Yes, very hard. Now be quiet."

Asmel probed his head with his fingers and found no obvious injury. "Are you telling the truth?" he asked.

"If you ask me again, I'll come in there and hit you in the head now," the guard said.

So Asmel stayed quiet. He did not know what day it was, or even if it was day or night, when the guards came and took him from his cell, but when they put a hood over his head and told him to keep silent, he assumed he was about to be murdered. He did not know the moon was full, and would not have remembered the significance of that fact even if he had. All he knew for certain was that someone had instructed the guards to hand him over to the goat-eyes, which sounded terrifying indeed.

He wanted to fight, but his arms were in such heavy irons there was nothing he could do, and he wanted to scream, but there was no one to help him. He had no friends. He didn't even recall ever knowing anyone, besides the men guarding him. He would die, he believed, unremembered and unmourned, and he felt sadder about that than about the end of his own life.

Asmel was marched up the stone stairs, and then put in the back of a cart or a wagon, and taken someplace else, and then he was made to walk on grass, and the air smelled of trees.

It seemed like a lot of trouble to move him so far in order to kill him.

Then he felt, for only a moment, as if he were passing through water, and nearly panicked, but it was over quickly and he found himself quite dry. Then a man who was not Asmel's guard said, "You aren't supposed to be coming through here. What are you doing?"

The voice of Asmel's guard replied, "We've been holding him for the guild. He's a mortal."

"Let me see his eyes."

Asmel's hood was removed, and he blinked in the bright beam of light that came from the ground nearby and shot upward into the heavens. Surrounding him was a host of men and women, all of them armed. The one who had demanded to see his face held up a glowing stone near his eyes, and examined them carefully before he said, "What do they want with him?"

"I don't make the orders," the guard said. "I was told to take him to the guild, so that's what I'm doing."

"We can't let you through to the city," the soldier said. "I'll send him with one of our people, but you'll have to go back through the gate."

"Fine by me, so long as you're taking responsibility." The guard reached into his coat and pulled out a sealed letter, and handed that over. "Give them this, too."

The soldier nodded, then beckoned over a young-looking woman, and told her, "Take him to the guild, then come directly back."

The woman took Asmel through a long, stone-lined tunnel, past a set of guards who, likewise, were not pleased to see anyone, and into another building where Asmel found himself locked in another cell. By and by, yet another man came, with an emerald earring in his left ear, and through the bars he asked Asmel, "Why were you looking for the gate?"

Asmel answered truthfully, "I can't remember."

The man looked very irked. He asked the guards in the room, "Didn't you already lay a truth spell on him?"

"Twice," they said. "He seems resistant."

"He can't be resistant, he's only a mortal." The man reached through the bars and pressed his thumb between Asmel's eyes, then repeated the question. "Why were you looking for the gate?"

Asmel answered again, "I don't know."

The man turned away from the cell and told the guards, "I haven't got time for this now. Kill him."

TOBA WOKE TO TSIFRA violently shaking her. She did not know how far the demons had carried them, or how long she had been unconscious from flying too high over Tarses's soldiers. "Get up," Tsifra said. "The demons have left us."

Toba put a hand to her throbbing temple and sat up. "Where are we?"

"Zayit. They fulfilled their part of the bargain and dumped us just inside the wall, but they're already gone. We must hurry."

"But we don't know where to find Rafeq!"

"They fulfilled that too," Tsifra said. "They left us a trail to follow, but I'm not sure how far ahead they are."

Indeed, Toba could see a glowing thread leading away from them into the heart of the city, about a foot above the ground. She followed Tsifra, and as soon as they passed each stretch of thread, it evaporated. "Hurry," Tsifra said again. "We're likely too late already."

✦ TWENTY-ONE ✦

DARKNESS HAD FALLEN on the night of the moon when Elena, together with a shade of Rafeq's, began the process of eviscerating Marah's safira in the machine. She estimated it would take three or four hours for the salt to render the jewel into powder, which she would then inhale.

Despite what Rafeq had told her, she was frightened, and while the shade turned the handle of the apparatus, Elena ruminated. Would she find herself crowded out of her own mind by her ancestor? Or would they learn to coexist?

It was a silly thought, but Elena wondered how much of herself was her memories, and how much was some other, elemental thing? The two Tobot, when both had lived, had shared all their memories, and yet they'd diverged. She'd wondered about that a great deal: Were the few experiences they'd had after their separation enough to justify their differences?

Elena tried to keep her mind on her work. It did not matter, really, if she were different after she inhaled the safira, because she would have to do it either way. She would do this, and she would free Toba from whatever fate Tarses had planned for her. The rest, she decided, were only minor details. She was an old woman. She'd gladly die to liberate her granddaughter—allowing her personality to be subsumed was no greater a sacrifice.

In the end, breaking down the safira took only minutes.

Elena put an ear to the vessel the shade continued to crank in a circle, and found that she could hear nothing besides the sound of the metal parts scraping each other. "Stop," she told the shade, who obliged. "It's done."

Rafeq and the old woman crept into the kitchen, keeping to the wall by the door. "How can it be done so quickly?" Rafeq wondered.

"I can't account for it," Elena said. "Perhaps the outer layers were harder than the inner. It also used much less salt than we planned; we still have nearly a third of it left." She breathed once, twice. "I'm going to open it now."

Extracting the safira particles meant disassembling the machine, which was not without danger. She put on the silk gloves Rafeq had made for her, and began by capping the bladder—which was fuller with miasma than Elena would have liked—and removing it from the rest of the apparatus. Then she unthreaded the receptacle from the bottom of the machine, confirming that it was mostly full of decayed salt. Sitting on top of this was the mass of Rafeq's magic, coated in blue. The killstone must have been absorbed into Rafeq's magic.

"It's done," Rafeq echoed. "You've done it. Are you ready?"

Elena put a hand to her throat. "I'm ready," she said, and then the glass of the window behind her exploded.

The room was filled with swirling demons, shrieking, "Traitor Rafeq, we have you at last."

Elena flung herself in front of the machine, hoping to block the demons from seeing her work. But it was too late. Later, she would muse on this and think that these were Rafeq's demons, they had his magic, and that they might already have known exactly what he was doing, and why, and there would have been nothing she could have done to prevent what happened next.

The demons hurled Rafeq back into the wall, smacking his head against the stones, and then, with a claw that came from within the swirling mass, took hold of the powdered safira that clung to Rafeq's magic, and sent the magic into a whirlwind that they breathed in, shrieking all the while, until it was gone. Elena made a grab for the amphora that held the rest of their salt, but found herself thrown back into the wall herself, her eyes darkening with the force of the impact. The last thing she saw, before she too fell unconscious, was the demons coalescing into a single mass that rose, growing taller and taller still, until it became a man with eyes as orange as Barsilay's, and in his hand was the killstone of ha-Moh'to.

TSIFRA WAS SO fast Toba could barely keep up, her feet flying over the cobbles, her hand grabbing Toba's wrist, pulling her along. "We can't afford to let them get so far ahead," she snapped over her shoulder. "If you can't go faster, I'm leaving you here."

But Toba had spent her growing years under the influence of an amulet that suppressed her magic. Compared to Tsifra, her legs would never be so long or strong, and she could not keep up. "Then let go," she said.

Tsifra only held tighter. Then, from an otherwise unremarkable house, Toba heard a man scream.

The door, of course, was locked. Tsifra backed up to kick it down, but Toba stilled her. "Faster this way," she said, and used Asmel's trick of making them both transparent, and then they were inside.

Rafeq was on the floor, just now stirring, a look of dawning horror on his face, while over him crouched a man Toba did not know, orange-eyed and dark-haired, wearing an exultant expression, his hand fisted around something he clutched so tightly his veins stood out blue against his skin.

"You were right, Rafeq," the man said. "I have all her memories. All of them, even this one." He opened his hand, revealing the starburst killstone. And he bent his head close to Rafeq and whispered a word Toba could not hear, and then, "Rafeq."

Atop his palm, the killstone glowed for an instant, and then Rafeq's eyes closed in death.

Toba stepped forward, but Tsifra threw out an arm in front of her. "Wait."

"But where are the demons?" Toba asked quietly.

"You fool," Tsifra said. "That man is the demons."

The man in question smiled and rose. "Birdlings," he said, "we have done it. We are Mazik. Do you see? We are Mazik at last." He held out his very solid hands.

"Why did you kill him?" Toba demanded.

"He abandoned us inside that mountain," the demons said.

"But he made you," she said.

"He did not make me! I made myself. And here I am, more Mazik than you shall ever be, and Rafeq the Traitor will never betray me again."

It was then that Toba saw there had not been one person on the floor, but two. The other was a woman, with an arm thrown over her eyes. Not just a woman: an old woman, which could only mean she was mortal. And no sooner had she realized this than she realized this was her grandmother. Toba cried out and went to her side, sliding Elena's arm off her face, and checking her breathing. A movement in the corner caught her eye, which she realized was Naftaly's old woman.

"What have you done?" Toba shouted. "She could have done you no harm!"

"She lives," the demon said. "She was only in my way."

Tsifra said, "You used the killstone. You know the command-word?"

The man said, "Yes."

"Then use it again. Kill Tarses!"

"Birdling," the demons said, "where is Asmel?"

"What difference does that make right now?" Tsifra asked. "You have the killstone. Use it now!"

"The second safira," the demons went on. "You have it, Courser."

"Are you mad?" Tsifra asked.

"I am not your servant!" the man screamed.

Toba rose from Elena's side. "You can't give it to him. You've promised it to me. That was our bargain: I would lead you to Rafeq, and you would give me Asmel's safira. You can't give it to him."

"Then *you* give it to me!" the demons snapped at Toba.

Tsifra took the second stone from around her neck and threw it to Toba. "Here; now there are no further debts between us and you may do with it as you like, but remember, both of you, we have one purpose. Or did you forget?"

"*You* have one purpose!" Toba snapped.

The old woman began to creep up from the floor in the corner, her eyes hardened. "Toba," she said quietly, "take Elena and go."

The demons said, "Do not move."

But the old woman had already taken a knife and cut the inflated sack attached to the machine there, turning it toward the demons, and a cloud of miasma more noxious than anything Toba had ever imagined poured forth. "Go!" she ordered Toba, who was already coughing.

The demons lifted their hand and blew the miasma back, catching the rest of the women in the cloud of it, and instantly Toba could barely see. Elena had been in her arms, but she found her muscles would not work. Then she heard Tsifra shout, and then the sounds of the wall behind her exploding outward, and then nothing at all.

THE GUARDS UNLOCKED Asmel's cell, and he was certain this time he was going to die.

He had so many unanswered questions, and nothing that had happened to him made sense, but he knew enough to be afraid. "What will happen?" he asked the guards, and even he was not really sure whether he meant *How will you kill me?* or *What will happen after?*

They had not answered when the door to the stairs flew open. The guards, turning toward the sound, were caught in a blast of flame so hot Asmel recoiled against the wall, sure he would be burned alive.

When he opened his eyes again, he found his guards burned to ash. Standing in the doorway of Asmel's cell was a tall man with dark hair and orange eyes.

"Are you here to kill me?" Asmel asked, still cowering against the stone. His knees had given out, and he was on the floor, inhaling the smell of smoke and burned flesh.

The man approached and crouched down before him. "Quite the contrary," he said. "My, you've had a hard time, haven't you?"

Asmel was trembling so hard he could barely speak, but he said, "I can't really say whether I have or not."

"No? You're in a cell, unfed and unwashed, and you aren't sure?"

Asmel thought it over. "Seeing as I can't say where I was before this, I couldn't tell you whether it was better or worse before. So no, I'm not sure at all."

"Oh," the man said, a drawn-out syllable. "I have missed you, Asmel."

"Is that my name?"

The man smiled sadly. "Have you forgotten even that?" He stroked Asmel's cheek. "You are like a child now. Don't be afraid. I've come to take you home."

"Home?" Asmel asked. "But I don't know where that is."

"I know," the man said. "But I do, and you will." He removed a glass phial from his jacket; it was filled with blue powder. "You have only to inhale this, and all will be well."

Asmel looked at the powder doubtfully. "That's a lot of powder to have in my lungs. I think I will choke on it."

"You won't. You must trust me on this."

"But I don't even know who you are."

"Asmel b'Asmoda," the orange-eyed man said. "I am the person who loves you best in all the worlds." He pressed the phial into Asmel's hand.

Asmel was unsure of any of this, but going home had to be better than staying in the cell. He removed the stopper from the bottle and smelled it carefully. It had no aroma at all. But still . . . so much material in his lungs.

"I don't wish to," Asmel said. "Please."

"But you must."

Asmel shook his head. "I think you mean to kill me."

"I don't, dear one." He leaned in and kissed Asmel carefully on the mouth. "You are dearer to me than anything. I would never harm you. Only take the powder, and then everything will be right for you."

Asmel said, "All right, then."

"Good," the man said, and with some magic Asmel did not understand, he pulled the powder out of the phial and into the air before Asmel, and said, "Breathe."

Asmel inhaled, feeling the powder slide down his throat and into his lungs, at first painful, like swallowing water the wrong way, but then warm and then hot. Asmel gasped, half expecting the powder to leave his lungs on the exhalation, but it remained.

The warmth in his lungs spread; he could feel it in his veins, in his heart, all the way to his fingers and toes. Then the pain came, in his eyes worst of all, and he cried out, and the other man put a hand on his shoulder. "It will be another moment only, do not fear."

But Asmel did fear, because his mind was turning itself inside out, reorienting itself to a world he'd forgotten.

He knew himself, who and what he was, and where, and why.

He did not know the man with the orange eyes who had helped him, though there was a familiarity about those eyes, about the expression on that face. "Who are you?" he asked.

The man said, "I am Marah remade."

EFRA LEFT TO meet with the Council, and Naftaly turned to Barsilay. "Why would the Peregrine identify herself to the Zayitis?"

"I don't know," Barsilay said. "What's more, I can't imagine how she was caught in the first place. It shouldn't have been possible, unless she allowed it."

"So you think she allowed herself to be captured and identified herself ... Why? She's hoping Tarses will find out?"

"That makes no sense, either."

"Well, should we tell Efra she's with us?"

Barsilay said, "Efra already suspects I may be working with Tarses. If I tell her the Peregrine is with me, it will only confirm it."

"But we can't very well just leave her in the dungeon."

"No," Barsilay said, "we can't. But until Efra trusts me a little better, I'm not sure how to get her out. She must have had some plan in mind when she was captured. Would have been nice to tell us what it was."

"Is it possible it isn't her?"

"An imposter? I don't think so. The Peregrine would have come back then. I think we have to assume it was her unless she turns up, and that she has some scheme in mind."

Efra then returned. "I've spoken with the Council," she said. "You"—here she indicated Naftaly—"are to stay with me."

Barsilay said, "I beg your pardon?"

"If he sees anything more, I want to be the first person who knows about it," she said.

"Then I stay as well," Barsilay said.

"As you wish. I'm on my way to inspect the wall. I've just ordered it resupplied, and I want to make sure they're keeping their reconnaissance high."

THE WALL OF Zayit was roughly fifty feet tall. The main gate was to the south, and the other walls had smaller gates that had, Efra told them, been sealed in advance of Tarses's arrival. The gate was barred each night at sunset, and the southern section of the wall was armed with the largest number of cannons. Efra spoke to a Mazik Naftaly thought must be the commander. Barsilay quietly explained that they were discussing whether they ought to have additional munitions on hand, which was itself dangerous because the munitions in question were highly poisonous. If someone were to drop a cannonball and it were to break open, it might kill half the men on the wall.

For this reason, most of the troops wore gloves and masks as they silently presented themselves for the Savia's inspection, which proceeded, Naftaly thought, far more slowly and deliberately than should have been necessary. Efra, it seemed, was being extremely thorough; every piece of equipment was catalogued, every munition counted.

"Why is this taking so long?" Naftaly asked Barsilay.

"I don't know," Barsilay said. "Either she's stalling or she's not used to doing this. I'm having trouble getting a handle on which."

By then, it had gone from mostly dark to pitch black. A fog had rolled in from the lagoon, blotting out the moon—which was full that night—and the stars. Somewhere, the gate would have opened by now. Either the fog was masking it or the soldiers in the grove were glamouring it somehow; Naftaly wondered which, but did not dare ask. Light-stones along the wall provided a bit of illumination, and the Maziks had grown quiet in the darkness. The leech behind Naftaly's ear had begun to itch, and he figured it was time to replace it with a fresh one, and asked Barsilay to give him some cover while he swapped it out.

The old leech glowed brightly in the darkness. "Good grief. Was this visible? Was I glowing in the dark just now?"

"Your hair was covering it," Barsilay said softly. He was standing between Naftaly and the outer edge of the wall. "I would have told you otherwise. Are you done?"

"Nearly. This new one isn't wanting to stick— There, it's on. I hate this, you know."

"I know, but it's worth it."

"Is it? There could be other things I ought to be seeing, and now I'm not. Useful things."

From farther down the wall, there was a call, echoed by several more, and then a general alert went up and a horn sounded. Barsilay took the elbow of the nearest soldier. "What's happening?"

The guard replied, "They've spotted troops beyond the northern wall. They're preparing to fire on them now."

Barsilay swore and took off up the wall, Naftaly on his heels. "Barsilay, wait," Naftaly called.

"Can't," he called back. "I want to see what's happening there."

"You shouldn't be there when they fire the cannons," Naftaly said. "There could be blowback. Everyone on that wall is at risk."

"Doesn't matter," Barsilay said.

"What is it you think you can do?" Naftaly managed to grab hold of Barsilay's arm and spin him around. "You don't know how to fire those cannons, and you won't be giving the order. You should be as far from that wall as possible right now."

But Barsilay either didn't hear or chose to ignore him, and they got to the wall just in time to see Maziks in full gear loading the cannons. They were covered head-to-toe in black cloth; even their eyes were invisible. "You shouldn't be here dressed like that," said a black-clad Mazik at Barsilay's elbow. By her voice and height, it was the commander again, a woman Efra had called Yel. "You should leave."

"What are they firing at?" Barsilay asked.

She hesitated, and then pointed out into the darkness. "There's at least a thousand Maziks out there."

"I see nothing," Naftaly said. "Shouldn't we hear the horses?"

"The horses aren't with them," she said.

"What?"

"Send a scout," Barsilay said.

"There's no time to send another scout. In twenty seconds, they'll be too close to the walls." She turned to her men, who had finished priming the first set of cannons. "Fire! Now!" she roared, and the sound of the cannons was deafening. Naftaly put his hands over his ears and nearly fell over from the explosion.

And then came the smell, acrid gunpowder, and something else vaguely familiar. The air was filled with smoke, and Naftaly's ears rang. The smell ...

"That's not salt," Naftaly told Barsilay. "It's something else."

"What do you mean?"

Naftaly ran to the Mazik loading the next volley and said, "Break this ball open."

"Who are you?" the soldier demanded. "I'm about to fire it, I'm not breaking it open!"

"Don't you smell this? If it's what I suspect, firing that won't do anything. Break it open."

"It will contaminate the entire wall!" the soldier said.

Yel, who had been watching this, said, "Do as he says. He's part mortal."

The Mazik who had been lifting the ball set it down, and swore, and directed a wave at it before reeling back and covering his face when the iron split open, revealing a core filled with compressed white grains.

"That's salt," Yel said, stepping back. By then Efra had caught wind that something was going on and returned. "What's happening?" she asked.

"Your Rimonis are confused," Yel said. "They oughtn't be here at all."

"No," Naftaly said. "Do you not smell it burning?" He reached forward, and took a few grains on his fingers, and tasted it, while the Maziks close enough to see exclaimed in disgust. "It's sugar," he said, turning to Barsilay.

Efra pulled the hood off her face. "Stop!" she called to the men preparing to reload. "Open all of them. Now." When they did, she turned to Naftaly. "Are they all sugar?"

Naftaly went down the line. He did not need to taste it, smell was enough. "Yes," he said, and then another guard called, "Adona!"

"What is it now?"

The man's scout, a bat the size of a well-fed rat, had just returned to him. "The troops down there ... They're all shades. There are no real men among them."

Efra said, "This is a diversion."

"Something's happening in the south," came the word.

"Somebody find me the quartermaster!" Efra roared. And when someone else said, "She's here," Efra said, "You have to resupply the wall now. Throw out everything that's been made in the past month—two months!" When she turned to go, she said, "Take him with you! When you get to the older stuff, make him sample the core. If it's sugar, throw out that lot, too. And start with the south wall!"

"And what if that's also sugar?"

"Then keep throwing it out until you find salt!"

Naftaly followed the quartermaster down off the wall, racing past panicking guards down several flights of stairs. "Where are we going?"

"Everything on the wall came in within the past two months," the quartermaster said. "We have to assume the stores are all compromised, which means we have to go back to the main supply room, and that isn't here."

"What happened to the supply that was here before?"

She said, "There wasn't any here before."

"What?"

"Keeping salt on the wall is dangerous! It's not just that there might be an accident; someone might steal it, so it takes extra guards. We've only had salt on the wall for the past two months. We used sand for our ballistics tests. No one wants to explode several hundred pounds of salt next to the city unless there isn't a choice." They'd come across the piazza at the base of the wall to what appeared to be a small, free-standing room.

"All the salt is in there?"

"It's mostly underground," she explained. "Take off your gloves. I need you to confirm what we're dealing with before we can resupply, or there's no point." The Maziks manning the depot leapt up when the quartermaster burst the door open.

"We heard the blasts—have they already—"

"Shut up and listen. The supply's been compromised going back at least two months. Take this man to the oldest munitions we have and have him confirm there're actually salt, and then resupply the wall, starting with the south. We're under attack, and we don't know which way it's coming from."

The man said, "How is he—"

"Just do it!" the quartermaster barked.

The underground depot seemed to extend back for several hundred yards, filled with neatly stacked pyramids of salt munitions. Both the quartermaster and the guard had slipped on the same protective gear they'd worn on the wall. "How can you tell when things came in?" Naftaly asked.

"I just know," said the guard. "Everything in the front half of the room is too recent. From this point back is three months, that might be good. I don't understand. How can you compromise salt?"

"We don't have time to fiddle with anything that *might* be good, we need the oldest munitions you have," the quartermaster said. "And it wasn't salt at all. The mortals in the salt guild betrayed us. Sugar for salt."

"But why?"

"Sugar's far more costly than salt on the other side," Naftaly said. "Someone paid the guild a great deal to do this."

"We shall kill them all," said the guard.

"Only if we survive the night," said the quartermaster. He'd shown her to the munitions along the back wall, and she pulled him a few steps back and directed a wave at one of the cannonballs, which broke open. Naftaly put his face by the exposed core and inhaled, while the guard cried out in alarm. "It's salt," Naftaly said.

"Are you absolutely sure?"

"If it's salt, how is he unharmed?" asked the guard.

"There's no time for that discussion. Start transferring these to the outer wall, now. Get everyone you have down here."

"But the protocols—"

"Fuck the protocols!" she said. "I'll take the first batch myself." She cast two shades, the guard cast two of his own, and they gathered the munitions into a series of baskets, three each, and Naftaly chased the quartermaster back to the wall.

The situation there was chaos, as the Maziks were sending bats out to scout the area, which kept coming back without having found anything. "What's happening?" the quartermaster asked a soldier, catching him by the arm as they ran past.

"Nothing," he said. "We can't find anything."

"Any word from the southern wall?"

"I haven't heard so," he said, and she released him. They rounded the corner to the eastern wall and kept going. "We're taking too long," she said. "We're taking much too long."

They were near enough to the southern wall to hear a commotion going up. Efra was already there. "Is this all?"

"There's more coming," the quartermaster said. "I wanted to get these here as quickly as I could."

"Load these in the central cannons," Efra ordered. "We have to fire now!"

"What's down there?"

"We don't know! Four scouts went out and never came back. Look!"

She pointed down off the wall. The entire area was covered in fog. "There could be a thousand soldiers down there, and we'd never see them. Get those cannons loaded, now!"

"Do you mean to fire indiscriminately?"

"There's nothing else we can do. Rotate the volleys," said Efra. "Every other cannon, fired at fifteen-minute intervals, so there's a steady round of salt going out there."

"But without knowing what we're firing at, how will we know when to stop?"

"We stop when we're out of munitions," she said. "Or when we get a clear view of what's down there. Or when whatever it is tries to come over the wall." From behind them, the Maziks shouted orders to fire, and Naftaly had just enough time to cover his ears as a dozen cannons went off at once, cannonballs vanishing into the smoke, and then he heard the sound of secondary explosions as the munitions hit... something.

"That wasn't the ground," said Yel. "They hit something solid higher up."

"You're hearing things," said Efra. "Your ears are still ringing from the blast. *My* ears are still ringing from the blast."

"I know what I heard," Yel said. She cast another bat out of the palm of her hand.

"Anything?" asked Efra.

"No. Wait! Perhaps."

"Reload!" called Efra, but Yel shouted, "Wait!"

The smoke from the explosions was beginning to dissipate, and so was the fog, and Naftaly smelled the acrid scent of burning salt. "Get your masks on!" he shouted. "They've detonated next to the wall!"

"Nothing misfired," said Yel. "They should have gone out half a mile at least." But she'd already got her mask on, and now the fog was dissipating as well as the smoke, and in the light of the full moon, they could see what Tarses's army had wrought two hundred feet from the main gate of Zayit.

It was a castle—cast from gray stone pulled up out of the ground, and half as long as the wall itself. There was no visible entrance on this side, but there were notches in the wall for archers, ready to shoot anyone who approached.

Not that anyone could approach from this side. The ground between the wall and the castle was now coated with salt and the remnants of the exploded munitions. The wall of the castle bore scorch marks from their impact, but no other damage.

"He's made a siege castle," whispered Efra. "Hashem help us all."

"I don't understand. Why didn't the munitions blow out the wall?" Naftaly asked.

"Our munitions were never meant to penetrate walls," Efra said. "They're meant to deliver poison. They won't work on something like that; they don't have the mass. They'll just ricochet off and dump hundreds of pounds of poison right next to the city. Which we've already done."

By then, Barsilay had made his way to the southern wall. He'd lost his arm somewhere along the way, and his sleeve was empty. "Then make some solid munitions!"

"Our cannons aren't built to fire solid munitions! They'll explode back on us!"

"Then build new cannons," Barsilay said.

"Be my guest," she said, waving her arm expansively. "Please. Create a new fleet of cannons capable of firing solid munitions, and then recast the munitions, too, while you're at it."

"Barsilay," Naftaly said, grabbing his shoulder. "Forget the cannons. Do you remember what the Peregrine told us, about why she was here?"

Barsilay's face went ashen. "Listen to me now, or things are about to get much worse. There's a Rimoni spy in your prison. You have to get her out, now. It may already be too late."

Efra scoffed. "I have no authority to release a Rimoni spy."

"Listen to me," Barsilay said again, jerking a hand at the siege castle. "The first thing Tarses did was build himself a base. He's not planning on sending a few people in to sabotage Zayit—he has people in Zayit already. They could have burned the city months ago, if that's all he wanted to do. He's here for your salt, and he's here for the gate, and he's not leaving, not ever. Now get the Peregrine out of your prison."

"How do you know this?" Efra asked.

"Because," Barsilay said, "I am Tarses's greatest enemy, and the Peregrine is my agent."

Twenty-Two

HIDDEN AWAY UNDER the Mazik salt guild, Marah leaned in to Asmel and kissed him, and Asmel was left reeling from the sudden return of himself. He pulled back, staggering under the weight of everything he remembered.

"No," he said. "Marah…"

"Is dead," the man said. "I am her memories. I am her magic."

"And something else, I think," Asmel said.

"Always so astute. Of course I am so much more than she. But I love you, as she did, and I will answer for her. Would you like me to prove it to you?" He took Asmel's hands. "Or shall I show you?" He took some piece of splintered wood from the floor and made it a bowl, then began reciting the words of a spell Asmel recognized: Marah's spell for the sharing of memory.

He'd only ever used it once, with Toba. Casting it had been the most intimate experience of his life. Asmel did not much want to use it on this person, who was certainly not Marah. "I won't do this," he said.

"I'm not casting it on you," the man said, misunderstanding Asmel's reluctance. "You're going to cast it on me." He whispered "*Redruna Delech*," and then a name Asmel had never heard before, and breathed a stream of magic into the bowl.

Asmel said, "That was not Marah's name."

The man said, "I won't compel you. But I know how you must have tortured yourself over what happened, and I am the only person with the answers you seek."

Asmel had indeed tortured himself, for the better part of the age. He'd been arrested by La Cacería and Marah had vanished the very same night. He had looked everywhere, cast every spell, begged every favor he might have left. She was simply gone, and 'til Toba had appeared, marked by her blood as Marah's descendant, he'd had no idea what had become of her. He assumed she'd died, and that was why there'd been no trace.

Of course, there had been a trace. She'd become mortal and had a child.

Toba had asked him, once, if she were like Marah, and he had told her no, mainly because the question was too painful to even consider. Later, he'd had to concede that they were not completely dissimilar. Toba was clever, as Marah had been, and headstrong, and creative in her thinking. But she was also forthright in a way that Marah never had been; there was a raw honesty to the woman that Asmel found disarming. Marah had spun layers of secrets around her work; she'd had to. But she'd also spun those secrets around herself. There was so much of her Asmel had never really known.

Asmel drank the magic and felt himself wake behind the eyes of the woman he'd planned to spend his immortal life with: Marah Ystehar of Luz.

She showed Asmel their last moments together, as he prepared to give his lecture about Aravoth. He saw himself through her eyes, dark-haired and flushed with the excitement of the moment. In her mind, she was already planning what she would do while he lectured. She was going through the gate to collect the Ziz and the book from Dawid ben Aron.

In her memory, Marah told Asmel, "The world has other problems apart from shifting stars," and Asmel said, "I don't believe it has."

Frustration, anger, resignation, in that order. Yet she'd said nothing.

And then another memory: Marah betrayed, unable to use the

killstone against Tarses, she in the mortal world, he in the Mazik, as he had long planned. Her choice was this: Pass through the gate and let Tarses have the Ziz, or remain in the mortal world and die.

There was so much to do, and the night was short, and to let Tarses have the Ziz was no choice she could make. She'd felt a deep regret for abandoning Barsilay and so many others who had relied on her, all her long life: Omer trapped in Te'ena, Rafeq beneath Mount Sebah, Dawid somewhere in Rimon, hoping she might yet prevail. Regret for leaving Asmel, who was unique in loving Marah for herself alone, asking nothing in return. But her greatest regret was for the work undone, for the terrible burden she would bequeath her heirs.

So many regrets and such an easy choice.

Asmel had always understood Marah's labors—in Luz, in ha-Moh'to—only as ambitions that ran counter to his own. He believed what he owed the world was his work. He had not understood, 'til he'd lived behind her eyes, that for Marah, her work *was* the world.

Marah pulled out her magic, and the memories stopped.

Asmel opened his eyes to the man who had Marah's memories, but who was not Marah.

"Come with me," the man told Asmel.

Asmel waited a bit before he answered, "There are promises that I must keep, which I cannot keep if I am with you. Debts I owe."

"Debts you gladly pay?" the man asked, and Asmel said, "Yes," and it was then that Asmel understood that if this had been Marah, if she had truly returned, he would have chosen the same. There was a debt he owed the world, which he paid from obligation. And a debt he owed Toba that he paid from love.

"Then I leave you here," the man said, "so that you may pay them."

"What will you do?" Asmel asked.

The man said, "You have forfeited your chance to find out, my love, in exchange for your hard-won debts. Go and pay them, and I shall pay my own." And one last time, the man who was not Marah kissed Asmel on the mouth, and then he was gone.

Asmel flexed his fingers, then ran his hands over himself, his magic mending his worn clothing and removing the filth of so many days in captivity. Toba would be expecting him through the Zayit gate, which meant that she would have to contend with all the soldiers in the olive grove.

If he hurried, he might find her on the way.

If not, she might need his help. He climbed the stairs from the prison under the salt guild, past several pairs of dead guards and the man with the emerald earring and made his way back toward the tunnel into the olive grove.

"I COULDN'T RELEASE the Peregrine even if I wanted to," Efra explained to Naftaly and Barsilay both. "That's far beyond my authority."

"Then find someone whose authority it falls under!" Barsilay said.

"You are trying me," she told him. "You have no power here."

"And I have no wish to claim it, but the woman in your dungeon may be the only person in all of Zayit who can tell you what Tarses means to do next and how to stop it. If you could just—"

Here, they were interrupted by the quartermaster, who had elbowed her way down the wall to Efra. "Something's happened in the city," she told her. "There was an explosion near the bridge. An entire house blew up, and many who saw it said there were demons involved."

"Demons? Here? There hasn't been a demon in Zayit for a hundred years!" Efra said.

"We had multiple accounts. Demons, an explosion, and some toxic miasma."

Efra glanced at Barsilay. "You think this is Tarses as well?"

"Tarses wouldn't have stopped at one house," he said.

She swore. "I don't have men to spare to investigate this. Every soldier in Zayit is either in the grove or on this wall."

"Then I'll go," Barsilay said. "Give me a handful of soldiers."

"I won't give you anything," Efra said. To Yel, she said, "You're in charge of this, and keep it quick. Take these two plus whomever else you think can be spared. I'm not taking my eyes off that castle."

Yel pulled four Maziks off the wall, armed Barsilay with a sword and—after a moment's deliberation—Naftaly with a knife, and they quickly made their way off the wall and into the heart of the city. "The air smells foul," Barsilay said.

"It does," Yel said. "What is that?"

"I don't recognize it," Barsilay said. "It's going straight through the mask, whatever it is."

Naftaly only smelled regular smoke, but as they grew closer he could feel something else, too: a burning sensation in his throat. They had to push their way through Maziks who were fleeing the area, coughing and covering their faces with their hands.

"Careful," Yel said, holding an arm out to stop their company before they got closer. "The reports implied the demons might still be in the house. No one saw them come back out."

"Blowing up a house does sound like demon activity," Barsilay said. "But the timing can't be a coincidence."

"Of course it's not a coincidence," said the Peregrine, who had suddenly faded into view from nothing. The soldier nearest to her made to draw his sword, but found his scabbard empty. "Don't bother," she told him, tossing the blade back to him. "I can just as easily take it away a second time."

Yel had raised her hands and was fixing to do some kind of magic when Barsilay forced her arm down. "Don't," he said. "She's with me. I thought you were in prison?"

"I was," the Peregrine said, and Naftaly wondered if Yel and the others realized they were witnessing a bit of theater. "Got in a bit of trouble tracking that other Falcon down and couldn't get out of it without killing a bunch of Zayitis."

"Doesn't sound like a problem for you," Barsilay said airily.

"It would have caused a problem for you," she said, "so I let them take me. Took the other Falcon an awfully long time to break me back out. Though I thought you'd have done it a little quicker, once you knew."

"I don't think—" said Yel.

"If she were planning on harming any of us, we'd have been dead before we saw her," Barsilay said. Indicating the house, he asked, "What happened?"

The Peregrine said, "I haven't gone in, so I don't know the specifics, but there were demons involved, that was true. Here is what you must understand: Tarses doesn't want to destroy the city, he wants to control it. What he's doing here is just putting himself in position to take advantage of the nastier work he's planning in the mortal world. That's where the bloodshed will be."

"By 'putting himself in position,' are you referring to the siege castle?" Yel asked.

"Siege castle?" the Peregrine repeated.

"You didn't know about that?" Barsilay asked.

"Tarses keeps things modular. There is much I don't know. But I do know this: Tarses has taken personal control of the Hounds, and there is a cell of them in the city, with a Falcon embedded in it."

"Not the same Falcon who freed you?"

"The same one," the Peregrine said. "Tarses sent them to locate the tunnel into the grove. As of an hour ago, they hadn't done it. But that's where the Hounds were headed—and my Falcon is with them. You haven't much time. I can't go with you and risk being seen."

Barsilay nodded, once. "Keep Naftaly with you."

"Barsilay, I'm going with you," Naftaly protested.

"We're going to fight a cell of Hounds, and you're completely untrained," Barsilay said.

"You were never a soldier, either," Naftaly said. "And if they have salt, I might be more useful than you think."

"He's right," Yel said. "Come on." To the Peregrine, she said, "Go and see if you can find anything in the house."

"I will," said the Peregrine, and Naftaly and the others continued on, following Yel to the entrance to the tunnel, which she explained was closer to the center of the city. The tunnel had been constructed by the salt guild, and its entrance was concealed inside a building they maintained near the main piazza.

The exterior door was unguarded, and they crept inside quietly, then down a long flight of stairs that went deep underground. At the bottom was a great wooden door, fitted with several metal locks affixed with different sorts of Mazik symbols. The door stood open, and the Maziks Naftaly supposed had been guarding it were all dead with no visible wounds.

"What happened to them?" Naftaly asked.

Zel only raised a finger to quiet him. She inclined her head toward the doorway. Beyond, Naftaly could see a tunnel carved into the ground, lined with rock. He could not tell how far it extended, but the grove was far enough outside of Zayit that it must have been miles. The Maziks rendered themselves translucent, which Naftaly could not do. Barsilay reached out and took his wrist. "Stay here," he said, "and stay out of sight."

"But Yel said—"

"I don't care what she said. Stay here."

Naftaly watched Barsilay and the others disappear into the tunnel, and waited miserably beside the bodies of the guards for sixty seconds before he quietly followed into the darkness.

The tunnel had a light-stone installed every ten feet or so, which was not enough to do more than provide enough illumination for Naftaly not to fall down in the dark. He strained to hear footsteps, and could not; probably the magic that had made them all insubstantial also tended to make one's feet soft on the ground. Then he remembered the leech behind his ear and wondered if it might be glowing in the dark again, so he quietly removed it, putting it back in the box with the others.

He continued walking. The air was so still it felt like a grave, and Naftaly felt a nausea starting to take him. He began to rethink removing the leech. And then, from ahead, came the sound of steel on steel. Barsilay and the others had caught up with the Hounds.

Naftaly broke into a run, and wished he'd had the sense to ask for some salt back at the depot. Probably they wouldn't have given it to him. Elena, if she'd been there, would have taken some anyway—the old woman, too—but it hadn't occurred to him until just then. If he'd had salt, he could have tried taking on the Hounds himself.

The Maziks were nearly impossible to see, shadows fighting shadows in the dark.

Hanging back was a figure Naftaly could only see because of her eyes, which were taking in the scene, darting between the fighters. It was, Naftaly knew, the Falcon. Her gaze took him in, and she said nothing.

Naftaly strained to see Barsilay. He found him, recognizable only because of the way he moved and then because he'd lost his arm. He was fighting a Hound with his right arm, which put him at a disadvantage—while the Hound could use magic with one hand and wield a weapon with the other, Barsilay could only parry and dodge—and then the Hound kicked Barsilay's leg out from under him.

Naftaly leapt forward before the Hound could strike. Not considering that the other man was stronger, better armed, and better trained, he wrestled him away from a screaming Barsilay, losing his own knife when the two hit the ground. Naftaly felt the Hound's blade in his side, a stab so quick he thought at first he'd imagined it.

Then the Hound pushed back from Naftaly and spun to face Barsilay, knife raised, and shouted, "What are you waiting for?"

This order was directed at the Falcon, a woman as small as the Peregrine, who had all this time been watching from the shadows—waiting, Naftaly thought, to see how things played out. And how things were playing out just then was that the Hounds were going to slaughter them all and then make their way into the grove, and if she continued her inaction, it would be reported to Tarses.

The Falcon pulled a pair of knives from her belt and walked out of the shadows.

Naftaly knew none of them could fight her, if she'd been trained by the Peregrine. She weighed the knives in her hands and cracked her neck—and then a ball of light the size of a cat streaked into the tunnel, growing brighter by the second as Naftaly threw a hand over his eyes against the white-hot light, and then everything went dark. Around him, he heard shouts in Rimoni and Zayiti both—they'd all been blinded—and then there was a crack and a muffled shout, and then silence.

Naftaly blinked a few times, willing his vision to return, and felt a small hand over his eyes, and then Yel was whispering something, and his vision was restored. There, standing with both hands outstretched, was Asmel.

The Hound who had been about to slit Barsilay's throat was dead on the ground, his head crushed by a rock that had been made to fall from the ceiling.

Another Hound called out, "Collapse it!" and began flinging magic wildly from his palm, causing more rocks to fall, but Asmel tossed a pebble from the ground into his forehead, and he slumped over; dead or unconscious, Naftaly could not say.

The remaining Hounds were all dead.

Asmel stood surrounded by rubble, covered in dust and filth, panting and staring at the group before him until his eyes came to rest on Naftaly. "I know you," he murmured, then more firmly, coming forward to meet him, "I know you."

From behind him, Barsilay had managed to extract himself from beneath the body of the man who had been trying to kill him. In a rough voice, he said, "Asmel."

Asmel stopped, his shoulders rose sharply. Then the two men came together and embraced. Barsilay's arm had gone again, but with the one that remained he dug his fingers into Asmel's shoulder, and Asmel, who was taller, pressed Barsilay's cheek against his own, and both of them were weeping. Finally, Barsilay leaned back long enough to say, "Your eyes—"

"Are my own."

Naftaly briefly closed his own eyes, feeling a momentary void. Asmel was the closest either of them had to a living father.

Releasing Asmel, Barsilay went to help Yel, who had taken a bad fall. The Falcon was against the wall, looking a little bemused, while two soldiers held her with swords drawn. "What were your orders?" Barsilay asked her.

"Get these men through the tunnel to break the wards in the grove," she said. "Or, if we could not, collapse the tunnel so the men there could not be resupplied."

"You did not fight with them," he said.

"She was about to," one of the men put in.

"My loyalty lies with the Peregrine," the Falcon said. "But my will lies with Tarses."

"That's most unfortunate," Barsilay said, and he reached out and laid his hand on the Falcon's cheek, and she slumped to the ground, asleep.

WHEN TOBA WOKE she found that the entire back wall of the house had been blown out, and neither the demons nor Tsifra were anywhere visible. Her throat was aflame, and the old woman was shaking her shoulder. Elena, beside her, was crouched over her with Toba's hands in hers and was muttering one of her quiet nursery rhymes. As Toba stirred, Elena let out a little sob and pulled her up into her embrace, saying, "My Toba."

Toba breathed in Elena's familiar warmth and thought of all the times she had held her, memories she'd borrowed from the elder Toba: stories told at bedtime, honey on her bread at New Year's, soup when she lay sick in bed, scoldings when she'd been a naughty child. Claiming them had felt like theft. But if she were Elena's Toba, then Elena was hers, too, and so were all those stories she remembered.

Elena, who had bribed the midwife to let her live. Elena, who had saved her from Tarses. She had claimed Toba at her birth, and she claimed her again now.

"Are you all right?" Elena asked into Toba's shoulder. "Are you hurt?"

"Me?" Toba said through her burning throat. "You were the one thrown into the wall. Is your head all right?"

Elena touched the back of her head. "It's not terrible." Toba set her hand to the spot and felt around with a bit of magic—there was a swelling there, and Toba did her best to reduce it.

"When did you learn to do that?" Elena asked, and then turned and saw the body of Rafeq, who looked as though he might have been sleeping. Elena whispered, "No," and hung her head.

"What happened?" Toba asked weakly.

"The Courser exploded the wall," the old woman said. "It's the only reason any of us are still alive."

"I can't believe you released the miasma," Elena croaked.

"That creature was getting agitated," she answered. "He was getting ready to kill us all."

"I don't think he was," said Toba. "He wanted Asmel's magic—" Which was when she realized she no longer had it. "He's taken it."

"He's done more than take it," said Elena, getting up with Toba's help. "The salt that was here is gone." She began an examination of the machine, which had only mostly survived the explosion, and disassembled the bowels of it. "He processed Asmel's safira and took the powder."

"You mean he absorbed that, too?" asked Toba.

"From what Rafeq said, absorbing that much magic would have killed him," the old woman said.

"He couldn't process all of it," Elena said, reaching into the basin beneath the machine. "He ran out of salt." She produced a blue shard, about a tenth of the size of the original gem, and handed it to Toba.

"That's all that's left?"

Elena had left Toba and was leaning over Rafeq's body, still prone on the ground. She reached out and took his lifeless hand, head bowed. Tears ran down her face, until Toba came and embraced her.

"Is there nothing to be done for him?" Toba asked. A juvenile question: What could be done for a dead man? Elena shook her head.

The old woman said, "We should gather what we can and go. There's poison everywhere and the Zayitis will come to see who blew up a house."

"The salt guild will be coming for the decayed salt," Elena said.

"They can gather it up themselves," the old woman said. "You know we shouldn't stay here like this."

"Where can we go?" Elena asked. "There is no place else for us."

To Toba she said, "We've lost Naftaly. We haven't been able to find him in weeks. For all I know, he's dead, too."

"No," the old woman said. "I won't believe that. We've been in this house too long, lingering over this cursed task. We'll find him now."

Elena nodded wearily. In the corner of the room, where it had been hurled in the explosion, was a large purse. The old woman said, "We should take that."

"No," said Elena. "If we take it, the salt guild will know Rafeq had an associate, and they might come looking. Leave it. And we must destroy the machine; I don't want the salt guild knowing how it works."

Toba used the largest extent of her magic to melt down the metal parts of the machine, transfiguring it until all that was left was a ball of iron Elena was able to fit in her pocket. She burned all of Elena's notes and plans and Rafeq's own edits of her work, and everything else the two of them had worked so hard on for absolutely nothing at all. The salt guild, when they came, would find Rafeq's body, and hopefully they would not know he'd had a partner with him, who also knew the secret of how to make decayed salt. She'd only just finished when a small, dark woman appeared in the doorway. Toba put herself between the newcomer and the old women, but then she recognized her as the Mazik she'd dreamed of in Rahel's tower.

The woman only looked surprised. "It's you," she said, not to Toba but to the others. "Is this where you've been all this time?"

Elena stared at the woman long enough to decide, "I don't have the faintest idea who you are."

"Are you very sure?" the woman asked, and Elena said, "Oh."

The woman said, "I'm the person who is going to take you to that boy you both adore so deeply. Provided he hasn't gotten himself killed."

The old woman said, "He'd better not have," and then, "Can we really trust her?"

Elena said, "She followed us all the way from Rimon and we're still alive, so I'd say yes, we can trust her. At least for today."

The woman smiled and led the others out toward the piazza just as the first light of day was hitting the horizon.

TWENTY-THREE

TSIFRA FOUND ATALEF in a dark alley near the salt guild, as if he'd been waiting for her there.

She wondered if the body he had made had been his design, or contained some version of Marah's physical being, and then she thought to wonder why he had not become a woman—if it was choice or something else. He was tall and orange-eyed, as Marah must have been, and dark and young and handsome, with severe lines to his jaw that reminded her oddly of Barsilay, until she recalled that Barsilay and Marah had been kin. His left hand was fisted, clutching, Tsifra was sure, the killstone. His right hand, which he must have used to touch salt, was blackened. "Where is Asmel?" she asked.

"I let him go," Atalef replied. "I was waiting for you."

"For me?"

"I knew that you would follow me here." Atalef opened his hand, revealing the small killstone on his palm.

"Atalef," she said. "Did you kill Tarses?"

He said, "No."

"Why? Why would you not, as soon as you could?"

"I have reconsidered."

"Reconsidered! We have the chance to be free, you and I. It's what we've been planning for months. Surely you're not saying you won't kill him?"

"Courser," he said. "There is much you do not know. My mind is so much larger than it was. There were things that Marah knew—"

"Was Marah not Tarses's enemy?"

Atalef said, "At the end. But not at the beginning. They were great friends, once. And Marah understood his gifts and burdens both. She knew Tarses told the truth when he said he saw what was to come."

She asked, "And what is coming, then?"

"The mortal world will run headlong into hell. The Mirror will drag us with them, and everything will be ended. Unless Tarses prevents it."

"Tarses cannot be so important."

"He is the only one with the will for what must be done. To harness the Mirror, it is a terrible thing, but it is the only choice."

"Is that Marah's opinion, or yours?"

Atalef said, "There were things that Marah knew, and there were things that Atalef knew. Together, our understanding is complete."

Tsifra felt a seething anger building inside herself. She said, "What you mean is that you have Marah's ideals and Atalef's lack of conscience."

"Is it lack of conscience if the entire world is at stake?" Atalef asked.

"That's Tarses's argument!" Tsifra shouted. "So you will continue as his slave, because you believe in his cause?"

Atalef gave no answer. Tsifra's fingers twitched, and she said, "Kaspit Rokedet, I order you to kill Tarses right now."

Atalef smiled and said, "I won't."

Tsifra went hot with rage. Atalef said, "Do you understand, now, Courser? I am no one's slave." He held up the killstone in his fist. "But Tarses will be mine."

"Marah . . . You have her name? The safira caused it to change?"

"Not Marah's name and not mine. A new name, new as the dawn, Courser. Tarses will rule the world and I shall rule Tarses. Can you not imagine it? Tarses will prevent our ruin, and I will see the firmament repaired, and then I shall be King of the new world. You will be my Courser," he said, reaching for her hand, which she pulled back. "You will rule the mortal world, and I the Mazik, and Tarses will serve us as I choose."

Atalef would become a new Caçador, a new Tarses. Tsifra had little time to decide whether this would be better or worse ... He was giving her a moment to choose him, to make herself his ally, but if she continued to hesitate, he would use her name and take her will, as Tarses had done.

"If you kill Tarses," she said, "I will be your Courser."

"I can't. I can't! If I kill him, then everything he built falls apart. Tarses has the names. Tarses sees the future. I need him to build my empire, do you not see?"

"He will betray you."

"He can't!" Atalef held up the killstone.

"It won't be enough! You have to use it now!"

"I don't take your orders, Tsifra," he said, and she gasped. She could see what would come next, as if she'd read it on a map. Atalef would use her name—the very name Marah had given her—to force her to his will. They would go against Tarses, and they would lose, and Tarses would kill them both.

She would not be made a puppet to a doomed cause. Before he could say her name a second time, she made her arm a blade and swung it at his throat.

Before she touched him, he became a flock of birds—no, they were bats—and then they were gone. The killstone was gone.

She shrieked, "You fool!" and there was no answer. What would he do? And would he give her part in this away to Tarses, in the end? Tsifra staggered in a circle, her arm still a blade, and she tore at her hair with her other hand. Plans upon plans upon plans, and she was worse off than when she'd started, any way she counted it. Atalef had been her one ally; Toba could not be, truly, so long as Tarses lived.

She recalled, then, what the Peregrine had told her: the King of Luz could give a Mazik a new name, as the safira had given a new name to Atalef. There could still be some chance for her, if she could find Barsilay, help him, befriend him.

It was so absurd she could not even complete the thought. Would Barsilay forget she'd broken his legs? That she'd cut off his arm?

Even if he could—which she could not quite believe—Tarses would be waiting for her with new orders the second she closed her eyes. She'd failed to carry out his last command.

If she remained in Mazik Zayit, she was a threat to any who might help her. She could think of no plan, no trick, to get around it. If she threw in with Barsilay, Tarses would order her to kill him; if she begged Toba to let her stay by her side, Tarses would simply order Tsifra to bring her back again.

Letting out a scream, she slammed her sword-arm into the ground and lowered her face, and wept, 'til the moon was low in the sky and she made her way invisible to the Zayit gate, past the soldiers of Zayit, and to the mortal city where Tarses would expect her to be.

BARSILAY WATCHED CLOSELY as Saba worked to knit Naftaly's flank back together with a thread of magic so fine it might have been spider silk.

They were inside the palace. Whether Saba had been given rooms there because of his relationship with Efra or for some other reason, Naftaly did not know, but he'd been carried there on the back of one of the Zayiti soldiers, all of them marveling over him because he should have been dead; the Hounds had been fighting with salted blades. A fortunate thing for Naftaly; it was likely the reason he was still alive. The Hound hadn't bothered to aim for a vital organ or do much eviscerating.

"Why are you doing it that way?" Barsilay asked. "Why not just heal the tissue?"

"Because," Saba replied without halting his work, "he doesn't heal like a Mazik. If I don't reinforce it, it might open up again."

Naftaly winced as Saba made another stitch with a needle that looked like it was made of silver. It was so thin it was nearly invisible except when the light hit it, and sharp enough that it didn't hurt nearly as badly as it might have otherwise, but he couldn't help but flinch every time it pierced him. There was some irony in the situation: the tailor being tailored. At least Saba was better at his job than Naftaly. "If you stop looking," Saba said, "it will hurt less."

Naftaly fixed his eyes on the cat snoozing on the worktable on the other side of the room. It had barely woken when they'd come in, Naftaly bleeding profusely and Barsilay shouting at Saba to hurry up, because the magical patch Asmel had used to hold his wound together wasn't holding on account of the salt. Saba had poured water over the wound three times, and still managed to burn his fingers when he'd started to examine it. Barsilay's face had been very white then.

"You kept it," Naftaly said, of the cat.

"Hm? Yes, well, she didn't want to leave. Getting too cold out, I expect, so I just brought her here with me."

Barsilay asked, "Were you able to repair the vascular system?"

Testily, Saba said, "Yes."

"What about the kidney?"

"The wound did not extend in that direction."

"Are you certain?"

Saba glanced up to Naftaly, taking his gaze from the sleeping cat. "I don't have the habit of sewing mortals back together much, so if you'd like me to do it correctly, please call off your mother hen."

"It might be better if you didn't watch," Naftaly told Barsilay.

"But I might learn something."

"If you want to learn then be quiet," Saba said. "And I'm nearly done anyway. Most of the damage was to the inside... It was a thrust, not a slash."

"Then you should recheck the kidney," Barsilay said.

"Barsilay," Naftaly said, "why don't you go check on Asmel?"

"You want me to leave." Barsilay said. "You don't mean that."

"I'm afraid it's for the best."

"But—"

"Please."

"All right," Barsilay said. "I'll go."

"Don't sulk."

"I'm not sulking," he said, stopping at the door. "I'm not."

Once he was gone, Saba resumed his work. "He'll be sulking for hours."

"Minutes," Naftaly said. "He's not persistent enough to sulk for hours."

Saba chuckled and went back to sewing. He was working in layers, from the inside out, putting things back together, and—as he'd told Barsilay—he was nearly done. Finally, he sat back and set down his needle, saying, "It's as healed as I can make it, but I'd like you to keep still a few days."

"Thank you," Naftaly said.

"Would you like me to give you something more for the pain?"

"Whatever you gave me before is still working," Naftaly said. "It doesn't hurt so terribly."

"Good," Saba said. "I'm glad to hear it. Now, since I have you here, how are your small friends?"

"The leeches?" Naftaly raised a hand to his ear and lowered it again, resisting the urge to fight with the creature stuck behind his ear, which he'd reapplied at Barsilay's insistence back in the tunnel, lest he suffer a vision while he was already injured. "I had to stop wearing them at night. They were keeping me from dreaming."

"I'd thought that might be possible. Are they working otherwise?"

"I haven't had any visions since you gave them to me. I was hoping I might not need them much longer? You said that I wouldn't need them permanently."

"I said you *might* not need them permanently," Saba said. "And it's far too soon to discuss going without them. Do you mind if I examine the area? I'll be cautious this time."

Naftaly turned his head to the left, allowing Saba to run a careful finger behind the spot where the al'qa was attached.

THE REPUBLIC OF SALT 325

"Do you mind if I remove it for a moment?"

"Go ahead," Naftaly said, and Saba carefully set it in a bowl before returning his attention to Naftaly. "Well, it's no worse but there's still some inflammation. It could be that you aren't wearing them enough."

"I'm not willing to give up dreaming," Naftaly said.

"If you just give it a month, for some healing to take place—" Saba began.

Naftaly cut him short. "No."

"No? Well, I suppose I understand, but this may be the best we can do."

"I have no symptoms anymore," Naftaly said. "I'm not sure what more I could hope for."

"You have no symptoms now, but they could worsen again with time. I'm only trying to prevent a relapse. But it is your decision, of course. No Mazik wants to give up dreaming." Saba lifted up the bowl and passed it back to Naftaly, who picked up the leech and reattached it, a bit resentfully. He felt strongly that there were things he ought to know. He'd seen Zayit burning, but without more details it was hard to give a decent warning. Maybe Efra had been right to order him to remove the al'qa.

The leech had been attached for several hours already, and seemed uneager to resume its work. Naftaly tapped it with his fingertip a few times to encourage it.

Unfortunately, he did not feel it put its mouth against his skin again, so when he tapped it a third time, he felt a jolt along the left side of his head. "Oh," he said to Saba, and then he fell off the table.

He was still in Zayit when he opened his eyes to the same scene he'd witnessed in his last vision, the city burning. The most notable difference was the gate stretching into the sky in front of him. Its point of origin was a familiar book on the ground.

There were only two people visible, Toba and a second, future version of himself. And she told the version of Naftaly that did not yet exist, "You must go first," and she pointed at a line she must have drawn on the ground, indicating, Naftaly guessed, an angle he was meant to take to pass through.

The future version of Naftaly turned his head, scanning the area.

"Do you see anything?" Toba asked.

"No," he said.

"Then go."

Naftaly watched himself step through the gate at the strange angle, and then Toba bent down and picked up the still-open book. She put her foot through the gate, and then looked back one last time and said, "Tarses will find Zayit's gate in six days."

Naftaly opened his eyes from Saba's floor. "I did tell you not to squeeze the leeches," Saba told him.

Naftaly was too stunned to respond with anything other than a shaky breath.

Saba said, "I don't suppose there's any good news this time?"

Naftaly closed his eyes again and said, "No."

ELENA HAD NOT wanted to let Toba out of her sight, but Toba convinced her to go to sleep in the next room, and then had a bath drawn by a shade made by some Mazik or other—she could not say who. Her modesty had given way under the filth of her misadventures; she hadn't washed properly since before her doomed wedding to Tsidon, and since then she'd run halfway around the world and been carried in the arms of demons, to say nothing of whatever was embedded in her clothes and hair from the explosion. The tub was made of silver—she'd never seen anything like it, even in the royal baths of Rimon—and the water was steaming and scented with perfume so strong it made her head ache. Her room—windowless, probably to stave off spies or assassins—was richly decorated with finely wrought furniture and ornate textiles on the bed that did not look to have been made by magic. She wondered if they'd been mortal-made and brought in through the gate, exotic luxuries made by lowly mortals on their way to a premature end.

Rafeq was dead. She wasn't quite sure how she felt about that. It was a loss, she knew, because Rafeq had been so old, and had been Marah's confederate once, and was the person responsible for the return of Asmel's magic. On the other hand, he'd also deceived her and stolen Marah's safira. Asmel did not know what had happened to the demon who had taken it, or to the killstone. If it had worked, if Atalef knew the command-word, then Tarses ought to be dead by now.

She wondered what had happened to her sister, who had saved them all from the miasma and then vanished.

If Tarses were dead, would his troops and his siege castle still be there in the morning?

She pulled herself from the cooling bath and let the shade put a shift on her, and crawled into the absurdly high bed just as Asmel appeared in the doorway. "I'm sorry," he said, hovering like a shade himself at the foot of the bed. "Barsilay had many questions."

It was the first time she'd seen him since Te'ena—since she'd abandoned him in Te'ena, with a little money and a little magic and a failing memory.

Now he was himself again, filled with magic, his eyes returned to their normal shape, the remaining shard of his safira hung around his neck on a silver chain. His entire carriage was different, less drawn in. There was no way for him to mistake her for Marah or the elder Toba now. He would know, always, precisely who she was, and this left her feeling slightly unmoored; she did not know how he would feel about her now. She could not embrace him, though she wished to. He sat down on the foot of the bed. "How are you feeling?" she asked.

"I feel," he said, "too much. My memories are jumbled and my mind is racing and I wish I had wine."

Toba took the pitcher of water by the bed and made him a glass of wine. "I could have done that," he said. "I forgot." He tasted the wine and laughed. "This is grape juice," he said.

"It's not!" She took the glass from him and sipped. "It is. I'll ferment it—"

"No," he said. "It's settling my stomach." He finished the glass in a long draught. "Thank you."

"It was only juice."

"I didn't mean the juice," Asmel said. "You went through a great deal on my account."

"I could say the same."

"I owe you my life several times over."

"Then we are equal in that respect."

"I think you are the most extraordinary person in all the worlds."

Here Toba's mouth snapped shut, because she did not know how to respond.

"I am not good at expressing myself," he said. He swayed a bit. "I think it was more than juice after all. You are angry."

"I'm not," she said.

"I have embarrassed myself with you."

Toba said, "Because you didn't always know who I was, you mean? You couldn't help that."

He sighed. "I was not always confused about that."

"Asmel."

He took her hand and said, "I am sorry."

"For confusing me with the others?"

"No!" He shook his head. "Yes! I don't know."

"I think you should rest."

"Toba," he said in exasperation, "please be quiet. You said you loved me, once, and I told you it was only because you were so helpless. For me to . . . to feel, or to act, it would have been wrong of me. But now, I think you are altogether different than you were then, and perhaps . . ."

Perhaps what? Toba wondered, as he trailed off, but she stayed quiet, as requested. He said, "I believe . . . I believe I have been in love with you for quite some time, and I was wondering if you might still . . . You're very quiet."

"You asked me to be quiet!"

"Yes, but now I think you should—" He got up. "I'm leaving."

"Hashem's sake," she said, getting up and pulling him around. "You're right. I don't need you. My magic is entirely under my control, and I know precisely who I am. Do you?"

"Yes," he said.

"Are you saying that *your* feelings are because I looked after you when you were weak?"

Asmel said, "No. Though I suppose it helped. If I am honest."

"All right then," she said, and she went up on her toes and kissed him 'til he swayed on his feet.

"Not juice," he said.

"Are you very drunk?"

"Oh, yes."

"Does that mean you didn't mean what you said just now?" Toba asked.

"No," Asmel said. "It only means I can't stand up any longer."

Toba rolled her eyes a little. "Then sleep," she said, "you impossible man."

"Here?"

Toba flushed in the darkness, and said, "You slept by me all the way from Rimon to Te'ena, unless you forgot."

"I didn't forget. It's only that you've washed and I haven't." He slumped a little, he was so tired. "I should call a shade."

"Don't bother. Come and sleep by me, Asmel."

Asmel used magic to peel off his filthy clothes and crawled into the bed without another word. His chest rose and fell, and Toba could feel the thrum of his magic within him.

He was quiet so long Toba thought he must have been asleep, but then she asked, "Do you think Tarses is dead?"

"I don't know," Asmel said. "Why not ask your sister?"

"My sister?"

"You didn't kill her, did you?"

"No," Toba said. "No, I didn't." *There are no further debts between us*, her sister had told her. But that was before she'd saved Toba and Elena both, and Toba was not sure if that amounted to a new debt or not. But she remembered then there was another issue, more important, and she asked, "Did you find Omer?"

Quietly, Asmel said, "I did. And he told me about Aravoth." He sighed. "I cannot go with you. No Mazik or mortal may go."

"No mortal or Mazik," she said. But she was not the only part-Mazik with a legacy to fulfill. Marah had left her to finish her work. And Dawid ben Aron had left Naftaly.

TSIFRA OPENED HER dreaming eyes to a place she'd never seen before: a stone chamber, without windows, lit only by a single candle burning in an alcove above a bed.

On the bed was Tarses, sleeping.

Tsifra did not know what to make of this. Was she not dreaming? Was it even possible to sleep in the dream-world?

She felt icy fingers at the nape of her neck that gripped her hard, and without moving her head, her eyes went to her left side. There stood a second Tarses. Could he have made a buchuk, she wondered—only that would not explain why one was sleeping. She felt the waking Tarses's magic creep into her muscles, freezing her in place. He did not speak.

An invisible door opened in the wall, and a man crept through. Tsifra realized, when he stepped into the candlelight, that it was Atalef—or whatever Atalef had become. Her eyes went again to the waking Tarses, who watched her closely without speaking. She could not ask what she was seeing, because her tongue was as frozen as the rest of her.

He was watching her reaction. Since Tarses knew what Atalef looked like now, this strongly implied she was seeing a memory. This was what Atalef had done after he'd left her. They were inside the siege castle, where Tarses slept.

Atalef approached Tarses's sleeping form. His right hand was balled into a fist, clutching—Tsifra assumed—the killstone. She made a great effort not to look at it.

"Wake," Atalef said, and Tarses, on his bier, opened his eyes and vanished. Atalef spun, trying to see where he'd gone, as several dark shapes circled the room, whispering indistinctly. Tsifra recognized them at once as demons. One nearby whispered in her ear, "Birdling, take care."

But did that whisper not imply the demons were more than memories?

"So you've made yourself Mazik at last, Atalef the Demon," said Tarses's voice, from somewhere hidden. "Don't look surprised; I knew what you were the moment you set foot in this castle."

"Who," Atalef said, his angry face lit by the lone candle set in the wall. "*Who* I am, not what."

"That matters little to me," Tarses said. "I know you don't intend to use the killstone in your hand, old friend, else you'd have done so already. You are here to bargain with me for my life. So go ahead, make your bargain. Perhaps I shall agree."

Atalef said, "I shall rule you, Caçador, and together we shall break the Mirror. Swear to me, on your name, to serve me, and I will let you live."

"Ah," Tarses said sadly, "I had hoped there would be more of Marah in you. Such a pity. You were something extraordinary, and you have made yourself common." At that, the flame from the candle rose from the wick, swirling like a whirlwind, and as Atalef tried to cast it away, it sent out a tendril that burned his hand, causing him to drop the killstone.

Tsifra did not understand why Atalef could not control the flame; it was within his power to extinguish it. Yet he gasped in pain at the burn, and in so doing, drew the flame into his lungs, and his orange eyes went wide with the agony of it. There was no air left in him, even to whisper Tarses's name to the killstone. The vanished Tarses reappeared, inches before Atalef.

"I've sealed your lips. Don't bother trying to fight. Did you really think you could enslave me? Did you think I would hesitate to kill you, because you hold Marah's memory? I'm too close to the end of my visions, demon, to allow you to steal what I have built."

Tsifra could smell Atalef's body burning from the inside, and she began to tremble as he collapsed, the flames exploding from his chest. He had not the breath to scream, but his face, in the moments before he died was pain itself.

Atalef was dead.

The flame that had taken him rose from his body and returned to the wick of the candle it had come from. Tarses lay back on the bier and closed his eyes again.

The waking Tarses dropped his hand from Tsifra's neck and went to pick up the killstone from the floor, where it had fallen. It was all Tsifra could do to stay on her feet.

"Did you know?" he asked softly.

Tsifra said, "I tried to stop him. I tried to kill him."

"So you did know. And yet you failed to warn me."

Tsifra said, "I came here as quickly as I could, Father."

"Call me not so!" he snapped. "Do you imagine I hold some tender feelings for you?"

"No," she said, and he grabbed her by the wrist, slamming it down on the stone bed by his own sleeping body.

"Were you in league with him?" he demanded.

"No!" she cried, and he cut off her smallest finger, and she screamed. It was not her real finger, she told herself. This was only a dream.

"When did you learn what he was planning?"

"Only now," she said. "Father, please—"

"Do not call me so!" he shouted again, and took her next smallest finger. "How can I trust you now?"

"I tried to kill him," she said, "once I knew—I swear it. I swear it!"

He dropped her wrist and she went down to her knees, clutching her bleeding hand. "Stop that," he ordered, because she was weeping from fear and pain both. "Do you know why I made myself Caçador? Why it was necessary? Because no one else had the stomach for what needed to be done."

He turned away, back toward Atalef's body, charred beyond recognition. Then he said, "Where is the other?"

Toba, he meant. Worse and worse. Tsifra said, "She slipped through my grasp. I am sorry."

Silence for a very long time. Then, "I see. I am surrounded by failure, it seems. I have chosen poorly in my lieutenants."

Tsifra wondered whether he included the Peregrine in this statement; she was usually his favorite as she was efficient and reliable both. She had been so strange the last time they'd spoken that Tsifra wondered whether something had gone wrong for her, too.

Tarses said, "Where are you?"

"Mortal Zayit," she said. "Where would you have me go?"

"I need you in Barcino. The Queen's fleet arrives in three days. You will take command of it there and return with it to Zayit."

She'd been expecting worse. But Tarses needed Zayit, and without Toba or Atalef, she was the only tool he had to operate in the mortal realm.

She nodded. "I will do as you ask."

"Courser," he said, "Zayit must fall. There is no need to restrain yourself now."

Twenty-Four

NAFTALY WOKE HALFWAY into the next day with the old woman huddled at the end of his bed like a cat on a cold day, her legs curled under her and a blanket obscuring everything but her face, which was turned to a fire burning in the hearth.

He'd nearly given up hope ever seeing her again.

"There you are," she said, as if she had not been absent for days. He'd missed her wrinkled face, her gnarled hands. She was, blessedly, less thin than she'd been last time he saw her; someone had been caring for her. Whoever it had been, Naftaly owed them a debt for it. She took his hand and patted it, again and again, and looked as if she might have wept while he'd been sleeping.

Naftaly was groggy indeed, and struggled to sit up. He was still without a shirt, and when he pulled back his blankets he could see the residual light of Saba's sutures in his skin. "Where have you been?" he asked. "I looked everywhere. I sent people—no one could find you."

The old woman's lip quivered, and then she threw her skinny arms around his neck and sobbed against him.

"I'm sorry," he said.

"You should be! I've been sick about you for weeks, and now look! That Mazik went and got you stabbed!"

"Barsilay didn't get me stabbed," Naftaly said. "I'm afraid I went and did that on my own."

"He should have been more careful," the old woman sniffled. "He knows you aren't a Mazik. I mean to give him a piece of my mind about it, too, the lout."

Naftaly said, "Barsilay feels bad enough already without you piling on. Where is he?"

"With that woman, the Savia," she said. "And Elena. And some other people, I stopped paying attention to their names. I'll take you to find him once you've eaten. They left us with one of those dreadful shadow-men, do you see it?" She pointed at the corner, where a shade seemed to be dusting the curtains. "It never stays still, but they said it will make you something to eat."

"Have you eaten?"

"Oh, twice. It makes a very nice chicken. You can hardly taste the lentils." She took him by the arm and helped him up, then took a snooze herself while the shade heated him some water to wash with and made him a bowl of soup, which was all he found he had the appetite for, and which he only ate because the old woman was not about to show him where Barsilay was until he ate something. Six days until Tarses found the grove, and he was eating soup and scrubbing his face with scented soap. Only when he was done, the old woman could not take him to Barsilay, because she'd fallen asleep again.

He had the shade lead him instead, down the covered walkways of the palazzo, down several flights of stairs, and across the piazza to the main armory, where Efra was yelling at several unhappy men while Barsilay looked on.

"Are you all right?" Barsilay said, squeezing Naftaly's shoulder while he held a stack of papers with his other, phantom arm.

"I'm fine," he said. "But I need to tell you something, and it's urgent."

"Everything seems to be urgent at the moment," Barsilay said.

Efra was tearing into the Maziks, and Barsilay winced. Naftaly asked, "What is she doing?"

"She had the entirety of the stockpile tested and re-inventoried. It's not good. There's more sugar than salt here."

"Then what happened to the salt? Is it elsewhere in the city, or still on the other side of the gate?"

"No one seems to know," Barsilay said. "She's brought in the head of the salt guild. If they were complicit somehow, there may be more wrong than we know."

"There *is* more wrong than you know," Naftaly said. "I had another vision."

Barsilay looked like he wanted to say a great many things about this, but Naftaly blazed on. "It was a continuation of my last vision," he said. "Zayit falls. I don't think there's any way to alter that."

"Nothing good so far."

"I saw myself with Toba," Naftaly went on. "She had the book. The complete book. And she was using it to open a gate."

Barsilay's eyebrows rose. "Where were you going?"

"I'm not sure . . . There was some angle marked on the ground, I don't know what it meant. But I can tell you we do get the book back. That's the good news."

"That's very good news indeed. What else?"

"Toba, in the vision, I think she knew I was watching. She said that Tarses will take the olive grove in six days."

Barsilay screwed his eyes shut. "She said that to you directly?"

"She did."

"You're sure it was Toba?"

"The future version of myself seemed to think so. I went through the Luz gate with her. Barsilay, this was a true vision. I would not lead you astray if I weren't absolutely certain."

Barsilay ran his thumb over his lower lip. "So we are about to lose Zayit and its gate both." His eyes went to the doorway because Asmel had just entered, still looking wretched but clean, at least. He made his way to Barsilay, saying, "I've been looking for you for hours."

"I'm sorry," he said. "Everything's gone bad. I've been here since the middle of the night— Don't look like that. Don't be . . . proud. I haven't actually done anything useful."

Asmel said, "I never suggested pride. Surprise, perhaps."

"That's better," Barsilay said.

"I would submit that responsibility suits you."

Barsilay sighed loudly.

Asmel said, "Keep your sighs, Barsilay. It's in the best interest of the world that you want this as little as possible." Barsilay smirked.

Seeing the three men conversing, Efra left off giving orders and joined them. "I heard you were looking for me," she told Asmel. "You have some news?"

Asmel said, "Before my magic was returned to me, I was imprisoned by the salt guild, and I overheard a number of disturbing things. The mortals have betrayed you."

"We're aware of the betrayal," Efra said.

"But not the extent of it," Asmel said. "They didn't only sell you sugar. The mortals have been stockpiling salt for Tarses. There's a thousand pounds of salt on the other side of the gate waiting for Tarses to send his Courser to claim it."

"That's enough salt to kill every Mazik alive ten times over," Barsilay said.

"It is," Asmel said. "And once he gets it here, there won't be a city in Mazikdom safe from him, not ever. You must prevent it, whatever the cost."

"Our best men are in the grove already," she said. "And Tarses failed to breach the tunnel last night. We can keep his forces away from the gate indefinitely with the wards up."

"Not indefinitely," Barsilay said. "We have six days, according to Naftaly."

"Six days!" Efra exclaimed. To Naftaly, she said, "You saw this? How can you be sure?"

"I was given a message," he said. "Last night."

Efra chewed her lip. Naftaly reminded her, "I saw the Prince of Zayit's dapple-gray stallion fall crossing the bridge. It broke its left rear leg." He touched his own calf. "Here. The bone went clear through the skin. Tell me it's not what happened."

Efra said nothing. Then, "But Tarses taking the grove, you did not see that yourself?"

"The messenger is unimpeachable," Barsilay said. "Tarses will get the wards down in six days. How long can the Second Division hold him off, once he does?"

Efra said, "Without the wards, if Tarses sends his full force against them, they won't last more than a few days at most."

"But you have all this salt," Naftaly said. "There's still the older stuff, from before the mortals started selling you sugar. What's the point of it, if you can't use it to win a battle?"

"We can't use salt in close combat without poisoning our own soldiers," Efra said. "It's only useful at a distance. Preferably when there's a wall between yourself and whomever you are shooting it at."

"Have you been in communication with P'ri Hadar?" Asmel asked. "Have you asked them to send their army?"

Efra breathed heavily. "I made that suggestion to the Council weeks ago, when Barsilay first arrived. They refused to consider it."

"But why?" Asmel asked.

"They fear that if P'ri Hadar puts soldiers in Zayit, they won't be willing to leave again. The city will become a colony of the Queen, and we'll lose our own rule."

"But that's better than losing the city to Tarses, surely," Naftaly said.

"They think they can hold off Tarses more easily than they can throw off the Queen once she has troops here. But I will remake the request. Circumstances have worsened. But even if they agree, P'ri Hadar can't get here in six days."

"Might there be some help from any of the closer cities?" Naftaly asked.

Efra said, "Anab and Tappuah have no standing armies, and they wouldn't help us if they did, after what we did in Habush. Everyone else is too far away to even consider."

Barsilay frowned to himself, and then said, "You all are looking at this backward."

"What is your suggestion?"

"If you cannot secure the gate with troops," he said, "then you must find a way to secure it without troops."

"Could you salt the grove?" Naftaly asked.

"Again, that would only slow Tarses down. All he has to do is wait for it to rain a few times and wash it away."

Naftaly said, "What if it didn't wash away? What if it were contained, somehow?"

Efra set her mouth in an irritated expression; to her, Naftaly knew, he was useful because he could touch salt and not much else. What did he know about defending a city, or a gate? Nothing, that's what. She said, "If you contain the salt well enough to withstand rain, what use is it?"

Except in this case, Naftaly did have an idea. He said, "What do you call those pyramid-shaped containers, the ones you use to store lentils?"

Efra gave him a nonplussed look. "The lentil amphoras?"

"Aren't they made to keep their contents dry?"

"Yes, but even if you filled them with salt—" she began, and then saw the direction his mind was taking. "You're not filling them with salt."

"Gunpowder and salt mixed together," he explained. "Then you only need something to detonate it when it comes into close proximity with magic. Can you make something like that? That would light a spark if a Mazik came close?"

She said, "We could. But if these are in the ground, eventually Tarses will find a way over the top."

"Don't put them in the ground," Asmel put in. "Float them in an unpredictable orbit around the gate. There will be no path through and even if he blows up some of them, the others will fill in the field again, and then there's salt on the ground and he'll have to wait for that to wash away, too."

Efra said, "It will take him months to get through it, and he'd be losing men the whole time. But how would we deploy it? If the amphoras detonate when they sense magic, we'll never get them assembled, let alone orbiting the gate."

"Elena and I can assemble them," Naftaly said. "As long as they're set only to detonate when they sense, say, a half-Mazik or more. You don't want him to be able to use shades to detonate it, anyway."

Asmel said, "The detonator would have to be calibrated very carefully indeed. But I think it could be done." He held out a finger and drew a sliver in the air that represented the gate, and then added several elliptical orbits around it and set them spinning. "I will need some time to think on the best way to construct the orbits."

To Asmel, Efra said, "Figure out how many amphoras you need. We need this up quickly if we only have six days."

"The detonator?" Barsilay asked.

"I have someone in mind for that," she said.

THAT NIGHT, INEXPLICABLY and for the first time, Toba dreamt of Tsidon the Lymer, the man she'd nearly married in a trap laid for her by her father.

They were in the garden of the King of Rimon again—the Queen, Toba corrected herself, since the King was dead along with all his sons. She wasn't sure how she'd arrived; she certainly hadn't wished to dream of Tsidon, but she guessed he probably had the ability to summon someone if he wanted. Which begged the question, why hadn't he before?

"Dearest," he said flatly, "you've come at last."

His left eye was encircled with an angry scar, and his face had lost the false smile he so often wore. Toba was not sure whether trying to run away would make things better or worse.

Tsidon liked to talk. So she decided to let him.

"Are you not pleased to see me?" he asked. "I've longed for you so."

"Is this necessary?" Toba asked him. "What's the point of a farce with no audience?"

His uninjured eye winced. "I went through a great deal of suffering on your account."

"Because I didn't marry you and let Tarses turn me into his slave? Shall I apologize?"

"You could apologize for my pain," he said. "It would be the kind thing to do."

Toba did not think it was safe to apologize, because admitting culpability carried its own implications. She said, "I am sorry you suffered."

He laughed. "That is no apology at all. You are so like him, you know." Like her father, he meant, and he had not meant it kindly. He added, "You would do well with him, I think."

"I'm not interested in your thoughts."

"Ah, she bites, still. Do you know you sent a dozen of my men completely mad with void terror? The Caçador had me kill them all myself as punishment for your escape."

"And yet you say I'd do well with him?"

He chuckled and plucked a small yellow flower from between the stones in the wall. "You have a similar nature when angry."

"You've never seen me angry."

"I've seen enough." He tucked the flower behind her ear, and she decided it was better to allow it.

"Why did you call me here? Why bother now?"

"Why do you think?" Tsidon asked.

"I assume it's because you want to know where I am."

"I don't care where you are," he said. "That's someone else's business."

She doubted the truth of that very much. "Then why?"

"I suppose it's only that I'm so hopelessly bored," he said. "Do you know where I am? Ah, I'll tell you. I'm in Rimon. I'm here all by my miserable self, while your father lays waste to the world."

"Why?"

"More punishment. For losing you. I have no Hounds to command here; they're all gone. The Alaunts are at the front. There's nothing for me to do, save guard Tarses's empty offices."

"I'm sure that's very important," she said.

"It isn't," he said. "There's nothing here for me to guard. I'm alone, day after day, with nothing to do but think about how you were nearly my wife." He'd threaded his fingers into her hair, and Toba thought she'd made a mistake in humoring him this far. She stepped out of his reach, but he only followed.

"How tragic for you, truly."

He ran a thumb down her cheek. "You act as if you don't care about my pain. But you should care, dearest, that you maimed me. Killed my men. Left me to suffer alone." He leaned in close. "And I want you to know I intend to do all the same to you."

TOBA'S EYES FLEW open in her windowless room in Zayit. Without a view of the sky, she was not sure what time it was, but she felt like it must still be night. Asmel was tangled in the bedding next to her, sleeping so deeply he hadn't so much as stirred when she'd sat up. She covered him with her own blanket before sliding out of the bed and out of the room. She needed advice from someone who knew Tsidon, and she could not think who that might be apart from the Peregrine, who she assumed must be hovering somewhere near Barsilay.

She was not, however, outside Barsilay's chamber, and Toba had just turned to go back the other way when she felt Naftaly's fingers on her shoulder. "What are you doing at this hour? Were you looking for Barsilay?"

The man himself rounded the corner and stopped. "It's late for a meeting in the hallway," he said. "Did something happen?"

"I was looking for the Peregrine," Toba said. "I assumed she'd be here."

Softly, Naftaly asked, "She's not, is she?"

Barsilay said, "No, and she hasn't been with me for a while. Was it urgent?"

"Possibly," Toba said. "I just had a conversation with Tsidon." She tapped her temple. "I'd like her opinion."

"You can't trust him," Barsilay said.

"Am I an idiot? Of course I can't trust him."

"Then you should just discount—"

"Just help me find her, would you?"

"I'll go with her," Barsilay told Naftaly. "You're still injured and you've been up too much already." He set his hand on his shoulder. "I'll tell you after." Naftaly agreed to this without argument and went into his room. Barsilay started down the hall with Toba at his elbow.

"We'll have a time finding her if she doesn't want to be found," he said. "And I'm not exactly a tracker."

The door behind them opened again and Naftaly stuck his face back through. "You can stop looking now. She's in here, and you'll need to come right away."

Toba followed Barsilay quickly into the room. Propped in the corner, next to the bed, was the Peregrine. She was dead asleep with her knees to her chest and her cheek propped against them.

"Oh, no," Barsilay said. He clapped his hands above her head. "Wake up, will you?"

"Do you have to be so rude?" Toba asked.

The Peregrine had opened her eyes; they were still swollen with exhaustion. "I'm sorry," she told Barsilay. "I couldn't help it."

"Why should she apologize for sleeping in the middle of the night?" Toba asked.

Barsilay gave her an irritated look. "Whom do you suppose she saw while she was asleep in the middle of the night?"

"Did you see Tarses?" Naftaly asked.

She rubbed sleep out of her eyes, saying, grimly, "Of course I did."

"What did he tell you?" Barsilay asked.

"Before we get to that, I'd like to know what Toba is doing here."

"That can hardly be more important," Barsilay said, but Toba had already answered, "I was looking for you, actually."

"Why?"

"I had a dream," she said. "About Tsidon."

"Were you hoping I could help you get the stink out?"

"No," she said. "There was something offhand he said. He told me he'd been left to guard Tarses's empty offices. There was no one there but him. Is that true?"

"I can't account for all of La Cacería," she said, "but from what I've heard, Rimon is largely cleared out, yes."

"Tsidon is out of favor," Toba said.

"He is. That's no secret."

"If Tsidon is out of favor, and no one else is in Rimon, then what do you suppose Tarses has done with the book?"

Naftaly startled. "The book?"

Toba continued, "It seems to me there are two possibilities: either Tarses left the book in Rimon under the care of Tsidon, whom he does not trust, or else he brought it with him."

Barsilay sat down hard on the bed. Glancing up at the Peregrine, he asked, "Is there anyone else he could have sent it away with?"

"There is no one left he trusts that much," she said. "And she's right. He wouldn't have entrusted it to Tsidon after the debacle at the wedding. But it doesn't necessarily follow he would have brought it to the siege castle."

"I may be able to confirm that," Toba said. "I need to speak to my grandmother."

"Even then," said the Peregrine, "I'm not sure what good it does us to know it."

Naftaly was quivering all over, and he said, "I think it does us a great deal of good, actually. Because I've seen the book, and I know we're going to get it back."

"That's wonderful news," said the Peregrine. "By the way, have you ever been to Anab?"

Barsilay looked taken aback by the turn in subject and said, "A few times. I had enough friends who left Rimon for Anab, after La Cacería took over."

"Of course you do," the Peregrine said. "Because their king runs the city well, wouldn't you say? He's good to his people."

"That is his reputation," Barsilay said. "Why are we discussing the King of Anab?"

"Because," she answered, "I've just been ordered to kill him."

BARSILAY SENT NAFTALY off to bathe, saying he needed half an hour to think on his own. Naftaly let a shade pour hot water over him, and comb out his hair, and put him into a long robe and a pair of soft slippers before he returned to his room to find the bed had been changed out for a round table, around which sat Barsilay, Toba, Elena, and Asmel, whom they must have awakened. The old woman, he assumed, had been left to sleep.

"I thought you wanted to think on your own?" Naftaly said in Barsilay's ear, as he motioned for him to sit down at his right hand.

"Yes, but I realized that never goes well," Barsilay replied.

"Where is the Peregrine?"

"I sent her off to sleep. No point in her continuing to exhaust herself now. And she shouldn't be part of this conversation, anyway."

"Shouldn't she?" Naftaly asked. "Do you not trust her anymore?"

"Everyone I trust is in this room," Barsilay said.

"You should recall," said Asmel, "that it is in the Peregrine's interest for Barsilay to prevail, but she is still very much under Tarses's control. She was ordered to take the page of the book from Barsilay, which she's done. And she was ordered to reveal Zayit's defensive strategies, which she's also done."

"Can't she kill Tarses?" Elena asked. "I don't understand that."

"Tarses has enough in his inner circle who would be happy to have him dead that we can assume it's impossible for them to kill him," Asmel said. "The killstone was probably their only chance, since they only needed to say his name and the command-word; they wouldn't need to touch him or use their own magic. So the question is, what is our alternative to letting her go?"

"She'll allow herself to be captured again and locked up." Barsilay tapped his fingers on the table. "I won't make this decision alone," he said. "The implications are enormous. Either I'm party to murdering King Yefet, or else I neutralize our most potent ally."

"She's only your ally until Tarses orders her to kill you," Elena pointed out. "Then she's your assassin, too."

"That's true," Toba said. "It might be a good idea to lock her up while she's willing."

To Asmel, Barsilay said, "What do you think?"

Asmel said, "I agree with the rest. She's extraordinarily dangerous."

Elena said, "On the other hand…"

Toba said, "We haven't allies to spare."

Naftaly said, "You just said to lock her up!"

"I said we should consider it," Toba answered.

"That's profoundly unhelpful."

Toba asked, "Is he a good king?"

Barsilay made a vague gesture. "He's fair. He's a fair king. He certainly doesn't deserve to be murdered."

"His people like him," Asmel said. "He's been King since the Fall, and he's treated his citizens well all that time. It's certainly why Tarses sees him as a threat: No one in Anab would think of betraying him. He's too popular."

"His heirs?" Toba asked.

Barsilay said, "He has no children I'm aware of."

"So," Elena said, "he dies and Anab is thrown into chaos, just in time for Tarses's army to show up."

"Precisely."

"That sounds like a terrible idea," Naftaly said. "We're handing Tarses another city. How bloody is that likely to be?"

There was an uncomfortable silence.

Asmel raised his hand to pause the conversation. "Forgive me the coldness, but you must parse through both scenarios before you decide. We let the Peregrine go, she kills Yefet, and then returns to the siege castle. What then? Can she help us from Tarses's side?"

"Maybe," Barsilay said. "But then he's going to order her to do something else. And it could be anything this time."

"If I may sum up …" Elena started, and Barsilay said, "Allow me. Either we choose to murder King Yefet and allow the Peregrine to potentially do something terrible later, or else we choose to risk the life of the Peregrine and lose any help she might give us. It's his life or hers." Barsilay sat back in his chair and said, "I'm no closer to knowing how to make that choice than I was half an hour ago."

Elena said, "What about the book? Toba and I were able to use the book's name to confirm it was in the siege castle. How do you plan to get it out? Someone's got to go in there and steal it, and I think we've determined the castle hasn't got a door."

"You think the Peregrine will be able to steal it?" Naftaly asked.

"She's the only friend we have with access," Elena said.

"Then Tarses would know immediately she'd betrayed him," Barsilay said. "And anyway she's been ordered to Anab at daybreak."

Toba said, "She could get me inside tonight, if she claimed to have captured me."

Elena said, "What?"

"Tarses still wants me. But if I go walking out of the city, I'll be killed by Tarses's archers before I get to the castle; they won't know who I am. I'll have to be escorted. It's the only way inside."

"You're suggesting," Asmel said, "that the Peregrine sneak you out of the city and dump you on Tarses's doorstep before proceeding on to commit murder."

"Well," Toba said, "yes."

"And then once you're inside," Elena asked, "how will you get the book? You won't be free to roam around in there."

"I'm not sure about that part," Toba said. "But listen, we know it works, because it's the only plan we have, and Naftaly's seen it. He's seen me with the book. Whatever we choose tonight will lead to that."

"That's quite an assumption," Asmel said.

"There's no other way for us to get it," Toba insisted.

"All right," Barsilay said. "We're running out of time. Let's put it to a vote: Do we let the Peregrine go, or call the Savia to lock her up again before she can kill King Yefet?"

Toba said, "I am in favor of letting her go."

Naftaly said, "As am I. I hate to say it, but we need the book."

Asmel said, "No."

Toba said, "Because you don't want me going into the siege castle?"

"No, though you won't believe it. I think losing Anab is too important."

Elena said, "I say no as well." To Toba she said, "It's a plan conceived in a rush based on supposition. I can't credit it. I'm sorry."

Asmel said, "It's up to you then, Barsilay."

Barsilay stared darkly at the table. "Should I condone the murder of a good man for my own benefit?"

"It isn't only your benefit," Toba said.

"The greater good," he said, disgusted. "That's your father's argument."

Toba sat back, chastened.

Barsilay rose sharply and said, "Then I suppose I'm a murderer. I'll go tell the Peregrine."

TWENTY-FIVE

THE RIMONI ARMADA was an overwhelming force, consisting of some sixty ships—overkill to take a single city, but when Atalef had assembled it under Tarses's orders, he'd wanted to take no chances. Further, this was the fleet that would go on to claim Anab, and then Habush, leaving troops to garrison every city all the way to P'ri Hadar, the great city of the east and the jewel in Tarses's new crown.

Zayit was his first target both for its proximity and for its salt, and the related wealth Tarses required to pay his soldiers. It cost a great deal of money indeed to convince a Mazik to risk his life, even if Mazik tactics were much less bloodthirsty than those of mortal armies. Mazik soldiers did not, as a rule, fight in close quarters unless absolutely necessary, preferring to lob projectiles—and occasionally salt—at each other from a distance until one side was forced to surrender. The Zayiti attack on Habush some centuries prior had consisted of Zayit opportunistically timing their attack to coincide with the mortal crusade. They'd laid siege to the city for three days with the threat of salt bombardment, the Habushis had surrendered, the Zayitis had gone in and removed the greater part of the city's wealth, and then simply left. According to the tales, no Mazik had actually died in that campaign, besides three Zayitis who perished in a salt accident and the lone soldier of Habush who had nobly sacrificed himself trying to stop the invaders from stealing the city's beloved bronze Zizim.

Even these sorts of battles did not happen much. There simply weren't enough Maziks to man a large-scale assault on another city, and since poverty was no real concern in a world where a lentil could become a feast and a tree could become a house, there was little one could offer a soldier to cause him to risk his immortality. This meant there were three types of Mazik soldiers, in general: those drafted under duress—usually by threatening a soldier's family, zealots willing to fight for a cause, and those who had found themselves in a bad circumstance through bad fortune or poor planning.

Only now Tarses had another group to recruit from: the victims of the lentil blight, which had spread from Tamar and into Erez and Katlav.

Tsifra, however, was operating under a different set of conditions on the mortal side. She was leading a crusade against the heathen lords of Zayit—she was not entirely sure why they were heathens, but then, she didn't need to be. She had plenty of troops who would fight in close combat, and who were eager for it, too.

Tarses meant to make an example of the city. He would capture it whole, with little blood—on the Mazik side, at least—and he would show the rest of Mazikdom that there was nothing to fear if they simply bent to his will.

The mortal city, on the other hand, need not be taken whole, so long as it was taken quickly. This last part was already in peril, because the fleet had been delayed three days by a storm. It should have been there by the moon, and its absence had caused a massive headache because Tarses was not willing to delay the construction of his siege castle. He'd lost contact with his operatives in the city and had become mistrustful. Things were moving quickly, and his orders were too slow to be relayed, so he'd put himself into an enchanted sleep to prevent his lieutenants on either side of the gate from making their own decisions. Tsifra had several vials of sleeping potion in the satchel that hung at her hip, so that she could speak to him in the dream-world if anything occurred he had not planned for, but she thought he was probably making a mistake. If he already mistrusted his lieutenants, then why trust them to go to the trouble of making themselves dream every time they needed direction? In trying to get tighter control, he was only adding another avenue for possible mistakes.

Tsifra found it difficult to force herself back to his will, having spent so many weeks planning his murder, but what was the alternative? Death was the alternative, and perhaps she deserved it. It would have been easier, certainly. Tarses's orders would not follow her once she died.

All her attempts to be clever about her betrayal had failed, and she wondered if that was the problem: She was trying to become Tarses, but she was not like him, not really. Machinations were not her forte.

Zayit's harbor, she'd been told, was filled with ships. The spies captured in Rimon had divulged the city's defensive plans before they'd died; the ships were in a defensive formation fanning out from the harbor, and she'd been told there were thirty. Apparently they hadn't counted on Rimon bringing its entire armada. It would be like crushing a walnut with a boulder. Her only concern was not losing too many ships, which would make it more difficult when they went on to P'ri Hadar.

"How long until they are in range of our cannons?" she asked the captain of their lead ship, a gray veteran who had the sense to be frightened to death of her.

"A day," he said. "If the wind holds."

There was to be no diplomatic overture. They would go in firing, until every ship was sunk. Then she'd make an offer, when there was no other hope to be had: Turn over the city to her, or she would set it ablaze.

It was a few minutes later when one of the ships on the starboard side of the Rimoni formation ran up a distress flag.

"How can they be in distress?" Tsifra asked the captain. "We're on open water, and we haven't even sighted an enemy yet."

"They wouldn't have run up the flag needlessly," he replied, and directed his own ship closer, which took a great deal more time than

Tsifra would have liked. Once they were in shouting distance, a sailor from the other ship called, "Plague!"

THREE HOURS WAS as much time as the Peregrine would allow Toba before they had to depart, and she went immediately to find Naftaly, who was alone and looked very surprised at Toba's appearance in his room. "Barsilay's not here," he told her.

"I'm here for you," she said. "I've been needing to speak with you since I got here, only there's been no time, and now there's still no time. I'm leaving. So what I have to say must be said now."

Naftaly, who had been sitting in a chair by the bricked-in window, got up. "What is it?"

"I have a message … No, not a message, exactly. I have information, about you and your book. What did your father tell you about how you got it?"

"Absolutely nothing," he said. "I didn't even know it existed until right before he died, and I didn't know what it was until Barsilay told me."

Toba understood all about family secrecy. She said, "I suppose the first thing I should tell you is that I dreamed of your ancestor."

Toba explained to Naftaly about Dawid, and how he'd escaped the Fall of Luz on the back of the Ziz.

"You've seen the Ziz," she reminded Naftaly. "I was there when you had that vision, before we rescued Barsilay from La Cacería. What more can you remember about it?"

Naftaly closed his eyes. "I remember the Ziz, but the rest is hazy. Someone said, 'Either you will succeed, or she will eat you.' So you are telling me that I am the descendant of the ugliest whore in Rimon and the half-Mazik who put the gate of Luz into the book in the first place?"

Toba said, "Yes."

It was, Toba knew, a lot to contend with. Though not so much as discovering one's father was a murderous tyrant who'd bred you like a dog. She knew it was unfair to make the comparison, but she found she could not help it.

Naftaly did not seem to know how to respond to this information, and said, "I have wondered how the book came to me. I suppose I'm glad to know the history, at last."

"It isn't only history, Naftaly. You know what I mean to do once I have the book: I have to go into Aravoth to find the Ziz. And we already know you go with me, you've seen it, but I didn't understand why 'til now."

"Hold on a moment, I saw the Ziz. That doesn't imply I saw Aravoth. Toba, slow down."

"I can't," she said. "I need you to understand because as soon as I get back, we will need to leave."

"Leave? Now? In the middle of all this? How could I do that to Barsilay?"

"This is your legacy, Naftaly—"

"My legacy," Naftaly said, huffing a laugh. "I lived my entire life believing my legacy was to be a tailor, and you see how that turned out. I won't live my life by such constrictions again. I don't care who my ancestors were."

"You certainly seem to care who Barsilay's were."

"Barsilay is acting for the good of us all!"

"We are doing this for Barsilay, don't you understand? Without the Ziz, there is no Luz. Without Luz, Barsilay can't be King."

"Yes, but that's all"—he waved vaguely—"in the future. Look, you haven't been here, you don't know how things have gone. Barsilay needs help. I won't leave him, and anyway I have hardly any magic. Take Asmel!"

"I can't take Asmel," she said. "It must be another part-Mazik, and you've already seen—"

"Neither of us knows exactly what I saw that day." He pushed his hair out of his face and exhaled. "I know your lineage is important to you. I understand. But being descendant from Dawid, it can't take the place of my own mind. I must do what's right, and for now, that means staying with Barsilay."

Toba said, "I can't force you, and I won't try. I don't need to convince you of what you've already seen. I just wanted you to know why you'd seen it."

"Toba—"

"I'm going," she said. "I'll see you when I return with your book."

Toba returned to her room, tore off her dress, and ordered a shade to bring her something more utilitarian to wear. She was not sure how long she would be inside the siege castle, or even if Tarses would let her keep her own clothes, but it was something to do, something to plan, and her mind was racing. She was irritated with Naftaly, who felt he had a right to stay by his beloved's side just because he wanted to. How many times had she left Asmel? "Selfish coward," she muttered.

Asmel, who had been waiting with her quietly as she stormed around, said, "The Peregrine will come for you soon. You must calm yourself."

"I can't," she said. "I must plan for what comes next."

"You are planning too much ahead," he said. "You must focus on what you are about to do. You can't be thinking about what comes after."

"I can't help it. One night," she said. "Since we fled from Tsidon, we've had exactly one night to rest without disaster looming, and now I'm leaving you again, and I don't think I can bear it."

Asmel drew her close. "I am sorry," he said. "But know this: I am not afraid for you."

She went up on her toes and kissed him, and he put his hands on her shoulders and embraced her for a long time. "One more plan? Just this one," she said into his neck.

"Yes?"

"After we put the gate back and Barsilay is King of Luz and Tarses is defeated ... After all that, what will you do?"

He smoothed her hair. "I imagine I'll go back to Rimon and reopen the university."

"Oh," she said, "that sounds lovely."

"Yes," he said, "it does."

"I think I would like that, too," she said. "To help with the university."

"I could certainly use your help," he said. "For as long as you're eager to offer it."

She smiled against his shoulder. It made an appealing picture, the university returned to what she'd seen in Asmel's memories, filled with bustling Maziks eager to learn and read and argue. "Would they accept me, since I'm not fully Mazik? I don't think there will be much space to keep it secret, after everything."

"La Cacería will be extinct," Asmel said. "The new age will be what we make it. Do you think I will let anyone treat you cruelly, after you've repaired the world?"

The door slid open and the Peregrine entered—she never knocked. "It's time," she said, holding out her hand. "Are you ready?"

Toba was not. But she embraced Asmel one last time, and she left.

She and the Peregrine crept out of the city through a tunnel used by Zayiti spies. "There's not much cover," the Peregrine told her as they were about to leave the safety of the underground passage. "Can you make yourself invisible?"

Toba, a little proud, made herself translucent, as Asmel had taught her.

The Peregrine laughed. "Is that all?"

"I went into Mount Sebah like this," she told her.

The Peregrine waved a hand through her. "You're very insubstantial, it's true," she said. "But look." She pointed at the ground, where in the light of the Peregrine's light-stone, Toba was still casting a shadow.

"Well, put your light out and I won't have a shadow."

"There will be moonlight in a few minutes," the Peregrine said.

"Can you do better?" Toba asked, a little grumpily.

The Peregrine handed her the light-stone, and then she was gone. Toba held up the light to where she'd been standing; there was no trace of her, no silhouette, and no shadow.

"Did you leave?" she whispered.

Toba felt the Peregrine pluck her earlobe on the other side. "Honestly," she said, "you're like a child."

Toba rather thought it was the Peregrine who was like a child, showing off her skills. "How are you doing this?"

"Same as you," she said. "Only I'm better at it."

"Did Tarses teach you?"

"Tarses taught me nothing," the Peregrine said, as they continued through the tunnel.

"So you were an assassin before you entered his service?"

"Not an assassin," she said. "I was a princess."

Toba stopped short.

The Peregrine said, "Barsilay didn't tell you?"

"You are joking."

"A minor princess," she said. "As far from a throne as one can be and still be a princess."

"And how did you come to serve Tarses?"

"Well, I didn't want to get married."

Toba had trouble keeping her pace with all this new information. "In general or to someone specific?"

"Both, I suppose. I didn't want to get married at all, but I really didn't want to marry the specific man they'd chosen for me."

"He was horrible?"

"He never smiled," the Peregrine said. "Ever. Like Asmel, but worse."

"Asmel smiles."

"Yes, that's my point. Asmel occasionally smiles. My intended did not. He never smiled. Never told a joke, never laughed at a joke, and also he was the lord of some absolute backwater where no one ever went, and I'd have had to stay there with him, for all time, looking at his sour face and wanting to die from it all. So Tarses made me a deal: Enter his service and he'd break the engagement." A pause. "I was very young then."

"He broke the engagement by killing your fiancé."

"Yes," the Peregrine said. "I did not quite understand what I was agreeing to. His cause seemed just to me then; they were protecting the world."

"And now?"

She paused, cocked her head to one side. "Do I think the Mirror will drag us all into hell? I think it's likely, yes. Do I think Tarses will make things any better? No, I don't."

"You think it will go to hell either way," Toba concluded.

"I do."

"Even with Barsilay as King?"

The Peregrine seemed to mull this over—a show, Toba knew, because of course she would have already considered this. She said, "I think Barsilay will make a dreadful king. His one redeeming quality is that he knows it."

"He let you go tonight," Toba reminded her.

"He did. I'm not sure it was the right choice."

"Will you kill the King of Anab?"

"Of course I will." The Peregrine hesitated. "He did ask me to try not killing him, Barsilay. As if I have a choice." They'd come, then, to the end of the tunnel. "We must be silent until we reach the siege castle. After that, let me be the one to speak. The Falcons inside will free you as soon as they're able. They'll just have to wait for Tarses's attention to be elsewhere."

There was a dark implication to his attention being elsewhere; if Tarses's mind were needed, it would be because they'd breached either the wards in the grove or Zayit's wall. "Any guess how long that will be?" Toba asked.

The Peregrine looked uncharacteristically grim. "I could not guess," she said. "Whatever happens, you must not give him your name, no matter what he might threaten or promise. Not to him, not to anyone else. And don't sleep if you can help it. Now be silent."

So Toba did not speak as they made their way back toward the south gate of the city, and stayed silent as the Peregrine laid a hand on her shoulder before the siege castle, making them both solid again. Then the wall opened up and she found herself pulled inside.

TWENTY-SIX

TOGETHER WITH ELENA and the old woman, Naftaly had spent the past several hours pouring salt into lentil amphoras that the shades had made from iron, since it had been decided that using ceramic would leave the mines too vulnerable to projectiles.

Asmel had designed the field to have three separate orbits at different speeds, and for all this, they needed four hundred and fifty mines, plus ten extra in case any broke on the way to the grove. The salt went in first. Once they were done with that, the Maziks would bring in the gunpowder, and then the detonator would go in last—assuming Efra had managed to make one by then. The old woman's hands were troubling her, and she'd already had to go out twice to get Barsilay to do some sort of warming treatment on them, which kept the swelling in her joints down for an hour or two at most. It was, Naftaly thought, colossally unfair to make her work this way.

Things were getting worse for the Zayitis, however, and Naftaly did not feel he had the right to complain. What they'd learned from the head of the salt guild—under torture, Naftaly presumed—was that they, too, had been complicit in Tarses's plans. They had concluded that Tarses was likely to win, and had gambled on helping him in exchange for keeping Cacería troops out of their business. The Prince, in their bargain, was to be replaced by the head of the salt guild, the Council of Ten abolished, and Tarses would be entitled to levy a tax on their trade.

They'd decided this was a better deal for them than allowing Tarses to take over the city and set his own terms. What had happened to the salt guild after all these revelations, Naftaly could not say.

He had just finished filling his twelfth mine since lunch when there came a knock at the door, and Efra's voice saying, "I need the boy."

"The boy is busy," Elena said testily, to which Efra replied, "I'm aware, but there's no one else who can do this. We're ready to test the detonator."

Naftaly exchanged a glance with his companions. Elena said, "I guess you'd better go. Don't do anything stupid."

"I'll do my best," he said, and went to the door, where Efra was waiting. Her hair was tied back under a scarf and she wore gloves to the elbow.

She said, "Do you know how difficult it is to make something that combusts when you touch it?"

"Did you manage it, then?" Naftaly asked.

"This whole enterprise is madness."

"So you did do it."

She pulled him into another room where Saba was working, dressed head-to-toe in heavy gray cloth, wearing his own pair of long gloves. "Ah!" he called. "How are your leeches?"

"Leave off about the leeches," Efra said. "We weren't certain how much magic you actually have. We need to make sure these won't explode when you're trying to move them, but they need to be strong enough to work on Tarses's Courser, if she shows up. We don't have a half-Mazik we can test this on, so we'll just use the strongest detonator we've got that doesn't react to you. Don't look so afraid. There's no explosive material in these, all they'll do is spark."

Naftaly said, "I don't see how you made all these without burning yourselves, if they're meant to ignite with magic."

"My brother created some long instruments for the final stages," Efra said. "For the initial ones . . ." She pulled off her glove and revealed her fingers were badly singed. "My brother came up with the gloves. After I burned myself twice."

"Not my fault it never occurred to you," Saba said.

"I'm a military strategist, not a scientist," she shot back. "This is your job. Anyway, anything that ignites when *you* go near it is too strong and must be discarded. We'll use the strongest of what's left."

"How close should I get?"

"To be safe, I think you'd better be pretty close. Don't touch them, though. We can't afford to burn your hands right now."

Naftaly saw that the detonators—silver disks about the width of his palm—had been left on a long table. He approached from the right, passing his hand over them; these were the weakest, and nothing happened. When he got to the fifth device, it sparked, and he pulled his hand back quickly. "It's this one," he called to her, while she stood watching from the doorway. "The fourth from the right." But then, as he pointed at it, it caught fire, too. "Damn it," he said. "The third. Use the third."

"Right," Efra said. "Can you put them out so they don't burn the table?"

"All right," Naftaly said, and leaned over to blow out the nearest one, while from the doorway Efra shouted, "No!" but he'd already done it, and the detonator flared up into his face, hot enough to knock him backward.

The air smelled of singed hair, which Naftaly realized was probably his eyebrows. Efra said, "Don't feed it more magic, you fool. Are you all right?"

Mainly he was embarrassed, and glad Barsilay had not been there to see it. "How shall I put them out, then?"

"Use your magic. Or can you not?"

Naftaly pursed his lips. "I can do it," he said, thinking it was unlikely that he could, but he lifted his hand again and ordered the flame to put itself out in his mind, and was rather unsurprised when it did not work.

"I'll manage it," said Saba, coming back into the room, while Naftaly stepped out and shut the door behind him.

"Very well," Efra said, once the door was closed. "Third one from the right. And we only have to make four hundred and fifty of them without killing ourselves." She set her hand to open the door, but Saba called, "Don't come in yet! The room's burning again."

"If this works," she muttered, "I expect a statue."

Saba called, "It's all right now … No. No, it's not."

"The statue," she said. "Make sure I'm taller than him."

Naftaly went back to filling amphoras with salt. When he entered the room, Elena looked up and asked, "Did they manage it? You're missing half an eyebrow."

"I think so," he said, adding, "Lucky I didn't lose my nose."

"Were you stupid?"

"Of course," he said. "What else?"

TOBA HAD BEEN inside the siege castle for nearly half a day, and she still had not seen Tarses.

When she'd first arrived, she'd been pulled inside so swiftly and so violently that she began to think she'd made a terrible mistake. Then a Mazik wearing a mask that came up to his eyes set a hand on her shoulder that left her body feeling two-thirds frozen.

Then some other Hound had put her in a room with no windows and closed the door, and from that moment everything was silent.

Toba hadn't seen much of the castle between the outer wall and her cell, but it did remind her a bit of the building she'd visited the one time she'd dreamed of Tarses, in some windowless fortress with too many stairs and doors that did not open. It gave the impression of being larger inside than out, and she'd been surprised to see no soldiers in it apart from the two who had taken her, though that could have been by design. Tarses would not want her to know their numbers. Barsilay had also warned her that she would be prevented from leaving the castle in the dream-world, so she would be completely cut off from her friends until she was able to escape.

In the room with her there was a bed, and a washbasin, and a pitcher of water that refilled when she took some, and a jar of lentils.

The jar of lentils gave her pause. It was very full, enough food to last for weeks.

There was also a chamber pot that emptied itself. She did not know where the contents ended up, and hoped she wouldn't find out later.

If Toba had been able to make a shade, at least she could have had someone to talk to, but she'd never bothered to learn how. She could make another buchuk, she mused, if she'd known how she'd done it in the first place.

Better not to, probably. Tarses would likely find some way to make use of a second version of her.

She put her ear to the door, as she'd done every ten minutes since she'd been locked in, and heard nothing. She tested it, and found it still locked. One of the Falcons would come and let her out at some point. That was what the Peregrine had told her.

She waited like that until what she presumed must be nightfall, and then came a quiet rap on the door, which quietly slid open to reveal the man on the other side, who was not Tarses but Tsidon.

Tsifra would have killed him, in her position. Toba considered it, but she did not think she would be able to. More than likely she'd only be forcing his hand into killing her, and then there would be no Tobas left in the world, and no one to steal the Luz gate back from Tarses.

"I thought you were in Rimon," she said stupidly.

Tsidon smiled. "I was in Rimon. Then I was called here."

"I thought you were out of favor," she said.

"I was. But it turns out the Caçador needed me again." He conjured himself a chair and sat in it dramatically. "He had someplace else to be. He's not available. If you were hoping to see him."

"I wasn't," Toba said.

"You should be," he replied. "Tarses wants you alive and unharmed."

"And you don't?"

"If I had my way, you'd suffer horribly and then die at my hand."

"When have you ever had your way?"

Tsidon looked miffed. He said, "I would be careful if I were you."

"Of what? You've already said you want to torture me as far as you're allowed. I can hardly say anything that would make things worse."

"You little fool," he said, rising from the chair and pinning her to the wall with one arm.

"You cannot touch me," she said. "Tarses will have your head."

Tsidon set a hand over Toba's scalp. "Worry about your own head, dearest."

Toba felt the wakefulness drain out of her. She pulled her magic up from the rest of her body into her mind, meaning to fight it, but there was no time, and she was not strong enough. Sleep took her.

When she opened her dreaming eyes, she was in the caldarium of the royal baths in Rimon. The only other person visible was the baths' hostage, whose eyes lingered just above the surface of the water.

TSIFRA'S FLEET WAS on the cusp of collapse.

She learned that the first ship to raise the distress flag had a man down with plague, but no sooner had the message been relayed than they'd discovered three others on the same ship, then five, then six. They'd hoped it was only a fever, but then the men had developed buboes, and there could be no doubt. At first, it was only the one ship, then another, then two more. The formation was strong enough, the captain assured Tsifra, that the fleet could easily make do without them. They ordered the affected ships to the rear of the formation.

Another ship raised the flag: five in total. Tsifra had already suspected, from the third ship, that this was not only bad fortune on the part of her fleet. A ship, two ships might be a coincidence. But five? In a port that was not already widely infected? It was the sort of maneuver the Zayitis were famous for, though she wasn't sure how they'd managed it on this side of the gate. They must have had mortal operatives outside of the salt guild, and Tarses had not known to neutralize them. He would be very angry when he found out. Probably the Falconry would be blamed, because someone would have to accept the guilt for this beside Tarses himself.

"We'll have to turn back," the captain told Tsifra. "We can't weather the loss of so many men, and if we send new sailors to those ships, they'll be infected, too."

"We can't turn back," she said, standing before the map of the Zayiti port she'd brought from Mansanar. "There is no way for us but Zayit now."

"Do you really feel safe assuming it's only going to be five ships?" he asked.

Tsifra did not. But it didn't matter to her how many of these men caught the plague, as long as they stayed upright until she'd taken Zayit. It wasn't as if she could do anything to save them, anyway. They would die on those ships, either before or after they accomplished their mission. She'd deal with the loss of them later, before they moved on to the next city, somehow. She would pretend this was not a disaster, that she wasn't likely to lose the entire fleet.

Tsifra was not used to commanding a force larger than herself. "Do you have a suggestion, apart from turning back?" she asked the captain.

The captain considered this, scratching the back of his neck. "We have to assume the entire fleet might be compromised. If you won't abort the mission, we have to push forward faster, before we lose the use of any more ships."

"Are any of the infected ships those carrying the garrison soldiers?"

"Not so far."

They were still a day out, if the wind held. They needed more wind. Her magic could power a single ship, but the entire fleet? She doubted it.

The alternative was failure.

She could let the mission fail. This was not her misfortune, after all, but Tarses's. Surely she could find some way to spin this to her advantage. Toba would find a way.

Tsifra could let the plague take the entire fleet, rendering the Queen toothless for months, or worse, leaving the ships adrift with dying men. It would take Sefarad years to rebuild. Tsifra could pretend to let the plague take her, too. Tarses might believe she could succumb to disease, like a mortal.

Of course he would not believe that. He would call for her, and she would go, and explain how she'd managed to lose sixty ships to rats.

Toba would find a way.

"I need to write a letter to the Queen," Tsifra told the captain, who handed her parchment and a quill. Slow. Everything with mortals was slow. She'd almost made the parchment herself, she was so impatient. She needed more men to replace those dying on their ships. They would not arrive before they got to Zayit and wouldn't do her any good even if they did; she would have to wait until the ships were no longer infectious before she could use them again. It was a bit of uncharacteristic optimism, to ask for men she'd need after she'd taken the city. The captain, when she told him what she'd written, looked surprised, and then sent the letter to be carried by caravel.

She waited for night, and then she cloaked herself in darkness and leapt to the ship behind them in the formation, then the next, then the next, 'til she was in the rearmost ship.

The men here were anxious. Tsifra could almost smell it. They did not know about the plague, but they would have seen the flags, and they knew something was wrong.

Quietly, she stepped off the back of the ship, her feet making contact with the sea, which froze, a thin skin of ice forming beneath her. She waited an instant to see if it would hold. When it did, she took another step, and another, until she was at the center of the rear of the fleet. Creating wings of shimmering air, she brought up enough wind to lift herself several feet above the water. She allowed herself to float, letting her magic reach down to the sea and up to the sky.

She was committed now. Either this would work, or she would drown.

Tsifra stretched out her arms and felt the air above the sea, looking for movement, as the demons had done when they'd carried her to Zayit. There, not far, she felt a wind, and she called it to her, urging it larger, as if it were a living thing she were simply willing to change a bit. Little by little it grew, until it was a great wave of air, which caught her and carried her forward.

It caught the fleet, too. She could hear the men in the nearest ships calling to each other to attend to the sails.

It was not so difficult now that she understood. She thought of all the energy she'd wasted fighting to make things instead of coaxing them to her from elsewhere, and she laughed, a strange sensation as the wind carried her forward with her fleet. And when the sun rose, Zayit's harbor lay before them.

She let her wings carry her back to the lead ship, and she touched down softly while the sky was still dark enough to conceal her. Or so she'd believed.

The captain stepped out of the shadow left by the railing, his eyes wide in the dark. He'd seen her wings. He might have seen her commanding the wind, too. Tsifra stepped forward, ready to take his head, only the captain said, in a whisper, "Are you an angel?"

Tsifra had spent enough time embedded in the mortal Inquisition to know he meant a Christian angel. She'd seen them depicted in paintings and frescos and statues all over Mansanar. She knew what an angel was. She understood the implication of his question.

Tsifra hesitated, only an instant, and said, "Yes."

TWENTY-SEVEN

SETTING UP THE mines around the Zayiti gate was a delicate operation. First, Efra explained to Naftaly, the mines would have to be taken out of the city through the very long tunnel, which meant loading wagons in the dark. Horses were utterly out of the question—the Zayitis had few of them anyway, and those they had would not set foot in the tunnel.

Besides this, the only people who could come within fifteen feet of the mines were Naftaly, Elena, and the old woman, and they'd decided that the old woman lacked the strength to move them. That left only the other two to load and unload four hundred and fifty mines from ten carts pulled by ten rather crabby Mazik donkeys.

The animals needed to move on their own accord without a driver, since the ten Mazik drivers they'd have needed would have detonated the mines. But Mazik donkeys, it seemed, were quite amenable to performing tasks independently when properly motivated. Naftaly and Elena traveled in a cart ahead of the others, which was filled with apples, and occasionally they would toss a few out to encourage the donkeys to keep moving forward.

"This is absurd," said Elena.

"So you keep saying," Naftaly said. "At least these beasts won't eat us."

"Are you sure? You said that about the horses, too."

"The doctor said they eat only vegetation. I don't think he'd have lied." He tossed out another apple.

They managed to get the mines through the tunnel and into the grove, where they found the Second Division as far away from the gate as they could get to avoid setting off the charges. The men had constructed a series of earthworks, a trio of concentric walls pulled out of the ground, each a dozen feet tall and cleverly made so as not to disturb any of the olive trees. Barsilay had explained earlier that the walls were imbued with a spell which made it impossible to rest any kind of ladder against them. Anyone who wanted to get through would have to burrow through the walls, or else under them.

Naftaly had not understood the point of such a thing, if they knew Tarses was not arriving for another two days, and that they would be finished with the mines by then.

"Will it stop Tarses?" Naftaly had asked.

"No," Barsilay had replied. "But it will slow his troops down a great deal. Tarses's forces won't fight in close quarters unless they have no other choice. Anyway, Efra insisted on it, in case we need the extra time to evacuate. We can't know precisely how long this will take you to set up. Something could go wrong, you know."

Naftaly was well aware that something was perfectly likely to go wrong, and when it did, it would be his fault.

Asmel and Efra were in the center of the grove, having set up the first orbit around the gate: a magical field, invisible to the eye, which rotated around the gate and would keep the mines suspended as they circled the aperture. Like the rest, it was a delicate business. The magic had to be powerful enough to keep the mines aloft and spinning, but not so strong as to trigger the detonator. Asmel and Efra had spent a great deal of time testing it. Asmel's hair looked rather singed from the effort.

"Is it finished?" Naftaly called, because there was no way to tell by looking.

Asmel reached down and picked up a small stone, which he threw into the air. Some unseen force caught it, and it began circling the gate in an oddly chaotic fashion.

"Are you sure the mines won't crash into one another? It's a messy sort of motion," Elena called.

"The distance remains constant, once the mines are in the field," Asmel called back. "A circular orbit would be too easy to get through, so it needs to appear chaotic."

Naftaly thought it must have been very hard to construct something completely unpredictable. It didn't even seem possible to make something with no pattern. But he would ask Asmel about it later, if they were still alive then.

The field had only one major vulnerability: any undeployed mines still on the ground. An accidental explosion of those risked blowing up the mortals and—if that wasn't bad enough—detonating any mines orbiting nearby. For this reason, the undeployed mines were kept at a distance of a hundred paces from where Naftaly and the others were working. Once the orbit was set, the remaining work involved Naftaly and Elena carrying the mines to the orbit, and then Naftaly using an almost imperceptible breath of magic to launch each one, since they were too heavy just to toss. There was also a matter of the timing, so that the newly launched mines would stay clear of the mines already orbiting. Asmel stood back and shouted orders about where to place them, occasionally stopping to argue with Saba about the best way to achieve the proper spin.

It was grueling work, and it took hours, after which Naftaly and Elena were so exhausted they could scarcely lift their arms. Saba came and used his magic to heal their muscles as best he could, and they ate and drank without speaking. Meanwhile, Asmel and Efra created the magic for the second orbit, far enough from the first that they would not risk detonating it by accident.

"We should sleep," Elena said, "'til they're done. We won't have time later."

Naftaly found himself unable to rest, though, and a few hours later he and Elena were roused by Saba and Asmel to put the mines into the second orbit, which took into the morning of the next day—the last day, Naftaly kept telling himself, until Tarses was set to arrive.

THE CALDARIUM WAS as stiflingly hot in Toba's dream as it had been in the waking world, and she could feel the water condensing on her skin. She tried to recall how she'd come there. Tsidon had enchanted her. That meant that Tsidon was the one who had sent her to the baths; she was not there of her own volition.

The hostage, Toba recalled, had been a prisoner of the crown of Rimon—and, by extension, La Cacería. The woman lifted a hand out of the water and set it on the surface, creating a series of ripples that flowed away from her. Toba realized that the ripples were writing, in Mazik script, and bent toward the edge of the pool to read, *I remember you.*

What was Toba doing here? She slowly approached the pool, and was surprised that even in the dream-world, the hostage was held by a thin silver chain around her neck.

"Can you speak here?" Toba asked, because in the waking world the hostage had her tongue cut out.

The hostage whispered, "Why have you come here?"

Toba watched her without replying, unsure if this was some kind of trick.

The hostage wrote, *I tried to warn you.*

This was true. She'd seen the hostage at the baths the day she'd come with Tsidon, looking for Barsilay. She hadn't known who Tsidon was then, or what. Still, it was safer not to confirm it. She said, "What is this place?"

The hostage looked up from the water and spoke aloud. "This is where the Lymer stores things for safekeeping." Her voice was low and rough, like it hadn't been used in recent memory.

"The Lymer keeps you here?"

"Yes," she said. "I've been here a very long time. I expect he plans to keep you here a long time, too." Toba looked up at the doors, and the hostage said, "Those won't work for you. But I have a secret. Come closer, and I will tell you."

This sounded like a trick indeed, so Toba said, "No, I don't think I will."

The hostage laughed. "I tried to help you once, do you deny it? I could not hurt you here, even if I desired it. This is only a dream. Come here. Unless you would rather sit there and wait for the Lymer to come back, and then I will be able to do nothing for you at all."

Toba did not like this, but it was true: the only other option was waiting for Tsidon. She lifted her skirt and climbed into the pool, finding the water every bit as scalding as it had been in the waking world. She came close enough to the hostage to see the place where the silver chain around her neck snaked down to the floor.

She leaned close to Toba, to whisper in her ear. "I can leave this place. Would you like me to show you how?"

"If you can leave, then why are you here?"

"Because," the hostage said, "I have no place else to go."

Toba met her gaze; her eyes were hazel and so blank she could almost believe it. "How do you get out?"

"Close your eyes," the hostage said, and when Toba did, the hostage gripped her by her hair and pulled her under the water.

Toba fought, kicking, clawing at the hostage's hands, and found that the woman was easily ten times stronger. She did not need to breathe, this was only a dream, but still, her lungs screamed and her throat was on fire from the hot water, and she felt herself losing consciousness.

She would wake up. Everything would be fine.

The water turned cold, and the other woman's hands were gone from her head, and then they were under her arms, lifting her out of the water. Toba came up sputtering and shoving at the hostage. "Are you mad?" she demanded, striking out again, and slapping her in the face. Her eyes were still too full of water to focus, and she coughed up several lungfuls of caldarium water, which burned worse going up than they had going down.

The hostage pinned her wrists together in one of her hands and said, "Stop that and open your eyes."

It was not the hostage's voice. It was Asmel's.

Toba scrubbed at her eyes with both hands until her vision cleared. It was the man himself, and she realized she was sitting in the middle of the fountain in the alcalá's courtyard. Toba gasped a few times, then sat up and pressed her face into Asmel's neck. "How?" she asked. "How did you bring me here?"

"I was worried for you," he said. "I've been calling you for hours, but you never answered."

"Calling?" she said. "How could you have brought me all this way?"

"All this . . . ? No." Asmel rose from the water and pulled her out along with him. "You are still asleep. Can you not feel it?"

Toba withdrew from Asmel's embrace and looked down at her hands, clenching and unclenching them. Truthfully, she was so new to dreaming that sometimes she had trouble telling the difference between the real world and the waking. They felt nearly the same.

"I was in the baths," she said. "With the hostage."

Asmel looked rather shocked.

"I think she was trying to wake me up," she said.

"Whatever she did allowed me to call you here, so I'm thankful for whatever effort she made. But you are still in a great deal of danger."

"Yes. The Lymer is keeping me asleep."

Asmel rose. "If he's keeping you asleep, you are in great danger indeed. Come. We have to stop him calling you back to him." He took Toba by the hand and led her through the alcalá, to the stairs and up to his observatory, leaving her to stand in the center of the room. "Don't move."

He began using his hand to paint a circle of golden sigils on the floor around her. "What will this do?" she asked.

"Buy us some time," he said, "until I can find a way to wake you. At least he can't summon you back to the baths."

"Even if you wake me, I'm still a prisoner," Toba said.

"Yes, but conscious prisoners can escape. Asleep, you are at his mercy completely."

"I've made a terrible mistake," she said.

"Don't worry," Asmel said, adding a second layer of sigils. "I am here for you now."

"But if you wake me, I'll be alone again."

"Stop being frightened," he said. "You've faced worse than the Lymer. Once you've woken, I have every confidence you'll find a way to escape." Asmel finished adding a third layer. "There," he said. "That will keep him at bay for now." He turned and began pulling books off his shelves.

"Are those real books?"

"They are copies," he said. "Sometimes I like to copy things out when I'm asleep. Helps pass the time."

"You copy them from memory?"

"Yes," he said. "Not all of us are having orgies in our sleep."

Toba reddened. "Are you speaking of your nephew?"

"Who else?" he said, putting the book back and taking up a second one.

"If you copied those from memory, why do you need to look through them? Don't you know everything that's inside already?"

"My memory can only hold so much at once," Asmel huffed. "Why do you write things down? Can you recall everything you've ever read? Now be quiet, I'm trying to find something."

He put the book down and took up a third, then a fourth. "I have it," he said. "It's one of my wife's. She must have made it for ha-Moh'to. Probably for a reason very much like this one, in case someone were captured and held asleep." He set the book down on his worktable. "It isn't a difficult spell, either. I only need two things: your dream-blood, and your name."

He took up his pen and ran his fingertips over it, recrafting it into a needle. He held it out to Toba. "Would you like me to do it, or would you prefer to do it yourself? I only need a drop."

Toba reached out and took the needle, which she used to prick the side of her wrist. Asmel then beckoned to the blood with his hand; the drop floated toward him and hovered over his palm. He looked back to her expectantly.

"Are you going to do it?" she asked.

"Your name," he said. "I need your name to complete the spell."

"But . . . you know my name," she said. In fact, it had been Asmel who had told Toba her name in the first place, after she'd called it in a blood spell, before she could read Mazik writing.

Asmel's eyebrows rose. "Do I? I can't . . ." He shook his head. "Forgive me, I did not mean to forget something so important."

But Toba was looking at him with increasing suspicion. "It does seem an awfully convenient thing for you to forget," she said.

"Hardly," he said. "It does make me wonder what else is missing." He tapped at his temple. "It's very upsetting . . . I am barely more than my memories. I'd hoped nothing significant would be erased, but now I realize I could have forgotten a great many important things, and I would not even know to miss them. Now, give it to me again, please, and I shall wake you."

Toba said, "How did I make my buchuk?"

Asmel said, "Do you not trust me, after everything I have done for you?"

"Answer me."

"Your buchuk . . ." He shook his head. "That's also missing."

"So anything I ask you, you can claim to have forgotten in the creation of your safira."

"I'm sorry," he said. "I did not realize that was so significant to you. Your name. Please."

Toba's mind began to spin, because if he were telling the truth, there could be no confirming it. No, that wasn't true. He should be able to remember things that happened after his memories were returned. Anything new should be safe. But so little had happened, and there was so little she could afford to reveal if she were wrong.

She could not divulge anything that had happened in Zayit, or anything about Barsilay, or the Peregrine, or what she was planning to do in the siege castle.

"What did we have for dinner, the night before I was captured?"

Asmel threw up his hands. "I will not be mistrusted this way! After all I have sacrificed for you. My home! My nephew! My memories! My very life, nearly, and this place!" He looked around at the observatory. "This place was all I loved best in the world, and I will never see it again, because of you. Every disaster that has befallen me has been because of you, and still, here I am, trying to help you, wretched creature that you are. And now you would make me grovel at your feet for the privilege of helping you? I won't do it. I won't beg to be your dog. Give me your name, and I will help you. Or don't and be damned."

"That was a very long speech," Toba said, and stepped one foot out of the circle of sigils.

Asmel's face went slack with alarm. "No," he said. "Go back in. I'm sorry. I am under such a strain from everything that's happened. I don't mean to take out my frustration on you, but you must understand—my mind is all I am, and when I find it lacking..." He gave a little gasp. "I cannot bear it. Please go back in. Let me help you."

Toba watched him go tense all over.

"Please," he said. "I only need your name to wake you. There is no other way. You must trust me."

Toba steeled herself. She said, "I can't."

She stepped her other foot out of the circle, and while Asmel called out for her to stop, she threw herself out the window.

The wind rushed by her, and she could not help but close her eyes as the ground hurtled toward her. She'd intended to float down on wings, as she'd seen Asmel do, but found herself unequal to the task.

The air went still, and then the ground came up to meet her and she gasped at the impact.

She opened her eyes to the inside of Barsilay's prison cell, in the heart of La Cacería. The floor was coated with Barsilay's blood, from the loss of his arm. And unfurling herself from the shadows was the Courser.

THE CAPTAIN COULD not quite look Tsifra in the face, now that he believed her an angel.

It was everything Tarses had ever warned her against—being conspicuous, drawing excess attention to herself. But as the captain gazed at her through awestruck eyes, she wondered if Tarses's admonitions had served as a leash to keep her from growing too powerful among the mortals. And what did it matter if Tarses did not approve? If she failed to take Zayit, there would be no future for her. He would take her eye, or worse.

He had wanted her to be Queen, but here was the possibility of something more: She could become an icon. They would love her, and fight for her, and die for her. These men, on these ships, would be hers. Not Tarses's, not La Cacería's, but hers alone.

"Plague cannot touch me," she told the captain. "I will go myself and see the situation on those ships, whether any men can be saved."

Tsifra knew, of course, that they could not—she had no ability to cure disease—but let him think she had some divine power. She would find some excuse later why none could be saved. What did mortals like to hear? None were worthy.

The ship she chose was manned by sixteen men and, of those, seven had plague in various stages. One had already died, and she turned her nose up in disgust at the body, stinking in life and putrid in death, beginning, already, to decay.

"Why has he been left here?" she asked the man she'd tasked with showing her the rest of the crew, mainly because he seemed to smell less offensive than the rest.

"He only died this hour," he said. "We were about to put him in the sea."

"Only an hour?" she asked.

"Yes."

"But why—" She stopped. This was what disease wrought, she supposed. She'd never lived among mortals closely enough to see it, the vulgarity of it. "Do it now," she said, and the man and one of his companions took the dead sailor under his arms and pulled him from the bunk where he'd been left to decay.

Six men with plague and ten healthy. They would all die, she knew; probably they knew, too. She had no special ability to prevent the spread of it. She got up and went back out to the deck, to the air that smelled of salt rather than of dying. A splash came from the opposite side of the ship.

"Do you wish to see the other men?" the sailor asked.

"No," Tsifra said. "I'll return to my own ship." Then, "Ensure your sail is open."

The man blinked at her stupidly. Why had she come? To witness them throwing their shipmate over the side? To bear witness to healthy men who were about to die?

Some of them might not. Plague was only mostly deadly. There might be one or two who made it. Such things were known to happen.

Back on the lead ship, she said to the captain, "None were worthy of salvation."

He gave no answer but a nod.

As the sun rose to port, Tsifra leapt again into the sky, the sun at her back to catch her wings of air and set them shimmering, and held herself there long enough to hear the men on the ships nearest her shouting in wonder. Word would spread, quickly.

It was not enough, she decided. She would be more than an angel appearing in the sky. She would be one they could touch, and the men did, falling at her feet, kissing her hands, weeping on her boots as she kept her face a mask. It was so easy to make them love her, she wondered that she'd never tried; it was easier, even, than killing them. They would follow her anywhere—into the sea, into death.

When she returned to the captain, she told him, "Move the plague ships to the front of the formation."

When they reached Zayit not long after, Tsifra sat in the prow of her ship and blew those with plague forward, before conjuring a bow and sending volley after volley of flaming arrows into their masts, their decks, 'til they were all alight. And when they were all subsumed in flame, she called enough wind to force them into the center of the Zayiti formation, which was too tight to maneuver away from the oncoming ships. She watched from the deck as the Zayiti ships, too, caught fire and sank, while the men cheered, and the captain stood just behind her with tears in his eyes—not for his dead sailors, but for her.

TWENTY-EIGHT

WHILE NAFTALY AND the Maziks were in the grove, the old woman was back in the palazzo with very little to do but worry, which left her feeling very, very hungry. Of course they'd had to take Naftaly—they needed someone to handle the mines, and she supposed it would not have done to take only Elena and leave the boy at home—but of all the things, for the Zayitis to march him around like a soldier, when he had so little magic compared to the others … A boy who could see the future ought to have been kept safe somewhere like a treasure, not dragged out to deal with exploding poison.

And now she was alone, again; the others probably hadn't even spared her a thought. Still, she'd managed to stay alive, and that was something. Rather than sulk over her abandonment, she was taking advantage and sampling the recipes in her shade's repertoire. It would not do, she decided, to starve, and who knew what was coming next? She was very good at choosing life for herself, no matter how dark things became. So she may as well put on a little weight while she was able. The old woman found she enjoyed Zayiti food, but the lack of salt left everything slightly bland to her, no matter how many expensive imported spices were added.

Fortunately for the old woman, she'd pocketed several spoonfuls from Elena's experiments, which she kept in a folded piece of parchment inside her pocket. She hadn't dared use it in front of

Naftaly or any of the Maziks—including the shade—but now that she was on her own, she went off in search of the kitchen.

Still veiled, she wandered around upstairs, then downstairs, then followed her nose into a kitchen in which one entire wall was made up of lentil amphoras, and the other two were lined with shelf after shelf filled with small glass jars, all labeled in Mazik writing.

Taking up most of the room were several large wooden tables stacked with ceramic serving ware glazed in bright colors, many bearing olive branches around their rims, others featured Zizim cavorting across them. One of these platters was filled with the single fanciest meal the old woman had ever seen: a small chicken or else some other kind of fowl, coated in a layer of some heady spices, and stuffed with a mix of breadcrumbs and what appeared to be walnuts. The plate was decorated with slices of citrus—possibly orange, but these were so much redder than the oranges in Rimon, she was not really sure.

Probably it was meant to go to one of the officials who worked in the palazzo, or even to the Prince of Zayit himself. Probably the shade meant to take it upstairs had forgotten it, or would be back to pick it up in a moment. The old woman eyed the door and heard nothing. With quivering fingers, she opened her packet of salt and sprinkled a good pinch over the chicken, then, taking a fork that had been put away with the serving dishes, she began to devour the finest meal of her life.

The chicken was perfectly cooked, and so fragrant with spices that she could detect no hint of lentil. The salt heightened every flavor, and the acid of the red oranges only made her want to eat more. The stuffing was made of some kind of sweetish bread, and the walnuts—they were indeed walnuts—made chewing it a thoroughly delicious experience.

About halfway through, she was quite full, having the appetite one would expect of a woman her age, but she realized she would have to finish it, or else leave a platter of poison in the kitchen. She might otherwise be inadvertently responsible for poisoning someone, even the Prince. Probably the Prince would not be served a half-eaten plate, but still, one could not take the risk. She finished everything, down to the bones, which clattered back into lentils as she set the plate down.

Setting a hand on her distended abdomen, the old woman turned her attention to the shelves of spices, jar after jar of them. She took one and removed the cork, holding it under her nose: pepper, that one, and a lot, too. She carefully replaced the cork and put it back on the shelf. It was an inconceivable display of wealth, this kitchen. The contents of this one room were worth more than every treasure in Rimon put together.

She opened another jar and smelled it: This one was smoky, another sweet. Another tasted like the fish she'd eaten from the vendor near the canal. One by one, she went down the row, smelling, marveling. Halfway down the row was a jar filled to the top with red filaments.

She'd seen saffron only once before, in a kitchen back in Savirra. It was worth so much that a plate of rice big enough for a party might only be flavored with three or four threads. Here were a thousand times that number. This one jar was worth as much as a castle, or more.

A shuffling sound alerted her to a pair of shades that had come in and were taking more lentils from the amphoras and arranging them on the empty platters. One of them paused before the empty plate of chicken and flickered its attention to the old woman, who still had the saffron clutched in her hand. Carefully, she dropped her arms to her sides and slipped the jar into her pocket along with her salt.

The shade turned back to the table and made a replacement meal of chicken and oranges. The old woman quietly slid from the room and down the hall again, where she promptly got lost finding her way back to the stairs. She'd passed through a door on her way to the kitchen, and they all looked so much alike she could not find it again.

Most of these doors were locked. The one she'd come through would not be, so she searched for one she could open. She'd just tried the fifth door when voices came down the hall, and the old woman quickly stepped through the next door—which was blessedly unlocked.

It was not the door she needed, and the old woman's first thought, upon looking around, was to wonder why it had been unlocked at all.

The room was filled with the bodies of dead Maziks.

Men and women had been laid out in various states of horror, some dozen and a half altogether. Some wore the emerald earrings she'd seen elsewhere in the city. Some were missing fingers, others bore the marks of burns, others the blackened areas she knew were the result of exposure to salt. They'd been tortured and killed, all of them, and the old woman realized this was the entirety of the salt guild.

Barsilay had told her Maziks valued life more than mortals, but the old woman thought if that had ever been true, it no longer was. Maziks, from what she could tell, valued their own lives only; violence seemed no less expected here than at home. The concept of immortal Maziks seemed as much a fairy tale as she'd once believed Maziks to be. Maziks died all the time. Maziks died horribly all the time. Maziks killed each other all the time. And maybe these Maziks—who had betrayed their city, after all—had deserved it, as the Hound Elena killed had deserved it, as Tarses would deserve it. The old woman was no Deborah to judge such matters. She only knew disingenuity when she saw it.

As to why the bodies were still here, the old woman could not imagine, until she realized they could not have been taken out of the city for burial with Tarses out there. Since there was no odor, she presumed they'd been magicked somehow to prevent their decay. The room was a makeshift mausoleum.

The old woman listened at the door until she was sure it was quiet, then went upstairs to say a prayer for Naftaly, who'd been turned into a soldier by the same Maziks who had killed the unburied behind her.

TOBA LOOKED INTO the Courser's dreaming eyes as she crossed Barsilay's cell and closed the book, shutting the dream-version of the Luz gate. She wondered if it was a real gate, somehow, and where she would have ended up if she'd crossed through it.

The Courser made her arm into a blade, and Toba wondered if

she'd made the wrong choice, not trusting Asmel. If that had been her one chance to be saved and she'd flung herself out the window instead. Toba said, "Wait."

"Wait?" the Courser said. "Why?"

"You have no reason to do this again."

"Again?" the Courser repeated, tilting her head to one side. "You've just freed my prisoner. I cannot let it stand."

"Freed your . . . What are you saying? Has Tsidon pulled you into this dream? Do you not remember anything?"

"My memories are of no concern to you, and this conversation grows dull," the Courser said, and before Toba could respond, she swung her blade through Toba's throat.

Toba did not have time to be terrified, even as the blade came toward her. She could not really believe her sister would kill her twice, and why, in a dream, when it did not even matter? She expected the action to wake her up. Instead, she felt herself slipping into the void again.

The horror of it crept at her from all angles; it was slower this time than the last time she'd died. First she lost her fingers and toes, then the void crept inward by inches, until all that was left was her screaming mind. Then, as she felt the core of her very self begin to extinguish, she opened her eyes again.

She was back in Barsilay's cell, the Luz gate still open, and the Courser unfurling from the shadows.

"What is this?" Toba asked her sister.

The Courser closed the book and walked toward her.

Toba begged, "Stop."

"Is that all the defense you have? To plead for me to stop?"

Toba's mind was at a loss. What reason could her sister have to want to kill her now? Unless Tsifra suspected that Tarses had her. "The Caçador doesn't have my name," she told her. "He won't have it."

"Good," said the Courser, and then she swung her arm and Toba was back in the void.

She opened her eyes again as the Courser stepped out of the shadow in Barsilay's cell.

"Stop," she whispered, begged.

This time, the Courser did not even reply before she killed her again.

NAFTALY'S ARMS WERE shaking. They'd concluded, during the night and somewhere in the middle of the second orbit, that the hundred paces between the undeployed mines and the field was causing too great a delay; Naftaly and Elena could not keep up their pace from the first orbit, and they would end up needing an additional half a day they did not have. Safety was compromised for speed and the remaining mines had been moved closer to the field.

They were well into the third orbit, and his back and shoulders felt as if they'd been pulled apart from the inside. He'd just stepped away from the field to tell Elena he needed another break when a noise he could not identify split the air: a crunching sound, one so loud the earth beneath him quivered. "What is that?" he called to Elena, who was several yards off, bringing him the next mine.

"It was from that direction," she said, indicating west. The earthen walls the Zayitis had constructed around the gate made it impossible to see more. Naftaly and Elena were too far away to speak easily to the rest of the Maziks, but Naftaly saw one of them send up a bat, and the same soldier then sent up an alarm, blowing a horn he'd seemingly pulled from the air.

Saba, who was at the perimeter of the field with Asmel and Barsilay, shouted a warning to his sister. Then there was another concussive noise, loud enough to cause Elena to clap a hand over her good ear. "What's happening?" Naftaly called.

"You must finish!" Saba shouted back. "The wards are down—we've run out of time!"

"But we have another day," Naftaly called back, rather uselessly. To Elena, he repeated, "We have another day!"

"We don't," she said. "What is that noise?"

Another crash, closer this time.

Through the wall burst the largest animal Naftaly had ever seen, taller even than the walls themselves. It was made of some combination of mud and stone, so massive it was able to collapse the walls where it ran into them, heedless of the pieces of itself that broke off in the process. Naftaly looked on as it turned and ran back through the wall parallel to the point it had already smashed, enlarging the opening. Its purpose was to demolish the earthworks.

"What is that?" Naftaly whispered. A behemot, he thought, made of mud and magic. How was anyone able to generate enough magic to create a creature so large?

Elena shouted at him to break his mind free from the fear of the thing, which looked like a cross between a boar and an elephant, with great stone tusks. "Let the solders deal with it!" she said. "We have to finish this!"

There was, of course, an alternative: they could have fled back through the tunnel. But there were still a large number of mines on the ground—and they were within feet of the field.

The mud behemot was knocking more of the walls down, leaving piles of rubble in its wake. One of the Zayitis shot a salt-tipped arrow at it; it glanced off harmlessly. A second managed to hit a softer area, and the mud surrounding it crumbled back to earth and fell to the ground, leaving a crater in the creature no more than a foot across.

"Stop!" cried Efra. "If we use all our arrows on this, we'll have no more for the soldiers."

"If we don't," came a reply, "it will trample us all!"

Indeed, as it looped back around from smashing more of the wall, it made a run directly at the soldiers, who had to leap out of the way.

Then the arrows began to come through the smashed bits of the wall.

The first volley took out three Zayiti soldiers before the others managed to shield themselves with makeshift barriers pulled by magic from the ground.

"Find cover anywhere!" shouted Efra, but there was scarce cover to be found, because now that the behemot had succeeded in smashing the wall, it was using its tusks to pull out the olive trees. It had pulled out half a dozen already, as if it were pulling weeds from a garden bed.

"She lied," Naftaly said, still watching the beast as it threw an uprooted olive tree at a trio of soldiers. Efra had ordered them into smaller groups to make them harder to trample, and these three managed to block the tree with a burst of magic that shot a blast of wind at it, knocking it aside. "Why would Toba have lied to us?"

Six days, she had said. And this was five.

Or else the fault was not Toba's, but his. The vision had been Naftaly's alone.

He could not see Tarses's archers yet, but they were advancing; it was obvious from the range of their arrows.

One stuck in the air, not three feet from Naftaly. It had been meant for him.

Asmel had stopped it, and it clattered to the ground. "Finish your task!" he shouted.

"The longer this takes, the more soldiers will die," Elena said, pressing a mine into his arms.

"This is my fault," Naftaly whispered, but before Elena could give him the dressing down he knew he deserved, the behemot made a run directly at them.

TOBA OPENED HER eyes again, collapsed to her knees, and heaved without bringing anything up. Her stomach, of course, was empty, because it was only a dream. Her body, she told herself, was safe. Where had she left it? With Tsidon.

She'd lost track of how many times she'd gone into the void. It was the same each time … She'd wake, the Courser would step out of the shadows, and she would cut off her head. Sometimes she would say something. Other times not. Twice Toba had attempted to make it to the Luz gate, hoping to escape this dream, assuming it were real, somehow. Both times the Courser had beaten her there and killed her before she could make it.

She'd tried to wake herself and found it impossible. She'd tried to dream herself somewhere else, or to someone else, and failed. She'd lost track of her deaths, and the time, and how many days it had been.

She'd begged Asmel to call her back, to put her back in his circle of sigils, to let her give him her name.

She slumped face down on the floor, because her dream-body had become almost as numb as it was inside the void. She waited to die again.

Only this time, the Courser said, "Do you want to wake up?"

Toba could barely answer. "Don't *you*? Aren't you tired of this yet?"

The Courser said, "I can wake you up, for a price."

"I have nothing," Toba said, and then the Courser killed her again.

Sometime later—it might have been moments or days—when she was back in the cell, the Courser said, "Is it the same every time? The void?"

"It's the void. How can you alter nothing?"

"Does it get easier? Do you get used to it?"

Toba said, "No."

"Then would you like to wake up?"

"Yes."

"Then give me something."

"I have nothing," Toba said.

"You have one thing. Give me your name."

Toba said, "No," and died again, and woke again.

"Give me your name and wake," the Courser said.

Toba was too exhausted from dying to think, but some needle of her own consciousness told her something was not right.

"My name," Toba muttered. "Do I have one, still? Maybe it's lost in the void." It did seem to Toba that not all of her was returning each time, like somehow she was growing thin, and some part of her was diminishing with each death. Maybe her name had peeled away, too, like the skin of a serpent. She was so tired, and her sister was only going to kill her again.

Her sister. The Courser was her sister. Of Marah's line, as she was.

Her mind was muddled from death, but then she remembered: The Courser knew her name, even better than Asmel.

Asmel could have forgotten, lost the memory with his magic. But the Courser would remember.

Toba rolled onto her back and laughed. "You can stop now," she said, "Tsidon."

Tsifra looked at her in a rage. Then her features sharpened into Tsidon's, and he knelt over her, his arm against her throat. "How?" he growled.

Toba ground out, "The smell."

"I can kill you as easily as the Courser," he said. "And I will."

"The Caçador will have your other eye for this," she said.

"I think he won't."

"Have you not parsed this out? What do you suppose will happen if I do give you my name? I will become the new Courser. And then the first thing I will do is cut your throat, you vile son of a pig."

He tightened his grip on her neck. "We'll see what you will do, once I present you to the Caçador with your name on my tongue, and he has reason to remember I was with him from the start, all these long years. This is all your doing, wretch. You cost me my master's trust, and now I have nothing left to lose."

Toba looked at him for a long moment, at this pathetic, desperate man. She said, "I would rather die a million times over than give you my name."

"Do you really believe so? Let's test it." And he produced a knife from somewhere and stabbed her through the heart.

This time, her trip through the void was different. Her limbs went numb, and then the rest of her, and then . . . she simply stayed there, her mind winking out one impulse at a time, each loss lasting what seemed like hours.

Toba did not know how long she stayed in the void, but when she opened her eyes again, gasping, she was shaking violently and found tears streaming down her face. Tsidon was leaning against the wall, dressed as splendidly as the first time she'd seen him. "I can hold you there as long as I wish," he told her. "That was one hour. Next time will be two. How will that feel, do you think? Then it shall be four. Then a day. Then a week." He came forward and leaned over her while she sobbed. "What do you think will be left of you after a week?"

"The Caçador," she whimpered.

"The Caçador is waging war on the entire world. He cannot save you from this." He reached down and set his hand on her throat, not roughly, but as if he were resting it there. "Give it to me, little fool." He began to squeeze, and behind her eyes, she saw stars.

He was cleverer than she'd credited him for. Pain she could withstand. But the void ... It was too terrible. Probably she was the only Mazik in the worlds who could be tortured this way. The others, they feared the void, but they did not know it. He was using her own mind against her, and she could not endure. She would have faced death. But this was so much worse.

"Tsifra N'Dar," she whispered, her breath hitching as her name trickled out of her.

"There," he said. "Tsifra N'Dar, open your eyes."

She felt a compulsion so strong it was nearly reflex, and her eyes met his. "Good," he said. "Now watch." And Tsidon lifted his knife and put it to her throat again.

"Stop," she said. "I gave it to you."

"You did," he said. "But you cost me a great deal. I think another few hours in the void will help me to feel better about it. I'll see you shortly, Tsifra N'Dar." And he pressed the knife into her throat.

TWENTY-NINE

BEFORE IT DREW blood, Toba felt a tugging inside her consciousness, and felt herself jerk awake.

She opened her eyes and found the Peregrine standing over her, glistening with sweat and with one hand on Toba's heart and the other on the crown of her head. "Thank the Name," she said. "I've been trying to wake you for almost an hour."

Toba sobbed. "You aren't real."

"Of course I'm real!"

"I'm still there," Toba said. "I'm still in the dream."

"This isn't a dream," the Peregrine said. "Stop this. We have little time."

"Please," Toba said. "Please stop."

"Damn Tsidon," the Peregrine muttered, and planted a kiss on each of Toba's cheeks. "Did you tell him we are friends?"

Toba shook her head.

"Then he could not know. You are awake, Toba, and it is time to do what you came for. Get up. It's time to go." The Peregrine pulled Toba by the arm from the room.

"How are you back so quickly?"

"It's been six days," she said.

"The King of Anab—"

"Don't worry about that right now. Tsidon will know someone is helping you, and he'll be trying to get here."

"Where is he?" Toba asked.

"In his room. I sealed the door, but he'll get it open in a moment. My Falcons were sent away before they could get to you. I'm sorry. You weren't meant to be here so long."

"Wait. I have to tell you— He knows my name. I gave him my name."

The Peregrine sucked in a breath. "There's only one way to deal with that. Stay here."

They came to a bend in the hallway. The Peregrine stepped out and flicked her forefinger and smallest finger toward a pair of masked guards in front of a door ... They collapsed instantly. Toba did not know if they were dead or stunned.

The Peregrine set a hand on the door, and a spiderweb of light appeared on its surface. "Not good," she muttered. "Tarses did these enchantments himself. There are too many layers here."

"What do you mean there's only one way to deal with it?"

"The door?"

"Tsidon!"

"I'll have to kill him, but right now it's only my second priority, so if you could just"—she tapped at a few of the sigils, and they winked out—"be quiet. Damn."

"Can you not open it?"

"I can undo the first six," she said. "But I don't know this last one." She turned to Toba. "I'll have to go through the wall." She touched the stone before her. "Which is also enchanted. Damn it, there's no time for this. I'm going to go up through the ceiling and then see if I can go through the wall upstairs and then come back down. I'll try opening the door for you from the other side."

Toba was staring at the sigils on the door. "I know this spell," she said.

"You can't know it. I don't know it."

"This is a ha-Moh'to spell."

"You aren't old enough to have been in ha-Moh'to."

But this was one of Marah's spells. Toba was not sure how she knew … It was some memory she could barely place, then she realized it must have been one of Asmel's, some latent memory from when she'd cast the *Redruna Delech* on him. She reached for the door and began unworking the sigils in the reverse of the order they'd been created, using a canceling formula her foremother had developed when the world had been much newer, before Luz had been at the bottom of the sea, when Asmel's hair had been black and Barsilay had dreamed of becoming a doctor and not a king.

She canceled out the last sigil, and pushed the door open. The Peregrine shut it behind them. Inside, the room was dark until the Peregrine lit a were-light in her hand.

The book was not there.

The Peregrine said, "Tsidon must have hidden it. He must have suspected you were here to get it back. It could be anyplace."

"I can find it," Toba said, drawing a circle on the floor, and changing her mind. "That won't be good enough—this building's not flat. Can you make me a model, somehow?"

"Not a good one," the Peregrine said. "This is the first time I've been here."

"Just give me something to show the size and shape," Toba said. She'd broken off a small chuck of stone from the floor, and used a pin she'd made to inscribe it with the name of the book, the name she'd learned from Dawid ben Aron. The Peregrine brought up a model of the siege castle, made from sand she'd created from the floor, and Toba swung her stone pendulum around and then through it. It came to rest on a spot on the left side.

"Do you know where that is?" Toba asked. "In relation to us?"

The Peregrine was examining it closely, counting off doorways, and said, "If I'm right, that is the room directly above where we are now."

Toba got up to go back out into the hallway, but the Peregrine said, "No time," and made Toba a shadow, and threw her upward through the ceiling, into a room with no door. In the center was a wooden table, and in the center of the table was Naftaly's book.

The Peregrine leapt up through the floor after her, as Toba reached into her hair and pulled out the pin she'd hidden there before she'd left Zayit. Setting it on her palm, she stroked it once, twice, and told it to return to its original shape: the last page of the book. With quivering hands she opened the book to the end and smoothed the last page into place, using a bit of magic to reattach it to the binding.

"Do you know how to use it?" the Peregrine said. "There can't be much time—"

The wall exploded inward, sending splinters of stone flying everywhere; only some quick working of the Peregrine prevented them both being eviscerated.

Tsidon was in the doorway he'd blown open, lit from behind by the lights in the hallway. Toba could not read his face, but he said, "Traitor."

The Peregrine rose to her feet. "Go," she told Toba.

Tsidon said, "Tsifra—" but before he could continue, the Peregrine flung out a hand, sending a bolt of red-hot iron from her palm which collided with Tsidon's mouth and clamped there, leaving him roaring with pain and rage. He pulled a blade from his belt and ran at the Peregrine, who was armed with nothing but her silver dagger. She dodged, parried, and ducked under Tsidon's arm.

"Go, you fool!" she screamed, and managed a blow that sliced Tsidon's shirt open from the cuff to the elbow, before he caught her in the hip with his blade. She only managed to deflect the sword with her knife after it had already drawn blood.

Toba grabbed the book and began reading, trying to will a gate to somewhere inside Zayit, but then she realized she couldn't do it, because she couldn't remember what anything in Zayit looked like and she could make no anchor. So instead, she decided to make a gate to wherever Naftaly was. After a few moments the room began to shake, and stones began to shift then fall from the ceiling as the gate bolted into existence from the center of the book.

Tsidon left off fighting the Peregrine and ran at her, sword extended, but the Peregrine managed to tackle him from behind. He rolled onto his back and kicked her into the wall, but she got her feet behind her and launched herself back at him just as he'd grabbed Toba's ankle, preventing her from moving toward the gate.

The Peregrine wrestled him away, and Toba picked up the book and stepped one foot through the gate. "I'll hold it for you," she told the Peregrine.

"Don't," she said. "Just go, Toba. I'll find you some other way."

"I can't leave you with him!" Toba said, and indeed, Tsidon had pinned the Peregrine face down on the quivering floor.

"Damnation," the Peregrine shouted, and held out a hand to Toba, who reached for it only to realize she was not asking for help but sending out a wind that knocked Toba through the gate, the book in her hands, and she fell through.

THE BEHEMOT WAS a dozen feet tall and ran as fast as a Mazik horse, barreling toward Naftaly and Elena as they stood rooted to the spot, its stone hooves thundering on the ground, while its stone bones made horrible grinding sounds with every move. "Does it have enough magic holding it together to detonate the mines?" Elena wondered.

"It doesn't need to detonate the mines to kill us," Naftaly said, taking her by the arm, but then a group of seven Zayiti soldiers managed to turn its direction by breaking up the ground in front of it. Enraged, it circled back again, lowering its head and aiming its tusks at the men who had thwarted it.

"I'm not thinking of us," Elena said, freeing her arm. To Asmel and Barsilay, who were still close enough to hear, she called, "Can we use undeployed mines against it?"

"It won't detonate them," Asmel said. "The detonator only works on living creatures. Naftaly, you must turn your back on this and finish. The soldiers will draw it off."

"How can they draw it off and deal with those archers?"

"Leave that to the Zayitis," Barsilay said. "How many mines do you have left in this orbit?"

"Ten," Naftaly said.

Barsilay looked aghast, realizing, at the same time as Naftaly, that the soldiers would not survive holding the behemot and the archers off so long. Already, the behemot had circled around the men who had blocked its path and was running through their formation, scattering them to either side while they threw up mostly useless impediments to its progress. They'd held it back the first time because they'd had some distance between it and themselves, but now it was nearly on top of them. Another cohort joined in, trying to draw it off, but were met with volleys of arrows that came through the broken wall; two of those men went down with arrows they could not block. The behemot tore out another tree and flung it into the brace of men trying to set up an earthen shield for the arrows.

They were being killed all around the grove, Maziks who had lived for hundreds or thousands of years dying like mortals.

If Zayit lost so many men, the city might never recover.

"You must finish," Barsilay told Naftaly. "Or all this is for nothing."

"What do you mean to do?" Naftaly asked.

"What I can," Barsilay said. "What you've asked."

Barsilay strode to the front of the grove, arrows glancing off the air before him as he walked, and stopped before the wall where it had been smashed open by the behemot. He lifted a hand, and the archers—who had been shooting at him consistently—stopped.

Drawing a breath, he called out, "Tarses b'Shemhazai, I would speak with you."

His voice was magnified by magic, thundering in Naftaly's ears. There was no immediate reply, and Naftaly expected the archers to resume, when there came a voice, low and flat: "You are not commander here, Barsilay b'Droer."

Barsilay glanced back at Naftaly. Through the dust of the battle, it was hard to read his expression. Turning back, he pulled open his shirt, revealing the mark of Luz, and called back, "I am commander everywhere."

The field went silent; even the behemot stopped its rampage. The only sound was the wind in the leaves of the olive trees that lay on the ground. Then Tarses strode through the opening in the wall, coming to stop a dozen feet from where Barsilay stood with his chest still revealed.

"I am your king," Barsilay said, "and I order you to withdraw."

Tarses laughed. "You are no king."

"I intend to take up the mantle of Luz," Barsilay said.

"I care not what your intentions might be," Tarses said. "Why have you called me down here, besides to crow like a child because you bear a mark upon your flesh?"

"I have called to give you an alternative to sending your men to unbroken death."

"My men are well enough," Tarses said. "Your Zayitis can do nothing but defend, it seems. And poorly."

"Your men are firing from behind cover," Barsilay said, and then glanced over his shoulder at Efra and nodded. She and several of her soldiers, whom Naftaly had not noticed, lifted their hands and brought the rest of the wall back into the ground, leaving Tarses's men, some hundred archers, exposed.

Tarses looked angry indeed, because if he seemed to discount the lives of his soldiers—those whose names he did not know—they might turn on him. He said, "My men are still superior. These Zayitis are untrained."

"You may test that assumption," Barsilay said, "if you do not mind sending your men into the void." He waited to make sure Tarses's soldiers had heard, and then said, "Or I offer you an alternative. You and I shall finish this ourselves."

"A duel?"

"Indeed, and no Mazik may fight or intervene in any fashion. My men will abide by the outcome. Will yours?"

Tarses frowned. Barsilay was manipulating him, and he was trying to find some way out of it, because really his soldiers did have the upper hand, so long as he didn't mind losing a few. A mortal commander, Naftaly knew, would never make this deal, because in a direct battle Tarses's soldiers would win.

Barsilay could see him wavering. He said, "I see you are still considering the welfare of your own men. They might prefer another master who values their lives more highly."

Tarses could no longer refuse.

"Very well," he said. "I will fight you for the olive gate, and no Mazik shall intervene in any fashion." He flung off his cloak and drew the sword at his hip. "Begin."

Barsilay passed his sword from his real hand to the phantom, which struck Naftaly as surprising until he realized Maziks typically used their left hands, and to do otherwise would draw attention to the false limb. The two men circled each other twice, and then Tarses sprang forward, more a test than a real attack, and Barsilay deflected it without much strength and spun away.

The Maziks of Zayit stood stock-still, hands on weapons, watching the archers and watching Barsilay, and then a cry went up. The behemot was charging again.

"We agreed no interference," Barsilay snapped.

"My behemot is no Mazik," Tarses snarled.

Barsilay smiled and inclined his head to where Naftaly and Elena stood. "And neither are they." Across the grove, his eyes met Naftaly's, and then he went at Tarses.

"We need the rest of the mines," Naftaly told Elena. "Help me."

But then the behemot changed course and was heading directly for the mines. The soldiers could not go after it without detonating the entire field.

Naftaly grabbed Elena around the waist and threw them both to the ground and rolled, covering both their heads with his arms. He peered up to watch the behemot thrusting its tusks into the orbiting mines, trying to destroy them in the air.

"They're going to explode," Elena said, but as the beast's tusk caught one of the mines in the third orbit, the amphora continued on its path, crushing the tusk as it completed another cycle.

The behemot stepped back abruptly, shaking its head. Its left tusk was shattered.

As Barsilay held off Tarses with a borrowed sword and a phantom arm, the behemot lowered its head. Either independently or under some invisible control, the beast decided if it could not take down the deployed mines, it would stop Elena and Naftaly from releasing any more. It ran directly at them.

Elena shoved Naftaly off her before grabbing him by the arm and pulling him through the minefield, dodging mines until they reached the center of the field, where the gate would eventually open. From outside the third orbit, the behemot pawed the ground and tried to find a way through without destroying itself.

"We're safe in here, but we can't finish the field," Naftaly said. "We have to find a way to get back out there."

"I'm thinking about that," Elena said. "Apart from the orbiting mines, that thing isn't vulnerable to anything, certainly not anything I can do."

"Is it being controlled, or moving on its own?" Naftaly wondered.

Elena considered this for a moment. "When Toba made mud creatures, they moved independently. If this one works the same way..." She took the waterskin from her hip and poured the contents into her hand, muttering one of her rhyming incantations, which caused the water to turn to mist and rise off her palm as she continued to pour until the skin was empty. "Now blow," she ordered Naftaly, who was not sure what she intended but complied, blowing 'til his lungs were emptied. She took his magic and used it to augment her mist, making it larger, denser, 'til it was all around them, and set it spinning—a whirlpool of fog—and now Naftaly saw what she was doing. "Blow again," she said, and when he did, the churning mist blew from the center of the grove toward the angry behemot, leaving it temporarily blind.

"That won't hold it long," Naftaly said, as Elena pulled him back through the field toward the remaining mines.

"It's made of earth," she reminded him, and through the thick mist, Naftaly could see the beast shaking its head side to side; the mist was softening its outermost layer, not enough to dissolve the creature, but enough to cause mud to flow into its eyes. It began to lurch this way and that, as if trying to find a target.

"Hurry," Elena said, handing him a mine, which he launched into the third orbit.

The sounds of the duel rang in Naftaly's ears, and he had to compel himself not to watch. Elena helped him launch another mine, and then another. And then the next he dropped with a metallic crash at his feet. Naftaly sucked in a breath, assuming he was about to be blown up, but the detonator stayed dormant.

The behemot lifted its head at the sound and charged.

A roar went up from beyond the perimeter: shouts, and then a rhythmic, concussive din that Naftaly felt in his teeth. The Zayitis were beating the pommels of their swords against their shields, giving Naftaly and Elena cover.

"You shall not interfere!" Tarses roared.

"They are not interfering," Barsilay said. "Or are you afraid of a little noise, Caçador?"

The behemot stopped and waited, head swiveling, before running toward the soldiers again.

Naftaly launched another mine and let himself steal a glance toward Barsilay as he danced away from Tarses, not quite fleeing, but striking just often enough to keep Tarses engaged and then retreating, dodging, deflecting when he absolutely had to.

What is he doing? Naftaly wondered as Elena handed him another mine. *He'll never win like that.*

Barsilay was tall, he was strong and graceful, but he'd never been a soldier. Tarses had been leading La Cacería for the past age; Barsilay, even before he'd lost his good arm, could never hope to match him.

Tarses's response to Barsilay's continued evasion was increasing rage, and he advanced with an uncontrolled aggression Barsilay could not equal. It was all he could do to block the blows, and he retreated, back toward the last tree in the grove, the only one the behemot had not yet torn from the ground.

Tarses swung his sword through Barsilay's phantom arm with a grim expression of satisfaction that was replaced with shock when the arm stayed whole. Tarses's sword had gone straight through and embedded itself in the trunk of the olive tree. He was forced to abandon the blade as Barsilay tossed his own sword from the phantom arm to his real one and struck back; Tarses only parried it by making a blade from his own right arm, wearing a grimace of agony.

"Do you have any idea how many Maziks realized that wasn't a real arm?" Barsilay asked. "You claim your vision makes you superior, yet you cannot even see what's right in front of your face."

Tarses only kept hammering at him with his sword-arm, but fighting with a sword was different than fighting with a blade growing from your own limb, and he'd lost his advantage. Barsilay continued, "You won't take this gate. You won't take Anab, or Habush, or any other city. You'll skulk back to Rimon, and that's where you'll die, Tarses, and may your memory be erased."

Tarses glanced briefly over his shoulder, and called out very loudly, "Come to me!"

The behemot swiveled its great stone face toward the dueling men and began to charge.

THIRTY

TSIFRA WAS ALIGHT with fury and beyond reason.

It was more dance than battle, so unevenly was she matched with the mercenary sailors. She was faster, stronger, the blade of her arm sharper than any forged weapon. She dominated the men on the first ship, taking heads, limbs, throats, and then, when none were left, she leapt to the next, slaughtering any who stood against her.

By the third ship, the men leapt into the harbor at her approach. She was just making up her mind what to do with no one to kill when a cannonball ripped through the hull beneath her feet. The next ship in the formation had seen her leap across and was firing, and this ship was quickly taking on water. Scanning the area, she realized the other ships were moving off, breaking formation to get away from her.

The next ship had already moved off far enough to make leaping impossible... She'd have to call the wind to blow her across, and had just made up her mind to do it when an arrow caught the top of her ear.

The next ship had archers. Another arrow struck the deck to her left as she dove out of the way, and she scrambled for cover, letting her arm return to flesh and pulling an arrow out of the mast, where it had stuck. With her other hand she coaxed a bow from splinters of the deck, then willing the arrow to catch fire, she sent it into the other ship's mast, too high for the men to extinguish. Then she pulled another and sent it into the throat of the man who seemed to be calling orders.

None could stand against her, these weak men with their weak weapons. She was an angel, the left hand of the new age, and the only ships that survived her onslaught were those with the sense to flee.

She let those go. They would return to the Uliman lands with tales that the Sefardi fleet was commanded by a demon with an arm of steel. It would only make things easier for her later.

Behind her, the Sefardis fought the ships that had not broken formation and fled; before her lay the city. The ships with the garrison troops were at the rear of her fleet, waiting for the battle to clear.

By that night, the fighting was over. Her ships had sunk a third of the mercenary fleet and she'd destroyed the men on another five ships, which she would use to replace the plague ships she'd burned. She was not sure how many had escaped. Tsifra was exhausted and exultant, and when the word came that the city wished to surrender, she would have accepted it, except for one condition they gave: the Sefardi commander was not to set foot on Zayiti land.

They knew, in some way, about the Mirror. It was a last effort by whichever Maziks were pulling the strings from their side of the gate to keep Tarses from their city, by keeping his Courser out of this one.

It likely would not matter. The city had been taken, and her presence in the city proper would not make much difference. She'd fulfilled her orders. Only, if she agreed, her men would see that she'd allowed Zayit to dictate terms to her, an angel. And that she would not have.

The garrison troops were hungry and as eager for blood as Alaunts. She told their commander, "Take the city. I will go with you."

They burned Zayit from the outside in, Tsifra's pulse racing with the excitement of it. This was what she was made for, neither smug Mazik nor frail mortal. Not to be clever, like Toba, but to conquer, to destroy. All around her were the screams of the dying, the wounded. She was as detached from it as she'd been from her men's kisses and weeping on the ships.

When the city was mostly burned, Tsifra strode into the palace, where she accepted the surrender of its prince in person, just before she took his head.

Not enough, she thought, to kill the Prince. Still, her mind itched with fury. So, because they'd made a deal with Tarses and not with her, Tsifra rounded up the mortal salt guild and killed them all, too. Not enough, she thought, to kill the salt guild. Toba had driven men mad, killed them with terror. How? Her death had made her powerful, a force of fear unlike anything else. That was what Tsifra wanted most of all.

She cast a buchuk, the first time she'd ever done so, and watched her own face look back at her, knowing her intentions. "Do it," the buchuk said, and Tsifra killed her with her blade, closing her eyes, waiting to see the void.

But the buchuk dispelled with her death; there was no void. Tsifra felt the pain of her own blade, but nothing more.

Death was all around her, but Tsifra's eluded her still.

THEY WERE DOWN to the final three mines when Naftaly fell down on one knee and found that he could not rise. "Get up," Elena barked.

But Naftaly felt as if he might faint. It was not a vision, he realized—he was out of magic. He did not have enough left to launch the remaining mines. "I can't," he said. "There's no more magic."

Elena's face went very panicky. "I don't have any I can give you," she said. She called to Asmel and Saba, who had stayed as close as they were able to offer some protection. "He's out of magic, you must help him!"

"The leech!" Saba called back. "The leech is full of magic!"

"How do we get the magic out?" Elena called back.

"Just swallow it!" he shouted.

"Do it," Elena said.

Naftaly hesitated. Without the leech, he would be vulnerable to having another vision, and if that happened, he would be unable to finish launching the mines, and he would be completely vulnerable besides. But if he didn't do something, the mines would certainly not go up. Elena didn't have enough magic to launch them. He was the only person who could do it.

Reaching behind his ear, he took the glowing leech, stared at it for a second longer, and swallowed it. He felt the magic bloom inside him, not much, but enough, as the strength returned to his limbs, and caught something in his mind.

His mind felt very far away.

He stumbled again, nearly dropping the mine he'd been about to launch, and then he saw the inside of a stone building, a woman on the floor, a book on her lap. Toba.

She whispered his name once, twice, and read from the book. She was opening a gate.

Elena was shaking his shoulders when he came back to himself, with a striking lack of weakness and a level of pain that felt only like a normal headache. He'd somehow managed not to drop the mine, and he launched it before turning away.

"There's still two more," she told him.

"Wait," he said. "Where is Asmel?"

"Asmel?" she repeated, but he'd thrust the next mine into her arms and broken into a run, toward the last place he'd seen the man, who'd been distracted by Barsilay and Tarses.

"Asmel!" he cried, when he was close. "Toba! Toba is coming. I've seen her. She's opening a gate—"

"Into Zayit?"

"No! Listen, she's not going into Zayit. She's opening it to where I am. She's coming *here*."

"Are you sure? Are you absolutely sure?" Asmel said, gripping his shoulders. "When?"

"Now," Naftaly said. "She's opening the gate now."

Asmel scanned the area, taking in the behemot still staggering blindly, the duel, the Zayitis standing just beyond the perimeter of the field. Naftaly's head swam a bit from the vision, but this one did not seem to have made him as ill as the others; he was still thinking clearly. "Asmel," he said, "if Toba opens the gate here, she'll risk triggering the mines."

At that moment, Tarses cried out and the behemot began to charge.

This seemed to snap Asmel out of whatever academic debate he'd been having with himself, and he ran forward, threw an arm around Naftaly's waist, and rendered them both invisible. "Hold your breath," he told Naftaly, and then, before he could ask what he'd planned, Asmel pulled them both under the ground.

Naftaly was so turned around he had to fight the urge to strike at Asmel as they dashed through the rocky soil with some magic Naftaly could neither see nor understand. He closed his eyes after the first moments and clung to Asmel's arm, and then they were up again, and Naftaly cried out because Asmel had brought them directly into the behemot's path, and Asmel pushed him down as the behemot made to trample them both.

A beam of light shot out of the ground only inches from Naftaly, just as the behemot would have crushed them, and the behemot gave a strange, metallic cry as the gate pierced its body. The great beast shuddered and disintegrated into rock above their heads. Asmel made some kind of shield above them to prevent them from being buried.

Naftaly slowly got to his feet, meeting Barsilay's eyes from not twenty yards away, so close the behemot had been to killing him. Tarses, behind him, was held to the olive tree by Barsilay's blade to his throat.

Turning back toward the gate that shot up out of the rubble, Naftaly gasped, "How did you know where to put us?"

Before Asmel could answer, Toba leapt through the gate, tackling Naftaly to the ground.

She looked up from Naftaly's chest and cried, "Tsidon!" and then from within the gate flew a gleaming sword meant for Toba's back. Instead it sailed another twenty yards, where it found Tarses and pierced him through the shoulder straight through to the tree behind him.

Barsilay watched as Tarses clawed at the sword with his other hand, trying to use magic to pull it free, his own blade discarded. It had hit an artery, it seemed, as the blood was gushing freely from the wound. "I cannot believe Marah ever trusted you."

Tarses laughed a little, saying. "You should be thanking me. She died without knowing how much blood you have on your hands. Do all these others know it was your idea to pull out the gate of Luz? Would they follow you, if they knew?" He panted against the pain. "Do you really think you could be King?"

Barsilay wordlessly raised his sword.

Without warning, a volley of arrows came flying from the Cacería archers; Asmel threw out a wave of magic to shield Naftaly and Toba. The archers were aiming, however, for Barsilay, who was about to end their master, and he turned just in time to knock away the arrows that would have pierced his throat and heart.

He was not fast enough to stop the arrow that shot across his right bicep, or the one that caught him in the calf.

Tarses began to laugh again. "You were right," he said, as his blood drenched the ground beneath the tree. "We die together."

"Fine by me," Barsilay said, lifting his sword again with his bleeding arm, just as another volley of arrows was released.

It was Asmel who stopped them, springing out of the ground again at Barsilay's back, shielding him with his magic.

"Uncle," Barsilay said.

"Finish this," Asmel said, breathing hard from the unaccustomed overuse of magic.

Barsilay turned back to the tree. Tarses—and the sword that pinned him there—were gone.

Barsilay swore loudly. "Let's go," Asmel said.

"I can't leave this undone," Barsilay said.

"Do you imagine that I hate him less?" Asmel asked, scattering incoming arrows. "There will be another day. I'm nearly at the end of what I can do, and you're no better." He gripped Barsilay's wrist and pulled him away from the last olive tree in the grove, toward the bands of retreating Zayitis, who were backing toward the entrance to the tunnel. Occasionally an arrow would find its way through, and there would be a shout, and then the men would have to decide between carrying one of their comrades –making themselves vulnerable to the archers—or leaving them behind.

They carried their comrades. Many of them died doing so.

Naftaly reached Elena, who pushed one of the two remaining mines into his arms. "I don't think we can do this," he said.

"We're not deploying them," she said. "We're placing them in the tunnel. This was Efra's order. We're bringing up the rear."

"The rear? But there's no one to stop the arrows. We won't make it!"

Saba, who was the requisite fifteen feet from the mines, called, "I'm the only one who knows how close I can get. I'll stay behind you."

Naftaly and Elena took the mines toward the tunnel, the Zayitis running ahead of them and the Rimoni archers advancing close enough behind that Naftaly could see their faces.

"The tunnel's too narrow for you to go around the mines," Elena said. "If you go through here, you'll set them off."

"I know," Saba said. "I know what I'm doing. Leave them and go."

"But—" Naftaly said.

Elena said, "Naftaly," and pulled him away.

They'd gone a few hundred feet into the tunnel when Naftaly heard the steps of the Rimoni soldiers, and then an explosion so powerful it knocked Naftaly and Elena off their feet. There was a second crash: the tunnel caving in. Naftaly coughed and helped Elena up. Some of the Zayitis ahead of them had started to come back, but Elena shouted at them to stay away. "There's salt in the air!" she called. She turned to Naftaly. "Was he in the tunnel when the mines detonated?"

"I couldn't tell," Naftaly said miserably. "He might have been."

They caught up to the Zayitis a minute later; they'd stopped to wait for them.

"The salt will keep them from building a new tunnel here," one of the soldiers explained. "Those mines probably saved the city." She pulled Naftaly by the hand. "Hurry on. We need to collapse the rest of this, once everyone's through."

They were through to the other side of the tunnel, inside Zayit, when a shaken Efra found Naftaly. "Why would he do such a thing?" she demanded.

"He said they were your orders," Elena said.

Efra's eyes were wet as she said, "No. They weren't."

"He may still be alive," Naftaly said. "We don't know if he was in the tunnel when it collapsed."

"The alternative is likely not any better," Efra said. "Tarses will want to vent his anger on someone." She shook her head. "I need to report to the Council." She turned her back and walked away, stopping only to say, without looking back, "You said six days."

"I hate this," Naftaly said. Turning away from the others, he went off to find Barsilay, who was someplace having his wounds treated by some other, lesser doctor, and to find Toba, to ask how they'd been wrong about the number of days 'til Tarses found the gate.

✦ THIRTY-ONE ✦

MORTAL ZAYIT SMOKED for three days, 'til the next hard rain. Tsifra disguised herself and wandered the streets, watching as the bronze gryphons of Zayit were pulled down from the top of the palazzo to be sent back to Rimon and the dead were dragged outside the city and burned, women and children among them. The detachment she'd felt as an angel began to fade, the numbness becoming something else.

Tarses could not have wrought this without her.

It was worse. She'd been more than his instrument: In becoming an angel, she'd become him, a savior of the worlds, a Mazik who was more than Mazik.

Perhaps Toba was right; she was, somehow, superior.

Tsifra had not yet slept, because waking she would not have to report to Tarses. She'd wrought more destruction than he'd ordered. She'd killed the Prince of Zayit. She'd killed the mortal salt guild. She'd made herself a religious figure to her men.

That was not what grieved her most. That was knowing that when she dreamt of Tarses, there would be new orders forthcoming. He would order her to Anab, and Habush, and to P'ri Hadar, murdering while her men worshipped her with their eyes and their swords.

They loved her while she killed them, just as Tarses had killed her mother.

She found she could not bear it.

Tsifra walked out of the palace, waving off the guards who

attended her like dogs, and walked through the smoldering city, and through the gate, all the way to the edge of the sea. And then she kept walking into the icy surf, and kept walking until the burning saltwater was over her head.

She would not swim back. She would die in the salt, as the cold water numbed her limbs. Closing her eyes, she dove into the water, down farther and farther until in the pitch black she no longer knew up from down, and she willed herself to drown. Dying was her last act of defiance, the only one left to her.

The cold and the dark reminded her of the void she'd pulled Toba from in their dream, some dream-manifestation of the real void—insofar as the void was a real place and not merely an absence. This was what she craved. Not a dreaming death, where she still might meet Tarses again, but quiet. There was nothing in her mind she wished to spare, no experience or friendship she wanted to linger. She felt her last breath leave her body with a sense of perfect relief.

SHE OPENED HER eyes to the dream-world, to a different, saltless sea. And in the middle of this was Tarses.

She was a stupid, unforgivable clod to have come here. Tsifra had not realized that a drowning person would lose consciousness before death . . . Why had she not cut her own throat? She turned her face from the scene and screwed her eyes shut. She was still alive, but only barely, and in a moment Tarses would know she'd passed out of the waking world. Tsifra had seen the dead in the dream-world before—it was a perceptible change.

"Come here," Tarses said from the sea, and like a dog she went.

"Tell me," he said, once she was close enough.

"Zayit has fallen," Tsifra said. "The garrison troops are in place. The Prince is dead. And the mortal salt guild."

Here, he turned his head sharply toward her. "Explain."

She did not care to explain. Her body was sinking to the bottom of the Dimah Sea, and in a few moments she would slip from being nearly dead to past utility. Already her lungs had stopped; Tarses, of course, had not noticed.

Tsifra did not know why she'd killed the Prince of Zayit. It had been unnecessary—the entire exercise had been unnecessary. But she wondered, for a moment, what sort of answer Toba might give, if she'd been in her place, so she said, "The Maziks in Zayit have mortal allies past the borders of the city. They infiltrated the fleet with plague. I believed killing the Prince and the guild was the best way to neutralize any allies that may remain outside the city."

She wondered that she'd come up with it. There was just enough truth to the statement that she'd managed to put it forth—a true lie would have caught in her throat. Everything she'd said had been true, but it hadn't been why she'd killed them.

Tarses thought on this a while and said, "You did well, Courser."

She bowed her head, unsure why she hadn't died yet. Perhaps Maziks needed less air than mortals. She'd seen mortals drown, and it went quick. Tarses continued, "You have become the Courser I have always wanted you to be." He began to walk back to the beach, conjuring his robe embroidered with stars. "I believe I've been mistaken in my assessment of your abilities. And in the abilities of your sister." He glanced back at Tsifra over his shoulder. "If you see her again," he said, "kill her. And there is something else you must do before you can proceed to Anab, now that Atalef is dead. Return to Mansanar. Make yourself Queen. And I will make you a promise, my daughter—I will never have another Courser, for all time."

Some small part of Tsifra's mind—possibly the part that thought the same way Toba did—wondered if he truly made this offer because she'd impressed him, or because he'd noticed she was dying.

What caught at her mind more than the offer was that he'd called her *daughter*.

Tsifra's eyes flew open and filled with salt; her lungs burned and she did not know which way was air and life and Tarses, and which was the bottom of the sea and freedom. But then some instinct took hold, some deeply held longing, and she could not argue. She wanted air and wind and breath, and her feet kicked and her face broke the surface.

Tsifra coughed up lungfuls of salt and gasped at the cold air. Her entire body was numb, save for the burning in her throat and eyes, but still, she began swimming back to shore. She'd chosen life for herself, yet again, and she finally understood that she could never do otherwise. She would draw one breath after another, 'til someone or something forced her to stop. She would live.

Only now, she would be Queen.

TOBA FOUND THAT the inside of the palazzo reminded her too much of the siege castle: too many windowless rooms, too much stone, and too little air. After Asmel went to bathe, she slipped out of her suite, past the guards, and into the city.

The streets were deserted, so much so that it almost felt like the dream-world—a sickening realization that made Toba think she'd made a mistake coming outside; at least in the palazzo were her friends and her grandmother, even if they were sleeping.

She wondered if she would ever sleep peacefully again, or if falling asleep would always feel like slipping into the void, or if she would always be waiting to see Tsidon in every person she dreamed of.

On the bridge before her was a tall figure she knew, one hand resting on the railing, the other sleeve blowing empty in the night breeze that still smelled faintly of sugar. Toba went to Barsilay's side and turned to see what he'd been looking at: only the canal, with the waning moonlight leaving rippled reflections. Toba suspected she had not found him by accident.

They stood side by side without speaking, 'til the sounds of a catfight under the bridge made them both laugh, just a little. "The palazzo," Toba said, "it's—"

"Stifling, I know. I can hardly bear to be inside it at all." Barsilay chuckled. "I am nostalgic for the time I spent fleeing La Cacería. At least then I got to sleep outside."

"You could sleep outside now," Toba said.

"I could, but Naftaly likes a bed and a door. I wait for him to fall asleep and then slip out."

"Doesn't he miss you in the dream-world?"

"He hasn't said so."

Toba wasn't sure whether to bring her quarrel with Naftaly to Barsilay's attention, but found she could not help it. "I asked him to go into Aravoth with me."

"Aravoth," Barsilay said. "He never told me this."

"He refused. He didn't want to leave you."

Barsilay smiled faintly.

"That pleases you, but Naftaly cannot always be your shadow."

"He's never been so," Barsilay said. "But it isn't my place to speak to him about this. It would be an insult, after everything. The mines were his idea, did you know?"

"Asmel told me," Toba said. She slumped against the railing; she was nearly asleep on her feet, but too afraid to close her eyes.

Without taking his gaze from the water, Barsilay asked, "Are you all right?"

"All right?" Toba huffed. "What does that mean?"

"I'll try again," he said. "Are you descending into madness?"

"Would I know if I was?"

"I'm not sure," Barsilay admitted.

"Are *you* descending into madness?"

"I'm not sure of that, either. I don't like to be confined, but I also can't abide being alone."

"Well, now you're neither," Toba said.

"Yes," he said, "and I feel grand, but I suspect this is helping me a great deal and you not at all."

He bumped her shoulder with his, and she smiled a little. "My problem," she said, "is that I'm not sure if I'm dreaming or awake. They feel the same to me, now."

He reached out and tweaked her nose, just hard enough that if she'd been dreaming, she would have woken. "Ouch," she said, batting his hand away.

"Better?"

"Yes," she said. "Actually, it is better." She rubbed her arms through her dress; it was cold, and she hadn't bothered to dress for the weather. Barsilay removed his own coat and settled it over her shoulders, stopping to take her wrist between his thumb and forefinger.

"All that work," he sighed. "All those pheasants."

"Believe me, I look forward to being fattened up again. I can hardly wait." She looked at him sideways. "But Asmel tells me you don't like pheasants."

"Oh, I don't, but they were very good for you," he said. "And it was highly amusing to watch you try to finish one by yourself."

"What do you like to eat, then?"

"Me?" He thought it over for a moment and said, "You know, I never told anyone this, but it's actually lentils. Not lentils turned into other things. Just lentils."

"Plain?"

"No one ever eats just lentils—I don't know why. But there was a stew I used to eat in Luz; they mixed the lentils with lemon. That was my favorite." He sighed. "I haven't thought of it in years. Marah and I used to eat it together, when we were homesick."

Toba felt into the depths of her dress pocket, where she still had a few random lentils, and pulled one out and handed it to Barsilay. He smiled at it on his palm, and bent down and kissed it, making it into a bowl of chunky soup, which Toba took from him, since he could not hold the bowl and eat at the same time. She made a spoon out of a hairpin and took a bite; the lemons made it very acidic, while the lentils tasted of earth and reminded her of her grandmother's cooking.

"My sister has returned to Tarses," Toba said. "Or so I presume."

"Did you think she would do otherwise?"

Toba thought on this. "I thought she would succeed in killing him, truly."

"You are young," Barsilay said. "It's natural to be hopeful. It speaks highly of you that you still can be, after everything."

"Young?"

"Hopeful."

"I never thought of 'hopeful' as a compliment."

"It is," he said. "At least until you slide into 'foolishly optimistic,' in which case the compliment becomes a curse."

"Hm. Barsilay, if we'd succeeded, and she'd killed Tarses, what would you have done?"

"I'd have been glad," he said.

"With my sister, I mean."

"What would you have had me do? Make her my friend?"

"You made the Peregrine your friend."

Barsilay sighed deeply. "If Tsidon came to you tomorrow and told you he'd had a change of heart and wanted to be your ally, could you accept that? Would you believe him?"

"No, but it's entirely different."

"How?"

"Because the Courser never chose Tarses—she was enslaved from birth. The Peregrine chose him, and you accepted her. Did she not hand you over to Tarses once, long ago?"

"She did," he said.

"Do you forgive her for that? It was because of that that Asmel was forced to accept the sigils of silence, all those long years. He was in pain from them, did you know?"

Barsilay was very quiet. "I think your concept of forgiveness may be different than mine. I have not forgotten what she did, but I've accepted that her interests have changed."

"Well, the Courser's only interest all these years has been staying alive when Tarses would have let her be killed. Her will was not her own."

"The Courser shattered my legs every day for weeks, and worse than that. She did things I will not tell you, because I don't wish you to live the rest of your life with those images in your mind. And that was all before she took my arm. You cannot ask me this."

"I know what she did!" Toba said. "Did you forget she murdered me? Cut off my head, Barsilay? You live every day without your arm, but I live every day knowing very intimately what it feels like inside the void, and I promise you it's a good deal worse. I don't ask you to love her, only to consider that she could have been otherwise, if Tarses had not made her, and she could be an ally."

"You ask me to consider her a weapon rather than a person? Is that what you ask?"

"I ask you to consider that she may have had no choice."

"But she did."

"But—"

Barsilay leaned forward and kissed Toba's forehead very tenderly, and said, "No."

Toba felt inexplicably sad, but she said, "I suppose it's a moot point anyway, since she didn't kill Tarses."

"No. She didn't. Though I would like to know what happened to the killstone."

Toba said, "I puzzled it out like this: Atalef had the killstone, and either he died or he lived. If he'd lived, then he'd have killed either you or Tarses, and since you are both alive, I can only surmise that he died. And if he'd given the command-word to Tarses, you would be dead then, too, so he must have died without telling him."

Barsilay nodded. "I think you must be right. And Marah never shared the command-word, not with anyone—it was far too dangerous. If Atalef's dead, the killstone's nothing but a relic and a curiosity. It won't be killing anyone."

"At least it can't be used on you, then," Toba said.

"Does that comfort you?"

"It does."

"Good," Barsilay said. "I'm glad."

Toba handed the spoon to Barsilay, who ate a bite, and the two of them passed the spoon back and forth until the bowl was gone and the moon had grown low, and then they returned to the palazzo.

THE OLD WOMAN was shuffling down the halls of the palazzo, hunting for the doctor's rooms.

She'd only just learned from Naftaly that he'd been left behind, and everyone was in a tizzy about what had to be done next to secure the city, and some business with the siege castle and Naftaly's magic book and so on. She'd fought with Elena, who had caught her adding salt to her breakfast and railed at her for possibly poisoning someone by accident and then taken her entire stash. Asmel was gone and Barsilay was gone and Elena and Toba were gone and Naftaly was some kind of war hero, and the old woman thought, *No one has remembered the man's cat.*

It seemed a trivial thing—the cat was basically a stray anyhow— but if it was locked in the doctor's rooms it would starve. The old woman had nothing much useful to do: She couldn't fight or do magic, and had not even been very good at putting salt into metal pyramids because she was old and feeble and weak, but she could let the cat out. Maybe she could even feed it, if she could find a helpful Mazik willing to make her some fish.

Also, it had occurred to her that there might be something useful in the doctor's rooms, something they should take with them to P'ri Hadar. Whatever the Maziks used for medicine, for example. Barsilay was too busy to have thought of this, but he would surely thank her later, when she showed him she'd made off with a stash of headache powder and cream for foot fungus.

She'd learned all about the battle in the grove from Naftaly—Naftaly being so brave and Barsilay nobly dueling Tarses to save the men of Zayit—and everyone seemed to consider it a victory. It was, the old woman had to admit, in that Tarses had failed to acquire the gate.

On the other hand, she worried. Tarses had been shamed, and the old woman had known enough temperamental men to realize that he would now be very angry and very dangerous. He might have been able to accept losing the duel, but being skewered with his own lieutenant's sword? That was a story that would spread. Someone would bear the brunt of that anger, and it would either be Barsilay himself, or it would be Zayit.

As she wandered the halls of the palazzo, the old woman wondered which way Tarses would go—if he was the type of man to go after the larger target or the more personal one. But as she got lost yet again—the palazzo was too big and too much the same inside—she concluded that Zayit certainly made a very large target indeed.

The old woman was forced to ask three different Maziks for directions. They all gave her the same horrified look as that one soldier Elena had fed to her horse, as if her face were a nightmare unimaginable to Mazik-kind, and maybe it was. Still, they could have been a bit more polite, tried to look a little less like she might have given them the plague. For all the Zayitis were meant to be so cosmopolitan, they were terribly rude.

She found the doctor's room locked, of course, but Zayiti Mazik locks did not seem to be much harder for her to pick than Rimoni Mazik locks, and she was quickly inside, where she was met with a mewling mess of patchwork cat.

"Oh dear," she told it. "It has been a while since someone's fed you, hasn't it? I'm sorry. Would you like to"—here, the cat raced for the open door—"come with me . . . I guess not." The old woman looked around the room. Books, endless Mazik books, none of them any use to her. Elena might have liked to see them; she'd learned to read a bit of Mazik from Rafeq, but someone had decided she was one of the "important mortals"—that was, every mortal besides herself—so she was off doing important-mortal things. She wondered if the Maziks made more of an effort to hide their affrontery at her wrinkles.

Unfortunately, someone else must have had the same idea, because the doctor's shelves had been cleared of everything besides the books. Not a jar or pot of anything remained. His sister had come through and collected things, or else someone else from the government.

She closed the door behind her and went back up the hallway, hoping one of the rude Maziks might lead her to wherever Naftaly had gone, but found, twenty paces down, the doctor's cat in the midst of eating a rat.

"I suppose I don't need to feed you, then," the old woman told it. The cat was very enthusiastic; she held a hand over her mouth and nose, because the whole scene was rather garish. "I'll leave you to it."

Then something caught her eye about the rat. It was slightly larger than others she'd seen—and as a beggar she'd seen plenty—but that could have just been a feature of its Mazikness; the horses were larger, too. But that did not account for what was attached to its back: a silver dome, like a small onion cut in half. She squatted down and reached for it, eliciting a series of hisses from the cat.

"Relax, I don't want your filthy vermin," she told it, and managed to pull the dome loose from the rat's half-eaten carcass. She turned it over in her hands a few times while the cat continued to eat. What an oddity. She put it in her pocket and would have continued looking for Naftaly, but then she saw another rat, further down, skittering from one side of the hallway to the other and disappearing into an impossibly small crack in the wall.

It, too, had been carrying a silver dome on its back.

Then came another, and another—an entire queue of rats, carrying parcels across the hallway.

"What the devil are they carrying?" she wondered, just as the cat came barreling toward the line of rats, scattering them and chasing one off down the hall. Once it was gone, the others resumed their trek into the crevice. The old woman took the dome back out of her pocket and turned it over, looking for some way to open it. There, at the base, was a seam the breadth of a strand of hair. She'd missed it before. Taking the pin she'd used to pick the doctor's lock, she worked to pry it open. It was very solidly attached, and it took all her strength, and then it gave way all at once.

The old woman shrieked, clawing at her face and hands, and then fainted dead away.

NAFTALY WOKE BEFORE dawn and found his bed empty and cold. He had not dreamt of Barsilay either, but when he rose to look for him he found the man had fallen asleep in the sitting room, still dressed. One of the Zayiti shades had laid out food, which sat untouched; probably Barsilay had been there for hours and the shade had been confused as to when to leave breakfast. Naftaly kissed the crown of Barsilay's sleeping head and took some fluffy bread from the plate, and, once quickly dressed, he thought he ought to check in with Efra.

He had not replaced the leech he'd swallowed, since his last vision had left him without pain or weakness. Saba had been correct: The al'qot had done their duty, and his mind had strengthened itself past needing them. Naftaly wished he could have told him. He wished that the two of them had not been made over into soldiers: Naftaly to become either a hero or a liar, depending on whom you asked, and Saba to become a sacrifice.

The guards told Naftaly that Efra had gone to the southern wall to check on the refurbishment of the cannons, which were meant to be fired at dawn. He was hoping to get to her prior; he was not sure what Tarses would do once they began firing on the siege castle, but he suspected there was something planned. What if the entire thing exploded, like one of Naftaly's mines?

It was still dark when he made it up the steps to the top of the wall, where he found Efra staring grimly ahead, several of her lieutenants standing silently behind her. All of the light-stones on the wall had been extinguished; only a bit of residual light from those on the steps showed him where she was.

"What do you see?" she asked Naftaly.

Naftaly waited a little for his eyes to finish adjusting to the darkness, and then said, "I don't see the siege castle. Have they glamoured it?"

"That would be the most reasonable explanation," Efra agreed, "but when we sent bats out, they flew right through. Give me another explanation."

"It's ... I don't know. Some sort of trick? An illusion?"

Efra said nothing.

"It looks like a trap, doesn't it?"

"It does."

It had grown very faintly light, just in the prior minute, and Naftaly could see that Efra was standing to the left of one of the new cannons. "We made four of these," she told Naftaly, "to fire solid munitions. For the sole purpose of breaking the wall of that castle, which is not there. We used nearly every bit of iron in the city." To the soldiers, she said, "Prepare to fire."

"At what?" Naftaly asked.

"Something's there," she said. "Something must be there. Did Tarses just suck it back down into the earth?"

Naftaly said, "Well, the wall was manned all night, surely someone heard something?"

"No one heard anything!" Efra shouted. "Not a sound, not all night. Not that I was here. I was in the grove watching a stone beast trampling my men and my brother die for you. Is the cannon ready?"

"It is, Savia," said one of the soldiers.

"Then fire!"

Naftaly clapped his hands over his ears as the cannon fired into empty space. They watched the shell sail through the air, unimpeded, and land in the empty field beyond the gate, so far out that Naftaly could not see it in the darkness. Efra cursed. "Where is it?" she shouted to Yel, who had only just returned. "The perimeter?"

"There is no sign of it anywhere from the wall," she said. "It's just—" She was cut off by a bat the size of a kitten that landed on Efra's shoulder; it had a tiny scroll attached to one foot, which Efra unrolled and read before it crumbled to ash. "I've been summoned by the Council," she said. She cast an eye back at the empty space beyond the wall. "I want this watched by at least two men at all times. If anything changes, come find me." She nodded to Naftaly. "You'd better come with me."

He followed her down the wall and back down the steps; the light-stones were winking off in the rising dawn as they passed. "Did they want to see me, too?"

"Yes. They want to meet the man who said six days instead of five."

Naftaly's empty stomach lurched, then he realized that was sarcasm. Of course the Council didn't want to see him. Seeing his discomfort, she said, "I don't want to leave you alone up here. Many of these soldiers lost friends in the grove."

Naftaly said nothing. She added, "You did prevent Tarses from taking the gate; I haven't forgotten that. But if we'd known the time frame—"

"We could not have installed the mines any faster," Naftaly said. "So what would have been different?"

Efra said, "I don't know." They walked across to the palazzo, and upstairs to the chamber of the Council of Ten, but the guards stopped Naftaly before he could enter. "They only want to see you, Savia," one of them told her.

"I'm bringing him with me," she explained.

"They were explicit," he replied, a little contritely. "They only want you."

"I'm not without power here," she said, but then Barsilay appeared in the corridor, and she said, "Were you summoned here, too?"

"I was told you were on the way here," he said. "I was looking for you, but I think it's best we both go in. Is there some problem?"

Efra said, "I'm not sure. I'll go myself and bring you in later."

She disappeared into the room, the doors shut behind her, and it was a quarter hour before she came back out, looking quite harried. "What happened?" Barsilay asked her.

"They won't see you," she said. "They're not happy playing host to the heir of Luz. They're meeting now to discuss what to do with you."

"What to do with him?" Naftaly asked. "He saved your gate from Tarses!"

"I know what he did, but the Council and the Prince are worried he means to seize power."

"I don't," Barsilay said. "Not here."

"They're also worried that keeping you in Zayit will further antagonize Tarses."

"It will," Barsilay said. "That much is true."

"I expect when things shake out, they'll ask you to leave," she said. "I'm sorry."

"It's fine," Barsilay said. "I need to start making my way to P'ri Hadar, anyway. But surely that isn't the only reason they summoned you?"

"It wasn't," she said. "The Council got a report from Anab this morning. The King is dead."

Barsilay closed his eyes. "When?"

"Three days ago. And in light of the siege castle disappearing, they've come to the conclusion that Tarses has given up on Zayit for now and is moving on to the next city."

Barsilay said, "They can't honestly believe he's given up on Zayit."

"They think Anab is a softer target, and now our gate's secure, the city's less of a prize."

"That's nonsense! There's still the salt stockpile."

"I did suggest that."

"We have a window of time," Naftaly said, "a very narrow one, and we have the gate of Luz. If we move quickly now, we can get the people out of the city before it falls!"

"They don't believe it will fall," said Efra. "They believe the siege castle is gone because Tarses has moved on. They think your work in the grove has given us an easy victory. They mean to give you an honorary title."

"Before they banish me from the city?" Barsilay said incredulously. "I don't want an honorary title, I want the people of Zayit not to be burned alive—who is running the Council?"

"I'm not sure what you mean."

"The salt guild was in league with Tarses," Barsilay reminded her. "How closely were they tied to the Council?"

"Are you suggesting the Council is actively engaged in betraying the city?"

"I'm suggesting either they are actively betraying the city or they are too stupid to rule. I don't know which it is. They're your Council, you tell me."

Efra said, "They aren't wrong about everything. If we evacuate the city, it hands Tarses a victory. We can't defend an empty city, and the economy will collapse. And what's also true is that Naftaly was wrong—Tarses didn't find the gate in six days. So I ask you, isn't it possible he's wrong again? Can you swear to me that he's not?"

Barsilay looked up at Naftaly, who said, "I don't know why the days were wrong. But I've seen Zayit burning, so I know it happens."

Efra said, "Whether I believe you or not isn't the issue. The Council won't. I'm sorry."

Barsilay nodded. "This isn't our city. If the Council wants me gone, I'll go. But I think you're making a terrible mistake not getting your people out while you can."

As the two men walked away, Naftaly said, "I wish I knew the truth about the days."

Barsilay said, "I suspect we'll find out soon enough. But either way, what you've done for this city is no less than heroic."

Naftaly felt a bit unequal to the compliment, so he turned back one of his own. "You were the hero of that battle, Barsilay. I know you fought Tarses thinking you would lose."

"But I didn't," Barsilay said. "I'm all right, Naftaly. And if there's ever anything you must do that takes you from my side, I'll be all right then, too."

✦ THIRTY-TWO ✦

ELENA HAD BEEN beating on Toba's door for several minutes before Asmel answered it, looking extremely unkempt. His safira, which he normally kept out of sight, hung openly around his neck; he clutched the shard in his left fist, as if worried someone might take it from him again.

"I've been out here for ages," she said. "Where is Toba?"

"She went out seeking Barsilay and Naftaly," he said.

"They left you behind?"

"I was sleeping," he said. "I'm not quite myself yet. So if you don't mind—"

"I need help," she said. "And you'll do." Without waiting for Asmel to answer, she pulled him out through the door and across to the room she'd been put in with the old woman, who now lay prone on the bed, unconscious and breathing roughly.

"What happened to her?" Asmel asked.

"I don't know," Elena said. "Some guard said they found her like this and dumped her here. Said they think she fell."

Asmel was already examining the old buzzard. "Where did they say she fell?"

"They didn't," Elena said. "And I can't wake her, either. Naftaly said the doctor knew what to do for mortals, is there something you can do?"

"I'm no doctor," he said. "Barsilay may be able to help when he returns."

"I don't want to wait for him," she said. "I want to know what happened to her. I won't believe she just fell, and I don't like being lied to."

Asmel was running his hands over the old woman's head. "He didn't precisely lie; she has a knot on her head. She did fall. But something else happened, too. Look at her hands. They've only recently been healed—were they injured before?"

"She could have been hurt while we were in the grove," Elena said. "But I wasn't told about it."

"Her face, too. This is strange. It looks like burns, healed in a hurry."

He was probing her head again with his hands; he seemed to be running a little magic between them, through the old woman's body. "Some broken bones, but those are very old, and the head injury's not so bad. I don't think it's what's keeping her unconscious—" He stopped. "Her lungs are very badly hurt. Burned, I think."

"At the same time as her hands and face?"

"Very likely," Asmel said.

"Why would they heal the external injuries, and not her lungs? Did they not know about that?"

"You saw how easily I found that issue," Asmel said. "But she's a mortal. I'm surprised they did anything for her at all, to be honest."

"Unless they left those injuries because they were hoping she would die," Elena said. "Can you heal her lungs?"

"Not well," he admitted. "I can try dealing with the worst of it, though, and Barsilay can do more when he's here." He set his hands on the front and back of her chest and closed his eyes. "This is very bad," he said. "I'm not sure I can help."

"Keep trying."

Asmel's palms glowed, and his face was pink with the effort of what he was doing. After another minute, the old woman began to cough, and sat up and coughed until Elena brought her a glass of water from the basin. "Are you all right?" she asked.

"No," the old woman wheezed, a horrible, sickening sound.

"Can you do more?" Elena asked Asmel.

"Wait," the old woman said. "Let me speak while I can." She wheezed again; her voice was only a strangled whisper. "Give me back the water." She took another drink and then said, "Rats."

"Rats?" Elena repeated.

The old woman nodded. "The Zayitis are using rats to take the salt"—she coughed again—"out of the city."

"The salt?" Asmel said. "From the salt stockpile?"

"No," the old woman said, her breath rattling. "Not the . . . Not the salt . . . the . . ." She pointed at Elena and had another coughing fit.

"Are you telling us," Elena said, "that the Zayitis are using rats to smuggle the *decayed* salt out of the city?"

The old woman was coughing so hard that Asmel had gone back to using his magic to try to heal her again, not waiting for Barsilay. Pushing his hand away from her throat, she said, "Yes."

It took Elena and Asmel several hours to find Barsilay, who was with Efra at the wall again, and ten minutes to explain what the old woman had seen. Asmel was quietly enraged, partly at the Zayitis and partly, Elena believed, at herself for making the poison in the first place.

She did not point out to him that if she hadn't, he would most likely be dead, and would certainly have no magic.

They found the Council and the Prince of Zayit not in the Council chamber, but downstairs in a room with walls inset with silver and emeralds. The Prince sat in a high chair dressed in purple silk; the Council flanked him on either side, five men on each, sitting at two arced tables. Efra had threatened the guard to get them inside.

"What is this?" the Prince asked as the four came inside. "If you are here to assert your authority as heir of Luz, no one will hear you."

"I'm here because we know you are smuggling poison out of this city," Barsilay said. "And I would know why."

"You aren't entitled to know anything," the Prince said crossly.

"Are you giving it to Tarses?" Elena asked.

Here, the Prince made a very sour face. "I have not consented, and will not consent, to be questioned by a mortal, Barsilay of Luz."

"That seems to be an expedient way to avoid the question," Asmel said. "Have you given it to Tarses?"

"Tarses," the Prince said, "is gone."

"So you keep insisting."

"So I know for a fact."

Barsilay said, "How?"

"All right," the Prince said. "I will answer your questions. I know Tarses is gone because we made a deal with him."

Efra's face went very stony. "You made a deal with Tarses? Why was I not told?"

"Because it did not concern you," the Prince said. "Or your army. This city cannot withstand a siege."

"We have enough lentils for months!" Efra said.

"We cannot use our gate, and we cannot trade with the other cities. We decided it was better to end the situation quickly rather than endure a protracted siege. Tarses offered us a deal: all our salt stores in exchange for him leaving—but that would have left us defenseless, so we countered with the decayed salt Rafeq of Katlav made for the salt guild. And Tarses accepted."

Barsilay said, "You fools. You gave lethal poison to the worst enemy this city has ever had!"

"Our duty is to Zayit," the Prince said. "And now Zayit is safe."

"You really think he'll leave this city standing, after we thwarted him in the grove? You're deluded," Barsilay said.

"Do you think we are fools? That we in Zayit would not know how to craft a contract? Tarses swore an oath on his own name," the Prince said, not a little smugly. "So greatly did he desire what we had. The contract is entirely comprehensive and unbreakable."

"So you say," Barsilay snapped.

The Prince smirked. "Would you hear our terms? All right. Tarses swore to leave this city, never to return. He swore that none of his men would ever set foot in Zayit for all time, nor their children, nor their grandchildren, for seven generations. He cannot use salt against the city, nor decayed salt. He cannot use weapons made by Maziks nor by mortals. He cannot use elements of nature. He cannot send troops nor animals, natural or otherwise. He cannot come himself. So you see, we are quite safe from him. If you want to continue to work against Tarses, I'd suggest you move on to Anab. They may have need of you there when he arrives."

Barsilay said, "You're mad if you think even that will stop him."

"Time," the Prince said, "will prove otherwise."

"In that case, you've just sold the whole world to the devil to save your own city!"

"And I am comfortable with that choice," the Prince said. "P'ri Hadar has an army. Let them deal with Tarses on their own lands." He threw out a hand, and the doors behind them flew open. "Now, Barsilay, heir of Luz, you may go."

TOBA HAD BEEN suffering all day with a splitting headache and cracked lips. The winter air was drier even than it had been in Rimon, which puzzled her. Would the lower elevation and proximity to the sea not tend to moderate the climate? She would ask Asmel about it when he woke, but her priority was to find Naftaly and make a plan for what had to come next. She hid the book under her coat and went out, thought it was afternoon before she found Naftaly wandering the streets near the piazza. He was much changed from Rimon, like a man carrying a great burden. She thought this must be the weight of his newly potent visions, a heavy gift for someone like Naftaly. She could tell the mood of the Zayitis had darkened toward him after the battle in the grove, when his warning had only been mostly accurate.

The warning had been Toba's, though, and she wondered which of them had made the mistake, or if it somehow could have been both of them who were wrong. Or else if something they had done had changed things, somehow. "What are you doing out here?" she asked.

"Wandering, I don't know," he said. "I needed some time on my own. No one will listen to me because I told them Tarses would find the grove in six days instead of five. What are you doing out here?"

"I hate the palazzo," she said, "and I was hoping to find you, actually. Are you all right?"

"No," he said. "I have this horrible sense there's something I ought to be doing, but I can't do anything, not on my own. Maybe we should just go."

"All of us, move on to P'ri Hadar?"

"If they won't summon help, and they won't help themselves, what's the point in our staying here, waiting for something terrible to happen we can't stop?" He shook his head. "I realized something, in the battle. I'm capable of more than I've allowed myself—and Barsilay needs me to be more than I've been. I need to go with you to Aravoth, to make sure this is done. Whenever you decide it's time, I will go."

Toba nodded. "I think we'll need to make sure the others are out of the city first. Have you discussed this with Barsilay?"

"Not yet," he said, just as Toba peered down into the canal beneath them and said, "Look at this."

Naftaly looked to see what she meant. All the goldfish in the canal were floating at the surface. "They're all dead," she said.

"Poison?" Naftaly said. "Salt? Would salt kill goldfish?"

Toba plunged her hand into the water and pulled it out again. "It's not salt," she said, holding her hand out to Naftaly so he could see. "It's oil. The surface of the water's been coated in oil."

"For what purpose?" Naftaly asked. "Why would anyone want to kill the fish?"

"No reason I can see. Is it just this canal?" They quickly made their way down the street to the next canal, which ran parallel on the next street. "It's the same," she said. "This isn't good. We have to tell Efra. Do the Maziks drink this water?"

"Yes, Barsilay said— No." Naftaly suddenly went very still. "No, Toba, this is how it starts. They aren't trying to poison the city. The oil is here to help it burn. The fire will spread through the canals, and the Maziks won't be able to get to the water to put it out."

Toba saw him turning in on himself, thinking, and she said, "Let's go. There's no time."

But Naftaly had cast his eyes skyward, and said, "It's already too late."

Toba looked up alongside him to see a volley of flames come over the wall—hundreds of small orbs of fire. The soldiers did their best to deflect them, but there were too many, and the men were too slow. The first volley set the canals alight. The burning was slow enough at first that Toba thought it might be extinguishable, with enough Maziks using magic on it, and then it seemed to catch in a wave of flame that went up like a roar through the city.

The second volley of flames went into the buildings.

✦ ✦ THIRTY-THREE ✦ ✦

TOBA WATCHED AS NAFTALY stretched out his arm, as if entranced, and murmured, "It's the same coat."

"What?"

He looked back up to the burning canal. "As in my vision. I'm wearing the same coat."

This was not helping anything, and Toba shook his other arm hard. "Wake up!" she snapped. "Tell me what else you saw. Where were we?"

"In the piazza," he said, and she took his hand and began pulling him back that way.

"That makes sense," she said. "The buildings in the piazza are all stone. It'll be safer there longer."

He yanked back against her. "But all these people!"

She stopped pulling and looked around. The Maziks whose homes and shops were burning had run into the street. They were using magic to try to extinguish the flames, but nothing they did seemed to be working. One of them was screaming about the burning canals; without that water, they had nothing useful to put out the fires.

A group of women had gathered in the middle of the street and was incanting loudly at the sky, with no obvious results. Toba ran up to them. "What are you trying to do?"

"Conjure rain," one of them told her. "But it isn't working—the sky's too clear."

Toba thought of her cracked lips that morning. "They've sucked the moisture out of the air," she said. "I haven't seen so much as a cloud since yesterday ... This won't work."

"If we extinguish the canals," one of the others said, "we'll have access to that water."

"We tried that," said a passing man, one of the Maziks with an emerald in his ear. "Everything we do just makes it worse. The fire's enchanted, I don't know how. Our magic won't touch it."

"Once the oil's burned off, we'll be able to get to the water," one of them said.

"Once the oil's burned off, the water will all be boiled away!"

"We have to get out," someone screamed. "Make for the wall!"

"Wait!" Toba cried, but many of them had already broken away and were running through the burning street.

"We need to get as many as we can to the piazza," Naftaly said. "You can open a gate there, and put everyone through to someplace safe. And I know Barsilay will come there, I heard his voice in my vision, too." He coughed; the smoke was growing thick and smelled of burning wood and oil. He grabbed at the nearest Mazik running past. "Come with us, we have a way to get everyone out," he said, in the best Zayiti he could manage.

But the Mazik only looked at him as if he were crazy and continued on. "What do we do?" he asked Toba.

She shook her head helplessly. "We need Efra, or at least some soldiers. All these people are panicking."

"There's no time to get all the way to the wall and back."

A Mazik man carrying a child ran back the other way, covered in soot. "What happened?" Toba asked him.

"We made it to the gate," he said. "There are archers, somewhere—I couldn't see where. They were shooting anyone who went through. We can't get out. We can't get out!" He would have kept running, but Toba held him with both hands. "Listen to me," she said. "Go to the piazza and tell anyone you pass. We have a way to get people out from there. Do you hear me?"

"The piazza is in the middle of the city. There's no way out from there!"

"We have a way," Toba insisted. "You must trust me."

"You're a Rimoni!"

"No," she said, "I am of Luz." Then a flock of larks sprang from her forearms, all of them crying in Toba's voice, "Make for the piazza!"

INSIDE THE PALAZZO, Elena turned away from the others, who were arguing about what to do now that the Prince of Zayit and the Council had betrayed the city to Tarses. There was some noise, coming from some other part of the building: an argument, raised voices, though Elena had heard none in all her time in Zayit. The Zayitis were too cultured to brawl in their palace. "Stop," she told the Maziks. "Listen."

Efra cocked her head. "Something's happened," she said. "I smell—"

"Smoke," Asmel said.

"Naftaly," Barsilay said. "His vision, it's begun. We have to find him, and Toba."

Heading back toward the entrance, they found the smoke heavier, and quickly saw why: the great oak doors were aflame. The guards were trying to put the fire out, but it only seemed to be spreading, somehow burning the stone.

"Didn't the Prince say Tarses could not use any elements of nature?" Elena asked.

"This isn't natural fire," Efra said. She told the guards. "Flee, and get out everyone you can."

"Savia, what will you do?"

"I'm going back to warn the Council," she said. "We can't slip out through the walls. They're embedded with salt to thwart assassins, and so are the floors. There's an escape route that will take us back through the Prince's chamber, but you'll have to follow closely, and one of you will have to take the mortal." She brought forth a light-stone from her pocket and rested it on her palm. "These walls are thick; you'll need light to avoid getting turned around."

Barsilay took Elena's hand in his, and the four of them became shadow and went through the nearest wall, down another hallway, and then through a second wall.

This brought them back into the Prince's locked chamber.

The Prince and the Council were all dead in their chairs.

"Assassins?" Asmel asked, looking the Prince over and seeing nothing.

"Suicide, more likely," Efra said. "They must have realized they'd been betrayed after they'd agreed to give up the city to Tarses. All of them dead in their chairs, no sign of any struggle. They simply entered the dream-world, the cowards."

"How is the fire spreading through the stone?" Elena asked.

"I don't know," Efra said. "But we'd better hurry before it spreads to the roof." She crossed to the far side of the room, and together they went through another wall.

She was about to lead them up a flight of stairs when Elena said, "Wait."

"We really can't," Barsilay said.

Elena could hardly believe she was going to suggest anyone risk their lives over this but found her conscience would not allow her to forget. Probably if the situation were reversed, Elena would have been abandoned. She was quite sure of it, actually. Nevertheless, she said, "We've forgotten the crone."

"Where is she?" Efra asked.

"The third floor, east wing."

"That will be hard to get to," Efra said. "Isn't she dying anyway?"

Barsilay said, "She's the one who discovered your Council had betrayed the city. We can't leave her to burn. I won't."

"I'll go," Asmel said, holding out his hand. "Make me a map of the walls I can use. I'll find you out in the piazza."

Efra looked like she might have argued, but instead she said, "It's too complicated, I'll have to go with you." She gave Barsilay a brief explanation of the six turns he'd have to make, and then she took Asmel upstairs.

Barsilay and Elena went through a wall, down a hallway, through another, and then found themselves in a long room lined with iron-barred cells. These were mostly empty, save one, which was occupied by a captured Hound. He must have been one of the men captured trying to go through the tunnel into the grove.

"Why have the escape route go through the dungeon?" Elena wondered.

"This isn't the dungeon," Barsilay said. "That's below the palazzo. This is a holding area. Most likely they'd been planning to question or execute him."

"How dreadful," Elena said. "Excuse us." And she pulled Barsilay across the room to the next wall.

"Wait," called the Hound. "I can be helpful to you."

"No," Elena said. "No, you can't."

"I know how to extinguish the demon flame."

Here, Barsilay paused. "What does that mean?"

"You've noticed the fire cannot be put out? This is Tarses's particular wonder. There is a trick to it, though, and if you prevent me burning alive, I will tell you."

"He's lying," Elena said.

"Almost certainly," Barsilay agreed.

"No one else can tell you," the Hound said. "If I burn, the city burns with me."

Elena turned to Barsilay and said, "No."

Barsilay pulled her aside. "If there's the smallest chance he's telling the truth, we need it. We have nothing else."

"And if he turns on you?"

Barsilay said, "I'll restrain him." He used some Mazik trick to open the cell door. "Put your hands behind you."

The Hound complied, and Barsilay took a piece of the iron bar and made it into a set of manacles he used to bind the man's hands. His phantom arm held a knife at the Hound's throat, his real one held Elena's hand, and Elena held a light-stone. They went through the far wall, and across another room.

They'd just passed into the next wall—the last one, Elena thought, before they reached the exterior wall—when the Hound slipped his bonds.

Elena could not tell how he'd done it. One moment he'd been bound, and the next the iron was on the ground. Barsilay pulled the knife into his throat but that arm, both phantom and shadow, was weaker than it should have been, and the Hound managed to pass directly through it, looking nearly as shocked as Barsilay. Once freed, he stepped behind Barsilay and put him in a chokehold. Barsilay's eyes went wide with panic. His real hand was holding Elena; if he let go, she'd go back to being solid inside the wall and die. Elena punched the Hound with her free hand, twice, three times, with no effect. Barsilay's eyes had closed. There was already no air inside the wall, and now he was losing blood to his brain. Once he was unconscious, the Hound would leave him inside the wall to die.

With her free hand, Elena groped in her pocket for the old woman's packet of salt, ripped it open with her thumbnail, and jammed it into the Hound's eye.

He let go of Barsilay and fell to his knees, his hand over the eye which was already blackening. Elena gave Barsilay enough of a shake to remind him where he was, and he pulled the two of them through the wall and into the next room, both of them gasping. A moment later, the Hound fell through the wall, too, blackness spread down half his face, and then he fell to the floor and was still.

Barsilay looked at her, aghast. "You've been walking around with poison this whole time?"

"I took it off the old woman," she said. "I was worried she might kill someone by accident."

"Yes. Well. We wouldn't want that," he said shakily. "Let's find our way out." Down this hallway, then right, then right again, then through the wall with the tapestry of the Maziks dancing in the olive grove, which Elena pushed aside.

Barsilay held back before taking them through. "Was that all the salt you had?"

"Most unfortunately, yes."

"Why do you look so relieved? I wasn't about to put salt in *your* eye."

"Right. I'm sure that never occurred to you." He took Elena's hand, made them both shadow again, and pulled them through the last wall.

TSIFRA WAS ABLE to make her way back to Barcino on the fleet's fastest ship; the rest she left behind to gather supplies and make ready for their next conquest. She would rejoin them, she told her captain, as soon as she was able, and then she rode hard from Barcino to Mansanar, nearly killing her own courser beneath her.

Tarses had given her latitude in how to make herself Queen, but she knew it would not be pretty—the real Queen would have to die. The question was how best to replace her and maintain loyalty among those who'd known her.

The Queen's confessor already was dead; he'd died of infection after losing his hand to Toba. At one time he'd been the Queen's closest confidant, closer even than the King. Tsifra wondered what the Queen had thought of him when he'd been possessed: how quickly she'd noticed, whether she might have preferred the newer version. Atalef, at least, had never been cruel.

She would have to kill the King, too. Their heirs she was not sure of. Better, probably, to let them live a while than draw attention by killing everyone at once.

Tsifra would kill the Queen and take her place and her face, and then, over the next five or ten years, allow her features to resume their normal appearance, slowly enough that no one would notice that the Queen's eyes had gone from blue to brown, or her hair from light to dark.

Tsifra killed the King in his bed and then she found the Queen in her own garden, where she was sitting outside, at night, in the winter. How odd.

"Why are you sitting out here?" Tsifra asked her as she approached.

The Queen rose quickly. She was tall, nearly as tall as Tsifra, and would have screamed, but then Tsifra allowed herself her wings of air, which shone in the starlight. The Queen fell to her knees. "Tell me," Tsifra said.

Without raising her head, the Queen said, "The cold air purifies my spirit."

"Does it?" Tsifra asked. "How?"

"I cannot say," the Queen replied. "Only it helps me settle my mind. It quiets me. What do you wish of me, angel?"

At that moment, only feet away, a beam of light shot from the ground into the sky, startling them both. The Queen covered her face and cried out. Tsifra waited, but no one came.

It was the gate of Luz, and only one person would have opened that gate to her. It was an invitation, and a message: Toba had the book. On the other side of the gate was her sister and the book, and whatever potential for freedom the Peregrine had risked her life for.

Behind her, the Queen cowered on the ground. Somewhere far away, Atalef was nothing but ash.

Tsifra took a step toward it, and then another, and then the gate closed.

Whether she would truly have done it, gone through, Tsifra could not have said. Not then, and not later.

She turned back toward the Queen of Sefarad, kneeling on the cold ground and shaking, and Tsifra cut off her head, and she made it an apple and planted it in the Queen's own garden along with the rest of what remained of her.

Then Tsifra took the Queen's face and went into the palace, and ordered someone to wake her advisors. When they came, she told them she'd be leaving Mansanar and the country would have to do without her for a while.

"But where can you mean to go?" they asked, and she smiled gently, as an angel might do, and said, "I have had a vision this night, that this crusade is mine. And for it to succeed, I must lead it myself."

After they'd objected, and begged, and left, she went back to the Queen's rooms and set the Queen's diadem on her forehead, and looked at herself in the mirror with her false face. The left hand of the new age. The image seemed inadequate to her; she was ordinary, the Queen. So Tsifra brought back her shimmering wings of air, and stood before the glass, and smiled.

THE ROUTE TO the piazza was littered with bodies of Maziks who had escaped burning buildings only to die of their injuries. Naftaly was beside himself, wanting to go into the houses and help anyone who might be trapped but Toba stopped him. "If we're killed and can't open a gate, then everyone dies."

So they continued back to the piazza while Toba's larks circled the city. "Have you found the others?" Naftaly asked her.

"No, but if they were inside the palazzo they should be safe for a little while; there's no wood in the building."

"How will they find us, though? Your larks won't be able to get inside."

"My grandmother can find anyone," she said, with such conviction that Naftaly felt he could not point out she'd failed to find him for an entire month.

In the piazza, the doors of the palazzo were on fire, trapping everyone inside. Worse, the flames had spread to the rest of the building and the stone itself was beginning to burn.

"How can stone burn?" Naftaly asked.

"These aren't normal flames," Toba said. "That's why the Maziks couldn't extinguish them. Naftaly, these flames are demons."

Naftaly stopped and watched the flames grow; the smell of burning stone was horrible. He said, "I think you'd better open the gate," and the two of them started trying to move the frightened Maziks back to make a space for Toba and the book on the ground.

Elena and Barsilay came outside to a sea of injured, burned Maziks. Behind them, Asmel came through the wall with the old woman in his arms, Efra at his side.

Fire roared on all four sides of the piazza.

Efra was the first to elbow her way through. "You're opening a gate? Here?"

"To P'ri Hadar," Toba said. "But I need someone else to do it. I've never been there. I was waiting for Asmel."

"I'm here," Asmel said, reaching for the book, but Elena held out her arm, blocking him. "You tried to open a gate to P'ri Hadar once before. You put us next to Mount Sebah."

"I was not quite myself then," he said. "I assure you—"

"Let Barsilay do it," Elena said.

Barsilay looked a bit chagrined and took the book from Toba, saying, "My, I've become the trustworthy one." He opened the book on the ground, and said, "My reputation is destroyed. I suppose there is no saving it." He began to read.

Toba gripped Elena's arm. "We must say goodbye here. I'm not coming with you."

Elena said, "You aren't thinking of staying here?"

"Not here. You know about the Ziz. You remember where she is, where Marah left her. Naftaly and I are going."

"You're going now? But—"

"It must be now," she said. "Grandmother, I'm telling you this because I love you." Elena stiffened a little. Toba said, "You must look after the others. There is no one I trust more."

Elena's eyes were wet, but she said, "You have my word, my love."

The flames engulfing the city began to swirl together, to coalesce on top of the roofs, and took on the shape of an enormous bird: a Ziz, made from flame. Its wings licked whatever surfaces had not already burned, leaving a layer of fire in its wake. In the piazza, the Maziks began to scream.

"You had better hurry up," Toba told Barsilay, who began to read faster.

"Listen to me," Naftaly told Toba, "my vision is about to begin. I'm going to see you, and you're going to tell me when Tarses finds the grove."

"I know. I'll tell you five days this time."

"No," he said. "Tell me six. If you tell me five, the Council will know we won't be able to lay the mines before Tarses gets there. They'll forbid us to try. And when the Prince of Zayit makes a deal to save the city, Tarses will do more than burn Zayit—he'll have the gate, too, and access to all the salt the guild has been stockpiling there for him. So tell me six days. Do you understand?"

"But—"

"Everyone will continue to mistrust me, I know, but the alternative is far worse."

Toba nodded sharply, and the gate shot into the sky. As the bird of flame circled the piazza and turned its fiery eyes toward the palazzo, Efra ushered everyone through 'til only Asmel and Barsilay were left with Toba and Naftaly. "You're not coming with us," Asmel said.

"Dawid ben Aron told me not to trust the Queen of P'ri Hadar with the book until I was ready to replace the gate. We can't come with you 'til we have the Ziz."

Barsilay said, "Naftaly," and Naftaly said, "My King."

Asmel asked Toba, "You remember what I told you, about the angle of entrance?"

"I remember," she said, and the bird of flame engulfed the palazzo with its wings, and the entire edifice exploded in fire. "Go!" she said, and then only she and Naftaly were left.

She closed the gate, because she could not risk the flame demons following the others through. Then she drew a line in the ash with her toe and marked off a semicircle around the book: ninety degrees, forty-five, until she'd marked the ten degrees on either edge. Then she put the book back down and began to read.

Any gate would take you into Aravoth, if you entered at the correct angle, so Toba opened one not to a place, but to a person. She opened one to Tsifra.

She didn't expect her to pass through it. She wanted only for the other woman to see it and know what it meant: that Toba had the book. And that she still had a choice to join her, to thwart Tarses, to become something else.

The gate opened from the center of the book, and she waited, just a single moment, to see if there was some small chance that Tsifra would come through. Then she told Naftaly, "You must go first," and she pointed at the line, showing him again the angle he must take.

Naftaly turned a circle, looking, Toba guessed, for himself.

"Do you see anything?" Toba asked.

"No," he said.

"Then go."

Naftaly stepped carefully through. Toba picked up the book, put one foot through the gate, and then looked back and said, "Tarses will find Zayit's gate in six days."

Thirty-Four

ELENA FOUND THAT she did not care for passing through the gate. It was remarkably similar to being pulled through the wall: no air, no light, and for one unbearable moment a growing certainty that she was about to be extinguished like a flame.

She felt the ground beneath her feet again and opened her eyes to P'ri Hadar.

They were not inside the city. Probably Barsilay had been right to put them in the hills outside, so as to avoid the major spectacle of a gate opening outside the moon, in the wrong place, and with a large number of Zayiti refugees to boot.

After her eyes adjusted to a night without great flaming birds illuminating the sky, she saw that they were in a citrus grove. Barsilay had taken them to the spot where a gate might be expected—to hide, Elena guessed, the fact that he possessed the book. The Maziks would wonder how they'd opened the gate at the wrong time of the month, but they might be led to believe it had been their normal gate that had opened, at least if these Maziks were very gullible.

Looking back toward where the gate had been, Elena could not help hoping to see Toba had followed her after all. But, of course, she was not there.

Asmel set the old woman on the ground, and Barsilay ran his hands over her. "I'd better do something for her lungs before we go any further," he said. "She's not good."

"She was in a bad way before she breathed all that smoke," Asmel told him. "She inhaled some amount of the decayed salt."

"Right," Barsilay said. "The decayed salt which Tarses now possesses. How's that?" he asked the old woman.

"I feel terrible," she said. "Like I inhaled broken glass."

"She sounds better," Elena said, and realized the old woman hadn't noticed yet that Naftaly was missing. She would, in a moment, and then she'd be in much worse pain than from her burned lungs. "She couldn't have said all that without coughing before."

"Come closer," the old woman said, and when Elena complied, she hissed, "I hate you."

"She's much better," Elena confirmed.

Efra said, "We should start moving these people into the city."

"Hm," Asmel said. "I don't know. If we show up at the gates of P'ri Hadar in the middle of the night with all these people, we may have a problem. I think we should keep everyone here and send a delegation ahead to explain the situation."

"And what situation are we explaining exactly?" Barsilay asked. "When have the P'ri Hadaris ever helped anyone?"

"It's harder to refuse the person on your doorstep than one you can't see," the old woman put in. "I suggest you find someone particularly pathetic to send." The Maziks all looked at her. "A pathetic-looking Mazik," she clarified. "Me they'll just put back through the gate. Or bake into a pie."

"You're suggesting the Queen is afflicted with a generosity of spirit?" Barsilay asked.

Efra said, "Ha."

A discussion was had, and it was decided that Efra would take Barsilay and Elena with her to negotiate for help: Efra as the Savia, Barsilay as the heir of Luz, and Elena as the person most likely to sniff out a trick. As dawn rose, the three of them entered the city and made their way to the palace.

They were brought into a room that was vast and nearly empty; their footsteps echoed on the sand-colored floor. The light in the room came through lead-glass windows set high in the walls, which left patches of different colors on the floor and on their faces. Efra strode up to meet the Queen and bowed, and Barsilay and Elena, two steps behind her, did likewise.

But the Queen's eyes were only on Barsilay.

"Barsilay b'Droer," she said. "The heir of Luz."

Barsilay went very white but said, "Adona—"

Efra put in, "We have many hundreds of injured Maziks—"

The Queen held up a hand. To her guards, she said, "Throw him in irons."

GLOSSARY

Note: ç (c-cedilla) is pronounced as in Medieval Spanish: "ts."

ADON/ADONA: Lord/Lady. A title among Mazik nobles.

ALCALÁ: Castle.

ALCÁZAR: Palace.

AMAPOLA: Extract of the opium poppy.

ATALEF: Bat.

BEHEMOT: One of the three mythical giant animals mentioned in Jewish scripture and folklore. The behemot is the King of the Beasts.

BUCHUK: Literally, "twin." Toba Bet is an example. She is notable both for having developed a separate persona from the original Toba, and for having survived after the original Toba's death.

LA CACERÍA: Literally, "the Hunt." The Mazik organization charged with protecting the gates, limiting contact with the mortal world, and bolstering the rule of the monarch of Rimon. La Cacería has two main divisions: the Hounds (and their elite force, the Alaunts), led by Tsidon the Lymer and responsible for Rimon and the dream-world; and the Falcons, led by the Peregrine, responsible for espionage and assassinations abroad.

THE CAÇADOR: Literally, "the Huntsman." The title for the head of La Cacería.

THE DREAM-WORLD: The shared dream-space of all Maziks.

THE FALL: The great disaster in which the mortal sages of Luz pulled out their gate and hid it in a book. The resulting tear in the firmament led to the inundation of Luz and the formation of the Dimah Sea. Te'ena was also made an island in this event.

HA-MOH'TO: A secret society once based in Luz, led by Marah Ystehar and devoted to resisting the rule of the Queen of Luz. Their watchword was Monarchy is Abomination. Most of ha-Moh'to's members were presumed to have died in the Fall; others include Barsilay b'Droer, Rafeq of Katlav, Omer of Te'ena, and Tarses b'Shemhazai.

KILLSTONE: A failsafe device used by a number of Mazik secret organizations. If an operative were to be captured, the holder of the killstone could order that person's death with the use of a command-word, enabling them to enter a dreaming death rather than being forced to endure torture and risk compromising the organization. Marah was the holder of the killstone of ha-Moh'to.

LA'AZ SEFARDI: The language spoken by Jews in Sefarad. Maziks refer to the language simply as "Rimoni."

PALAZZO: In Zayiti, "palace." The palazzo in Zayit houses the administration of the entire city.

PIAZZA: In Zayiti, "plaza."

SAFIRA: A blue gemstone made of magic removed from a Mazik, either voluntarily or as a punishment. After the removal of their magic, the Mazik will quickly lose their memories and sense of self. However, the removal of their magic also makes it possible for a Mazik to survive in the mortal world outside of the full moon.

SAVIA: Literally, "wise person," in Zayiti. One of the important officials tasked with the oversight of the running of the city. The Savia della Mura ("Wise Woman of the Wall") is in charge of Zayit's defense.

THE VOID: Nonexistence. Maziks may experience two types of death: a dreaming death, in which a Mazik will permanently remain in the dream-world, and an unbroken death, in which a Mazik will cease to exist completely, usually as the result of violence. All Maziks share the void terror; most are unwilling to put themselves at significant physical risk because of it.

ZIZ: One of the three mythical giant animals mentioned in Jewish scripture and folklore. The Ziz is the King of Birds and is said to be able to blot out the sun with its enormous wings. Marah Ystehar hid the Ziz in the realm of Aravoth to conceal her from Tarses, believing the Ziz was necessary for the restoration of the gate of Luz.

Acknowledgments

THANK YOU SO much to Hannah Bowman and the rest of the team at Liza Dawson Associates for so much continued support.

Enormous thanks to both of the editors who have approached this series with so many keen insights, Amy Borsuk at Solaris/Rebellion and Sarah Guan at Erewhon. Thanks also to the rest of the team at Solaris/Rebellion: Jess Gofton, Chiara Mestieri, Lin Nagle, Sam Gretton, Gemma Sheldrake, and Micaela Alcaino; and to the team at Erewhon: Viengsamai Fetters, Martin Cahill, Kasie Griffitts, Cassandra Farrin, Kelsy Thompson, Sarah Webb, and Alice Moye-Honeyman

Thank you to my father-in-law, Dave, who passed away before this book was finished but who taught me so much about how to build and shred and rebuild a sentence, and how to maintain my equanimity in the face of a page covered with more red ink than black.

Finally, thanks to my family, for sharing their love and creative spirits.

STAFF CREDITS

Thank you for reading this title from Erewhon Books, publishing books that embrace the liminal and unclassifiable and championing the unusual, the uncanny, and the hard-to-define.

We are proud of the team behind The Mirror Realm Cycle by Ariel Kaplan:

Sarah Guan, Publisher
Diana Pho, Executive Editor
Viengsamai Fetters, Assistant Editor

Martin Cahill, Marketing and Publicity Manager
Kasie Griffitts, Sales Associate

Cassandra Farrin, Director
Leah Marsh, Production Editor
Kelsy Thompson, Production Editor

Alice Moye-Honeyman, Junior Designer
and the whole publishing team at Kensington Books!

Learn more about Erewhon Books and our authors at erewhonbooks.com.

X/Twitter: @erewhonbooks
Instagram: @erewhonbooks
Facebook: @ErewhonBooks

THE
GAL'IN

KINGDOM
OF
SEFARAD

ZAYIT

RIMON

TE'ENA

TAMAR

EREZ